Books by Elisa Braden

MIDNIGHT IN SCOTLAND SERIES

The Making of a Highlander (Book One)
The Taming of a Highlander (Book Two)
The Temptation of a Highlander (Book Three)—Coming soon!

RESCUED FROM RUIN SERIES

Ever Yours, Annabelle (Prequel)
The Madness of Viscount Atherbourne (Book One)
The Truth About Cads and Dukes (Book Two)
Desperately Seeking a Scoundrel (Book Three)
The Devil Is a Marquess (Book Four)
When a Girl Loves an Earl (Book Five)
Twelve Nights as His Mistress (Novella – Book Six)
Confessions of a Dangerous Lord (Book Seven)
Anything but a Gentleman (Book Eight)
A Marriage Made in Scandal (Book Nine)
A Kiss from a Rogue (Book Ten)

Want to know what's next? Connect with Elisa through Facebook
and Twitter, and sign up for her free email newsletter at
www.elisabraden.com, so you don't miss a single new release!

Ever Yours, Annabelle

ELISA BRADEN

Cover design by Dar Albert at Wicked Smart Designs

Excerpt from *The Madness of Viscount Atherbourne* copyright © 2015 Elisa Braden

For more information about the author, visit www.elisabraden.com.

ISBN-13: 978-1-950805-01-3
ISBN-10: 1-950805-01-8

Chapter One

"Children are like potted plants. They must be watered with
wisdom from time to time, whether or not they consider
themselves children or their elders wise."

—THE DOWAGER MARCHIONESS OF WALLINGHAM in a letter to the
Marquis of Mortlock, answering said gentleman's laments about his
grandson's resistance to sound advice.

Dearest Robert,
Mama says I may begin writing to you, provided I also write to John.
I do not wish to write my brother, as he is daft and likes to tease me
about my nose being too small. Papa says older brothers tease their
sisters as a matter of coarse. I answered that he is vexing, not coarse.

Papa laughed, but I assure you it is true. Whilst you are at Eton together, perhaps you will improve John's character. I miss you much more than I miss him.

Ever yours,
Annabelle Huxley
P.S. Please do not tell John what I said. I do miss him sometimes.
P.P.S. I have enclosed a sketch for you. John is the ~~goat~~ dog, and you are the ~~horse~~ knight. I shall do better next time.

—Letter to Robert Conrad dated October 7, 1803

July 30, 1809
Nottinghamshire, England

LADY ANNABELLE HUXLEY HAD LOVED ROBERT CONRAD FOR her entire thirteen years of life. Yet, in all that time, she'd never imagined him naked.

What an appalling oversight.

Perhaps it was because he was her brother's best friend. Perhaps because, until now, she'd been keener on his solemn smile and solid, capable character. Likely it was because the last time she'd seen Robert without a coat and cravat, she had been nine years old, well before it occurred to her that she was destined to marry him. Before he'd grown shoulders wider than the span of her arms.

But now, here, crouched in a tangle of shrubbery above the River Tisenby where Robert and her brother, John, were swimming, she confronted her appalling oversight with stark fascination.

He gleamed like a marble god.

"Con!" shouted John from ten yards downstream, pointing at the water near his waist. "We should have brought our rods, by God. The trout are bloody swarming."

She ignored her idiotic brother. She ignored the bead of sweat dripping down her nape. She ignored the bramble thorns snagging her best pink gown.

Robert Conrad was wet. Muscled. Riveting.

Naked.

A small smile curled his lips as he ran a wet hand through dark, rumpled hair. "Next time, Hux."

The muscles of his abdomen tightened and rippled when he raised his arm.

And he had nipples. Fancy that. His were a light copper color, twin coins upon his smooth flesh.

But his arms fascinated her most. They swelled with hard, bulging muscle. Extended from broad, heavy-boned shoulders.

She was afraid to blink. Who knew when he would dive beneath the sluggish water and remove himself from her view? The Tisenby's swirling depths disguised whatever nakedness lay below his waist too well. She could just make out the waistband of his breeches resting low upon his hips.

"You're off to battle the Corsican Tyrant soon. Not too many 'next times' left." John again. She didn't bother sparing him a glance. Her brother was a year younger than Robert. Leaner and more lighthearted. For years, he had called her "Anna-smell" when he was vexed at her for chasing after the pair of them. In fairness, she'd chased them frequently. To the river. To the village. To the wood where they'd climbed a giant beech and declared it their fortress.

"Go home, Anna-smell," John would shout from a high limb. "Why must you follow us everywhere?"

One such day, after she'd slipped and scraped her knees while clinging to rough bark, Robert had shoved his best friend's shoulder and told John if he ever called her Anna-smell again, he would darken his daylights. Then, he'd dusted her off, taken her hand in his warm, dry grasp, and walked her home.

Robert had never liked for her to be hurt. It was why she loved him.

Loved him as a lady loved her favored knight.

Once, she might have said she loved him as a brother.

Not today, by heavens. Today, he was naked. Wet. Fascinating.

She studied his form—the bones of his shoulder blades broader and thicker than before, the lesser muscles of his torso ridged and flexing where his waist tapered into his hips. Tufts of hair were dark beneath his arms. The hardened jaw was squarer than it had been at fourteen.

His voice was deeper, too. Deep and solemn.

Robert had always been a serious boy.

Man, she corrected herself. *He is a man now.*

"We must find you a woman," her daft brother called over his shoulder. "No man should hie off to battle before he's had a proper ride."

Robert gave a grunt of protest. "I've ridden."

John's head cocked to one side as he examined the water. "Twice. Scarcely qualifies. Perhaps I'll recruit Red Bess to the task. No finer bosoms in three counties."

Annabelle glanced down at her own bosoms, flat beneath pleated pink silk and white ribbons. She swallowed her dismay. Mama had assured her that bosoms grew with time. She prayed it was true, for if Robert required a wife with bosoms, then she must have them. She longed to be everything he wanted, to have him look upon her with the same adoration that filled her too full to be contained.

John's arm shot beneath the water's surface then quickly emerged holding a wriggling silver fish aloft. Drops splashed onto his Huxley-brown hair as he turned a triumphant grin toward Robert.

"I can catch my own fish," Robert replied darkly. "Never needed your help in that quarter."

John grinned wider and tossed the wriggling trout back into the water. "Females are selective, Con. They fancy a bit of charm, not a man so dour he could snuff a candle with a single glance."

Robert waded deeper into the river's center until water lapped at his collarbone. "I shall be an officer in His Majesty's army. The only charm I require is the gleam upon my sword."

"The point is to polish your sword thoroughly before facing the bloody French cannons."

Annabelle's stomach lurched. She'd known Robert had purchased a commission. He was the second son of Earl Conrad and the grandson of the Marquis of Mortlock. If they didn't wish to become clergymen or useless rakes, second sons bought commissions. But more than that, Robert was born to be an officer—she pictured him seated boldly upon his mount, scarlet wool and golden epaulets decorating his broad, broad shoulders.

She sighed.

Ever since Robert had written to her of his plans, she'd only thought how perfect he would be. He was her heroic ideal— noble and serious, strong and protective. Now, he would be England's hero.

But that was not what would happen. He would not simply don a pair of gold epaulets and parade through London on his gallant steed.

He would be fighting. Leading other men into battle. Where he might be shot. Blasted with a cannon. Skewered with a sword.

He might ...

She swallowed and rubbed at the icy ache beneath her breastbone.

... die.

A splash sounded as he dove beneath the water, swimming toward the long shadow cast by Packhorse Bridge. The old stone buttress directly to her left was covered in damp moss and anchored deep in rocks and mud. Above her head, looming branches full of heart-shaped leaves rippled like the water's surface. Behind her, the low buzz of a curious bee and the distant nicker of a horse intruded on the harsh *whump-whump-whump* of her pulse.

Robert could die.

She reached into the pocket of her best pink gown. Felt crinkled paper. Blinked until the tightness in her throat eased.

Another splash. Robert's dark head emerged just below her. Then his shoulders. Then his arm, raising a fish twice the size of John's. "You see?" He blew out a spray of droplets and ran a hand over his face, brushing heavy brows downward above his eyes. "You make your catches, Hux, and I shall make mine."

John laughed, the sound grating. Didn't he realize? Robert could die.

Suddenly, the caricature she'd drawn for him last evening— a sketch featuring Robert presenting a trussed-up Bonaparte with a dish labeled *Coq de feat*, and saying, "Another serving, monsieur?"—seemed a dreadful folly. Her fingers tightened upon the folded edges in her pocket. Ice bloomed in her stomach, at odds with the stifling heat of summer.

This was wrong. Robert Conrad must stay here, in Nottinghamshire. With her. And his grandfather, of course. He was ever so fond of his grandfather. No, he did not belong on some faraway battlefield where even marble gods cracked and bled when the cannons fired.

How would they marry if he were ... dead?

She shifted as heat prickled and nausea swarmed. Her foot slipped on the slick leaves beneath her boots. Without thinking, she reached for a handhold to steady her balance. Sharp thorns dug into her palm and fingers, jabbing as deep as a dressmaker's needles.

"Argh!" Her pained cry echoed, high and shrill, across the river's banks. She froze, one leg overextended down the leafy, pebbly slope. Below her, a masculine shout and violent splashing made her heart pound.

"Who's there? Annabelle?"

Oh, heavens. He was coming. Naked. Wet. Coming, as he always did, to rescue her from her own foolishness.

Thorns dug deeper into her palm as she grappled and grasped. Her feet dug deeper into slick leaves, scrambling to climb. Away from him. Away from the shame of being caught ogling a boy—no, a *man*—in her best pink gown. She glanced down. It was ruined, the pink silk stained green and red with leaves and blood, the thorns snagging once-pristine fabric.

Heart pounding, she released the brambles. Her feet slid, her legs stretching apart painfully as she strained to climb the slope. She fell. Brown added to green and red and pink, smearing and grinding where her knees gouged into the river's long, steep bank. Pebbles pattered and fell.

"Annabelle!" The roar was hoarse and panting. Closer.

No, no, no. He must not see her this way. He would never view her as a lady, then. As the woman who should be his wife.

The thought spurred her toes to dig, her hands to yank at the snagged silk. Thorns were in her hair now, velvety-rough leaves stroking her cheek as a needle clawed fire along her jaw.

She whimpered. Not because of the pain, but because he would see her. Humiliated. Desperate. Ugly and wild and strange.

She was the odd Huxley girl who followed him like a dandelion tuft chasing a strong wind. Helplessly. Naturally. Propelled by forces she did not understand.

He'd always turned back for her, no matter the years that separated them. He'd always taken her hand in his, strong and dry. He caught her when she fell, protected her—often from herself. Once, he'd carried her home when she'd broken a toe while demonstrating her ability to leap from a fallen log. *Watch*

me, Robert, she'd called to his retreating back. *I can keep up!* The
pain had robbed her of breath. All she remembered was gasping
for air as the boy she adored had scooped her up onto his back.

At five, she hadn't weighed much. But he'd been only ten—a
child, himself—and his arms had been thin on his lanky frame.
Her home had been two miles away. Yet, after sending John to
fetch the physician, he'd carried her the entire way, those not-
yet-muscled arms shaking with the strain, his blue eyes grim and
unrelenting, even as a boy. She'd clung to his neck, her tears
dampening his rough linen shirt.

Robert *belonged* to her and she to him. He must not die on a
battlefield. He must *not* see her this way.

"Annabelle! Answer me!" Frantic eyes locked upon her
through a veil of leaves. Blue flared bright and fierce.
"Annabelle!" Her name was a command.

She ignored it. Shoved hard to her feet. Yanked and heard
silk tear. Clambered up the slope. Up and up and up.

Glanced back. He was near. Broad shoulders. White, wet
skin. Dark, heavy brows. Muscles straining and long arms
sweeping brambles aside as he climbed in great, furious strides
over wet rocks and pebbled soil.

She ran. Up and up and up. Another thorn dug at her bare
arm, but she scarcely felt it. She reached the top of the bank and
veered toward Packhorse Bridge. A sharp rock jabbed at the
sole of her boot, nearly piercing it. Again, she ignored the pain,
carrying on a limping race for her dignity.

She was a third of the way across the bridge when she lost
that race.

"Annabelle, stop," came the deep bark just before a large,
strong hand closed around her arm.

She halted. She had no choice. He was twice her size and
obviously furious.

And, one mustn't forget, naked. Well, apart from his
breeches.

She snuck a glance at his bare feet. They were big and wet on the slick stones of the bridge. They were also a bit bony. His smallest toes rode awkwardly atop the adjacent ones. He was not precisely perfect, then, was he? Not so god-like, at least his feet.

"What the devil were you doing?" A long finger stroked her jaw gently, where the thorny gouge stung. "You've hurt yourself."

She opened her mouth to tell him it was nothing, but was interrupted by John's shout from below. "Bloody hell, Annabelle! You agreed to stay home." John's voice turned first to a mocking singsong then a disgusted indictment. "'I shall see you both at dinner,' you said, pretty as you please. I'd forgotten what a pest you are, little sister. Now, I suppose you've turned an ankle, and once again, all merriment must cease because of your bloody-minded obsession." During his rant, John waded to the south bank of the river on the far side of the bridge and began climbing.

She blinked as she realized his drawers were transparent, displaying his pale buttocks. She hadn't seen her brother's naked backside since he was eight and she was four. John had persuaded her it would be great fun to chase the newest litter of piglets about Mr. Eggleston's sty. Mama had taken one look at their head-to-toe muck, stripped them both naked and tossed them in a tub, then promptly scrubbed them pink again.

Not long afterward, John had stopped playing with her, preferring the company of his best friend, Robert.

The boy she also loved. The man who now held her arm.

"Let me see your hands," Robert said quietly.

She kept her eyes on the incline of the bridge's arch. Rough, medieval stones were clothed in moss. The bridge was narrow and seldom used. A canopy of green made it slick, even in summer.

Taking a shuddering breath, she focused upon all the things that, unlike the man behind her, were not mortifying to her soul. Along the river's edge, lime and beech rustled in a green dither. Below, the Tisenby's water dallied and swirled. At the end of the bridge, rocks tumbled as John crested the top of the bank, cursing angrily at the thorny, white-bloomed brambles that caught his elbow.

"Your hands, Annabelle," Robert commanded, deep and hard. Harder than she'd ever heard him. "Now."

The skin of her cheeks and neck pulsed with heat. She blinked away tears, swallowed away shame. Curled her fingers into her palms, feeling the sticky wetness of her own blood. "No," she choked.

He grasped her right wrist. Pried open her fingers.

She grunted her resistance, but there was no fighting his strength.

All he did was sigh. Then murmur, "Now you've done it, Bumblebee. How will you wield a pen to write me all those letters of yours with such injuries?"

Though his voice softened with affection, she hated his words—the implication that he would leave soon, the nickname he'd used for the girl who invariably "bumbled" into calamity. She'd only ever done so around him. Trying to prove herself. Trying to remain close.

He was leaving. Oh, God. Robert might die.

Her stomach felt sick. Cramping. Her throat felt tight. Burning.

She wanted to scream at him. But she could not even look at him. She squeezed her eyes closed.

His thumb stroked the back of her wrist. "You may turn round, you know. I am relatively decent." He paused. She pictured him glancing down at his own bare chest and wet breeches. "Well, nearly so."

She tugged at her arm. "Let go."

"Not until you tell me why you followed us. Hux said you'd promised to—"

"I did not promise. And what if I had? Breaking such a small promise is a tiny matter—nothing at all, really—considering what *you* are planning to do!"

A long pause had her picturing those shaggy dark brows lowering over brooding blue. "I am lost, Bumblebee."

"Do *not* call me that." She didn't care that she sounded shrewish and shrieking. The heat inside her was caustic. Suffocating. Like smoke expanding in billows. She needed to let it out.

Another sigh. "Annabelle, then. *Lady* Annabelle, if we are being proper, I suppose."

"You are l-leaving. For war." Her words emerged as a low, bitter accusation. She hadn't meant to say them. But they wanted out.

First, silence. Then, "I have a commission. That is my duty."

"No." She shook her head for emphasis. "Your duty is here. *Here.* With your grandfather and ... us."

"Annabelle—"

A ball of clothing sailed past her, flung by her brother and—presumably—caught by Robert. John had already donned his own breeches and shirt, along with thunderclouds of fury. He stalked toward them, tight-lipped and narrow-eyed. "Go home, Annabelle," he barked. "You've had your eyeful of our naked backsides. I hope your curiosity is satisfied."

The heat in her cheeks felt like a brand.

Robert had released her arm to dress, or at least, she assumed so. She still hadn't summoned the courage to turn around and look at him.

"Leave her be," Robert said quietly.

John ignored him to glare at her. "I assumed you'd outgrown this tedious infatuation. More fool me."

"Hux."

John's eyes—a match for their father's hazel—flashed bright gold in the dappled sun. They bored into hers. "It's only worsened, hasn't it? Now, look at you." He waved an impatient hand toward her bloodstained skirts. "You've injured yourself again. And for what?" He pointed to the boy—*man*—behind her. "He is not your beau, Annabelle. Not your knight or your suitor or your future husband. You are a *child* to him. A pest. He treats you kindly because he pities you."

Pressure seized her chest, tightening and tightening and tightening. Her throat hurt. Her heart hurt. Her face burned. It was the only part of her that felt warm.

"Huxley!" The growl from behind her was a warning. A warning John did not heed.

"She needs to hear the truth, Con. Unlike you, I am not so fearful of damaging her feelings that I cannot speak it."

"Stop this."

Hazel eyes came back to her, hard and determined. Her brother's features blurred as her throat tightened further. She clenched her fists and stuffed them in the pockets of her skirt. Her right knuckles brushed paper. The pain in her palm reminded her there was something beyond the unbearable pressure inside her.

"Grow up, little sister," John snapped after lowering his face nearer to hers. His finger nudged beneath her chin, his touch far gentler than his words. "Behave as the lady you should be, rather than the pathetic pup we must constantly rescue from her own foolishness."

The sob caught her unawares, emerging as a grinding gasp. The aching pressure in her chest did not ease. Another whimper escaped before she caught it.

John's hand was violently swiped away by a bearish paw attached to a long, muscled arm. Then broad, linen-clad shoulders moved in front of her. A hard shove sent her brother backward.

Dimly, she thought the two young men might start brawling. They were shouting at one another, but she missed half the argument, too focused upon trapping another humiliating sob inside. She could not let it out, though her shoulders shook with the strain.

"... no call to be so cruel, you bloody arse!"

"Look at her! She's covered in lacerations. She might have fallen down the bank, cracked her head, drowned, or broken another damned toe!"

Robert gave his best friend a second powerful shove, sending John stumbling backward toward the south bank. "Leave. I will bring her back to Clumberwood." His voice was a low roar, rippling with anger.

"Haven't you realized by now coddling her makes everything worse, you porridge-headed—"

"Go! Or, so help me, Huxley, I'll break that charming face of yours into blackened bits."

John threw his arms wide before gesturing toward her. "Very well. Let it be upon your head to explain her injuries to my mother and father."

"Go."

With a disgusted snort, John pivoted and stalked toward the south end of the bridge, muttering about where he'd left his boots.

Robert turned. He was breathing heavily. His jaw was stiff, his eyes closing briefly as though he sought to regain command of himself. When he looked at her, a swooping pain gripped her belly. There, deep in the blue, was controlled anger, old affection, remorse, and ... pity.

She swallowed against the ache in her throat. "It is true, is it not?" she whispered. "That is what I am to you. Pathetic."

An instant before he shook his head and raked a hand through dark, wet hair, she saw the truth. It stabbed through her middle. It made her bleed.

Because his eyes dropped away for the barest instant. His discomfort produced the briefest wince before he schooled his expression into his customary solemn lines. Robert might intend to spare her feelings, but his honorable nature did not allow for ready deception. Had she cared to look, she might have seen it sooner. Instead, she'd imagined his every glance had been a connection, his warm, dry hand affection, and his rare smile a promise.

How wrong she had been.

"Bumblebee." His voice was as rocky as the river's banks. He did not seem to know what else to say. Only that—the name he'd called her forever. Since she was a ... child.

Suddenly, the future she'd imagined began to crack apart like a tumbling rock bursting open along its faults. Their first dance together at their betrothal ball would have been at Clumberwood Manor. She would have worn blue silk, and he scarlet wool with gold epaulets. He would have kissed her behind the walled garden.

Their wedding would have been at Rivermore Abbey, where he and his grandfather lived. The chapel there was lovely, with rainbow light pouring through stained glass onto ancient stone. She would have decorated the worn, walnut pews with ivy and orange blossoms. She would have worn lace in her hair.

They would have had babes together, she and Robert. Little, sweet-smelling babes she would have cradled and nurtured and loved. On a summer day like this one, they would have taken their family for a carriage ride to visit Mama and Papa and her four younger sisters. Their children would have laughed and wriggled and teased one another. And all the while, Robert would have gazed upon her, love glowing in his blue eyes.

Not pity. Never that.

She wanted to vomit. She wanted to wail. The jagged pieces of her future—once shimmering brighter than diamonds—crumbled to dust on the stones of Packhorse Bridge.

He was leaving.

For war.

He might die.

And he did not love her.

Not as he should. Not as she loved him.

She crossed her arms over her chest, gripping and holding herself together. The pressure was agony. It wanted out. She breathed faster. Staggered backward away from him, the source of her pain.

"Bumblebee, don't. I never wanted you to be hurt."

She could not speak, only squeeze her arms tighter. Another step back. The bridge's stones slipped beneath her boots.

He closed in, his heavy brows crashing into a frown. "Stop. Annabelle, stop."

She shook her head, continued backing away. She could not be near him now. She must find a place to let the pressure out. Somewhere she would not be pitied or humiliated.

"Bloody hell," he gritted, lunging toward her. "Stop!"

She did not think. She must get away. Her feet scrambled faster.

And lost their grip.

And her calf snagged on the low parapet.

And trees became sky.

Her breath left in a soundless scream at the disappearance of the stones beneath her feet, the sensation of nothingness at her back. Her arms failed to loosen in time to catch herself.

Which was why she reached for him so late. Why, when he reached for her with his strong, dry hand, all he caught were her fingers, which were slick with blood. Still, his grip was ferocious. Painful, even.

Her gaze flew up to his, bound by the blue. "Robert," she mouthed, no air available to produce sound. "Pl-please."

He'd fallen to his knees. His jaw flickered, his shoulders shuddering with the strain of holding her, dangling above the Tisenby. But his eyes were the worst. Desperate. Horrified.

Her fingers were slipping.

"Annabelle." His muscles shimmered. "I—I cannot ... much longer. Reach for me."

She wanted to. How she wanted to. But she was frozen. Her feet kicked out for stone but found only air inside the bridge's arch.

"No! My wrist. Use your other hand. God, Annabelle. Help me."

He gripped the parapet with his free hand, stretching his torso and making himself a rope between the bridge and the abyss below. She glanced down. They were just inside the river's edge. If she fell, she would not hit water. She would hit rocks.

Those rocks rippled and spun in her vision. Someone whimpered like a pup in distress. It was her voice, she thought, but younger than thirteen. A child, really.

Two things happened at once. Her free arm unfroze, allowing her to swing it upward and claw for a grip upon his wrist.

And Robert let go of the parapet to reach for her.

Her eyes met his. Saw his fear. His shock at losing his balance upon the stones of Packhorse Bridge. She felt his grip upon her elbow, even as her bleeding hand circled his thick wrist.

Then, she felt them both falling. Felt his grip swinging her, his strength astounding as he forced her weight toward the center of the river like a fisherman tossing a net into deeper water. He let go at the farthest arc. She could not hang on, not with the blood on her palms and the momentum of his swing.

She fell.

Bridge and leaves and sky disappeared.

Water swallowed her with a concussive clap, a consuming chill. Her legs folded beneath her as they met the river's bed. But she did not hurt. Apart from swallowing a bit of water, she was ... unharmed.

Good heavens, Robert had saved her. Again.

She shoved upward through murky water, her pink skirts dragging and fighting her legs. No matter. The river was not terribly deep, and John had long ago taught her to swim.

When she broke the surface, she immediately looked for Robert. Had he managed to catch himself? Surely a man of his strength would have done. Or had she seen him ... fall?

The pressure in her chest built as she treaded water, frantically searching the bridge above, the heart-shaped leaves at the north end, and finally, the river's bank near the abutment.

Where rough rocks now were stained red.

Where Robert—who belonged to her, and she to him—lay like a fallen god.

Silent.

Still.

Broken.

She screamed loud enough to quake the trees. Screamed his name, over and over. She gulped water. Fought her skirts. Kicked at the current, which wanted to drag her past him. Her feet found pebbles and sand. She shoved her body toward him, ground her knees on rocks for the second time that day.

Reaching him, she saw his collarbone protruding grotesquely against his skin. Saw his leg bent at an unnatural angle. Bone piercing through. Blood staining rock. She reached for his jaw. Brushed his eyelids with her thumbs. Stroked his heavy brows over and over.

She could not tell if the blood that streaked his face was hers or his.

And she did not realize how loudly she'd been screaming—how relentlessly she'd been chanting, "Robert, please. Wake up. Wake up. Robert!"—until she felt her brother's arms tighten around her from behind.

"Come away, Annabelle."

"No!"

"Let me help him."

"Robert! Wake up!" Her hands trembled so badly they felt disconnected from her body. Numb. "Why won't you wake up?"

"Annabelle!" John forced her up onto her feet with a huge heave. He spun her even as she kicked and clawed to return to Robert's side. He shook her and forced her to look into shockingly hard, steady hazel. "Fetch my horse. Ride to Clumberwood Manor."

She shook her head.

He shook her again. "He will die, Annabelle. If you do not fetch a surgeon, he will die. Is that what you want?"

"No," she sobbed, her voice frayed after all that screaming. "Please. John, it is my fault. He mustn't die."

John's jaw hardened while his eyes melted into liquid gold as their father's sometimes did when gazing upon his children. Her brother gathered her close, his arms wrapping her too tightly as he cupped the back of her head. Her chin dug into his shoulder. His breath was hot against her ear. "He won't, little sister." He pulled back, the gold blazing. "We love him too much to let him leave us, don't we?"

It was only after she'd climbed the bank, after she'd struggled onto John's saddle and raced the half-mile to Clumberwood that she lost her hold upon it—the pressure inside her. As her home came into sight, the pressure burst, forcing its way out as gasps.

Robert might die. Not in battle, but at her careless hands.

She'd fallen into the river earlier. But only now was she drowning.

Chapter Two

"How swiftly childhood ends.
How brutal is the world that makes it so."

—THE DOWAGER MARCHIONESS OF WALLINGHAM in a letter to the
Marquis of Mortlock reflecting upon the vagaries of youth and fate.

Dearest Robert,
Perhaps you heard I turned my ankle last week. I blame our new dance
tutor, Monsieur Garcon, who became distracted when Eugenia
accused him of not speaking French. Though she is only five, her
observation was quite correct. I suspect he hails from Birmingham.

Still, the thought of you when I was injured brought comfort. I

remembered how you would always catch me, always carry me. When
you are near, I never have cause to wonder whether I am safe. With
you, I always am.

Ever yours,
Annabelle

—Letter to Robert Conrad dated May 14, 1808

August 1, 1809

ROBERT'S HEAD FLOATED HIGH ABOVE HIS BODY. THE
laudanum, he supposed. A pity it did nothing for the agony
clawing fire outward from his leg, neck, shoulders, back—and
the aforementioned head.

Not enough, at any rate. That would require oblivion. Or death.

His grandfather sat on the foot of his bed, square shoulders
curved forward in rare defeat. "It is done, my boy."

Falling from a bridge produced myriad gradations of pain in
his body, from mild bruising around his wrist to screaming
anguish where bone had pierced flesh from inside.

But nothing hurt as badly as this.

He let his gaze fall to the side, glaring at the queer square of
light shining around his bedchamber draperies.

"Commissions do not sell as readily during war," his
grandfather continued, the old man's voice rasp and flint. "Too
much risk a man might have to earn his laurels." A wry grunt
signaled the Marquis of Mortlock's disgust. "Pale, pampered
whelps," he muttered. "Nevertheless, yours has sold. Sir Harold
Standish's boy appears eager to join your regiment."

The square of light wavered, silver and blue. "No longer mine."

Grandfather hummed his agreement. Slowly, the old man stood, bracing himself against the bed's post. "A pity, indeed. Martin Standish might be eager, but you were born for it. Runs in your blood." He glanced over his shoulder to where Robert lay propped against a pile of pillows. Iron-hued brows creased and lowered. A big, bony hand gripped the bedpost as broad shoulders sagged. "You've your own battle ahead, my boy. Not the one you anticipated. Less glory, to be sure."

Robert let the silence thicken. Perhaps Grandfather, in his gruff way, meant to inspire resolve in his broken grandson. Instead, Robert wished the rocks of the Tisenby had done a more thorough job.

"It will require every ounce of Conrad steel you can muster," the old man continued. "God knows you've inherited your share." He shook his head, then glanced down at his own big, gnarled hands. "Built like me. Always were." Turning, he placed a hand beside Robert's on the blanket, spreading his fingers, comparing the two—one showing the wear of more than seventy years, the other young and scabbed and bruised. "Your father, your brother. They take after your grandmother's side. The Northfields pride themselves on being thoroughly domesticated. Not a soldier in the lot." The gnarled hand patted the blanket as though it wished to comfort but did not know how. The old hand withdrew. Grandfather drifted toward the bedchamber door, pausing before he disappeared.

"You will fight, Robert." His voice was as rough as his knuckles. "That is what we were made to do."

Robert did not want to fight. His steel was not Grandfather's steel. His hands were not Grandfather's hands. They shared a name, a bloodline, a resemblance. But Nathaniel Conrad had been one of the youngest captains in His Majesty's army to earn not only a promotion to lieutenant colonel but an additional title—the Marquis of Mortlock. He'd been a second son, like Robert. He'd purchased a commission at sixteen, fought in the Seven Years' War. When his elder brother had died, Nathaniel had inherited the title Earl Conrad. And though he'd done his duty by taking a genteel wife from the "thoroughly domesticated" Northfield family and producing an heir, he'd never been anything but a soldier.

A ferocious, fearless fighter whose blood ran thick with the steel of Saxon warlords, Norman invaders, and Prussian crusaders.

Nathaniel Conrad had been a mere six-and-twenty when he'd led his men into the jaws of certain death during the Battle of Belle Isle. Previous attempts to take the French island had failed, but Captain Conrad had never been an ordinary soldier. He and his men had scaled impossible cliffs, beat back French forces into retreat, and set the stage for the siege that later claimed the island. Belle Isle was strategic territory, its proximity to mainland France making it an ideal base from which to launch future attacks. The victory had positioned England to greater advantage in the negotiations for peace with France two years later.

By then, Captain Lord Conrad's heroism had become legend, earning even the king's admiration. Indeed, His Majesty had bestowed a rare honor upon Earl Conrad, making him a marquis and granting him a small but coveted property near London.

Grandfather had accepted the title and the property, naturally, but he'd never worn the cloak of refinement well. He preferred the ancient stones of Rivermore Abbey to the civilized symmetry of Mortlock Manor. He preferred the title of lieutenant colonel to that of lord. And he preferred the company of the grandson who was most like him, rather than the heirs he regarded as "more Northfield than Conrad."

For his entire life, Robert had understood his place. He was

Grandfather's boy, a living legacy. He hadn't the ready charm of John Huxley or the fine manners of his father and elder brother. He scarcely knew which spoon to employ during the dessert course. But the outsized hands that felt oafish with a teacup gripped a sword with perfect dexterity. The warrior's gaze that found ballroom machinations incomprehensible could predict battlefield maneuvers with little trouble.

Grandfather had it right. Robert was made for war.

He shut his eyes against the taunting square of light. Let his head float. Gritted his teeth against the pain.

The fall had broken more than his body.

He glanced briefly at his hands. They hadn't been strong enough. Bloody hell, *he* hadn't been strong enough to pull her up. Without proper leverage, he'd barely managed to swing her to the middle of the river.

She'd survived. A few bruises on her arm, scrapes on her knees, scratches on her cheeks and hands, according to Hux. But she was alive and whole. It was his only consolation. The only thing that mattered, really.

Still, rescuing Annabelle exacted costs. This one had been particularly steep.

He gripped the blanket beside his hip, the fabric of his sling. His neck and shoulders screamed through the laudanum's haze, forcing his fists to loosen. Fists were pointless, now, weren't they? He was useless as a broken sword.

A firm knock sounded at the door—two taps, then the twist of the knob. He didn't need to glance up to know who it was, so he elected to keep his eyes on his hands. The sound of liquid sloshing inside glass confirmed it.

"Con. You awake?"

He raised his gaze. Still no sign of John Huxley's ever-present grin. His best friend had come to see him several times since the accident. He hadn't grinned once.

Huxley moved hesitantly toward the bed. The scrape of a

chair being dragged closer felt like saw teeth grinding Robert's bones.

"Brought you some relief." The other man raised the bottle, sloshing the amber contents inside. "Later, perhaps."

"Why do you keep coming, Hux?"

Huxley stretched to set the brandy on the table next to Robert's laudanum. He sighed and ran a lean hand through thick hair. "I should have taken her home."

"No."

"She is my sister. My responsibility."

"We argued about her. Nothing new."

"Yes." Huxley's mouth twisted. "And you leapt to her defense. Nothing new there, either."

"You had the right of it," Robert admitted, noting his friend's bloodshot eyes and tense jaw. "Coddling her made everything worse. My fault, not yours."

Hux blew out a breath. For a bare moment, his mouth relaxed into a quirk of affection. "Annabelle. Ever the exasperating pest. I should have known better than to leave you both ..." His voice rusted, and the flicker of amusement vanished. "Good God, Con." He gestured sharply toward the odd apparatus the surgeon had applied—a splint that elevated and immobilized his fractured leg. Hux seemed about to speak before thinking better of it, instead hanging his head and glaring toward the brandy bottle. He strummed his jaw several times with his knuckles before speaking again. "She wants to see you."

"No."

"To apologize—"

"I don't want her apologies."

"What of mine?" Haunted hazel eyes met his. "I am sorry, Con. For ... for everything that happened."

"I don't want your apologies, either."

Silence fell between them like a bramble thicket.

"Very well," Hux said after a long pause. "Be vexed at me, if it helps. Bloody hell, I'll stand still for the thrashing you'd like to give me, once your shoulder heals. But do not deny her this."

His head might be floating, but his gut burned. "What am I denying her?"

"She is tormented. She blames herself."

"Blame changes nothing." He sounded low. Mean. Bitter. But his tone was misleading, for he felt none of those things. Quite the opposite, in fact. He loved her. He always had.

"She hasn't eaten in days. Wanders about like some phantom." The charming, insouciant John Huxley swallowed as though he might retch—or weep. "Please, Con. Let her have her say."

Robert closed his eyes. There, in the dark, her face appeared. White with innocent horror. Mouthing his name. Silently begging. Those deep brown eyes—Huxley brown—had always dominated the round lines of her nose and chin, giving her the look of a wild sprite crossed with a cherub. Now, he could only picture them filled with terror, remember the moment he'd known they would both fall.

He could not bear to keep reliving it—the sensation of her fingers slipping from his grip, the sickening thought that he hadn't done enough to save her.

He blinked his eyes open, banishing the image. "Very well."

As though aware just how close Robert was to reversing his decision, Hux rushed to the door. A moment later, he ushered her inside Robert's bedchamber.

She had always been small. Her rounded features gave her the look of plumpness, but Lady Annabelle Huxley was as delicate as a teacup. Presently, in fact, she was the color of bone china, her lips bloodless, her eyes enormous and dark. The fiery scratch upon her jaw was the only bit of color he could see.

She stood weaving in place, her hands folded neatly. Long, white-muslin sleeves covered her arms to the wrists, so he was unable to discern the extent of the bruises he'd left upon her.

The very thought burned his stomach, dwarfing the pain of his injuries.

He dropped his gaze. This was a mistake. She was too young to witness the blackness inside him.

"R-Robert?" Her voice warbled. Muslin swished as he sensed her moving closer. When he glanced up, her bowed lips quivered and curved down.

"Say what you came to say," he ordered softly, hoping she would leave. He could not bear this much longer.

Frantic and pooling, a brown gaze combed his immobilized leg and arm, his blackened neck and bruised eyes. Tears spilled over bone china cheeks as her delicate throat bobbed on a swallow. "I—please." She covered a gasp. When she lowered her hand, he spotted the scabs on her palm.

Fire burned deeper, burrowing into his bones.

"I am so very sorry, Robert." A faint sob shook her chest. She moved into the golden light cast by the lamp at his bedside. Swaying as though waves knocked her to and fro, she suddenly collapsed to her knees.

From his position in the shadows near the door, Hux rushed toward his sister, only to halt when Annabelle held up a hand and shook her head. She placed her palms upon Robert's bed, her fingers spreading near his hip.

"I wish it had been me." Her statement was a mere breath. But he heard. And the words detonated something inside him.

"But it was not," he replied, scarcely able to whisper, to do the hardest thing he'd ever done.

"I beg of you, Robert." Her voice twisted. "I beg your forgiv—"

"Do not. I shall not grant it."

She fell silent, dark eyes searching and swimming—tormented, just as Hux had said.

It was Huxley to whom he next spoke. "Take her home."

"Pl-please," she sobbed. "What can I do?" Delicate fingers brushed his left wrist, the one she had gripped desperately only days before. "Let me earn your forgiveness. I shall visit every day until you are improved. I shall bring you broth from Clumberwood's kitchen and books from Papa's library. I shall—"

"Stop." His guts felt like molten lead.

"—do anything you ask. Anything. Please."

He summoned the strength he'd lacked for too many years—strength bred into him by Saxon warlords, Norman invaders, and Prussian crusaders. His grandfather had been right. He had a battle ahead, one requiring Conrad steel. Bone china teacups would never survive it—nor should they have to.

"Do you mean it?" he asked. "Anything?"

She knuckled away her tears, nodding frantically. "Anything you wish. You enjoy my drawings, do you not? I could sketch a new one each day. If you prefer, I could write letters like the ones I sent when you were away at school. At least it might offer a bit of amusement—"

"Here is what I want most, Lady Annabelle." He forced the words from his throat. Forged them with bitter cold that was both cruel and necessary. "I wish never to set eyes upon your face again."

He'd imagined she could not get any paler. He'd been wrong.

Her lips were gray. She swallowed reflexively. Panted like a wounded pup.

"Bloody hell, Con." Hux's rasp sliced through the long silence.

Robert could not let it dissuade him. He kept his eyes upon hers, held her gaze so that she could not mistake his resolve. Conrad steel must be wielded decisively. "If you truly wish my forgiveness, then you will do me the favor of removing yourself from my sight. Not merely today, but forever."

She'd gone still. Even her breathing appeared to have stopped.

He must finish it. "If you see me on the road, you will change direction. If you hear that I might attend the fair, you will avoid the same. If I must visit Clumberwood Manor to speak with Lord Berne, you will confine yourself to an unseen chamber until I have departed."

Her lashes fluttered. Her gaze fell.

He crooked a finger beneath her tiny, rounded chin, forcing her back to him. "Perhaps one day, you will imagine my terms must ease, that I spoke in haste at the apex of my despair, and that, in time, I shan't mind your presence again. This, I assure you, would be an error. You have cost me my commission. You may have cost me my leg, for the surgeon doubts whether he can mend it before the rot sets in."

She pressed her lips together. Tears were a constant stream now, but she did not look away. He should have been surprised, but Annabelle Huxley had always been braver than a girl her size had any right to be.

"Leave me now," he said, rending something he knew would never be mended. Something precious and dangerous. "Leave me always."

Long after John Huxley helped his sister to her feet and guided her gently out of Robert's life, long after Robert had drained a bottle of brandy so that his head both floated and spun, he could still see her.

Every time he closed his eyes, there she was. His Bumblebee. Mouthing his name as he strangled her tiny, delicate fingers in his big, oafish paw.

Slipping from his grasp. Falling into water.

Disappearing an instant before he shattered into a million pieces.

Chapter Three

"*The benefits of feminine influence upon a man's life are both myriad and essential. Proper meals. Motivated bathing. Decorative pillows. One supposes men are useful, too. I once had a carriage wheel that required repair, for example.*"

—The Dowager Marchioness of Wallingham in a letter to the Marquis of Mortlock regarding the sad state of his grandson's attire.

Dearest Robert,
I saw you in the village today, outside Mr. Parnell's smithy. You did not see me, of course. My skill at ducking into doorways and hiding behind coal carts now surpasses a pickpocket's. You've grown too thin. John assures me you are improving, but I cannot bear to see you in

such a state. I have asked him to ensure Rivermore's cook prepares your favorite beefsteak every day until you are fully recovered.

I don't know why I keep writing letters I shall never send. Talking to oneself seems the height of futility. Yet, I've found emptiness a far worse companion than futility. Perhaps someday, this will change. Perhaps someday, you will forgive me.

Ever yours,
Annabelle

—Letter to Robert Conrad dated August 4, 1810

February 8, 1816
Rivermore Abbey

"YOU NEED A WIFE."

Robert wiped the back of his neck with the corner of a horse blanket and picked up the bucket near the stable's entrance. He threw his grandfather a skeptical glower. "I asked why I should travel to London, not whether it is time to marry."

Grandfather grunted. "Same answer to both queries."

Sighing, Robert retrieved his cane before limping into the stable yard. The groom, a yellow-haired lad Robert had recently employed, tipped his cap and murmured, "Good day, Mr. Conrad. My lord." The Marquis of Mortlock's gait was even slower than Robert's, but the boy stood at attention like a footman serving supper until they'd both passed by.

The processional was a slow one. Robert's efforts to mend his broken body over the past seven years had been precisely the battle Grandfather had predicted—brutal, glacial, and riddled with setbacks.

In the first year, he'd fought to keep his leg. The third surgeon had agreed to allow it but warned he was likely to die from putrefaction within a sennight. A fourth doctor had given Robert crutches and told him such severe fractures rarely mended well enough to support a man's weight. A fifth doctor had given him a cane and warned him to expect pain "like you've never known."

In the second year, Grandfather had summoned Robert to his library, glared at his thinning frame and listless, unshaven face before barking, "My estate manager is leaving for York. Wants to work for his wife's father or some such. You will take on his duties." Robert had shaken himself out of his laudanum stupor long enough to protest, but Grandfather had cut him off with a disgusted glare. "He leaves after the harvest. I suggest you use the time wisely, my boy. You've much to learn."

Robert had needed his wits, so he'd reduced his intake of laudanum. He'd needed his writing hand, so he'd fought to restore the strength in his right shoulder. He'd needed to visit Rivermore Abbey's farms and examine its damaged fences and arrange the chapel roof's repairs. So, despite his physician's warnings, he'd fought to strengthen his leg enough for riding.

It hadn't gone well. The leg had healed badly and proved his fifth doctor correct. Atrophied muscles punished him with weakness during the day and excruciating pain at night. He'd sweated through horrific knots above and below his knee, nearly gagged upon his agony as, again and again, he forced his thigh muscles to lengthen, his calf muscles to limber around awkwardly mended bones.

In the third year after Robert's accident, he'd finally worked up the courage to mount a horse again. His companion in the endeavor had been Colby, the old stable master who'd lost a leg to a Frenchman's musket ball at Belle Isle and later followed his captain into employment at Rivermore Abbey. Colby only ever spoke to horses, but that day, as Robert sat in a saddle for the first time in three years, the old major had squinted up at him, patted his own amputated leg, and said, "Best keep yer seat. I ain't liftin' ye when ye fall."

The gelding Colby had selected for him was the slowest and oldest in the stable. Methuselah's smooth gait, heavy bones, and patient nature made riding bearable, if not pleasurable. Since then, Robert had seen little reason to change mounts. The horse might be a touch swaybacked, and yes, he occasionally fell asleep in the middle of a ride, but he was steady and loyal. Despite appearances, Methuselah had a useful life left in him.

Robert sometimes wondered if the same could be said of himself.

In the fourth and fifth years, he had gradually improved until his strength surpassed that of his youth in all but his injured leg. In the sixth and seventh years, his skills as Rivermore's estate manager likewise progressed until he knew the accounts without looking, understood the estate's rhythms better than his own heartbeat, and could predict his suppliers' lowest prices down to the farthing. Crop yields were up year over year. Rents were high and tenants' complaints were few. Rivermore Abbey was prospering.

All the while, Grandfather's health was declining. At first, Mortlock had merely taken to napping in the afternoons. Then, he'd ceased riding with Robert, instead spending hours each day corresponding with old acquaintances, an activity he'd previously derided as "the impotent reminiscing of dying men." Over the past several months, he'd developed an alarming pallor and a rattling, persistent cough that chilled his grandson to the core—when Robert allowed himself to contemplate it.

"A wife will civilize you," Grandfather said now, eyeing Robert's dusty coat and shaggy hair. "Bed you. Give you children. A bloody haircut."

Opening the gate to the east courtyard, Robert grunted and waited for Grandfather to shuffle past. Rusty iron groaned as he pulled it closed behind the old man.

The subject of women and wives was not new—Grandfather had made his position plain over the past few months, often with an irritated tone, as he had now.

"My brother is the heir," Robert reminded him as they entered the east doors into the abbey's service corridor. "William is civilized enough for both of us. And he is married."

Grandfather released a disgusted snort. "For all the good it's done him. Ten years. No babes. Potent as a raindrop in a barrel of brandy."

Robert continued along the dark corridor past the archway to the kitchens, which bustled with clanking pots and servants' chatter. Distantly, he noted one of the flagstones was cracked and would soon need repair.

"It will be years before his lack of offspring becomes a concern," he murmured, wondering if he should hire the same tradesmen who'd repaired the entrance hall last winter. They'd been slow but reliable.

Behind him, Grandfather's shuffling steps halted. "Not so many years as you might think."

Robert stopped. Turned.

Grandfather slumped against the casing for the door to the east stairway. His head hung low. His skin was white. Iron-gray hair had thinned enough to reveal his scalp. Blue eyes once sharp as sapphires were now milky and exhausted.

Robert's ribs squeezed until breathing was a chore. Grandfather was dying. They both knew it. The thought tinged every moment of Robert's days like smoke in the draperies—an acrid reminder.

"Earl Conrad inherits first," Robert pointed out. "Then William. At best, I am third in line." Leaning heavily on his cane, he shifted closer, moving carefully to avoid a cramp. His leg always pained him worst just after a ride.

"Your father and brother share a weak constitution and a fondness for overindulgence. Typical Northfield get. I'd wager you have fifteen years at most."

"William could still produce an heir—"

"Stop acting the fool!" Grandfather barked. Stooped shoulders straightened as he shoved away from the wall. "Ten years and not even a by-blow. There will be no heir, apart from you."

Robert ground his teeth and tore his gaze from the old man's. Pivoting on his cane, he muttered, "I've work to do."

An old hand, weakened by time but strengthened by determination, grasped his sleeve. "You need a woman."

Robert tugged loose, but he twisted to meet his grandfather's gaze. "I need to work."

"Obstinate whelp. Think I gave you this position because I could not find another to fill it?"

He narrowed his eyes upon the old man. "Rivermore has prospered in my—"

"Bah! You needed a battle to win. Managing the estate gave you one. Congratulations on your victory."

"The work suits me."

"The work will not birth your sons."

Robert shook his head, vexation beginning to burn in his gut.

Heedless, Grandfather continued, "The work will not make this great pile of stone a home." He clapped the corridor wall. "You spend too much time in the company of old warhorses. Major Colby. Me. Work is a fine thing, my boy. But a man needs more, lest his soul wither like a muscle seldom used."

Glancing down at his twisted leg, Robert swallowed his reply. Sometimes withered muscles were all a man had. Sometimes the damage was too great to repair.

Cold rushed in like a north wind. He wanted to deny it, but he'd recognized it himself. His nature had always been taciturn, and the grinding struggle of the past seven years had further callused him until nothing seemed to matter any longer. Even his Grandfather's impending loss was simply another battle he must wage with gritted teeth. He was a soldier without a war.

Or perhaps life itself was a war. Hard men won. Soft men got crushed.

Robert's lips twisted as he nodded down at his cane. "Know many women who would willingly shackle themselves to this, do you?"

"Don't need many. Just one. God willing, she'll have a fine set of bosoms."

What a stubborn old goat. Grandfather did not understand. Even before his accident, Robert had not found much success with the fairer sex. The handful of times he'd managed to coax a woman into his bed, he'd had John Huxley to thank for it. Hux could woo not only his own quarry but her companions, as well. Since then, Robert's prowess had not improved much.

He imagined wooing a wife would be doubly difficult. And to be worthy of such herculean efforts, she must be exceptional. In truth, the only female with whom Robert had ever formed a true connection had been a girl, not a woman. He'd loved her as a child loved another child. No, that wasn't quite right. As a soul loved another soul. Yes, that was closer. The feeling had a purity he'd never been able to explain. Golden, shimmering, inexorable.

Perhaps that was why their bond had eclipsed anything less powerful—which was everything. He might feel simple lust for the Nottingham widow he visited sporadically, or appreciation for the kindly Miss Thatcher, who'd helped her physician father tend his grandfather's ague last month. But nothing compared, really. Even years after he'd severed it, the bond cast a long shadow

He closed his eyes, forcing golden memories to gray and recede back into their corner. Over the years, he'd found it best to forget.

"What do you want of me?" Robert heard his own voice, tight and graveled.

"To see you married before I go."

All of Robert's arguments—with his grandfather, with himself—curled up and disappeared. The stark words, the calm certainty in those milky blue eyes, spoke the truth.

He was going to lose the one man who mattered most. And this was the one thing he could do to bring that man peace. Could he deny him that?

The battle would be misery, just as all the others in the past seven years had been. But Robert's adversary was not Nathaniel Conrad. It was time. Time was less forgiving than the rocks of the Tisenby.

Robert steadied his weight upon his cane. He glanced to where his grandfather's hand rested on the stone wall. Then he came back to focus on a weathered, old, beloved face.

"Very well." His voice was tight. He cleared his throat. "I shall write our new neighbor to the north—Thatcher. The physician. He and his wife are hosting a dinner week after next."

Oddly, Grandfather's glower deepened. "Bollocks. Major Colby has more bosom than the Thatcher girl. No, you must go to London."

Robert frowned. "Why?"

"Proper breeding matters. The woman you marry will be a marchioness one day." Grandfather patted the wall again, his eyes roaming the corridor with fond melancholy. "Before that, she will be mistress of Rivermore." His gaze came back to Robert, strong and sure. "Most of all, she will have the thankless task of civilizing you. Best find a lady trained for such endeavors."

Robert let his silence convey his skepticism.

Grandfather gave an impatient grunt. "That scowl of yours is likely to send the civilized chits scurrying for their mothers. Try smiling."

Robert kept his expression unchanged. Why should he pretend? Smiling indicated happiness, which was the last thing he felt.

Sighing, Grandfather continued, "I've been corresponding with an old acquaintance, the Dowager Marchioness of Wallingham. She's agreed to guide you during the season." He huffed a small chuckle. "Brace yourself, my boy. She'll not be gentle." He wagged a half-crooked finger up and down in Robert's direction. "But, by God, you need her help. That waistcoat should be put out of its misery along with the swaybacked nag you call a mount."

Robert glanced down at his rough riding coat and woolen waistcoat. Threads were frayed along the waistcoat's edges. His shirt was worse—holes beneath both arms needed mending. He hadn't worn a cravat or suffered a haircut in over a month.

Blast. Perhaps Grandfather had a point.

He tightened his grip upon his cane. "So, you want me to go to London for the season and find a pampered aristocrat to marry."

Grandfather nodded. "A good one. Fertile. Look for ample hips."

Robert sighed. "Anything else? Blonde hair, perhaps?"

"The sooner the better. At my age, delays are perilous."

April 20, 1816
Mayfair

AFTER SEVEN DAYS IN LONDON, ROBERT COULD HONESTLY SAY the season was not as painful as he'd anticipated.

It was worse.

Lady Gattingford's fete might be the first ball he'd attended, but it would also be his last, by God. He winced as a tall, thin gentleman who reeked of onions and port slammed into his bad shoulder.

"Oh! I do beg your pardon," the man slurred before weaving on his way.

Leaning heavily on his cane, Robert moved tighter against the wall of the crowded ballroom. His leg ached in repeating pulses. The air was hot and dense, the ball a crush of bejeweled ladies and black-clad gentlemen. His mouth had gone dry a quarter-hour past, but Lady Gattingford's lemonade was little more than tart water. Nearby, an obnoxious Scot named Mochrie guffawed at his own jest. Among the dancers in the center of the marble floor, a bulge-eyed fat man ogled a buxom lady. She wrinkled her nose every time the forms of the quadrille forced her to circle him.

Why did Robert continue attending these gatherings? They were excruciating. He could not dance. He loathed the stifling air created by too many peacocks in one place. None of the women Lady Wallingham had urged him to pursue showed signs of being charmed. Rather, they seemed vexed by his silences, intimidated by his frowns, disconcerted by his limp, and disappointed to discover he'd been wounded in a mundane fall from a bridge and not a heroic charge at Waterloo.

Worse, he hadn't found a single lady he would pursue across a busy street, much less into matrimony. The entire venture was disastrous.

An elderly man with stooped shoulders and iron-gray hair passed in front of the dancing couple. It was a reminder. Everything he had—his very life—he owed to Grandfather. Robert could damn well endure the vagaries of a London season for his sake. He'd promised he would try, and so he would.

He gritted his teeth and gripped his cane. Shoving away from the wall, he began a path through the throng toward the opposite end of the ballroom. As he rounded a group of young gents debating top speeds of high-perch phaetons, he scanned the room for prospects. Some ladies were familiar to him from the spate of dinners and other assorted gatherings Lady

Wallingham had insisted he attend. He dismissed them all.

Then, as he contemplated how long a man must remain in a place before he could leave knowing he hadn't missed anything of value, his eyes snagged upon a pair of hips. He frowned, hearing his grandfather in his head. Ample, yes. Also beautifully rounded and attached to a surprisingly petite frame. The owner of said hips was flanked by two companions—one blonde and wearing large ear bobs, the other plump, dark-haired, and wearing spectacles. The one with the ample hips had bent forward to listen to her bespectacled companion whisper in her ear.

He tilted his head, eyeing the fall of silver silk over her backside. Slowly, he followed the tuck of her waist, the flutter of her gloved fingers. He noted her skin was the same color as the pearls decorating her hair. Brown curls played with her white nape. A gentle pink flush shone on her cheek as she turned toward the thin blonde on her opposite side. She smiled wide. Her lips, too, were pink, he noted. She licked them, her tongue dashing as though she were thirsty.

Then, she laughed. Not a polite titter or a dainty giggle. A full-throated laugh complete with a crinkle beside her dark-fringed eye and a dimple in her gently rounded cheek.

Good God. Why had he not seen her before? Had she recently arrived in town?

Without thinking, he moved closer, using his cane and his size to forge a path. He wanted to hear her. He did not know why, but it seemed important.

When he finally did, the sound moved through him like the flashing burn of good brandy, sweet and head-spinning. Her voice was pitched lower than her blonde companion's, overlain with a faint, husky rasp. To him, most of these frivolous debutantes sounded like girls. Not this one. She sounded ... womanly.

He circled closer. Close enough to make out her words.

"Blackmore? Handsomer than Atherbourne? Lucinda. Dearest." She shook her head. "Ordinarily, I might advise such false flattery. He is a duke, after all. And male." She tapped her blonde companion's arm with the tip of her fan. "But Blackmore shot the man's brother in a duel. I doubt he would appreciate the comparison. Besides, no man is handsomer than Lord Atherbourne. He is—good heavens, when he entered the ballroom, every female within viewing distance lost the capacity for speech."

Robert frowned. He'd noticed the crowd's response earlier when the black-haired viscount had sauntered through Lady Gattingford's ballroom doors. He supposed most women would find the man handsome. So, why did it irk him that this one did?

The blonde girl with the ear bobs protested, "I would much prefer to become a duchess than a viscountess."

"Of course," came the wry reply. "You have never lacked ambition, dearest."

"Atherbourne may be splendid, and his valor at Waterloo admirable. But Blackmore is also exceedingly handsome. Given the choice, I should think the more esteemed title settles the matter."

A faint snort sounded from the silent, bespectacled girl, who then mumbled something about lemonade and ducked into the crowd.

The blonde continued as though she hadn't noticed the departure. "You are friendly with his sister, Lady Victoria Lacey."

The siren with the ample hips and pearlescent skin and dimpled cheek chuckled. Unexpectedly, the husky sound sent arousal rippling from the base of Robert's spine down through his groin and thighs. He'd never had a similar reaction merely from hearing a woman laugh. What the devil?

"As I warned earlier this evening, Lucinda, using her as a conduit to Blackmore is a mistake. Lady Victoria is polite enough to listen, but you will doom your chances with her brother in the attempt. They are rather ferociously protective of one another."

"The finest catch of the season refuses to make himself available to be caught. No, his sister is the key. Margaret agrees."

The siren shrugged. "She is your twin. You think in similar ways. Which only means you are both mistaken."

The blonde bit her lip and appeared conflicted. "Your information is usually impeccable."

"Usually?" The siren sounded irritated.

"That is why we adore you, of course. Nobody has a finer ear for gossip."

"How you flatter me, dearest Lucinda." Her sarcasm made a grin tug at Robert's lips, but her tone escaped the blonde's notice.

"Oh, but it is true! When Matilda Bentley claimed Lord Stickley would offer for Miss Meadows, and you suggested that was nonsense because he'd already set his cap for Lady Victoria, it was clear who had the superior sources, particularly in matters of matchmaking."

The siren squinted suspiciously at the blonde. "You and Margaret already petitioned Lady Victoria about Blackmore despite my warnings, didn't you?"

The blonde sputtered then protested, "We had to! Now that she is betrothed to Stickley, our opportunities to approach her at events such as this have diminished—"

Popping open her fan with a flick of her wrist, the siren clicked her tongue. "Cross Blackmore off your list, Lucinda."

"Oh, but—"

"You and Margaret should set your sights upon targets you have a faint hope of striking. Sir Barnabus Malby, perhaps. Rotund and toad-like, yes, but eminently reachable. Surely one becomes inured to offensive odors. Eventually."

Again, the siren's wry, matter-of-fact manner brought an unexpected grin to the unlikeliest of places—Robert's mouth.

Even before the accident, he'd not been the smiling sort. But this woman made him want to laugh. And view her face fully, rather than in profile. And draw near enough to decide whether he liked her scent. He suspected he would.

He liked everything else about her.

Working his way around a pair of matrons arguing about opera, Robert sidled nearer to his siren. He wanted to see her face. And perhaps her bosom.

He drew a shuddering breath as he circled her, his gaze caressing the slopes of her shape. Yes, definitely her bosom.

Across the ballroom, an explosion of murmurs near the terrace doors overtook the noise of musicians and conversations. His siren turned away, rising up on her toes to see what had caused the furor.

Blast. Now, she was drifting in that direction—away from him. Frowning, he pushed past an older man chiding his two daughters about the evils of gossip. He planted his cane against gray marble and forced his way through the crowd.

He needed to see her. Wanted to know who she was.

Like a swelling tide, the crowd surged in the direction of the glass doors, and as it did, the spaces between bodies tightened. Several people moved between him and his siren, but he could still see her. Silver silk. Pearls amidst dark curls.

A loud, shrill, feminine voice echoed through one of the open doors, berating some unfortunate soul over wanton behavior. Apparently, a scandal was erupting. Now. At Lady Gattingford's ball. The furor was separating him from the one female for whom he'd felt the slightest twinge of interest since arriving in London.

God preserve him from the ton's hypocrisies.

Scowling his frustration, Robert watched as three more bodies pushed between him and his siren. This was not going to work. From her brief conversation with her blonde companion, he'd gathered she enjoyed gossip. Short of shouting to draw her attention—which would only make him look mad—she was unlikely to find him more compelling than the salacious goings-on occurring on the terrace.

He halted, letting the crowd flow around him. Bloody hell. He must find another way. Perhaps Lady Wallingham could help. He knew the blonde companion's name—Lucinda—and the girl's twin sister was Margaret. He doubted many twins occupied such aristocratic circles. The dowager likely could identify the siren from her association with them. Once he knew who she was, he would obtain an introduction. A proper one. Face to bosom—er, face.

Turning against the flow of the crowd, Robert fought his way toward the ballroom's raised entrance. He wondered whether eight was too early to call on Lady Wallingham. Probably. To the beau monde, any hour prior to noon was deemed impolite. His leg protested as he climbed the two steps onto the raised end of the ballroom where the doors to the entrance hall stood open. Just as he passed through the nearest set, he paused.

He could not say what stopped him. An odd shimmer of heat on his neck. A queer hesitancy to leave her behind.

Whatever it was, it turned him around at precisely the right moment. Or, perhaps, the wrong one. She'd drifted to the rear of the crowd, halted in the center of the emptying floor. And she was facing him. Looking at him. Indeed, staring at him.

Something seized him hard in its grip. Fire and pain. Longing so deep it was starvation.

Her skin was pearl, her hair twists of honeyed chocolate. Her nose and chin were round, as were her eyes, darkly fringed, too big for her face. She was part cherub and part sprite. Her lips trembled. Formed his name.

Robert.

Bloody, everlasting hell.

This was no siren. This was his Bumblebee.

Without thinking, he examined her from pearls to slippers, shamefully pausing at her bounteous bosom. He swallowed. It could not be. Annabelle Huxley was a girl. Precocious and funny. Small and innocent. She was not lovely and curved with a wry, womanly laugh and ample hips.

Annabelle Huxley did not make him hard.

His eyes came back to hers. The plump, bespectacled companion from earlier tugged at her arm. Annabelle shook her head. Pressed pink lips together. Blinked as sadness replaced surprise. Retreated a step. Grimaced as though she fought a grievous pain. Then slowly pivoted away, letting her companion tug her toward the terrace.

It should not be her. Could not be her. And yet it was.

Annabelle. She was here.

Blood pounded in his ears. And in other places where it had no right.

Seven years. Seven brutal years.

He gripped his cane. Leaned into it, ignoring the jagged tension in his leg after hours of standing. Hux hadn't warned him she was in London—not that he should have done. Robert had long ago forbidden him to speak of her.

A fool. That's what he'd been.

A starving man might avoid gazing upon food, might never hear it mentioned. But the hunger remained.

And, as he staggered out of Lady Gattingford's ballroom, as he mounted Methuselah and forced his leg to bend, as he rode from the lamp-lit mews into a colder, blacker alley, he wondered for the first time in seven years what a starving man might do when reminded of his deprivation. Faced with that which once nourished him, what might he do to possess it again?

He gripped the reins and glanced up at the crescent moon, faintly glowing behind a shifting cloud. An answer came quickly, but it brought no comfort. On the contrary. It chilled him deeper than the frigid night.

He was a Conrad. He had the steel of Saxon warlords, Norman invaders, and Prussian crusaders running through his veins. Warriors might sacrifice for a cause of sufficient importance. But, in time, their true nature would always rise.

Warriors did not go hungry.

Warriors saw what they wanted. And fought to claim it.

Chapter Four

"A young lady's pastimes must be just interesting enough to be sufferable. Anything more entertaining than tepid tea invites gossip. Which is why the clever girls make gossip their pastime."

—THE DOWAGER MARCHIONESS OF WALLINGHAM in a letter to the Marquis of Mortlock regarding proper assessment of matches for one's offspring.

Dearest Robert,
My drawings have improved of late—even Jane says so. I suspect the cause may be all the time spent rambling about the countryside with my sketchbook, trying not to think about you. Needless to say, I have found greater success with the former than the latter.

Ever yours,
Annabelle

—Letter to Robert Conrad dated April 14, 1811

"IS IT YOUR AIM TO GIVE ME APOPLEXY?"

Annabelle Huxley's heart stopped before resuming its rhythm with a hard kick. Glancing over her shoulder, she arched a brow at her sister Jane and tucked her package beneath her arm. "I shall specify what was *not* my aim—to be followed."

Jane nudged her spectacles higher on her nose and gave a snort. "Obviously. You managed to leave Ned and Estelle behind easily enough," she said, abandoning her post near the shadowed brick doorway on Catherine Street and falling in alongside Annabelle as they headed for the Strand, where their footman and lady's maid waited with the coach. "But you forget how well I know your methods of evasion."

Annabelle clutched her package tighter. "Let it be, Jane."

"What business have you with a publisher?"

Nodding a greeting as they passed a finely dressed couple she recognized, Annabelle feigned nonchalance. "I enjoy Mr. Green's paper."

"*Green's Daily Informer* is nothing but scandalmongering disguised as news."

"Yes. And?"

Jane chuckled. "I thought you preferred to be the wellspring of gossip. Its grand deliverer, if you will."

"I do. A grand deliverer must have the finest sources if she is to maintain her influence—"

"By the time a rumor appears in the *Informer*, it is already days old. Weeks, in some instances."

Silently, Annabelle cursed her sister's perceptive nature. Jane was a year younger, yet she often seemed a great deal wiser than other girls of nineteen—or twenty, for that matter. "It is worth reading. Even Lady Wallingham thinks so."

"Rubbish and rot. Your allowance is sufficient to have that paper delivered to Berne House every morning, should you desire. There is certainly no need for an elaborate ruse in which you enter the publisher's premises and exit with a mysterious package you clearly wish me to ignore."

Annabelle cast her sister a sidelong glance. Considered by many too shy, plump, and plain for success in the marriage mart, Jane did not seem formidable to most. But Annabelle knew her best—well enough to be alarmed by the determined gleam in her eye.

"Jane—"

"You are one of Mr. Green's sources, I suspect."

Annabelle's stomach tightened. She slowed their pace, pausing to pretend perusal of a jeweler's shop window.

Jane stopped beside her. "The truth, now," she murmured, sidling closer. "I shan't tell Mama and Papa, if that is what concerns you."

"You mustn't tell anyone."

"Agreed."

Annabelle sighed. Looped her arm through Jane's and drew her in tight against her side, leaning into the window as though they examined the trio of gold crosses gleaming in the afternoon sun. "You have seen the work of Edward Yarrow Aimes, have you not?"

Behind her spectacles, Jane frowned and blinked. "The caricaturist? The one Lady Wallingham has vowed revenge upon for his portrayal of her as an imperious purple dragon wearing a ridiculous plumed turban and an ermine cape?"

"The very same."

"He is deeply despised, Annabelle. Do not say you are acquainted."

Annabelle kept her eyes upon the crosses. She cleared her throat. "Acquainted. No. I would not say that."

"More than acquainted?"

Finally, Annabelle slid her gaze to meet her sister's. Jane's eyes were much like hers—large, dark, and round. Their brown hair was similar, too. Their noses. Their voices. Certainly, few would mistake them for anything other than sisters. They even shared a tendency to flush at the slightest provocation. Yet, they were vastly different people. In a crowded room, Jane's shyness drove her to freeze into silence or hide amongst the wallflowers, whereas Annabelle viewed large gatherings as opportunities for friendship, connection, and information. Jane loved nothing better than to wallow in a good book with a steaming cup of coffee. Annabelle preferred the stories of those around her—real people in the real world—to works of fiction. And she liked tea. Coffee was too bitter.

Although they were close, their differences meant they did not always understand one another. But no one was a truer or more loyal friend than Jane. Of that, Annabelle had little doubt.

"He is me." She whispered the confession, barely a breath.

Jane's eyes rounded to ridiculous proportions behind her small spectacles. "You ..."

"I am him. Or is it 'he'?"

"You ..."

"His work is—"

"You ..."

"—mine. That is why I was—"

"You are ..."

"—visiting Mr. Green's offices."

"... Edward. Yarrow. Aimes." Jane's voice was even raspier than usual.

Patience eroding, Annabelle tightened her grip upon her sister's elbow. "Remember your promise."

Nodding, Jane nudged her spectacles higher. "Bloody hell, Annabelle."

Annabelle frowned and glanced around the bustling street, relieved to see no one paid them any attention. "Mind the vulgarities."

She snorted. "Vulgarities I learnt from you."

"Which makes it no more acceptable—"

"Do you realize how many people have wished for your premature demise? Aloud. And loudly."

"Only the hypocrites."

"That is *everyone*," Jane hissed.

Annabelle raised her chin. "My work exposes the truth of who they are. If they find it objectionable, they should write a letter of protest to themselves."

"Annabelle." Jane's small hand clutched her wrist. "Quite apart from the ravaging your reputation shall suffer should anyone discover you have masqueraded as a man—and for a rather *extraordinary* pursuit, I might add—you have angered a great many powerful people. It is too dangerous. You must stop."

"Don't be silly." Again, she raised her chin. Jane did not understand. Annabelle needed her work—it gave her a purpose, filled vast chasms of emptiness that had plagued her for years. Well, perhaps "filled" was overstating the matter. At least her caricatures offered a distraction. "I am good at it," she explained.

Jane clicked her tongue. "That is not the point."

"Then, what is? Nobody else knows my secret. Even Mr. Green believes I am Edward Yarrow Aimes's sister."

"Are you certain?" Jane squinted, tapping her own temple. "A bit dim, is he?"

"No. Quite astute, actually."

"Assume he knows, then. Bloody hell, Annabelle."

"Stop saying that."

"What is in the package?"

Annabelle tightened her jaw and gripped the brown-paper-wrapped bundle. "Nothing of import."

Jane's lips pursed. "If that is true, you shouldn't mind telling me."

She blew out a breath of exasperation. "Oh, very well. My last submission was ... declined. Mr. Green has requested a new one. The package contains his notes and the preliminary proof for—"

"Declined? For what reason?" Jane's ferocious frown forced her spectacles down her nose. Her knuckle pushed them up impatiently.

Warmth spread outward from the center of Annabelle's chest. She swallowed a smile and squeezed her sister's hand. How lovely it was to have such support. For nearly a year, she'd done this alone. Mr. Green was not the gentlest of editors.

"He felt my treatment of Lady Victoria Lacey's scandal showed too much sympathy for Lady Victoria and too much condemnation of Lady Gattingford's display of outrage."

Jane blinked. "But Atherbourne *seduced* her. He clearly meant his actions as retribution against Blackmore."

Shrugging, Annabelle sighed. "Yes. Unfortunately, Mr. Green believes readers of the *Informer* will be more gratified by a simpler tale: A duke's saintly sister falls from her lofty perch, breaking her engagement and her halo in one disastrous night."

"Do you agree?"

Annabelle pulled her sister into motion, pretending to browse the Strand's odd assortment of shops, before answering. "I agree it is in Man's nature to prefer simple answers—and to revel in the downfall of those we envy." She glanced at Jane, noting her frown. "But, do I think appealing to those preferences moral? No. The aim of my work is to reveal truth. Mr. Green's aim is to sell more papers."

Jane nibbled her lower lip. "At the Gattingford ball, Mama was acting as Lady Victoria's chaperone."

Yes. Their mother's guilt over the incident had made Berne House a rather weepy, distressing place over the last two days.

"If you accede to Mr. Green's demands—"

"It will make everything worse," Annabelle finished. "For Lady Victoria and for Mama."

They passed a bookshop, and as though books were magnets and Jane made of iron filings, Annabelle quickly found herself tugged toward the shop's window. "He is your publisher," Jane murmured, peering longingly at a three-volume set titled *Sense and Sensibility*. "What will you do?"

This was not the first time Annabelle had been forced to choose between the moral path and the commercial one, but it was more personal than such a quandary had ever been. She *knew* Lady Victoria Lacey. She knew the Duke of Blackmore. And she certainly knew her own mother. These were not mere figures of gossip. They were real people making difficult choices, making mistakes for which the consequences were dire.

She understood. She'd made mistakes of her own.

"I don't know, Jane," she whispered. "But I must decide soon."

"You should refuse his revisions."

"He will stop publishing my work."

"Splendid. All the better."

"Jane."

Her sister nodded toward the novel she'd been eyeing. "You see that? Good sense should prevail above the whims of sentiment. I don't wish to echo Lady Wallingham—"

"Heaven forefend."

"—but, no matter how much you enjoy this pursuit, straying from convention causes *problems* for a lady, Annabelle. Your work has incurred enemies. The risk of discovery is too great to continue."

Annabelle raised a brow. "I note this novel of which you are so fond was written '*by a Lady.*'"

Jane sniffed. "An entirely different matter."

"Not so different. I, too, am a lady."

"Her stories are fictional."

"Mine are truthful."

"Precisely! The ton *loathes* truth. They will truss you up and roast you like a leg of lamb should they ever discover your connection to Edward Yarrow Aimes."

"So long as you tell no one, they will never know, will they?"

"Hmm. A perilous assumption, I daresay." Predictably distracted when a customer exited the small bookshop carrying a sizable stack of volumes, Jane drifted toward the shop's entrance.

Annabelle rolled her eyes and tugged her book-mad sister toward their coach. "Come. Ned and Estelle will be wondering whether we have been carted off by brigands."

On the return to Mayfair, Annabelle contemplated the alterations she must make to her illustration. Her original drawing had portrayed Lady Victoria—previously dubbed "The Flower of Blackmore" for her graceful, virtuous demeanor—as a white rose being robbed of her petals by a roguish, masked highwayman while a braying donkey in a gown made of rotting lemons declared Victoria spoiled goods.

Mr. Green wanted her instead to draw Victoria as a tarnished, wilting bloom casting off her own petals in a deliberate seduction of an intoxicated highwayman.

"Tell Aimes to make her a temptress," he'd barked, shoving his notes across his desk and tapping the package with an ink-stained finger. "Like Eve. Put an apple in her hand, if it helps. And dispense with the ass. Readers won't like their own judgments coming out of a donkey's mouth."

Annabelle had gritted her teeth before carefully considering her answer. Ordinarily, she communicated with Mr. Green through correspondence, which gave her ample time to formulate her responses to his demands. But this had been short notice—he expected a new illustration within a few days' time. So, sitting across from the white-haired, large-toothed publisher, she'd had to bite her tongue until it bled.

"Do you think it wise to portray the Duke of Blackmore's sister in such a fashion, Mr. Green?"

His head had remained bent over the column he appeared to be editing out of existence. "I think it is what readers want, Miss Aimes. What dukes want matters little."

She'd cleared her throat, pushing past his arrogant dismissal. "I fear I must disagree. Respectfully. Sir."

The white head had come up. Sharp eyes had pinned her in her chair. "Oh?"

Mr. Green was a cold man bristling with impatient energy. His white hair might appear grandfatherly, but he was neither kind nor paternal. Ruthless would be more apt. His success stemmed from his cleverness with profits, charging readers the usual seven pence for the paper alone or one shilling for the paper with an Edward Yarrow Aimes print tucked inside. But he spared no mercy for anyone—be it a duke's sister, a lowly typesetter, or the poor wretches he paid a pittance to run paper through iron presses. Within moments of meeting him, Annabelle had understood how the *Informer's* popularity had surged in such a short time. It was why she always trod carefully with him.

"Blackmore is powerful," she'd continued, using the truth as her best argument. "If he chose, he could destroy your publication within a fortnight."

Shrewd eyes had narrowed upon her, dropped to the closures of her pelisse then risen to the ribbons of her bonnet. "Deliver my notes to Aimes. Tell him I expect the revisions first thing Friday next."

And with that, she'd been dismissed.

Now, she must decide what to do. Beyond the coach window,

she watched the shops and bustle of the Strand become the shops and bustle of Pall Mall before becoming the shops and bustle of Piccadilly. Ordinarily, the energy of London excited her. Everywhere was movement and sound—the turning of wheels, the clopping of hooves, laughter and chatter and shouts to gain the notice of passersby. In Mayfair, the energy was less boisterous, but it was still there, glittering like a faceted jewel. Some might be dazzled by its light, but Annabelle saw the sameness beneath the flash. That had always been a comfort—how similar people were, regardless of their circumstances.

Today, nothing was a comfort. Not the glittering energy of London. Not the challenge of her work. Not a blessed thing. The decisions she must make pecked at her like crows upon carrion. And the choice Mr. Green had demanded, while onerous, was not the greatest dilemma among them.

She frowned as the coach turned onto Park Lane and trees rustled outside her window.

No, her greatest dilemma was deciding whether a promise made by a girl must be kept by a lady. And whether the cost of breaking that promise could possibly be higher than the cost of keeping it.

She swallowed against the aching emptiness that stretched its horrid hand up to grip her throat.

It seemed unlikely. Keeping her promise was a pain that never ceased.

"I cannot abide more than an hour," Jane whispered as the coach pulled to a stop outside the large, white-stone townhouse of Lady Wallingham. "An hour. Then, we leave. Agreed?"

Annabelle squeezed her eyes closed before gathering herself enough to turn and smile at her sister. "We shall do our best, Jane. But you know the dragon sets her own timetable."

Jane shot her a puzzled squint. "Why do you look sad?"

Quickly, Annabelle forced her customary sparkle back into her eyes. It was a trick she'd learned years earlier. Seven years, to be precise. "Don't be silly. I enjoy Lady Wallingham's luncheons. They are the premier venue for gossip."

Snorting, Jane retorted, "Only you would find being repeatedly scorched by a dragon enjoyable."

Indeed, as an elegant footman welcomed them into Wallingham House, the dragon's trumpeting voice swept down the stairs and ricocheted off the white-paneled walls of the entrance hall.

"Leave London? The season has scarcely begun, yet you wish to abandon the field of battle without so much as a volley? Bah! I have eaten soup with more spine!"

Annabelle glanced at Jane, who arched a brow and tilted her head as if claiming victory in an argument. Distantly, she heard a quieter, masculine voice replying. She could not make out his words, but his tone did not suggest he was spineless. Rather, he sounded steady. Solid. Unmovable.

The footman showed them upstairs to Lady Wallingham's parlor. As she approached the open door, Annabelle first only saw the dragon. The Dowager Marchioness of Wallingham's white hair, tiny stature, and bird-like appearance belied the tidal force of her personality. Annabelle had known the woman for many years—her mother was one of Lady Wallingham's dearest friends. Yet, the juxtaposition of such an imperious character and loud, resonant voice emitting from a tiny, elderly woman still confounded her. It was why she had portrayed Lady Wallingham as a dragon. No other guise captured her true nature.

The caricature had caught on to the point that many in the beau monde now referred to the dowager as "dragon"—not in her presence, of course, but with regularity. Annabelle remained uncertain whether the comparison pleased or displeased the lady in question, but she suspected the former. Otherwise, such references would have ceased. Lady Wallingham wielded astonishing influence among the ton.

"When I offered my assistance, young man, I did not realize

your mind was as damaged as the rest of you. Do crutches exist for such an affliction? A curative tonic for absence of cleverness, perhaps?"

The dowager's posture as she stood swathed in blue velvet and fairly bristling suggested her displeasure was genuine. Her glare attacked a single target.

And, as Annabelle gingerly entered the room, she followed the old woman's line of sight toward the windows. Suddenly, she comprehended the reference to damage.

For, there stood Annabelle's dilemma.

Heart pounding, she halted. Scoured him from dark head to broad shoulders to black boots. Traced his heavy brows and solemn blue eyes. Drew him in like breath.

He glared back at the dragon, gripping his cane with undue ferocity. "I've little reason to remain and every reason to leave," he snapped. "Whose cleverness should be in doubt, my lady? Mine? Or yours?"

Good heavens. Had Annabelle not lost all breath the moment she'd set eyes upon him, she surely would have done so at his retort. No one spoke to Lady Wallingham in such a way. No one questioned her cleverness. It was akin to questioning His Majesty's right to rule—absurd.

But, then, Robert Conrad was quite unlike other men. He was stronger, more deeply rooted inside himself. Even at five-and-twenty, he possessed a solidity most men at five-and-fifty would envy.

Annabelle did not feel envy. She felt longing. It pierced her abdomen, achingly hot. She'd felt the same upon seeing him so unexpectedly at Lady Gattingford's ball. Then, she'd reeled beneath the shockwave. Feasted upon the sight of him. Marveled at how much larger he was—wider shoulders, thicker arms, more muscular neck—than the last time she'd caught a glimpse. Even his wrists appeared bigger. Stronger. She'd tried to turn away, to leave before he spotted her. But it had been too long. Years. As their eyes had locked together, she'd only managed to breathe his name.

Jane had pulled her free then. Now, Annabelle clutched her sister's arm, eliciting a concerned frown. She struggled to control her racing heart.

Drat. She must regain her composure before he noticed—

"Ah! Lady Annabelle Huxley! And Lady Jane," trumpeted Lady Wallingham. Jewel-green eyes speared her. "A fortuitous arrival. Late. But fortuitous."

"Steady," Jane muttered beneath her breath. Annabelle didn't know whether the reassurance was meant for her or Jane, herself. Shyness often caused Jane to freeze up like hunted prey.

Feeling her sister's tension, Annabelle concluded the latter. The thought strengthened her. She was the older sister. She must protect Jane.

Raising her chin, she nodded to Lady Wallingham. "My lady, we are most grateful for the invitation. As always."

"Of course you are. As I have repeatedly informed Mr. Conrad, there exists no richer trove of information in all of England." Lady Wallingham raised a single white brow, glaring pointedly at the man now glowering at Annabelle. "A young man seeking a bride would be wise to make use of such a treasure."

Bride? Another dizzying wave rocked through her body. Robert was seeking to marry?

Her eyes flew to his, her stomach heaving.

Of course. After the Gattingford ball, she should have realized. He'd spent the past seven years in the country managing his grandfather's estate. Robert hated London, rejected the beau monde as meritless and frivolous. He would hardly have left Rivermore Abbey to attend the theatre and waltz across Lady Gattingford's marble floor.

Her gaze fell to his leg—the one that remained twisted where bones had failed to mend properly. No, he was not in London to waltz. He was here to find a wife.

"You are long acquainted, I take it. Neighbors, yes?"

The whoosh in Annabelle's ears made a reply difficult.

Robert answered the dowager's query first. "Neighbors. Indeed."

His tone was dark. His eyes were brooding.

Beside her, Jane cleared her throat. "M-Mr. Conrad. As it has been some time since you last saw us, perhaps a reintroduction is in order."

"No need. You appear well, Lady Jane." He was not looking at Jane, but rather glaring at Annabelle. A muscle flexed in his jaw. "Lady Annabelle."

"Well, now," said Lady Wallingham. "Fortuitous, as I said. Lady Annabelle is precisely what you need, Mr. Conrad."

Heavy brows crashed into a scowl. Blue eyes flashed and flared directly into hers as though lightning ignited the air between them. After a long moment, he finally released her to focus on the dragon. "How so?"

"A gifted gossip. She knows the secrets of this season's female stock. The good. The bad. The tedious."

Annabelle turned a frown of her own upon the old woman. What was she proposing? That Annabelle act as a matchmaker? For *Robert?* She would sooner eat one of Jane's books. Leather binding would be less likely to make her vomit.

"Were you not mere moments ago touting the vast 'trove' of your own knowledge and resources, my lady?" His question was dry and irritated.

"Yes," the dragon snapped. "A treasury you have abandoned with the haste of a startled cat. Foolish boy." She sniffed and waved an imperious finger in Annabelle's direction. "She attends the sorts of gatherings you must navigate. I am too old for such fiddle-faddle. She will assess your performance and recommend improvements."

"I will?"

"No, she will not."

Lady Wallingham ignored their overlapping protests and continued addressing Robert. "If you think she will attempt to land you for herself, you needn't worry. Lady Annabelle has *many* suitors. One, in particular, shows great promise. Captain Martin Standish. Returned from Waterloo with nary a scuff upon his buttons, or so I understand."

Annabelle blinked at the woman known for her cleverness and wondered if age had finally come to claim the dowager's mind. Captain Standish had, indeed, been amiable toward her this season. But so had two-dozen other gentlemen. They were all friendly enough. None had proposed marriage. None had begged for a second or third dance. Her interactions last season and this had produced one conclusion: Annabelle would always be cast in a sisterly light. Perhaps it was her features—more than one fellow had called her "charming" rather than "comely," as though she were a pup performing an amusing trick. Or perhaps it was her wry humor and discomfort with flirtation. Most of her conversations with gentlemen ended in one of two ways: The man walked away either laughing or mulling information she'd given him about another lady—one who was comely instead of charming.

All of which made Lady Wallingham's assurances to Robert profoundly strange.

Robert's reaction was even more so. As though he'd been shoved in the back, he moved forward several paces, gripping his cane until his knuckles turned white. Then, he gritted, "Standish. Is that true?"

Annabelle opened her mouth to set him straight, but Lady Wallingham answered first.

"Indeed. Dashing fellow. Favors sporting his uniform about, regardless of the setting—balls, suppers, a morning ride. I'd wager his epaulets have seen more daylight this season than they did on the Continent." Green eyes grew calculating. "You know, that scoundrel Lord Atherbourne refuses to be addressed by his military rank despite his heroics on the battlefield. Some nonsense about losing too many good men to accept such honors." The dowager chuckled. "Captain Standish has taken the opposite approach, it would seem. Still, he cuts a fine figure in scarlet. Lady Annabelle is quite taken with him."

As Lady Wallingham spoke her addled madness, Annabelle watched Robert Conrad's expression darken. The entire exchange was dashed odd.

Jane leaned close to murmur in Annabelle's ear, "Have I missed something? When did Martin Standish begin courting you?"

"He didn't. I think she's gone daft."

"Lady Wallingham?" Jane whispered, shaking her head. "Likely she has some manipulation in mind."

Robert closed in upon the old woman, his gaze hard and fierce upon hers. They appeared to be in a battle for supremacy. He was a foot taller, twice as broad, and heavily muscled. Yet, Annabelle would have wagered a year's allowance that the dragon had the upper hand.

"I am leaving London." Robert's rumble was edged with desperation.

Slowly, Lady Wallingham smiled. "Your grandfather will be most *disappointed* to hear it, young man."

Robert's head jerked. His posture stiffened.

"Mortlock's time grows short. He took great comfort in the assurance that his favorite grandson would be well settled with a wife before his death." She sniffed her triumph. "Pity."

Annabelle cleared her throat. "Lady Wallingham, perhaps Mr. Conrad would prefer another lady's assistance. Miss Matilda Bentley, for example, has excellent connections—"

"Rubbish. Miss Bentley is, at best, decorative and, at worst, a marvel of vacuity. I am astonished when she manages a coherent greeting. No. It must be you."

Opening her mouth to protest, Annabelle stopped when the dragon pivoted to Robert with a challenge.

"Mustn't it, Mr. Conrad?"

Though the tension in his shoulders increased, Robert did not reply. Instead, he turned toward the door. Without another word, he limped out of Lady Wallingham's parlor. Along the way, he passed Annabelle and Jane, but he did not so much as glance at their hems.

By contrast, Annabelle's eyes followed him helplessly, as Jane's might follow a cartful of books. His hair overlapped his coat's collar. The thick, dark strands needed trimming. His boots were worn and creased. His cane was stout and serviceable—no elegant silver or inlaid ivory. He wore no gloves.

As she eyed those naked hands, her breath caught.

Robert Conrad was not the man she remembered. His years of hardship had roughened him even more than rumors had suggested. She knew of his grandfather's failing health. She understood Lord Mortlock's desire to see Robert wed, knew that Robert would benefit from having a wife who would ensure his hair was trimmed and his brow was stroked to ease its tension.

Inside, Annabelle understood the wisdom of it. She wanted to want this for him. But she could not. He was hers. He'd always been hers.

She squeezed her eyes closed as he disappeared into the corridor. Clenched her teeth tight. Gripped Jane's arm. Forced her expression into neutral lines.

Heavens, how she'd missed him.

"Come, my dears," crowed the dragon. "Let us have tea and discuss Miss Bentley's shortcomings, shall we?"

As they crossed the yellow parlor to settle onto a rose velvet settee, Jane leaned in to whisper, "She clearly believes she has won, but for the life of me, I cannot discern the prize."

Neither could Annabelle. But whatever the dragon's goal, she suspected neither Robert nor she would be well pleased in the end.

Chapter Five

"My son is positively horse-mad. If he expended half as much effort searching for a wife as he does acquiring broodmares at Tattersall's, I should have a vast herd of horse-mad grandchildren by now."

—THE DOWAGER MARCHIONESS OF WALLINGHAM in a letter to the Marquis of Mortlock regarding obstacles to helping one's offspring recognize his procreative duty.

Dearest Robert,
Lady Wallingham has advised me to cease moping, as she claims my face reminds her of an overwatered cabbage. So I have taken to riding with Jane during her ladyship's visits. Enclosed is a sketch of said rides.

I am content with the cabbage riding a pony. But do the flames from the dragon's mouth look too much like ribbons?

Ever yours,
Annabelle

—Letter to Robert Conrad dated June 29, 1811

THRONGS OF EAGER MEN PACKED THE COURTYARD AT Tattersall's. Half of them eyed the gleaming black mare on display. The other half wagged their jaws at one another.

Robert leaned his good shoulder against a post and wondered why he was there. Then he remembered.

Don't come home without a good woman and a decent mount, my boy. He heard his grandfather in his head, along with the old man's graveled laugh. 'Course, some might say they're one and the same.

Grandfather had a rough sense of humor, but he wasn't wrong. Robert intended to leave London without a wife. The least he could get out of this miserable trip was a new horse.

"Sold to Lord Wallingham for forty-eight guineas!" the auctioneer called, rapping his gavel upon the rostrum before waving forward the next offering, a bay gelding with a lively gait.

Wealthy peers and lowly traders alike turned as one to mutter their envy at the Marquess of Wallingham. Lady Wallingham's son was lean, tall, and distinguished with subtle graying at his temples and an air of quiet supremacy that was well deserved. He'd cultivated the finest stable in England with an unparalleled eye for horseflesh and a will as formidable as his mother's. Holding court as much as the iconic fox perched inside the grand cupola at the yard's center, Wallingham stood beside a man holding a leashed hound. That man had the fine coat, high cravat, and tousled hair of a dandy.

Robert recognized the dandy as the Marquess of Stickley. He watched Stickley's eyes follow the bay around the courtyard as the auctioneer recited its pedigree and began the bidding. Wallingham displayed less interest, but Robert would wager he had little need for geldings—racing and breeding were his game.

"This one might suit," came a rumble from behind him.

Robert glanced back to see a giant emerge from the subscription room. Only the outline of his six-and-a-half-foot frame was visible in the deep shadows beneath the colonnade. By his side was a black-haired man of about Robert's height, but with a face that was a study in sardonic symmetry.

Atherbourne.

"No," he answered the giant. Dark eyes roamed the yard in a distracted fashion, skimming over the bay gelding before settling on Stickley. Atherbourne's glare went hot with menace. "Unless he bids. Then, I shall take it from him gladly."

The giant grunted. "Haven't you taken enough from him?"

Atherbourne didn't answer. Neither did he look pleased.

Turning in Robert's direction, the giant paused. "Conrad?"

Only when the dark-blond, granite-faced man moved into daylight did recognition strike. "Tannenbrook. Bloody hell."

A giant paw clapped his bad shoulder, making him wince. "Aye. Bloody hell, indeed. Never fancied seeing you in London. Thought you'd buried yourself in that great pile of stone you call an abbey."

Robert shook the Earl of Tannenbrook's hand. "Likewise. Do they allow your sort in Tattersall's?"

A deep chuckle. "Think they could keep me out if they were of a mind?"

"Not likely." The man was the size of a mountain.

He'd known Tannenbrook for years, though they saw each

other infrequently—the last time had been three years ago in Nottingham. Tannenbrook's estate was in the neighboring county. Unlike most peers, he did most of the land management himself. Robert's position as steward of Rivermore took him to fairs and auction houses and merchants in both counties. When he ventured to Derbyshire, he occasionally encountered the towering earl. Their similar natures—dogged, pragmatic, and skeptical of false airs—had led to a solid rapport.

Presently, Tannenbrook introduced him to Atherbourne then asked, "What brings you to town?"

"Mortlock is getting on. Wants me to find a wife. And a new mount."

Atherbourne's mouth twisted into a sardonic half-smile. "In that order?"

"Grandfather claims a woman will civilize me." Robert glanced around the yard, where a landaulet was now being offered for sale. "Failing that, he'd prefer my mount were younger than he is."

"Do not say you are still riding that old nag," said Tannenbrook.

Robert frowned. "Methuselah is sound enough."

"It took you two days to travel from Derby to Nottingham. That's fifteen miles, Conrad."

"He's a good horse. Steady."

A grunt. "Half-dead, more like."

Atherbourne changed the subject. "How goes the wife hunt?"

Robert noted the viscount had resumed staring in Stickley's direction. "Poorly. Ladies seem to favor dancing."

Glancing to where Robert loosely clasped his cane against his twisted leg, Atherbourne's face whitened even as his eyes darkened into a black storm. He appeared frozen, unable to look away.

Tannenbrook carefully set a hand upon his friend's shoulder. "The injury is from a fall he took as a lad, Luc. Not in battle."

Robert frowned, wondering why such an assurance was necessary. Then, he remembered that Atherbourne had been at Waterloo. According to most accounts, he'd approached death twice—once while leading a charge of his men, and again after discovering he'd lost half his regiment in the ensuing slaughter. Some claimed he'd gone mad with bloodlust. Others said he'd not wished to live after losing so many men.

At the moment, Tannenbrook looked worried. Little wonder. Atherbourne had gone bloodless, his eyes glassy.

"It's true," Robert said, keeping his voice low and even. He lightly tapped his cane against his boot. "Broke it when I fell from a bridge."

The viscount swallowed hard. Sucked in a shuddering breath. Finally, haunted eyes came up to meet Robert's. "A bad break, by the looks of it."

Robert nodded. "Surgeon wanted to take my leg."

"You refused."

"I like to keep what's mine."

"Yet, you didn't die."

"A near thing. Bone broke the skin. With such injuries, surgeons always remove the leg rather than watch a man rot to death." He was deliberately blunt, as it seemed to be what Atherbourne needed—reassurance that a man could survive against all odds.

Atherbourne's tension eased, his color returning somewhat. "You didn't die," he repeated.

"No. Good thing. My grandfather would have been mightily displeased to outlive me." He shrugged as though his survival had not been a torturous, impossible act of will. "I don't like to disappoint him."

Swallowing, Atherbourne nodded an acknowledgment. He seemed to return to himself enough to half-smile. "Well, a new mount is easy enough to acquire. What happens if you return without a wife?"

Robert had the same thought. But what choice was there? He could not remain in London. He could not watch Annabelle flirt and dance and laugh her womanly laugh with Martin Standish—or any man, really.

Tannenbrook shook his head. "The marriage mart is no fit place for brutes like us, Conrad." The giant gave a disgusted grunt. "Ladies prefer the dandies."

Glaring once again in Stickley's direction, Atherbourne observed, "A dandy is only a vain man with a good valet. We are all uncivilized beasts beneath our cravats."

Robert turned back to the yard for a moment, wondering why Atherbourne seemed to despise Stickley so much. According to Lady Wallingham, Stickley should be the one doing the despising—Atherbourne had seduced the man's betrothed beneath his nose.

Presently, Stickley crowed at something Lord Wallingham said and pointed down at his hound's snout. He appeared to be simultaneously bragging and begging for Wallingham's approval. Perhaps the young lord *was* a bit dandified. His hair was expertly trimmed along the sides, expertly tousled with faint curl on top. Vain, indeed. He'd also reacted poorly to his betrothed's moment of weakness, denouncing Victoria Lacey with a vehemence Robert considered scurrilous—calling a duke's sister a whore, whatever her indiscretions, went beyond the pale.

Still, Atherbourne's low-boiling fury was odd.

"If you wished to see her better treated," murmured Tannenbrook to his friend, "you might have refrained from luring her into scandal."

"She is better off," Atherbourne replied darkly. "He talks of nothing but hounds. Within a month of marriage, she would have perished from tedium."

"Aye. Nevertheless, he'll be a duke one day, which would have made her a duchess." Tannenbrook paused, softened his tone. "What is she now?"

Inside the yard, voices buzzed their excitement as a magnificent chestnut hunter pranced and gleamed around the yard. Yet, despite the din, Atherbourne was near enough that Robert heard his reply to Tannenbrook.

"Mine," the viscount breathed, seemingly unable to keep the word from escaping.

So, that was how it was. Atherbourne had been caught in his own trap.

Robert considered himself fortunate to have avoided such ensnarement. Females were complex and mysterious. Even the most virtuous had secrets. Men, by contrast, were simple and preferred straightforward explanations. If a woman was out of sorts, a man in love might feel compelled to dig for answers until his fingers bled. He might imagine her faraway gaze dreamt of a new lover—or an old one. He might picture that man's hands upon her, invent jealousies, and find himself thoroughly consternated. Meanwhile, the woman's secret might be no more than disquieted digestion.

No, Robert preferred his work. It was reliable. Unambiguous. Like Methuselah. One always knew where one stood with Methuselah—especially during a mid-ride doze.

"Sold to Lord Atherbourne for seventy-four guineas," announced the auctioneer.

As Atherbourne left to claim the fine-looking hunter he'd just purchased, Robert felt Tannenbrook move to his side.

"Apologies for his questions about your leg," the earl said in a low rumble. "Since Waterloo, he's had some ... difficulty."

Robert waved away the concern. "I was raised by two old soldiers. One lost a leg after Belle Isle. I've seen the reaction before."

Tannenbrook nodded. "You handled it well. He doesn't appreciate being cosseted."

"Men of courage rarely do."

They fell silent as both watched another large, deep-chested hunter being escorted around the central cupola. This one's gait was more plodding than prancing. Robert eyed the animal's coat, a medium brown with a white blaze running from between its eyes down to its left nostril. The marking gave the horse a lopsided look. The auctioneer described the animal's parentage—hardly illustrious, but it was a gelding, so pedigree mattered less. Next, the man waxed on about dependability, stout bones, and a "remarkably calm temperament."

Tannenbrook nudged him. "You should bid."

Frowning, Robert studied the horse's eyes, which appeared unimpressed by the fancy cupola and the finely dressed crowd. Indeed, the animal seemed in no hurry to be sold, his pace lackadaisical, his tail twitching only to swat a fly.

"You and that horse were bloody made for each other. He's only six years. Would last you another fifteen, if you treat him well."

The auctioneer cajoled and wheedled, but no one bid as the groom led the horse in another turn about the yard. "Come now, gents. Dewdrop could go for days with nary a complaint."

Behind him, Robert heard a snicker and someone whispering, "Days, aye. That's how far behind a man would be, should he take that tortoise into a hunt."

"And what of that blaze?" the auctioneer continued. "A handsome mount, indeed."

Perhaps it was the name. Dewdrop. Ludicrous for such a massive, muscular animal. Perhaps it was the unhurried gait or the bones that looked like they could haul a London townhouse. But Robert wanted this horse.

Tannenbrook was right. They were made for each other.

He raised his hand to bid, offering ten guineas.

The auctioneer pointed at him with relieved excitement. "Ten guineas! Excellent, sir! Do I have twelve?"

Out of the corner of his eye, Robert saw a flash of red. It was a sleeve. On an upraised arm. Attached to a man he'd like to flatten until nothing remained but scarlet wool and brass buttons.

"Twelve! Splendid, Captain Standish." The auctioneer turned back to Robert with eager expectancy. "Do I have fourteen, sir?"

Standish. By God, that worthless usurper was wearing his *uniform* at Tattersall's. And, once again, he was determined to filch what rightfully belonged to Robert. Narrowing his eyes, he took the usurper's measure. Sand-colored hair. Weak jaw with a marked overbite. Slim frame.

What the devil did Annabelle see in him?

"Fourteen, sir? Do I have fourteen? Just look at that blaze."

Standish glanced Robert's way, eyes assessing his reaction, mouth twitching into a faint sneer. That's when he knew. The usurper thought this was a competition. And he bloody well thought he would win.

Robert raised his hand and nodded to the auctioneer.

"Fourteen, indeed!"

The bidding war continued until Dewdrop's price reached a number as ludicrous as his name. In the end, Tannenbrook stepped in to end the battle with a bid of his own. Evidently, Standish was not so keen upon defeating the giant as he was on winning something away from Robert's grasp.

Not keen enough to spend fifty-two guineas on a ten-guinea horse, at any rate.

"I expect repayment, Conrad," Tannenbrook grumbled.

"You'll have it," he replied.

Scowling at the retreating scarlet usurper, Robert expected to feel satisfied by his victory. He did not. His gut still burned, his fist closing around the head of his cane over and over.

"This is not about a horse, I take it."

Robert slanted a glance at the giant. "He bought my commission after I was injured."

Tannenbrook stood silent, arms crossed. Waiting.

"He wears that uniform as if he'd defeated Bonaparte singlehanded. He was a *coward* in war. Now, he struts about like a peacock. Bloody galling."

More silence.

"He's been doing this for years, making everything into a competition. I've no patience for it."

A long pause. Then, a low, rumbled reply. "No. Those are sound reasons to dislike a man." Tannenbrook eyed Robert's hand where it fisted his cane. "But hating one—that's usually caused by a woman."

He didn't bother answering. Tannenbrook didn't seem to require it. The giant simply gave him his address in Knightsbridge and told him to bring the blunt when he came to claim the horse.

As Robert exited Tattersall's, he looked about for signs of an unearned scarlet coat, but he didn't see one. The area around Hyde Park Corner was bustling with riders and carriages entering the park, leaving the park, and striving to be noticed like the peacocks they were.

Bloody hell, he needed to leave this town. Maybe now that he'd found a new mount, he could do so.

Slowly, he made his way from the yard's entrance toward the trough where he'd left Methuselah to doze and drink at his leisure. The horse was still sleeping.

"Mr. Conrad!"

He halted mid-stride. Closed his eyes to gather his patience. Strongly considered feigning deafness.

"Don't bother pretending you cannot hear me, boy."

How could he? Her voice carried like a trumpet's blare.

"Your leg may be lame, but there's nothing wrong with the rest of you." A supercilious sniff. "Nothing a clever wife couldn't remedy, at any rate."

She sat perched inside an open carriage twenty feet away. The faint breeze caused the plumes of her bonnet to bob and rustle. Her gown was purple, but her feathers were as white as her hair.

"Lady Wallingham," he called, tipping his hat. "Waiting for Lord Wallingham, I take it."

She folded the newspaper she'd been reading and raised her chin. "I do not *wait* for my son. If I require his presence, I command it and he complies."

Despite the vagaries of this day, amusement quirked his lips. She really was unlike any other female he'd encountered. "I stand corrected."

"Do stop shouting across this muddy field, young man." She waved the folded paper in a commanding gesture. "Come! I have an errand to attend. You will join me."

He began to explain that he had other tasks and would gladly call upon her tomorrow, but she glared at him until he ran out of words.

"Get in the carriage, Mr. Conrad. We have much to discuss."

Before she announced their destination to her coachman— before he'd realized his mistake—he'd already climbed up into the barouche and lowered himself onto the seat beside her. "The Strand?" he asked incredulously. He'd assumed her errand would be in Mayfair. Surely the Dowager Marchioness of Wallingham did not venture far from Mayfair. This could take hours. "How long do you expect me to—"

"As long as our conversation requires, Mr. Conrad." She raised a single white brow. "Are you still intent upon leaving London?"

He ground his teeth. "Yes."

"Then, I expect we shall need an hour. Two at most."

As the barouche ambled along Piccadilly at a snail's pace, the white-haired termagant regaled him with cautionary tales about gentlemen she'd known in her youth who had come to piteous ends for want of a wife. In one example, a desperate baronet "involved himself with a vulgar barmaid who robbed him blind and left him naked in a churchyard on Sunday morning. An appalling sight, a naked baronet. Past eighty, little remains of a man but sagging flesh and despair."

In another example, an earl's third son humiliated himself by pursuing a rector's daughter. In truth, the rector did not have a daughter, but he did have a milk cow with unusually long lashes. "It took the villagers two years to persuade the pitiful wretch he'd been suffering poor eyesight and brandy poisoning," she explained. "His bovine pursuit waned, though some claimed they'd spy him on moonlit nights from time to time, standing at the rector's gate like a heartsick swain."

He watched a heavily burdened wagon pulled by a single, ancient horse pass them by. "Mightn't we go a bit faster if we wish to reach the Strand by nightfall?"

She harrumphed. "This is not one of those high-perch phaetons in which you young men are so eager to careen to your death. We shall keep to a sensible pace. My time on this earth will end soon enough. I see little need to hasten the process."

For the following hour, she opined on the topic of wives—primarily their importance in the care and proper maintenance of men. Her reasons for declaring them "essential" ranged from preventing rampant venereal disease to ensuring tasteful upholstery selection. When she suggested he risked permanent physical damage by denying himself frequent access to an accommodating wife, he called a halt.

"Lady Wallingham," he bit out, well past the end of his tether. "There are women in Nottinghamshire, I assure you. Scores of them. Some might even make acceptable wives. I do not have to remain in London to find one."

She dismissed his claim with a wave of her newspaper. "Rubbish. Do you wish to marry a barmaid and find yourself stripped of your fortune and your unmentionables for the entire congregation's amusement?"

He opened his mouth to answer but released an exasperated sigh instead. She obviously had an agenda, and reasoned discourse was not it.

"Your best hope—dare I say, *only* hope—of finding a suitable bride lies here in London. With my capable guidance, of course."

Eventually, they reached their destination. Not before he'd decided a preferable fate would be to leap from the barouche and break his one good leg, but the dowager's endless, relentless diatribe did halt. As the carriage pulled to a stop—in front of a decrepit cobbler's shop, no less—he threw the door wide and gathered up his cane.

"Do not even contemplate it, young man." Her voice was an icy, imperial command.

Suddenly, he understood why this woman's son answered her summons with compliance. Still, he could not spend another two hours trapped in the kingdom's slowest carriage being lectured about the dangers of insufficient marital congress.

"I'm afraid I must go, my lady."

"Go?" Green eyes flared. "Go *where*, pray tell?"

Anywhere. Anywhere was better. "I'll take a hack. I must retrieve my horse."

"You will wait here," she snapped as her coachman assisted her from the carriage. "I won't be a moment."

He shook his head, bracing his hand on the side of the carriage.

"Mr. Conrad, if you are not here when I return, I shall be sorely vexed. Your grandfather will hear of your refusal of my assistance." Her narrowed gaze blazed emerald fire. "Perhaps you do not care for *my* opinion of your worth, but I suspect you do care for his."

The last sentence, spoken in a quiet tone, hit him hard. He lowered himself onto the seat. Closed the carriage door. Watched her wave away her coachman and enter the cobbler's shop, unconcerned by its cracked window and dented door.

For the first few minutes, he wondered what the devil he was doing. She was an old woman, for God's sake. A friend of his grandfather's, it was true. But still, just a woman. She could not dictate whether he must sit or stand, nor prevent him from going where he pleased.

It was also true that some people—male or female—commanded respect. The Dowager Marchioness of Wallingham was one.

He rubbed his eyes, slumped against the seat, and sighed. When his hand fell, it brushed paper. The newspaper she'd been reading was folded in half, opened to one of the interior pages. There, tucked inside, was a separate print. A caricature. The sketch featured a round, bloated prince in front of a gilded mirror, asking a tall, long-nosed general whether he should wear the large gold crown or the larger gold crown for his war victory ball. The prince was portrayed as a slovenly boar draped in ermine and jewels while the general was represented as a lean, noble hound wearing a suit of armor.

Robert smiled at the wit.

Then frowned at the familiarity.

He traced a finger along the forms of the boar, the points of the tusks. The hound's eyes, disappointed yet accepting.

Why did it seem so familiar? He searched for the artist's name.

Edward Yarrow Aimes. He'd never heard of him.

But there was *something*. The use of animals with exaggerated features, perhaps.

It reminded him of ...

Annabelle. She'd drawn in a style much like this. Amusing sketches of her family and neighbors, mishaps such as John's first attempt to drive a phaeton. She'd captured them all, sending him dozens along with her many letters. The eyes of the animals were always most telling.

Once again, he traced the hound's features. The artistry was more polished, to be sure, yet somehow the same.

Quickly, he refolded the pages to view the title of the publication. *Green's Daily Informer*. The contents included advertisements for "miraculous" face creams, lady's maids seeking employment, and lengthy columns of gossip. It took only a minute's reading to conclude the caricature was better quality work than anything in the entire publication, yet they shared the same publisher.

Perhaps Edward Yarrow Aimes had published his work in the past, somewhere Annabelle would have seen it when she was young. She must have mimicked his style of caricature to tell stories about her own life. Yes, that made sense. She was simply a follower of this man's work. He wondered if she was still sketching away in her little notebooks. He hoped so. His Bumblebee was a rare talent.

He turned back to the caricature for one last look. Again, it made him smile.

When he set the paper aside and glanced up, a jolt shook him. He felt disoriented, as though he'd conjured a vision from his thoughts. For there, on a side street across the bustling Strand from where he sat, was Annabelle. She was arguing. With a man.

Inside his chest, darkness pounded like a battle drum.

The man was of middling height. Lean. Wearing a plain coat and worn hat. His hair was white, his teeth too large for his mouth.

Cold sliced through his belly. Annabelle was small and lovely in her green spencer and white skirts. Her shallow-brimmed bonnet failed to disguise the challenging tilt of her chin, the flush upon her cheeks.

The man stood close to her. Too damned close. He was leaning forward, saying something she didn't like, for her lips tightened and gloved hands clutched the package she held tighter against her middle.

No lady's maid hovered nearby. No footman. Not even one of her sisters. Just Annabelle and this white-haired man arguing on a busy thoroughfare at midday.

What in bloody hell was she thinking? And who in bloody hell would dare behave in so familiar a fashion with an earl's daughter?

With *his* Bumblebee.

Everything inside him coiled tighter. Forced him to rise. He threw open the barouche's door and yanked himself down to the street. It only took a moment to grasp his cane and close the door. But by the time he'd found an opening to cross the Strand, the white-haired man was disappearing down the side street.

And his Bumblebee was climbing into a hack, alone.

The hack pulled away before he could reach it. Before she knew he'd seen her meeting a strange man in an even stranger location. As he watched the black vehicle roll westward, only one thought occupied his mind.

He must stay in London.

"You did not go far, boy. That is to your credit."

Reluctantly, he took his eyes from the disappearing hack. Lady Wallingham stood beside her barouche wearing a faintly smug expression. Her plumes bobbed in the breeze. She raised a brow in expectation.

Robert returned to hand her up into the carriage, then followed to lower himself onto the opposite seat. Resolve hardened his gut. "I shall be staying in London," he said, his voice resonant with a purpose he hadn't felt in years.

She sniffed. "Good."

"I will require your assistance."

"Naturally."

He breathed, steadying himself with the rhythm, forcing his fists to relax on the seat. He glanced about, focusing on the side street where he'd seen Annabelle. His eyes fixed upon the spot until Lady Wallingham's carriage pulled into motion.

"Tell me, my lady," he said softly. "What do you know of Annabelle Huxley's suitors?"

Chapter Six

*"The best advice I can offer is to follow my advice.
This one simple rule improves mortal existence
in ways both great and small."*

—THE DOWAGER MARCHIONESS OF WALLINGHAM in a letter to the
Marquis of Mortlock regarding advice for grandsons attempting to
navigate the marriage mart.

Dearest Robert,
My brother is both perfectly daft and utterly charming. This morning,
he dressed in a footman's livery—wig included—to deliver crumpets,
bacon, and tea to my bedside. He insisted he'd taken gainful
employment within the household because he'd spent his last farthing

on a map of the Pyrenees.

What a silly goose. Plainly, his aim was to comfort me. During my fever, the nightmares have returned. I cannot tell Mama and Papa or even Jane, for none of them will understand.
I ached to feel your hand around mine when I awakened. John offered his instead. It was not the same, but it was something.

Perhaps I was wrong. Perhaps John is not so daft, after all.

Ever yours,
Annabelle

—Letter to Robert Conrad dated December 27, 1811

"GOOD HEAVENS. WHAT IF HE MARRIES A SPANISH GIRL?" Meredith Huxley, the Countess of Berne, glanced up from her son's latest letter, brown eyes round and wide. "I don't speak a word of Spanish."

Annabelle raised a brow at her mother and closed her small sketchbook to take a sip of tea. "John is touring the Continent, Mama." She nodded toward the newly opened crate cluttering the center of the parlor. "I am certain he intended Mr. Goya's painting as a gift to you and Papa, not a declaration of matrimony."

Mama frowned toward the crate, which Annabelle's two youngest sisters, Eugenia and Kate, were gleefully emptying of its straw and miscellaneous contents. "Genie, do stop elbowing your sister," Mama admonished.

Eugenia huffed and planted her hands on her hips. "Katie

pinched me first!"

"You stole the bonnet he sent me!" Kate protested, tugging Genie's arm and reaching for the apple-green silk confection.

"It doesn't suit you," Genie answered flatly, holding the bonnet high to force Kate into leaping. "Your head is too small. Perhaps when *you* are thirteen—"

"I am almost twelve."

Genie snorted. "In ten months."

"Give it back, stupid Genie!" Kate snapped. "John meant it for me—"

Mama blew out a breath and resumed examining John's letter. "Kate, do stop calling your sister stupid."

Kate narrowed her gaze upon Genie with a gleam of vengeance. "Thou hast no more brain than I have in mine elbows."

"Katherine Ann Huxley," came Mama's warning. "What did I just tell you?"

Kate's cheeks flushed as she fumed in Genie's direction. "I did not say 'stupid.' I was quoting Shakespeare."

"You will both conduct yourselves as ladies, or you may both retire to your bedchambers until dinner."

Genie's triumphant grin made Kate's fists curl at her sides.

"Eugenia, give Kate her bonnet."

Genie's grin faded. She harrumphed—or as nearly as a girl of thirteen came to it—and tossed the green bonnet onto the crate's remaining straw. Kate snatched it up promptly.

Annabelle's youngest sister was small for her age, as Annabelle once had been, so the bonnet slid down comically over Kate's ears and brow. Genie crossed her arms and smirked. Undeterred, Kate tied overlong ribbons beneath her chin, tucked and plucked the hat into a more appropriate position, and paraded about the room as though on stage at Drury Lane.

"Do you suppose they serve lamb in Spain?" Mama nibbled her lip and turned John's letter over as though searching for clues. "If he brings home a Spanish bride, I should like her to feel welcome in her new home."

Annabelle shook her head and glanced toward Jane, who sat curled in a chair near the fireplace, reading. Jane was *always* reading. Annabelle had even caught her with her nose in a book at Lady Gattingford's ball. At this rate, the only husband Jane might hope to land was a bookseller.

Annabelle attempted to catch her third-youngest sister's gaze, but Maureen was preoccupied with staring wistfully out the parlor window. At seventeen, the prettiest of the Huxley sisters often stared wistfully. Annabelle suspected it had to do with waiting to have her own season. More than anything, Maureen longed to be swept into soul-stirring love with a dashing suitor then danced into a life of domestic bliss. But Papa could only afford to launch two daughters at a time.

Annabelle should probably marry soon and spare the family any more of Maureen's melancholy sighs. At the thought of marriage, she stifled a grimace. Thus far, few gentlemen had made a lifetime of mingling sundry bodily fluids worth contemplating.

Only one. The one she could not have.

"Spaniards are a handsome people. Perhaps she will be beautiful. Oh, I do hope so."

Annabelle rolled her eyes. "Mama."

"Surely she could learn to speak English."

"A month ago, you were convinced he would bring home an Athenian. Before that, a Venetian."

"Thank heaven he did not take up with a French girl. Too haughty by half. Although, the dinner menu would have been far easier."

"Not everything is about food, Mama."

"A surprising number of things are, dearest."

"John falls in love with *places,* not women. New art, new lands, new adventures. He is infatuated with exploring."

Annabelle took a sip of her tea, which had gone lukewarm. "I'd wager he shan't marry until that particular appetite is quenched, which will not be for some time." She returned her cup to its saucer and flipped open her sketchbook. "The world is a big place."

Mama *hmm'd* and squinted suspiciously at John's letter.

Annabelle studied her most recent drawing—the one Mr. Green had demanded, refusing to bend an inch, growing ever more impatient. Yesterday, she'd gone to see him again, and they'd quarreled. She'd argued her case for running the original caricature. He'd glared with dismissive contempt and said if she did not deliver the revisions he'd ordered, he would find another artist who would.

At this point, she could not decide which she hated more— her publisher or the drawing she'd just finished.

"It is a lie," she whispered to herself. Gritting her teeth, she tore the page from her sketchbook and crumpled the drawing into a ball. Then she heaved to her feet and tossed the ball into the fire. Wandering to the window where Maureen sat pining for her own season, Annabelle laid a hand upon her sister's shoulder and released a wistful sigh of her own. A soft hand came up to cover hers.

"Annabelle," Maureen murmured, searching Grosvenor Street as though it held clues to life's deeper mysteries. "Do you suppose a lady recognizes the man she is meant to wed? Upon first sight, I mean."

A twist of sadness squeezed and tightened. "Some, perhaps." Annabelle certainly had, for all the good it had done her.

"I wonder." A wistful sigh. "Lady Victoria Lacey appeared most content with her betrothal to Lord Stickley, and yet she was lured away by a stranger." Maureen shook her head. "Was it a failing of character? Or might she have accepted Lord Stickley too soon?"

Annabelle's chuckle was wry. "You haven't seen Lord

Atherbourne, dearest. I believe that might answer your question. Heavens, the man could seduce a lamppost. Or a block of frozen marble. Even Lady Wallingham, should he venture such a horrid enterprise."

Distracted from her melancholy, Maureen turned her gaze up to Annabelle's. Like Papa's and John's eyes, Maureen's were more gold than brown. Her hair was also a lighter shade than the other Huxley sisters, and her features similarly rounded, but daintier. She was lovely. Yet Maureen's form was not her most appealing aspect. No, her substance—kind, sincere, sweet—made her a favorite with everyone she encountered.

Now, she grinned and twinkled. "The dragon? Oh, I should like to see that."

"No, I don't think you would." Annabelle gave a mock shudder. "Nauseating thought. Better to imagine the lamppost."

"He must be very handsome, indeed."

"Hmm. Yes. Devastatingly so." Annabelle had considered drawing him as the fallen angel Lucifer but had decided against it. He might be devilish in some ways, but the viscount had recently suffered great losses—his entire family, in fact—and he was a war hero, besides. Inwardly, she grimaced. Caricaturing was beginning to feel less like truth-telling and more like cruelty.

She glanced back at the settee, where her sketchbook lay on the blue-silk cushion. Then she looked at her mother. Regret over failing in her duties as Lady Victoria's chaperone had eroded Mama's cheerful determination. Worrying over imagined foreign brides was the least of it. Annabelle had recently discovered Mama and Papa arguing in Papa's study. Mama had been weeping while Papa murmured that it was two in the morning, and she would feel better once the sun had risen. Annabelle did not know if Mama had felt better after sleeping, but given the redness of her eyes, she assumed not.

How much worse might matters be when Lady Victoria's fall

from grace was mocked by the pen of Edward Yarrow Aimes? Still, Annabelle must answer Mr. Green's demand for revisions somehow. Her deadline was mere days away.

"Oh! Papa has returned from his club," Maureen observed. "With a companion, it would seem."

Annabelle turned back to the window, spotting their father's lean, distinguished form striding down Grosvenor Street. He spoke animatedly to the man at his side. Broad. Dark-haired. Solid. Larger than Papa, though of similar height. It was his shoulders. They were intimidatingly wide. And his arms were heavily muscled beneath his greatcoat. Through the rain's soft veil, she watched him. He walked with great assurance for a man with a cane.

"Is that ...?"

Annabelle's stomach flopped like a fish. "Yes."

"Do you wish to see him?"

The concern in Maureen's voice echoed Annabelle's despair. She could not answer, could not say what her heart roared.

Yes.

Yes, yes, yes.

But seeing him would never be enough.

As it happened, she hadn't any choice in the matter. Papa entered the parlor with his dark, dour companion within minutes.

"Stanton!" Mama cried, popping to her feet and crushing John's letter to her bosom as she spun toward the door. "I did not expect you to return from White's until two." She paused, her eyes flaring as Papa's companion followed him into the parlor. "Who is ...?" The man removed his hat and leaned upon his cane. "Oh my word," she murmured, her voice choked. "R-Robert? Dear boy, is that you?"

Papa's grin was wider than the sky. "Indeed it is, Meredith. And doesn't he look well?" He clapped a hand on Robert's broad shoulder, shaking him a bit like a proud father whose son had come home from Oxford. Or from war.

"Lady Berne," Robert said, inclining his head. "It has been too long."

Mama was having none of his formality. She dropped John's letter beside her tea, bustled around the sofa, and closed in upon him in two blinks. Clutching his upper arms, she drew him down into her embrace. "Oh, my dear, dear boy." She rocked him to and fro. "How we have missed you."

Papa discreetly swiped the corner of his eye with his knuckle and patted Mama's shoulder. When he spoke, his voice was hoarse. "Ran into him at the club, of all places." He cleared his throat. "I'd no idea he was in town. He asked after the family, and I told him he must see everyone for himself."

Mama pulled back to view Robert's face through welling eyes. Gently, she cupped his cheek. "Too long, indeed. I'll not abide such absences again, no matter the cause."

As he gazed down at Mama, Robert's brows drew together. First, he seemed startled and a bit confused. But only a moment passed before his eyes darkened with pain. Regret. As though he hadn't realized until that moment what he'd done.

"You have been a part of our family since you were too small to carry Stanton's boots," Mama continued, her tears overflowing onto rounded cheeks. "Do you remember that Christmas?"

He nodded.

"Annabelle was still a babe. Your mother had died. You'd just come to live at Rivermore Abbey. John was over the moon to have another lad to play with. He insisted we bring you to Clumberwood for a proper pudding."

A small smile curved one corner of Robert's mouth. "He always did favor pudding."

Mama chuckled and patted his jaw. "You had such an appetite. Ate like you'd never tasted food. Yet you refused to smile, our serious little boy. The only one who could manage to coax you into it was Annabelle, tiny as she was. It gladdened my heart." She pressed her lips together before whispering, "A mother's heart."

His jaw flickered. His gaze dropped. He seemed to be battling grief.

Mama reached for his hair. "This needs trimming." She sniffed. "Have you eaten?"

He nodded. "At the club. Lord Berne insisted."

Giving her husband a watery, approving smile, she patted Robert's shoulders and took his hands to draw him farther into the room. "Let us have tea while you tell me everything."

"Everything? Rather a long conversation, my lady."

She tugged him to the sofa. "Then we will need a fresh pot, I daresay."

To Annabelle's eye, he appeared chagrined, yet he allowed Mama to manage him—mother him, even—without a word of protest. Perhaps he had missed the Huxleys after all.

Not Annabelle, of course.

No, in the seven years since their bitter parting, he'd gone to great lengths to avoid so much as hearing her name. He'd held himself apart from the family that had treated him as one of its own. At first, Mama and Papa had assumed his convalescence kept him away from Clumberwood and caused him to refuse their calls at Rivermore.

But, soon, the truth had become obvious: He blamed Annabelle. Hated Annabelle. Wanted nothing and no one near him that reminded him of Annabelle.

In time, Mama and Papa had taken the hint and kept their distance, even while hoping for reconciliation. But Robert had evinced no change of heart, no sudden bolt of forgiveness. For if he had, John would have said so. Her brother—who had refused to be banished from Robert's life—had argued doggedly on her behalf for the first year after the accident. Eventually, Robert had ordered him never to speak of her again unless he wished to end their friendship.

Annabelle had begged John to make the concession, and so he had. He and Robert had remained friends, albeit more distantly than before. Perhaps the distance was because John had attended Oxford while Robert remained at Rivermore. But, to her everlasting regret, she suspected she was to blame.

Her brother loved her. John had seen her pain and resented its cause. Her separation from Robert might as well have been an amputation. For seven years, she'd lived without a part of herself.

At first, unable to bear the loss, she'd sought glimpses of him from afar—in the village, along the road through the wood, across a field where her family's land adjoined Rivermore's. She'd hidden behind barrels, trees, tall grass. Even a privy, once. When she'd realized seeing him only deepened the emptiness, she'd stopped.

Now, he was in London. Seeking a bride.

After giving a general nod to her and her sisters, he glanced at the open crate and sat beside Mama, propping his cane beside his knee. She watched as he conversed with her parents, solemn and respectful.

Was this a sign that he sought to reconcile with her family? Mama and Papa appeared to think so. Mama chattered on about John's travels and cooed over how much Kate and Eugenia had grown since Robert had last seen them. Papa, always a jovial sort, glowed like a lantern as he took the second chair near the fireplace.

In the first chair, Jane leaned forward and caught Annabelle's eye. Hers were questioning behind her spectacles. Concerned.

Annabelle gave a subtle shake of her head.

Maureen's hand tightened around hers as she turned on the settee. Then, she tugged Annabelle down to sit beside her. "If you wish, we could make our excuses," she whispered. "You needn't stay, dearest."

Forcing a smile, Annabelle murmured, "I am fine."

Was she? She watched Robert's face—quiet and patient—as Mama chattered away and Kate spun in place to show off her new bonnet. She watched his eyes—creasing at the corners a bit more than when he was younger—as Genie explained with exaggerated clarity why the bonnet should have been hers.

And inside Annabelle's center, above her stomach and below her heart, a fire lit.

How dare he?

How bloody *dare* he wander back into the Huxley parlor like the prodigal hero after all this time? After all he'd done to reject her family?

His absence had not just harmed her—though heaven knew it had—but Mama, Papa, and John. The stubborn, unforgiving, graceless wretch.

She had been thirteen. *Thirteen.* And, yes, she had often behaved recklessly around him, and never more so than that day on Packhorse Bridge.

But ... thirteen. She'd been Eugenia's age. A young, besotted girl.

She dropped her gaze to where Maureen still held her hand. With a gentle squeeze, she tugged loose, stood, and moved to the window. Rain misted the glass. A post-chaise rolled by, yellow and black.

Between her stomach and heart, fire blazed and spread.

He'd been grievously injured. Denied the future he'd planned for himself. His recovery had been slow and, presumably, agonizing.

Every day since the accident, she'd swallowed the guilt of that like medicine.

Or poison.

The fire in her middle caught kindling. Her skin prickled. Her jaw clenched.

Why should she continue to swallow something so bitter? Was she still expecting to be forgiven?

No. He'd punished her for seven years. Why should he suddenly forgive her now?

And even if he did, what difference did it make? He'd hurt her family. Why should *she* forgive *him?*

Eugenia and Kate continued arguing until Mama ordered them both to take their gifts to their bedchambers. As the two girls left the parlor, Ned entered. The footman approached Papa and whispered in his ear.

Papa nodded, looking faintly surprised. "Show him in at once."

Within moments, a tall man with a knife-edged jaw, stiff cravat, and highly erect posture strode into the room, surveying them through wintery eyes as though they were an exotic menagerie. He had the golden hair and refined features of a well-favored god—and power to match—so perhaps his arrogance was justified. At the moment, she was inclined to agree with Lucinda Aldridge: His handsomeness did rival Atherbourne's.

"His grace the Duke of Blackmore, my lord," the footman announced quietly.

Naturally, everyone in the room flew to their feet. Well, all except Robert, who had to retrieve his cane before slowly rising.

Blast. There came the guilt again, bitter as ever.

"Lord Berne," said Blackmore, colder than January frost. "Lady Berne." He inclined his golden head. "Forgive the intrusion."

Following introductions, Papa offered Blackmore refreshment, which he declined, and a seat, which he also declined. "Well, now," said Papa in his affable way. "What brings you to Berne House?"

"A wedding."

Mama stared at the duke, then swept her three oldest daughters before flying back to the duke. "I—I thought you did not intend to marry this season. Of course, if you are here to inquire about Annabelle—"

"I am not." Clipped. Precise. The duke was like a blade of ice. Blue-gray eyes scanned the room without landing. He paused a moment on Jane, but only to frown at her slipperless feet, which she tried to hide by slouching into a permanent curtsy.

Mama blinked. "Er—Maureen has not yet made her debut, your grace. Although, I am certain you will find her charming after spending a bit of time—"

January frost returned to slice into Mama. "You mistake me, madam. The wedding is that of my sister, Lady Victoria."

Round eyes grew rounder. "She is to be wed? To whom?"

A muscle flickered in Blackmore's jaw. "Atherbourne."

Mama gasped. They all did, really. Good heavens, Victoria Lacey was to marry her seducer? Granted, he was handsome. And, according to reports, so valiant a soldier that even Wellington had sung his praises. But Atherbourne despised Blackmore. Ruination was the entire purpose of the seduction.

Wasn't it?

Annabelle frowned. Marriage would ease Victoria's scandal, to be sure, but for Atherbourne, the move made little sense unless his goal was to force his way into Blackmore's family. But to what end?

Glancing about the room, she could see everyone else was equally shocked.

Except Robert. He stood silent and brooding as though he'd anticipated this very outcome. And, of all things, he was watching *her* with unnerving intensity.

A flutter heated her belly. A blush heated her cheeks. Get hold of yourself, Annabelle, she thought. He is Robert. He broods. If he's doing so in your direction, that is mere coincidence.

"The wedding will take place at Clyde-Lacey House in three days," the duke continued. He clasped gloved hands behind his back, posture rigid, jaw tight. "Victoria wishes you to attend."

Mama and Papa reacted with predictable delight.

Annabelle's mind went in several directions at once. Firstly, she was relieved for Victoria. The duke's fair-haired sister was as pristine as a fresh sheet of paper. Unlike her brother, she was not cold, but rather delicate. Innocent. Soft. The sort of creature who would not bear up well under the vicious gauntlet of scandal.

Indeed, every time Annabelle pictured Victoria as she'd been on Lady Gattingford's terrace—swollen lips, wounded gaze, fiery cheeks turning ashen as she realized what Atherbourne had done—she cringed for the girl. While marriage to one's own Lucifer might not be ideal, it would spare Victoria a lifetime of such mortification, which must be the reason Blackmore had agreed to it. Atherbourne had left the duke little choice.

Victoria was fortunate. Most men would not set aside their pride for the sake of their sister's happiness. And Blackmore's pride towered like Mount Olympus. Such brotherly devotion was heartening to witness.

Very well, Annabelle was not merely happy for Victoria's sake, but for her own. Now, redrawing the caricature for Mr. Green would be easy: Keep the flower, the highwayman, and the donkey. But instead of the highwayman stealing the flower's petals, he would secretly present her with a bouquet. The donkey's misinterpretation of the scene would seem asinine.

She stifled a grin. Oh, yes. Much better.

Next, her gaze drifted to Mama, who was grinning in a joyful-yet-teary-and-befuddled fashion. Maureen and Jane had crossed the room to flank her, offering comforting pats and encouraging murmurs. Annabelle sighed. Dearest Mama. She had been through too many trials of late, not least of which was to have been suddenly confronted with ...

Robert.

Oh, dear.

He kept staring at Annabelle with the queerest expression.

Once again, her belly fluttered and her skin warmed. She fought the sensations, surprised at the battle. Hadn't she been vexed with him earlier? Perhaps she should cease swooning over his brooding blue eyes.

Blast. It was harder than one might suppose.

Fortunately, Papa broke her line of sight as he strode forward to shake Blackmore's hand. "Your grace, we would be honored to attend," he assured quietly. Papa had a talent for setting everyone at ease, like warm, honeyed milk with a generous splash of brandy. He was, in Annabelle's opinion, the perfect father.

Oh, yes. That was why she'd been vexed with Robert. He'd treated Papa—indisputably the best Papa in the world—no better than a pair of unfashionable boots. Easily discarded and forgotten.

She nearly harrumphed. But she was not Genie. So, she merely sniffed and narrowed her glare upon Robert.

His head tilted questioningly.

As far as she was concerned, he could stew in his own confusion. No one treated Papa in such a way. Or Mama, for that matter.

Say what you would about the Countess of Berne. As a grand deliverer of gossip, Annabelle had heard plenty of sly digs about her mother—too round, too plump, a short nose, a tendency to giggle at her own jests. But Mama was warm where others were cold, merry where others were dour, eccentric where others were tediously conventional. She was a gale of maternal affection. And she'd long treated Robert as one of her own.

Only an ungrateful, bitter wretch would reject such kindness for *seven years*.

Annabelle fumed and glared harder at said wretch. Robert leaned heavily upon his cane, his shoulders hunching and his brow furrowed as he limped toward her.

Making a ploy to increase her guilt, was he? Well, he might

try, but she was wise to his game, so he'd best watch his step. Or his limp.

Blast. Did his leg really pain him so?

Blackmore's stiff farewells served as background while Annabelle pondered whether to confront Robert with her indignation.

"What the devil are you scowling at?" he growled as he reached her.

She crossed her arms and scowled deeper. "An ungrateful wretch, that's what."

"Have you lost your mind?"

"Ha! That *would* be the first thing you say to me, wouldn't it?" She lowered her voice to mimic his. "'Have you lost your mind?' Hmmph. A fine way to end a seven-year pout."

Blue eyes flared in disbelief. "Pout."

Her chin went up. "Mama and Papa have shown you nothing but kindness your entire life, Robert Conrad."

His shoulders rolled as though trying to cast off something sticky. Like a cobweb or well-deserved guilt.

"After seven years, you waltz blithely into Berne House—"

"As you can see, Lady Annabelle—"

"—expecting to be greeted with huzzahs and confetti—"

"—I do not *waltz* anywhere these days."

"Well, you'll not spin *me* into a dither with your ridiculous shoulders and heavy brows." She poked a finger into his lapel. "You forget how familiar those brooding blue eyes are to me. I'll not be swayed, *Mr.* Conrad. Mama may coo about how much pudding you ate when you were six." She flicked the lapel she'd just poked. "Or lament how threadbare your coat is. Or tell you your hair needs trimming." She frowned up at him. "Which it does, by the by."

"I came here for you."

"But I am not such a softheaded ninny that I will so easily forget ..." She blinked. "What?"

"I came for you."

"For what purpose?"

Ridiculously broad shoulders shrugged. "Lady Wallingham suggests you may be of help to me."

For a moment, she had no words. Then, she snorted. "I would sooner turn myself into a pudding and let you devour me whole."

Oddly, his gaze dropped to her bodice. "Grandfather wishes me to marry." Those brooding blue eyes came up to meet hers. "This"—his cane tapped lightly against the parlor's carpet—"only looks dashing when a man doesn't need it to cross a room."

Guilt that had always tasted bitter returned in a flood. Now, it burned her throat. Soured her stomach. Tightened her neck. "You're implying I owe you a debt."

"Am I?"

"Perhaps you are right. But I do not owe you a wife."

"A wife is what I need."

She shook her head. She would be dust in the grave before she helped Robert Conrad marry someone else. If he thought he could manipulate her with guilt ... well, he could. She'd kept her distance for seven years, hadn't she? But nothing could convince her to play matchmaker for the man who should have been hers. Not one blessed thing.

She gestured with a flutter of her fingers. "A new coat may improve your odds."

"Two-thirds of courtship is dancing. I cannot dance."

"I suppose you must rely upon your winning charm, then." She raised a brow. "Perhaps you should acquire some. Less costly than a new coat and more persuasive than properly trimmed hair."

He inched closer, lowering his head. A dark lock of improperly trimmed hair fell across his brow.

Her fingers itched and tingled.

"I shall follow you, Annabelle," he muttered, blue eyes burning her skin.

Her stomach heated. Her thighs squeezed. Her heart

stopped. "Wh-where, precisely?"

The faintest quirk of his lips nearly made her groan. Then he spoke a single word: "Everywhere."

And the groan escaped her throat. Oh, God. How had it come to this? She'd *groaned*. Aloud.

She was thirteen all over again. He was naked and wet all over again.

No, no, no. Mustn't picture him naked.

Helplessly, her eyes traced his ridiculous shoulders and his strong jaw and his heavy brows. *Another* groan. How embarrassing. That must be why she felt so ... hot.

"I shall plague you," he said, his warm breath falling upon her forehead and nose. "Ballrooms. Music rooms. Assembly rooms."

"Everywhere." She swallowed away the sudden breathlessness. Cleared her throat of its sudden rasp. "Yes, I got that bit."

"I shall hunt you down as you once did me. Wherever you are—"

"There you shall be. Your point has been made, Robert. And yet, I still refuse to play matchmaker for you and some"—she struggled for a term to convey the appropriate degree of loathing—*"woman."* The term was lacking, but her tone was right.

Heavy brows drew down. "I cannot dance."

Because of her. The implication stung, as truth often did.

"I recall many occasions when you required help, and I was there to provide it. Surely aiding me in this endeavor is the least you can do."

Any other endeavor, perhaps. Finding a competent valet. Acquiring a new townhouse. Stealing one of Lady Wallingham's turbans. She would have done anything else. But not this. Never this.

"Technically," she replied, "the least I can do is nothing. Which, coincidentally, is what I intend."

His eyes narrowed. "Then, the chase is on, it seems."

"Indeed. Do your worst, Mr. Conrad."

Slowly, the quirk of his lips spread into something she hadn't seen in seven years. The sight of it caused an implosion inside her chest, like sunlight and tumbling water and the rustle of heart-shaped leaves.

"Have a care what you invite, Lady Annabelle." His smile deepened as brooding blue dropped to her lips. "I am not the boy you remember."

Chapter Seven

"In the matrimonial hunt, some ladies are prizes whilst others are decoys. An able hunter knows better than to pursue empty plumage. But he should remain wary. Decoys can become hunters, too."

—THE DOWAGER MARCHIONESS OF WALLINGHAM in a letter to the Marquis of Mortlock regarding concerns about the proper focus of a gentleman seeking a wife.

Dearest Robert,
The vicar's wife, Mrs. L., reported a happy tidbit from her sister's daughter's husband at dinner last evening. Is it true you are now taking daily rides? This is happy news, indeed.

Much happier than the other tidbit Mrs. L. shared about her sister's daughter's husband's preference for wearing his wife's petticoats. One shudders to imagine a portly solicitor harboring such predilections. Though to be fair, Mrs. L. was quite sotted at the time, so perhaps she was simply rambling nonsense.

I hope not. You always did adore riding.

Ever yours,
Annabelle

—Letter to Robert Conrad dated February 3, 1812

"ARE YOU AWARE THAT A MAN WITH A CANE IS STARING AT YOU?"

Annabelle gaped at her silly friend in a pretense of daftness. "Why, no, Matilda! Did I forget to mention I'd gone blind prior to this evening's entertainments?"

Matilda Bentley fluttered her faint golden lashes in Robert's direction. "That is your Nottinghamshire neighbor, is it not? Mr. Conrad? My, he is rather brutish." The girl shivered and worked her silk fan until the careful curls along her forehead floated upward. "Those shoulders."

Downing the last of Mrs. Bentley's appalling orgeat punch in a single swallow, Annabelle slammed her cup down on a nearby tray and exhaled her annoyance. Matilda took little notice, too bloody fascinated by Robert's ridiculous shoulders.

It was infuriating.

Annabelle searched the Bentleys' pale-green music room for Jane. She found her bespectacled sister in a corner wearing a look of trapped misery. On one side sat the ancient and deaf Lady Leech. On the other sat Mama, who appeared to be chiding Jane. If Annabelle had to guess, she'd wager their mother's disapproval stemmed from Jane's habit of bringing a novel to a husband-hunting party.

Annabelle had told her sister to be more discreet, but Jane was obsessed with books, assuming Mama would ignore her as most gentlemen did. But after Mama's failure with Lady Victoria, she'd become more focused than ever upon helping her daughters find spectacular matches—whether they wanted to be matched or not.

In short, the Bentleys' soiree was a bad time to be caught reading.

The Bentleys were, in fact, known for their small-but-fashionable gatherings designed as prime matrimonial hunting grounds. Wealthy and ambitious, Mr. Bentley sought to purchase a place within the ton through marriage—first his own and secondly his daughter's. Mrs. Bentley possessed all the intellect of her orgeat punch, but she was a Northfield cousin, which gave the family valuable connections. Their daughter, Matilda, had inherited her mother's mental prowess and her father's ambition. She had a keen eye for eligible men and was a reliable gossip, which made her popular. Or, rather, Matilda was a reliable *conduit* for gossip. She was as feather-brained as Lady Wallingham had claimed, so Annabelle never expected insightful analysis. But, if a rumor needed passing along, Matilda could be an unquestioning tool. Like a pipe or a wheelbarrow.

Annabelle narrowed her eyes upon the slim, willowy blonde currently examining Robert's overlong hair with unseemly intrigue.

"He cannot dance, you know."

Matilda breathed a daft, syrupy sigh. "Dancing is not so important."

"It is two-thirds of the season's activities."

"That leaves at least ... oh, a quarter or so that is *not* dancing."

"He is also a dreadful bore. Conversation?" She snorted. "Only if you enjoy debating the merits of oxen over plow horses. Or enduring treatises about stable cleanliness. Equine disease is not a subject for delicate ears, I assure you."

"His father and brother are more slight. Elegant men, both, but much smaller. Do you suppose he wears padding beneath his coat?"

"He rarely smiles. Almost never. A more dour, sour, disagreeable gentleman I've yet to meet."

"It seems impossible to achieve such thickness in one's arms. Yet, they appear genuine. Extraordinary."

"You are related. He is part Northfield."

"From a different branch. My mother would be his fourth cousin once removed."

"Practically siblings."

Matilda giggled as if Annabelle had made a jest. "Silly. If I avoided every gentleman related to Northfields, I should never find a husband. Besides, he is Earl Conrad's son."

"*Second* son. You'd do just as well to marry a chimney sweep. Better, in fact. Have I mentioned how disagreeable he is?"

She grasped Annabelle's forearm. "Oh! He is coming this way." Her fan worked harder, tossing her yellow curls about like froth upon a wave. Or spittle from Lady Leech's ancient, pruned lips. "You must introduce us."

No. What she must do was find a way to avoid him. But, for a man with a cane, he moved fast. By the time she decided she'd rather wedge herself on the settee between Lady Leech and the malodorous Sir Barnabus Malby, Robert had already crossed the room.

"Lady Annabelle," he murmured, inclining his dark head. "I thought you hated orgeat."

She glared up at him. How could brooding be so attractive? His coat did not even fit properly. While it was made of fine, black wool, the seams strained across those wide, wide shoulders.

Matilda's elbow dug into her side.

Furthermore, when a lock of that almost-black hair fell across a heavy brow, it nearly met his eyelashes. Of course, nothing veiled the crackling resentment in those blue eyes. For a man in search of a wife, he seemed rather displeased.

All the better, in her estimation.

Matilda cleared her throat.

Annabelle ignored her. "Everyone hates orgeat."

"Yet, you've had three cups," he observed softly.

"Counting, are you?"

"Three cups of something you hate."

"Partaking of refreshments is what one does at a soiree, Mr. Conrad. Refreshments are at least a quarter of every London season."

His head lowered. "Particularly when delivered by a suitor, hmm?"

She blinked. Suitor? What suitor?

Matilda chose that moment to stop being ignored. "It was most gallant of Captain Standish," she simpered, strategically resting her closed fan atop her pleated bodice. "He fetched us each two cups. My head is positively spinning."

Annabelle rolled her eyes. "There is no liquor in the punch, Matilda."

"Perhaps a man of your ... impressive proportions might offer a steadying arm?"

"A man of his proportions who requires use of a cane would be a poor bet for steadying."

Matilda extended her long, slender hand toward Robert. "I am Matilda Bentley." She fluttered both her fan and her near-invisible lashes. "And you are Robert Conrad."

Robert grasped Matilda's lengthy fingers. They both wore gloves and the contact was light, so Annabelle's reaction should have been milder.

Instead, it burned like boiling stew.

She wanted those brooding blue eyes upon *her*. She wanted that large, strong hand holding *hers*. She wanted the man who belonged to *her* to cease touching, approaching, or otherwise seeking to wed other women.

But, as she'd learned long ago, wanting and having were worlds apart.

True to his word, for the past ten days, he'd followed Annabelle to event after event in search of a wife. The Bentley soiree was only the latest in a string of similar encounters: She arrived; he arrived. She ignored him; he approached her. He inquired about this lady or that; she explained why said lady was best avoided—scandalous forms of pox, breath like a chamber pot, a lurid taste for stable boys, a history of drowning ducklings. Eventually, he'd ceased asking about other ladies, but he had not ceased speaking with them.

Drat and blast, it was aggravating.

"Miss Bentley," he uttered before releasing Matilda's fingers. "A pleasure."

"Your grandfather is Lord Mortlock, if I am not mistaken."

"Indeed."

Matilda tittered. "How generous of him to cede Mortlock Manor to your father." Her dainty nose wrinkled. "Far lovelier than some crumbling abbey. Lord Conrad hosted my mother and father at Mortlock Manor for dinner recently. Our country house is likewise in Buckinghamshire, quite nearby. Such a gracious gentleman, your father. So *elegant*."

As Robert's expression cooled, Annabelle's fists began to unclench. If Matilda wished to impress him with her knowledge of his family tree, she was headed in precisely the wrong direction. Robert hadn't spoken to his father in ages, apart from dutiful correspondence at yearly intervals. They did not hate each other, but neither were they close. His grandfather—and the "crumbling abbey," for that matter—was another story entirely.

Matilda would have done better to poke Robert's eye with

her grotesquely long, willowy fingers.

"When I spoke with your brother, Lord Tatterton, at the theater last month, he indicated he and Lady Tatterton are spending the season in Bath. How unfortunate you and he will have missed the chance to enjoy London together."

Now, Robert appeared bored. "Unfortunate. Yes."

"But I suppose Lord Tatterton's health must come first."

"I suppose it must."

"London is much improved by such an *elegant* presence as Lord Tatterton. And Lady Tatterton, of course."

"Elegant. Quite."

Annabelle's hands relaxed fully as she watched Robert's gaze flatten with a hint of annoyance. By heaven, she could not have asked for a more perfect performance if she'd been wielding Matilda like a puppet. Stifling a grin of satisfaction, she casually rearranged her bronze Kashmiri shawl over her arms and folded her hands at her waist.

Ordinarily, this would be the moment when she stepped in to rescue Matilda from her own obtuse nature. And she would have, were the willowy fribble attempting to impress any other man. But this was Robert.

Robert was hers.

"Are you fond of dancing, Mr. Conrad?" Matilda cooed.

Robert did not bother glancing down at his cane before replying, "I'm afraid not, Miss Bentley."

Missing his dry tone, Matilda once again tittered. "Of course, a man of your *vigorous* nature must certainly enjoy exercise in some variety. I know! Riding. Perhaps we shall see one another at the park—"

This time, Annabelle intervened. "Matilda, your mother is summoning you."

Matilda blinked, turning this way and that. "She is?"

Gently, Annabelle spun her in the direction of the punch bowl. "You should assist her. Immediately. I sense she requires your *elegant* touch with the cup arrangement."

"Oh! Yes, she does rely upon my elegance." The willowy fribble cooed her pleasure at meeting Robert before drifting toward her mother.

Robert was silent for several heartbeats before commenting, "Miss Bentley is well informed about my family."

Annabelle raised a brow and casually resettled her shawl. "Her mother is a Northfield."

His frown cleared. "Ah. Northfields do value their connections."

She hummed her agreement and smoothed the gold silk of her skirt.

His frown returned, this time more vexed than perplexed. "He is not watching if that is what concerns you."

For a moment, she felt as Matilda must feel most of the time—utterly at sea. "He?" She shook her head. "He who?"

"Standish."

"Captain Standish?"

"Yes," he gritted. "Bloody *Captain* Standish."

"What would he be watching?"

"You."

"Why?"

"Why would he bring you punch?"

Now, *she* was frowning. Somehow, she'd lost her ability to translate English into English. "He brought punch to Miss Bentley."

"And you."

"Only because I was standing next to Miss Bentley."

"You expect me to believe that."

She glanced around, wondering if, in fact, there was liquor in the orgeat. Perhaps she was in her cups. Or perhaps he was.

"No, Robert," she snapped. "You've made it quite clear I should not expect anything from you. Anything at all."

"He watched while you played earlier. Never took his eyes from you."

"I was playing the pianoforte. Everyone watched. That is the point of a musical performance. To be observed."

"You should discourage his attentions."

She squinted up at him. His jaw was tight, his eyes flashing. He'd moved close enough that his breath washed across her forehead. She wanted to brush aside that overlong lock of hair. She wanted to stroke his lips with her thumbs, brush his mouth with her own.

Wanting and having. Worlds apart.

"If I wish to marry, then discouraging a gentleman's attentions would be counterproductive, wouldn't you say?"

"He is a coward. He wears that coat as though he earned it. He did not."

"One might say the same of half the officers who survived Bonaparte's armies. Shall I avoid them, too?"

"You should marry a man worthy of you."

All air halted inside her chest. When she managed to breathe again, her words emerged softly, but they might as well have blasted from her like a cannon. "Worthy? According to you, my worth is rather dismal."

His jaw flexed while fury sparked. "I never said any such—"

"Did I misremember? Silly me. Perhaps the laudanum caused you to demand never to see my face again." She tilted her head to a mocking angle. "Strange. I would swear laudanum's effects could not last longer than five years. Six at most. But surely not seven."

"Annabelle." Her name growled in that familiar, warning way gripped her insides and twisted. It choked and squeezed. It nearly undid her.

But she was no longer thirteen. She'd paid her price. Whatever her sins, she would not continue to stand for his punishment.

"Leave me alone," she whispered.

He shook his head. "No."

She had little choice. If she remained there, gazing up into those fierce, beautiful eyes, she was going to lose herself. Do something mortifying like weep or collapse or beg.

So, instead, she pivoted on her heel and marched through the nearest door. As it happened, the door led into a narrow passage, poorly lit with a single sconce. A footman carrying a tray full of cups shot her a startled glance as she rushed past him down the long stretch of parquet wood and assorted doors.

"Annabelle." There it was again. That growl.

She glanced behind her. Ten feet back, a furious man with shoulders nearly as wide as the corridor bore down upon her. In the darkness, he was but a shadow. A looming, angry shadow.

Her heart thrashed and bucked. Panic made her skin prickle in warning. She did not think, merely seized upon the next door she came to. It opened into a black space, tight and close. A closet, she thought.

She slipped inside, holding the knob tightly with both hands. Seconds later, it twisted and yanked from her grip.

"Do not bloody well run from me." He reached for her.

She shoved his arm away.

He grunted, but rather than retreat, he advanced. Moved inside the tiny space. Closed the door behind him, forcing her back against the closet's wall and trapping them both inside utter blackness.

"Is that very clear, Annabelle?" The growl was low and throaty, now. Near enough to tickle her skin.

She could not see him, but she felt him. Felt his arm brace on the wall beside her ear. Felt his breath wash against her cheek. Felt his heat and size surrounding her like a furnace.

"Never run from me," he rasped. "I will always catch you."

Her head fell back against the wall. Her breath came faster. He was too close. Too big. Too much.

"Robert," she whispered. "Why can you not leave me alone? After seven years of ignoring my existence, one would think it would be a simple matter."

"You are reckless. You've always been reckless."

"Do you hate me so much?" She loathed sounding weak, pleading, but she needed the answer. His nearness after so long was torture.

"Hate is not the word I would use."

"Despise, then. Abhor. Resent." Her chuckle escaped as an orphaned sound. "Whatever it is, no punishment on earth will unmake my mistakes. You must let me go."

He crowded into her until his chest pressed her flat. The pressure against her breasts was a pleasure unlike anything she'd imagined. And she'd imagined a great deal.

"Never again." His lips brushed her ear, sending swirling tingles down to her toes. "I did that once. It nearly killed me."

Another reminder of the accident. Of her guilt. She gripped his coat in her fists, battling both him and herself. "What do you want? Do you want me on my knees?"

He groaned, long and pained. His head came down to rest upon her shoulder, the cool strands of his hair tickling her bare neck. "Yes," he whispered. "Yes, I do."

"I did that once," she whispered back. "It nearly killed me."

His head rocked to and fro. He grunted, and she felt a hand at her waist. "Not what I meant."

"I am tired, Robert. Whatever it is you seek, make your demand and let's have done with this ... torment."

Something soft and damp caressed a sensitive spot between her jaw and her ear. "I told you already, I seek a wife."

Her hands wadded his coat into fists. "Then find one," she gritted, "and leave me out of it."

"I cannot."

"I won't stand for this punishment any longer."

Gentle lips brushed her brow, her cheek, the corner of her mouth. "There is one way to end it."

She squeezed her eyes closed, used her grip upon his coat to pull him in tighter. "Finally," she murmured, breathless and panting. "What is it? Shall I be pilloried? Exiled to Greenland?"

"I need a wife."

She groaned.

"If you will not help me find one ..."

She waited. "Yes?"

His grip on her waist strengthened. Pulled her hips into his. "Then you must accept the role, yourself."

Everything inside her froze. Surely, he did not mean what she thought he meant. No. He could not. He wanted nothing to do with her. "You are a hard man, Robert."

"You noticed."

"But I never thought you cruel."

Oddly, his breath came fast, now. And, she noted, the hand at her waist had become an arm across her lower back. His thighs were wedging and rubbing in the strangest, most heat-inducing fashion. His lips were wandering from her jaw to her throat and back to hover near her mouth. "You asked for my demands." Hot breath washed across her lips. "I need a wife, and soon."

"But not me, surely."

"You'll do."

She shook her head. The motion swept her temple against his jaw. She could feel his whiskers beneath his skin, rasping and causing her lower belly to clench. "No. This is some new punishment. Marry Annabelle and force her to scrub Rivermore's chamber pots for the rest of her days. Well, I shan't do it."

"Bloody hell. I don't need a servant, I need a—"

"Wife. Yes." She tried to gather her thoughts, but he held her so tightly, was so hard and hot against her that she could scarcely remember her own name. "P-perhaps we could lie. We shall tell your grandfather we intend to wed then settle into a long engagement. That would ease his mind, but neither of us would be trapped—"

"No."

"It is a sound plan."

"I refuse to lie to him."

"So, instead you will bind yourself to me, the woman you hate enough to punish forever." She laughed, but the sound was bitter. "Or, perhaps that is the point—a punishment which never ends."

Inside the closet's blackness, the silence was broken only by their breaths, their heat.

"Give me your answer," he demanded.

She opened her mouth to refuse him.

But he must have anticipated her rejection, because the next thing she knew, his lips had seized hers in a long, sliding caress.

Oh. Dear. Heaven.

Kissing.

Robert was kissing her.

She moaned as the sensations hit her bloodstream, zinged along her nerves, fizzed out to her fingertips and her bosoms and the very roots of her hair. They effervesced inside her thighs.

Why had nobody told her?

How the stroke of his tongue and the heat of his breath and the squeeze of his fingers into the flesh of her hips would tip her upside down.

How deeply she would want him deeper.

How badly she would want him closer.

How vexing it would be that the only way to lengthen and strengthen their glorious kiss would be to kiss him in return.

Which she did. Oh, how she did. She gave him her tongue. She gave him her arms around his thick, strong neck. She gripped him hard and drew him down and devoured him.

Dear God, she was burning alive.

This was no sweet, glancing brush of lips or chaste holding of hands.

This was lust. Clawing. Raging. It *hurt* to want something this much.

She found herself gripping whatever she could reach—his overlong hair, his under-starched cravat, his ridiculously wide shoulders.

He ground his mouth against hers, his tongue a sleek, pulsing invasion. He gripped her backside, slid her up between the wall and his thighs. She felt it then, the ridge. Sizable. Determined. Hard as heated stone.

Her feet left the floor.

He grasped one of her thighs, bent her leg, forced his hips up into hers, lifting her higher.

Then, he groaned. Tore his mouth away. Cursed.

She followed blindly. She wanted him back. His sleek tongue and demanding hands.

"Bloody hell." It was a growl, and it sounded ... pained. He lowered her to the floor. She heard him panting. Shifting his feet in an awkward rhythm.

"R-Robert?"

His breathing was harsh, like a horse ridden too hard. "It's nothing."

Her fingers slid from his neck to his mouth. Even through her silk gloves, she could feel the brackets of pain on either side. "It is your leg, isn't it?"

There was a long silence while he held himself still and breathed against her. "Sometimes the muscles ... seize up."

Suddenly, everywhere she'd felt melting heat cooled to a chill. While he'd been giving her pleasure, she'd been causing him pain.

Wasn't that a familiar tale?

To Robert, she'd never been anything but pain. She'd cost him the future he'd wanted. She'd caused him endless agonies. She could not even kiss him without ...

Nausea rose up in her throat. She swallowed it down. Stroked his cheek one last time.

"I am sorry, Robert," she whispered.

"It will pass," he gritted. "Give me a moment."

"What can I do?" She remembered asking the same question years ago, begging him to allow her a path to forgiveness. He'd denied her then.

Now, he offered her a single chance. Just one. The one that might destroy her.

"Marry me."

Perhaps it was the shock of their kiss or the blackness of their surroundings or the remnants of his pain and her guilt, but when she opened her mouth to answer, she might as well have been cup-shot on liquor-laced orgeat. For, every wise and sensible thought fled, leaving only one: She would belong to him, and he to her.

In all her life, she'd only ever wanted one thing badly enough to risk everything else—her pride, her pain, her plans. Perhaps he meant his demand as a punishment. Perhaps she deserved to suffer. But in the blackness, she could only see orange blossoms and ivy on walnut pews. Smell the sweetness of their babes cradled against her. Hear the bells of Rivermore's chapel calling them on Sunday morning. And feel the warm, dry clasp of Robert's hand around hers.

"Very well," whispered her guilty, foolish, besotted heart.

He went utterly still. Silent. She could not even hear him breathing. "You agree to become my wife?"

Could he hear her blood pounding? The sound was deafening to her.

"Annabelle."

"Yes." The word emerged scratchy and near soundless. So she said it again, even though it was likely the daftest decision she'd ever made. Years and years of heartache lay ahead. His pain. Her pain.

But he would belong to her, and she to him.

The alternative was to watch him marry someone else. Someone willowy and obtuse like Matilda Bentley.

"Yes," she repeated, a bit shaky, but at least audible. "I will be your wife."

She could not see him—not his brooding eyes or wide shoulders or heavy brow. But the moment she spoke the words, she felt something of his reaction.

It reminded her of the day he'd carried her home after she'd broken her toe. He'd been exhausted, arms trembling with strain. Refusing to set her down on gravel or grass or even carpets, he'd taken her directly to her father and insisted Papa lift her from his back and deliver her to her bedchamber.

Papa had done it, of course—he was the best papa in the world. But, before he'd carried her away, he'd turned to Robert. "You've done well, son. Go and rest. We shall take care of her."

In a face streaked with sweat and dust, those blue eyes had flashed their defiance. She'd reached for Robert, and he'd taken her hand in his. "I will stay with her, my lord," he'd said. "She is mine, now."

Papa had looked startled, but even as a child, Annabelle had understood. She'd felt it, too—the connection no words could explain. A shimmering, golden thread between them had hummed with power.

And, after seven years of emptiness, here inside a place with no light, she felt it again. The thread. The power. The hum. Before Robert opened the closet door, before the faint light revealed his usual stoic expression, before he straightened his cravat and grasped his cane and led her into the corridor, she heard the words echoing in her head as clearly as if he'd spoken them aloud: *"She is mine, now."*

Chapter Eight

"*Do not underestimate the value of a fine head of hair.*"

—THE DOWAGER MARCHIONESS OF WALLINGHAM in a letter to the Marquis of Mortlock regarding his grandson's potential advantages in the marriage mart.

Dearest Robert,
Keeping myself informed about your health has become impossible of late. Why must you constantly dismiss your valets? They make excellent sources, but only when employed.

Ever yours,
Annabelle

—Letter to Robert Conrad dated May 8, 1812

AS ROBERT GUIDED DEWDROP ALONG GROSVENOR STREET, it occurred to him how fortunate he was that John Huxley was currently traipsing about the Pyrenees and not in London.

He didn't fancy being beaten to death with his own cane.

Indeed, a beating was precisely what he deserved. And, if Hux knew how Robert had manipulated Annabelle, kissed Annabelle, groped and nearly debauched Annabelle inside the Bentleys' hall closet, he reckoned their friendship would meet a swift and bloody end.

The shame of last evening weighed upon him until he imagined Dewdrop going as swaybacked as Methuselah beneath the burden.

He drew up outside Berne House, using his left leg to dismount. His right was still smarting from the vicious cramp he'd suffered when he'd tried to position Annabelle for his pleasure.

He should have taken it for the sign it was. He should have told her the truth then and there—that she was not to blame for his injuries. That she should feel no guilt and had no obligation to let him kiss her.

But he'd needed her to agree to marry him. It was the only way he could protect her.

The blasted woman was out of her mind. Over the past ten days, he'd followed her everywhere, just as he'd promised. But he hadn't confined himself to ballrooms and drawing rooms. He'd followed her to the Strand. He'd watched her enter and exit the plain brick building on Catherine Street, where the publisher of *Green's Daily Informer* printed the work of Edward Yarrow Aimes.

Whose work was just like Annabelle's.

Because it was Annabelle's.

He'd long known she was reckless, but he'd always thought her impulsive behavior centered upon him—trailing him into danger, leaping to impress him, taking wild risks to remain by his side. This was the entire reason he'd forced distance between them. Annabelle had put herself in harm's way over and over. The last time she'd done so, she'd nearly died. So had he.

Their separation had been a kind of death—no other pain he'd suffered could compare—but it had been necessary, he'd told himself. For her sake.

He'd been wrong. Not about her recklessness, but about its cause. He'd assumed by removing himself from her life, it would disappear. She would be sensible. Measured. She would never risk herself again.

He wanted to laugh. There was nothing sensible about her producing caricatures scathing enough to make the artist the target of violence. And a *female* artist? What consequences would she suffer if the true identity of Edward Yarrow Aimes were discovered?

No, if anything, she needed him far more than he'd ever suspected. Needed him to keep her safe from her own foolishness. And, as Lady Wallingham had observed, if he wished to do it right, he must marry her.

"For a woman, a man's useful purposes are few," the dowager had advised during their barouche ride returning to Mayfair. "Begetting offspring. Occasional gifts—jewelry is preferred. And amusement. Men are most entertaining, often unintentionally." Her mouth had quirked as though recalling a fond memory. Then, she'd turned stern. "But offering the protection of his name may be a man's greatest value. Make yourself into a shield, Mr. Conrad. There is but one way to ensure she does not suffer the consequences of flawed judgment. Marry the girl."

Lady Wallingham had suggested a scheme in which he insisted Annabelle help him find a bride. In her view, the mutual project would cause marriage and Robert to mingle in

Annabelle's mind and draw them closer so he could reestablish a rapport. At the time, he'd thought the plan reasonable.

Reasonable. Good God. That alone should have set alarms clanging.

Annabelle's reaction to the charade had been rampant hostility. When she wasn't dancing with other gentlemen or ignoring him entirely, she'd glared daggers and cut him to ribbons with her sharp tongue. After ten days of nonsense, he'd discarded Lady Wallingham's plan for his own more direct approach.

It had worked. Annabelle had agreed to marry him, and now Robert must coax her to follow through on her promise. But first, he must tell her the truth about their past. He could not ask her to trust him otherwise.

The footman who answered the door at Berne House—a pleasant fellow named Ned—showed him into the oak-paneled entrance hall. "If you've come to see Lord Berne, I'm afraid he has not yet returned from his club."

"Actually, I am here for Lady Annabelle. Is she at home?"

Ned appeared startled. "Er—yes, I believe ... that is, I shall inquire." The servant bowed and turned toward a set of doors off the entrance hall. He spun back around. "May I ask, sir, do you have an aversion to cats?"

Robert frowned at the odd question, noticing the disheveled state of the footman's livery. "Not particularly."

Nodding in a relieved fashion, Ned straightened his wig and continued on his way.

As Robert stood waiting, he heard several thuds above his head. A door slammed. A female squealed. A male shouted. Feet shuffled and thumped. Then, Ned reappeared looking even more disheveled than before. "This way, Mr. Conrad."

He took him to the drawing room, which was directly above the entrance hall. Inside, two of the five Huxley daughters sat calmly in the chairs near the fireplace. One was Jane, whom he still had trouble reconciling with the shy little mite she'd been seven years ago. The other was Annabelle, who held a pencil poised above her open sketchbook. On the sofa near the tall windows, a plain-faced lady's maid sat wielding a sewing needle on a tattered scrap of linen. Her white cap was askew.

"Why, Mr. Conrad," said Annabelle in a theatrical tone. "Quite the surprise. Have you come to see Papa? He is out at the moment. Perhaps you would care to leave now and return later this afternoon."

He glanced back at Ned, who hovered nervously in the doorway, then at Annabelle. "What the devil is going on?" He'd been asking that question with disturbing frequency since arriving in London.

Annabelle's eyes widened. "I don't know what you mean."

Jane adjusted her spectacles before setting aside her book.

He nodded toward the young woman's hands. "Lady Jane, why are your knuckles bleeding?"

"She scraped them," Annabelle answered quickly.

"On what?"

"Books."

Jane snorted. "Not books, silly. What a ludicrous notion."

"Well, it seemed the obvious answer," Annabelle retorted. "Given your preoccupations."

He frowned. Looked about the room with its blue silk walls and gold draperies. Came back to Annabelle, whose posture was too stiff for such a casual tone. "I return to my original question." He moved farther into the room, edging his way around a satinwood table and past the nearest of three windows. "What the devil is going on?"

Suddenly, he jolted as a creature of claws and viciousness landed upon his nape. With a feral hiss, it dug needles through his cravat and into his skin. He forced himself into stillness. The pain was no worse than being snagged by a bramble. He reached up with his free hand then smoothly grasped the tiny, furred animal.

It did not care to be removed. It yowled and writhed. He tore it free, trying not to crush the thing, and brought it around where he could see it.

The kitten was gray. Its long fur stood on end. Its blue eyes were panicked and outraged. Its claws gouged spasmodically at his glove.

He held the terrified creature out toward Annabelle, who had leapt to her feet the moment it pounced and now stood wringing her hands a few feet away.

"The answer to my question, I presume," he said.

"Katie discovered them inside a broken old cart left abandoned in the mews."

"Them?"

"She knows Mama is fond of cats, so she gathered them up and brought them all inside. Her intentions were good."

"All?"

"We've managed to find three so far. This one"—she leaned forward to examine the hissing, clawing, belly-side-up thing in his hand—"is number four."

"Cats make your father sneeze."

She sighed and nodded. "Uncontrollably, yes. It's been ten years since Mama's last attempt to bring a cat into the house. Katie is too young to remember the disaster that was Mr. Moonshine."

Robert had been at Eton with John at the time, but he recalled Annabelle's letters and sketches illustrating Mr. Moonshine's savage path of destruction. He'd never laughed so hard in his life.

Annabelle had always made him laugh. Always.

Now, she waved Ned forward and asked him to take the kitten. The footman winced as Robert transferred the angry feline into his hands.

"How many more are there?" Robert asked.

"One. Goodness knows how we shall find him before Papa arrives home."

Jane stood and offered a suggestion. "We must search each room and close the doors as soon as we finish." She peered about the drawing room. "I think it's safe to close this one. I shall rally the maids to search the remainder of the house."

"Use a grid pattern," he advised.

Jane did not meet his eyes, but she nodded as she passed him. Still a shy one, he noted.

"Estelle," Annabelle said to the maid near the window. "Would you be so kind as to lend your assistance to Lady Jane?"

The maid appeared alarmed by the request. She glanced first at Robert then toward the closed door then back to Annabelle. "Are you certain you do not wish me to stay, my lady?"

"I am certain."

With visible reluctance, the maid tucked her sewing into the basket at her feet and did as she was told.

As soon as they were alone, Annabelle sighed, her shoulders sagging. She rubbed her forehead with her fingers. "If you are here to speak to Papa about our marriage, you may wish to wait until tomorrow. We will ensure the kittens are gone before he arrives, but the presence of their fur will cause him some misery. He is fond of you, but he will not be in the best of spirits until the draperies and furniture are properly cleaned."

For long seconds, he allowed himself to look at her. She wore a simple blue gown with a darker blue sash. The neckline was rounded, giving him a glimpse of the pearlescent skin of her throat. Wisps of brown hair fell along her jaw and ears and nape.

God, he'd forgotten how delicate she was. His teacup. Small and fine.

And she was tired. He could see the tension in the lines of her neck, in the curve of her shoulders. Bloody hell, he wanted to take her in his arms again. He wanted her to tell him everything so he could tell her all would be well.

"We should have the wedding at Rivermore," she said, crossing toward the chair where she'd left her sketchbook. She picked it up and began making notes. "This is for your grandfather's benefit, after all. He will wish to attend."

Grandfather. Right. She believed his demand had been about pleasing Grandfather. Because that was the lie he'd told her.

He started to answer. Intended to confess everything—how he'd lied seven years ago, wounding her in order to prevent her from following him down a hellish path. How he'd stayed in London to ensure she did not fall prey to that worthless, craven peacock Martin Standish. How he'd followed her from place to place because he needed to protect her. To be near her. To hear her laugh. To feel that strange, resonant connection again after seven years of deprivation.

And how he'd let lust and greed and hunger wear away his control. How he'd seen her pain, her defiance, her fury, and let everything ruthless inside him have its head. He'd seized what he should not have, using weapons he should never have used.

Because he was ravenous. Even now, standing in her family's house, he was bloody ravenous.

But, before he could utter a word, she continued, "The chapel is lovely." A smile curved her soft lips. "I always pictured ..." A sigh. She fluttered her fingers and made another note. "In any event, I am unable to leave London for at least another month. So, we have time to plan. You may wish to write Mortlock and inform him—"

"Why a month?"

"Hmm?"

"What is keeping you here?"

"Oh, this and that." Another flutter. More notes. She evaded his gaze. "A lady has obligations, you know."

He closed half the distance between them. "What obligations?" he asked, keeping his voice soft. Was it Standish? Someone else? Or her dangerous hobby?

"My family, for one. We cannot simply cut short Jane's season and return to the country."

Gut churning, he moved closer. "You agreed to the marriage. I see little need for delays. We will leave next week."

Finally, her eyes came up to flash over him. A single brow arched. "Write to Mortlock. Inform him we are to be wed in two months' time."

"Two? What happened to one?"

"You have vexed me."

He fisted his cane and inched closer.

Her chin tilted. Her brow arched higher. Her eyes snapped.

He halted. "Annabelle."

"Yes?"

"My grandfather's time runs short."

"Not that short."

"How could you possibly know that?"

"I am exceedingly well informed."

He blew out a breath and ran a hand through his hair. She was punishing him. If he vexed her any further, she'd break the engagement. Revealing his past mistakes would have to wait.

"Besides," she continued with a blithe air, "we shall require sufficient time to hire you a new valet. Or at least visit a barber."

Frowning, he dropped his hand, feeling a prickle of heat touch his face. "What the devil does that mean?"

Her fingers fluttered in his direction. "Your hair needs trimming, Robert."

Bloody hell. Why was everyone so preoccupied with the length of his hair?

Thick-lashed brown eyes scanned his shoulders. "Out of charity, I shan't elaborate upon the state of your tailcoats." She wrinkled her nose and clicked her tongue. "Hair first. Garments later."

"If my hair so offends you," he growled, "trim it yourself."

"Very well." She marched to the maid's sewing basket and withdrew a pair of shears. Then, she pointed the sharp end toward a cane-backed chair at a desk near the third window. "Sit," she commanded pertly.

He scarcely knew what to make of her. This was no bone-china teacup. No funny, worshipful girl willing to follow his lead. She accepted his challenges and issued her own. She grew "vexed" with him. She demanded two months instead of one.

This Annabelle fired his lust to an alarming degree, just as she'd done in the Bentleys' closet.

"Glare all you like," she said. "But you *do* need this."

Grudgingly, he moved to the chair and sat, resting his cane against the leg of the desk. "Have you ever done this before?" he asked the vexed woman standing behind him with a pair of shears.

"Hmm. Let's see. There was the time I thought Kate would look better with short hair than long." She patted his shoulder with a delicate hand. "Not to worry," she purred near his ear. Her proximity—the warm wash of her words, the scent of a summer night filled with honeysuckle—made his vision blur. "It only took two months for the right half of her head to match the left. Fortunately for you, hair grows back. Eventually."

If he'd been capable of standing right then, he might have leapt to his feet. She was taunting him, of course. He had no fear she would mangle the job. Annabelle was impulsive, not incompetent. Rather, he feared his control would break when she touched him. Already his thighs tensed against the surge of arousal.

Behind him, he heard a delicate sigh. He waited.

And waited.

"Annabelle?"

"Hmm?" Lazily, her fingers sifted through his hair, causing ripples of sensation to zing from his scalp to his groin.

He swallowed but could not speak.

"So thick," she murmured. "I've long admired it, you know."

Sift and stroke. Trace and tickle. By God, she was driving him mad. His eyes drifted closed. "My hair?"

"The brown is so dark, it is nearly black." The snick of the shears was quiet and rhythmic. Cool metal slid along his nape. *Snick, snick, snick.* "Mine is lighter. Not as light as Maureen's, of course. Plain, middling brown." She chuckled, the sound a sensuous temptation. "What could be duller?"

"Nothing about you is dull."

Another chuckle. Another snick. Her finger traced the top of his ear. "Clearly, you haven't seen my embroidery. Eugenia said it would benefit from incompetence, for then at least there might be something to remark upon."

He almost smiled. "She does not mince words."

"No, indeed." Her breasts brushed his shoulder as she leaned forward. A dainty fist deposited a handful of his hair upon the desk. "I suspect her honesty may lead her into trouble one day."

Annabelle continued speaking, but he could not hear. His blood pounded hard enough to concuss the walls. He went rigid as stone while she fluttered about like the Bumblebee she was, lightly touching, never landing, buzzing and playful.

"... genuinely dismayed that John sent a bonnet to Katie instead of her." Annabelle laughed with affection then sighed. "Genie forgets how he likes to tease. I do hope he returns soon. We all miss him so."

Her chatter should have been a distraction. But desire had exploded into every fiber of his body the moment she touched him. Before then, actually. Every minute in her presence stoked the flames higher until fantasies played out behind his eyes.

Annabelle Huxley's lush breasts and pearlescent skin bared to him.

Her naked arms extended above her head.

Her naked wrists in his hands.

Her hips writhing for him.

Her thighs silken and wet for him.

Her lips chanting his name. Begging for his invasion. His dominion.

The vision was obscene, but he could not stop. He opened his eyes, stared blindly out the third window at the newly dampened street. It didn't help.

She kept touching him, her fingers dancing over his forehead and along his jaw. Her voice, with its womanly rasp, had gone lower, breathier.

By God, he wanted to take her mouth again. He wanted those dainty hands threading his hair with passion, not routine grooming.

"... much better. It grows long so rapidly, and with such thickness, we will have to tend it with great frequency, I suspect."

He suspected the same. In fact, he suspected the first month or two of their marriage would be spent in his bed. Perhaps he would let her leave for meals. Perhaps he would bring her trays and feed her himself.

The snick of the shears ceased. She stilled for a long while before laying them on the desk. Then, soft hands brushed at his shoulders. Long, lingering brushes. Caresses, really, as though she wished to take his measure. Or push him past his bloody limits.

He reached up and snatched her wrist. Ignored her gasp. Drew her palm to his lips. Breathed her in. Summer nights and honeysuckle.

God, he hurt. Wanted her so badly, he felt like he was dying.

Nothing had ever been this ferocious. Of course, nothing had ever been Annabelle.

She leaned against him, her soft cheek coming down to nuzzle his. Her breasts flattened against his back. "P-perhaps we shouldn't hire a valet just yet," she whispered.

He felt her panting breaths along his jaw, rhythmic pressure against his back.

"If you like the way I trim, I could—"

"Yes," he growled, scraping his teeth gently against her inner wrist. Licking the abrasion. "You."

He made no sense, grunting and growling and hungering like a savage beast. His head clouded with primal urges. *Take her. Make her mine.*

"Robert," she whispered, rubbing her cheek against his, clawing her hand into his shoulder.

Yes. Want my name on her lips. Want inside her.

"Another punishment?" She murmured the question as though she hadn't meant to ask it.

Distantly, he heard the door open. She startled upright and jerked her hand away before he could tighten his grip.

"The last rascal has been found," announced Jane. "He was in the larder frightening Mrs. Dunn witless. She thought he was a ... oh!" Annabelle's sister cleared her throat. "Oh, my. Yes, well. I ... thought you would like to know about the ... I shall leave now, shall I? Yes, I think I shall. Books to read. Draperies to clean. Carry on."

The door closed.

In the silence, he breathed. Annabelle had moved away. He hadn't bothered looking anywhere except the window, but he felt cold settle where her honeysuckle sweetness had been.

He could still taste her skin.

"You should ..." Her voice was hoarse. Breathless. "Wait a day or two before approaching Papa."

He did not want to wait. Not a day or two, and certainly not a month or two. But enough blood had returned to his brain to restore some measure of caution. So, he did not say what he wished to say, which was that she belonged to him, and he would claim her now, here, in this drawing room on this very desk, if he thought she would allow it.

"Once my family knows of our engagement, you should write your grandfather with the news. It will bring him comfort." Slowly, as she spoke, she seemed to gather more authority. "I daresay you might even carry the news to him yourself. No reason for you to remain in London. Surely you'll wish to resume your work at Rivermore Abbey. We can be married when I return to Clumberwood with my family after the season is—"

"I am not leaving London without you." He sounded like a beast.

So be it. She had little notion of his true nature, but she must learn swiftly. For, as he'd discovered over the past hour, nothing provoked it more powerfully than she did.

The knowledge left *him* reeling. It would shock her senseless. "Don't be silly. You hate London."

He used his good leg and a tight grip on the desk to rise from the chair. Grabbing his cane, he spun to face her.

Her cheeks were crimson. Her eyes glinted with a complex mix of emotions—wariness and desire and provocation among them.

He crossed the room as quickly as his leg and the lingering hardness in his groin would allow. When he stood before her, he lowered his head. Held her eyes. Let her have a tiny glimpse of what drove him.

She blinked rapidly, fingers fluttering to her throat in a protective gesture.

"I am not leaving without you."

"S-so you ..." She swallowed. "You intend to simply ramble around inside some rented townhouse whilst I attend the obligatory functions of the season?"

"I intend to be wherever you are."

Her mouth worked in disbelief. "But ... you will be miserable. *I* will be miserable. No. You cannot mean it."

His head tilted nearer. He inhaled honeysuckle. "Every word."

"Robert. That is daft. And unnecessary."

"You need watching."

A spark of outrage flashed. "I am a grown woman from a respectable family, not a wayward kitten intent upon shredding the draperies."

He nearly told her what he knew—that she'd risked her reputation and perhaps her safety by posing as a male caricaturist for a rubbish scandalmonger. But he wanted her to tell him the truth on her own. He wanted her to trust him, to let him protect her. Annabelle could be infernally willful. The best way to keep her safe was to have her cooperation.

So, instead of explaining that the longer she stayed in London, the greater the danger grew, he gave an answer she might accept. "We are betrothed. My presence ensures you keep your promises."

Her eyes narrowed and fired hot with temper. "Every promise I ever made to you has been kept, Robert Conrad." Her voice trembled with rage. "Every. Bloody. One."

"Then, you won't mind having me close."

Brown eyes flashed ominously bright. "Three months," she bit out, her chin rising to an infernally willful angle. "Care to try for four? September weddings are so very lovely."

Helplessly aroused, he looked to her lips, the rise and fall of her bosom, the flush of her cheeks. "Punishing *me* now, are you?"

"Preserving my sanity."

He smiled. It seemed to further incite her temper, but he couldn't help himself. She'd always made him smile. And laugh. She hadn't always made him lust like a primitive beast. No, that was new. But he thought he might grow accustomed to it.

She must marry him soon, though. Desire this potent could not be denied for long.

Leaning forward until their faces were level, his lips brushed hers softly. Lightly. Once. Twice. "Sanity has never been a part of what's between us, Annabelle." He straightened before she tempted him into further intimacies. "So long as you are in London, I shall be in London. So long as you partake in the season's offerings, so shall I. You may end the misery at any time. Just say the word."

Her gaze went mutinous. And moments before he left the Berne drawing room laughing, she smiled with sinister intent and said the word. It was precisely the wrong word, of course.

"Four," she snapped.

His amusement seemed to baffle her, but she would understand eventually. Four months? Sweet, naïve Bumblebee. She'd be lucky if he allowed her four days.

Chapter Nine

"Call it what you will—part of marriage is battling for one's ground. One may settle matters through warfare or negotiation or means far more pleasurably sly. But never doubt the battle exists. One need only observe the victor's triumphant gleam to understand who has lost and who has won."

—THE DOWAGER MARCHIONESS OF WALLINGHAM in a letter to the Marquis of Mortlock settling an old argument on the nature of matrimonial harmony.

Dearest Robert,
Cultivating a new source at Rivermore Abbey has been a trial. I despaired of finding one to last longer than a month. You've made so

*many changes to the household, it almost seems we are engaged in a
pitched battle, you and I.*

*Happily, I discovered Major Colby's weakness—and as of this morning,
he has agreed to supply me with weekly reports in exchange for weekly
deliveries of Chelsea buns.*

In chess, I believe the term is checkmate.

*Ever yours,
Annabelle*

—Letter to Robert Conrad dated September 20, 1812

"AH-*CHOO!*" PAPA'S EYES WERE SWOLLEN AND RED, HIS FACE
wreathed in misery. Although they'd reversed yesterday's feline
invasion before he'd arrived home, bits of fur yet lingered. The
maids had been attempting to beat it out of the carpets and
draperies for the past twelve hours.

Annabelle glanced at her poor Papa, who was on his fourth
handkerchief of the morning. "Perhaps some tea will help," she
suggested. "I could—"

"Never mind me, sweet girl." He smiled through his misery,
sounding clogged. "I shall improve in no time at a—a—a-*choo!*"

Wincing in sympathy, Annabelle stood from her end of the
breakfast table and delivered her napkin to her poor, suffering
father. She patted his shoulder and returned to her seat.

Earlier, Mama had taken Eugenia and Kate shopping for hair
ribbons, while Jane had dragged Estelle and Maureen along to
the circulating library, so Annabelle and Papa were alone in the

morning room.

Her red-nosed papa buttered a slice of toast before clearing his throat. "I've been informed I should expect a visit soon. Is this true?"

Annabelle's eyes flew wide. She took a sip of tea before replying, "Visit?"

"From a certain suitor."

Drat. Who had told him? Jane, perhaps? She replaced her cup with a gentle clink.

Despite his malady, Papa smiled in that don't-bother-obfuscating-I'm-your-father way. "Why haven't you said anything?"

She sighed. In truth, she didn't know. Something in her didn't believe it, she supposed. Any minute, she expected Robert to reveal his proposal had been a cruel hoax intended to humiliate her. But Mama and Papa would not understand. They doted on Robert. To them, he could do no wrong. "I thought to give you time to recover your health, Papa. That's all."

"But this is happy news, is it not?"

She forced a smile and nodded.

"You were so close as children. Rarely saw the boy smile unless you were in sight. What was it he called you? Bumblebee. Yes, that was apt. Such a restless little mite you were, forever wanting the next flower and the next. But as soon as Robert arrived, all the fuss turned into a singular focus. Nobody could stop you. Three years old, and we'd find you trailing him into the garden." He chuckled. "Your mother and I always assumed you'd marry him one day."

She dropped her gaze to the crumbs on her plate. She'd thought so, too, until she'd destroyed his life. That diminished the odds of matrimony rather decisively.

"Annabelle."

She met Papa's eyes, red-rimmed yet glowing gold.

"Sometimes a man feels he must bear his hardships alone, so as not to burden those around him."

Immediately, she cringed with remorse. "Goodness, Papa. I am sorry I've kept you. Perhaps you should go to your club, where at least you'll enjoy a few hours of relief."

"Thank you, sweet girl, but I wasn't speaking of myself."

She sat back and blinked. "Oh."

"Robert distanced himself from us, I think, because he feared being a burden. Perfect rot, of course. But young men do have their pride." Papa wiped his nose. "I remember that age. My world was small, but by heaven, I had mastered everything in it. Only later did I realize how much more world there was."

Annabelle smiled. "A mistake common to us all, I daresay."

"Indeed." Papa sneezed, wiped his nose, and then grinned. "He loves you, though. That much I do know."

Loved her? No. Papa only remembered how Robert had been as a boy who'd carried her two miles on his back. He didn't know what Robert had said to her as she'd begged on her knees for forgiveness. He didn't understand what she'd done to turn a boy's love to hate.

But, rather than argue, Annabelle pasted on the smile she'd practiced for hours upon hours when she was thirteen—the one with the twinkle. "Of course he does," she lied. "Why else should he wish to marry me?"

Papa's sneezing worsened, and she suggested they go for a ride. Papa complained about the rain, and she advised at least he must retreat to his club. He conceded, kissing her forehead before he left. "Tell Robert to come speak with me soon," he said. "So long as you are content with the match, I could not be happier."

For a long while after Papa left, Annabelle sat staring down at her hands lying folded upon lilac silk skirts.

In the two days since she'd agreed to marry Robert, she'd given his motives a great deal of thought. Why, of all the ladies he might choose, would he choose her, the one he must surely loathe most? The answer could only be that he wished to exact a greater price for the suffering she'd caused him. What could be greater than seven years of banishment?

The bleak weather mirrored her answers to that question.

A husband had absolute dominion over his wife. He might be kind, like Papa. Or cold, like Blackmore. Or ruthless, like Atherbourne. He might cosset his wife, protect her and strive for her happiness. Or he might revile her, turning her life into a winter without end.

Perhaps that was the source of his urgency. He feared she would realize his intentions and escape punishment.

She'd dreamt of Robert's fall the previous night. Not since the nightmares had begun to recede at the age of fifteen had she been plagued with one so vivid. She'd awakened sobbing loudly enough that Jane had rushed over from the adjacent room.

Annabelle hadn't been able to explain. Always before, she'd had John, if only through correspondence. John understood because he'd been there. After the fall. After the banishment. Jane had been too young. And last night, Annabelle had been in no condition to explain. Her sister had hugged her and wiped her cheeks. She'd assured her it was just a dream.

How Annabelle wished that were true.

Suddenly, she needed to write. She needed to tell the truth to someone who could never be hurt by it, spill her bitterest thoughts onto paper. Her fingertips itched. She shoved to her feet. Rushed from the morning room to the parlor, sat at the little writing desk between two windows, and began as she'd done for many years: *Dearest Robert.*

She'd written almost an entire page when she heard Ned's knock at the door. She glanced up, noting the rain had turned to misty drizzle. "Yes?" she called absently, dipping her pen in the inkwell.

"A visitor for you, my lady."

"Is it the Aldridge twins, Ned? Because if so, I fear I've been stricken by a grave malady of some kind. Call it a lung complaint."

"No, my lady."

"A putrid cat scratch, then. Dreadful sight." She waggled her fingers in Ned's direction. "Same answer for Miss Bentley."

"It is Mr.—"

A deeper voice intruded, halting her heart and her pen. "My thanks, Ned. Lady Annabelle would like tea. Fetch it for us, won't you?"

She stiffened, waiting until the door closed before she turned. His shoulders were damp, his newly trimmed hair glistening in the light from the window.

"Papa has gone to his club." She kept her voice casual, though her heart pounded. "The kittens had their usual effect."

He stood motionless in front of the door, his cane propped beside his foot. "Before I speak to your father, I wish to ..." He glanced at his boots, wet and worn. "I need to speak with you."

Not since she'd plummeted into the Tisenby had she felt such a shock of cold. This was it. He intended to cry off the engagement. After a few breaths to regain her sanity, she snapped, "Go on, then. Let's have done with it."

He frowned at her. Scowled, really. "Why are you angry?"

"Oh, no reason at all." She snorted. "I suppose you'll pursue Matilda Bentley, now. Men do seem to enjoy being the more intelligent half of a pairing. By the by, Papa already knows we'd planned to marry. If you think I'm vexed, wait until *he* finds out what you've done."

His eyes narrowed. "Which is?"

She stood and jabbed her pen into its holder, then folded her arms beneath her bosom. "Do not pretend, Robert. This is insulting enough. I am hardly daft."

"Perhaps I am, because I haven't the slightest idea what you're on about."

"The engagement. You've come to break it."

"Why the devil would I break it?"

She threw her arms wide. "I don't know! Punishment? Some

bizarre need to humiliate—"

Within seconds, he'd charged across the room and cupped her chin in his free hand. His thumb stroked across her lower lip with disarming sensuality. "Damn and blast, Annabelle," he muttered. "I've no reason to punish or humiliate you. No reason whatever."

Between his touch and the contradiction between his statement and her expectations, she suddenly needed something solid. Something strong. His shoulders would do nicely, she decided. The moment she stepped into his arms, he wrapped her up tight. No hesitation, no puny pressure. When Robert held her, he meant it. Muscular arms cinched around her back, drawing her flat against him. A large hand cradled the back of her head while she rested her cheek against his coat's lapel.

"I don't know how you can say that," she whispered against the wool. Like him, it smelled like fresh air. "I don't know why you asked me to marry you."

She heard his sigh in his chest, heard his heart's deep, thudding rhythm. She closed her eyes and let it calm her, as it had always done.

"Because I want you as my wife," he rumbled. "As to the rest, that is what I came to discuss."

She didn't want to discuss anything. She wanted to wallow in his nearness, the reassurance that he still intended to marry her. Fancy that. She was going to *marry* Robert Conrad. Relief suffused her like heat from an oven.

"Bumblebee."

She shushed him and snuggled tighter.

"I need to tell you something."

"I was wrong. You are perfect for steadying."

A brief silence was followed by a deep chuckle. "Happy to be of service."

"It is lovely here, Robert. Can we stay like this forever?"

Another silence. His thumb stroked her nape. "Afraid not,

Bumblebee." His tone, quiet and solemn, suggested she would not like what he had to say.

She braced herself. Squeezed her eyes shut. Took a breath. And asked, "What did you have to tell me?"

He waited so long to speak, she began listing calamitous possibilities in her mind: He was unable to father children. He was about to be hanged by the crown. He would accept nothing but turnips at his dinner table. He wanted her to wear turbans. He'd only pay for one pair of slippers a year. He'd invited Lady Wallingham to stay at Rivermore indefinitely.

Oh, God. What could it be?

"I never blamed you for the accident," he said.

She blinked, waiting for him to finish his thought. But he said nothing else. That was it? An obviously false reassurance? The minuscule slipper budget would have been more upsetting.

Men. They could be baffling. She patted his arms and drew back to look up at him. Brooding blue eyes roiled like storm clouds.

"Did you hear me?" he asked.

"I'm standing right here, Robert. Of course I heard you."

His hands fell to his sides. "Why are you not ... I don't understand."

She retrieved his cane from where he'd propped it against her chair. Handing it back to him, she sniffed. "The past is done. There is no need to lie about it."

Now, he looked frustrated. "You don't believe me."

"I was there," she pointed out.

"You've never wondered why—"

"No. You told me why. And you were right. Had I not followed you, the accident would not have happened. You'd have taken your commission. You'd have gone to war. You might have died. Or you might have lived. You might have been injured in battle. Or you might have come home a hero. In any event, that is not what happened. Instead, you must walk with a cane for the rest of your life. And that is my fault. It is what I live with."

He raked a hand through his hair. He looked pale. Sickened. "Bloody hell, Bumblebee."

"If you've forgiven me, just say that. Rewriting the past is foolishness."

"Listen to me."

She shook her head. "Let's speak about something else."

"Annabelle." He looked tortured, now. Tight-lipped and tense. "Please listen."

"No."

"I never blamed you."

"Stop it."

"Not then. Not now. Not ever."

Her throat tightened until she couldn't breathe. "Robert. I don't want to talk any longer. I think you should—"

"I drove you away—"

"—leave."

"—because you were bound and determined to ruin your life for my sake."

"Please, Robert," she whispered. Her chest was collapsing. She reached blindly behind her, bracing against the desk. "Stop."

"I could not let you sacrifice yourself. I spoke harshly so you would stay away. So you could be free."

Covering her mouth with her hand, she gritted her teeth and stared at his boots. They were wet from the street.

"I was wrong to let you believe it was your fault. I thought it the only way to protect you. Perhaps it was, but I am no less sorry." He went quiet. His boots shone gray in the misty light.

"Why ..." Her voice emerged as a muffled croak, so she tried again. "Why say any of this now?"

"You deserve the truth before we marry."

"Marry. You've just informed me the last seven years have been a lie."

His boots inched closer. His voice came from above her

head. "Our separation was necessary, Annabelle. Without it, you'd have been ruined within a year or two. It would not have mattered that I could scarcely lift my arm, much less debauch anyone. A young woman cannot remain constantly in the company of a young man and keep her reputation, even a girl whose only intention was to care for an injured friend."

"Perhaps if you'd simply said that—"

"You would have refused to leave me. Tell me that isn't so."

A long silence fell before she forced the truth past the rocks in her chest. "I cannot," she whispered.

He paused. "My survival was ... uncertain for a long while. Had I died, you'd have been left no remedy to repair your reputation, not even marriage to a crippled man."

"If you'd died, my reputation could go hang. I would not have cared a whit."

"That was what worried me most."

For minutes, she simply stared at his boots, trying to absorb this new version of events. In a way, it made sense. Everything he'd claimed about her was true.

But how was manipulating her with guilt better than blaming her for an accident that had nearly killed him? It wasn't. At least his bitterness had been understandable. But this—this decision he'd made for both of them—this was maddening.

Humiliating.

How pathetic she must have seemed to him.

Slowly, she slid her gaze upward. Past his twisted knee and thick thighs. Past narrow hips and trim waist and wide shoulders. Up to blue eyes that should have seen better. Should have seen *her* better.

"Arrogant, high-handed, stubborn man," she muttered.

He frowned. "I understand if you're—"

"No! You understand nothing."

His mouth closed tight. He rolled his shoulders. "Probably true."

"I should have had a choice, Robert. You should have given me that."

He took the safe ground of silence.

She shook her head, fighting the urge to wail and shove at him and demand that he take it back. Instead, she gripped the edge of the desk. Felt the corner of the letter she'd been writing when he'd entered. How many had she written through the years? Letters to a phantom. What a piteous fool she was, too obsessed to relinquish him entirely.

He'd had no such trouble forgetting her, had he? But then, she'd always done the chasing. Sooner or later, he'd been bound to grow weary of it.

"Why pursue marriage with me?" She hadn't meant to ask, really. The question escaped before she could squelch it.

He seemed caught off guard, opening his mouth several times as though searching for an answer safe enough to satisfy a madwoman. "It is a good match."

"Lady Wallingham would give that answer," she snapped. "You all but blackmailed me into consenting to become your wife."

"As I told you before, that is what I want."

"But why? If you thought we were better off apart, what sense does it make to suddenly decide—"

"I realized you need me to keep you safe. You've had trouble controlling your impulses since you were a girl. I assumed that behavior was confined to our ... connection. Recently, I realized it is simply part of your character."

Her mouth gaped. "Unbelievable." She could scarcely credit his arrogance. "This betrothal has been about *managing* me like an unruly pet?"

Heavy brows crashed into a V. "No. That's not—blast. I am not good with ... You take unacceptable risks. Do rash things without thinking about the conseq—"

"What sort of fool would I be to marry a man who thinks I must be manipulated into self-preservation?"

"Bloody hell. Do not break the engag—"

"The sort too daft to bother with, I daresay."

"Stop this, Annabelle. You agreed."

"And you lied." Those lies had shattered her heart so badly she still felt the abyss left in its place. Nothing filled it. Not even the work she loved. She'd thought marrying Robert her best chance to regain some of what she'd lost. But he did not love her—he pitied her. He always had.

At the moment, he looked frustrated. "I had good reasons."

"No. You had *your* reasons. And I am calling a halt to this disastrous union for *my* reasons. I want you to leave."

"Annabelle."

"Oh, is that rash? As a weak-minded girl incapable of managing her impulses, it is a wonder I do not relieve myself on the carpets like an untrained hound." She shoved away from the desk then pointed at the door. "Leave. Or I shall ask Ned to assist you out to the street."

He did not leave. He did not even step toward the door. No, in typical Robert fashion, he instead crowded closer. "You agreed to marry me," he gritted.

Heavens, he was close now. Her hip brushed the desk as she tried to gain some breathing room. "That was before realizing I am an ill-behaved ninnyhammer whose judgment should always be questioned." Reaching back to steady her balance, her hand slid on a sheet of paper. She watched in horror as the page—her letter to a phantom Robert—flew past the actual Robert, who watched it flutter past his boot with frowning curiosity.

She had scant seconds in which to panic. To run through her options. To imagine the dreadful scenario in which he retrieved the page from behind his boot—and read it.

Only one distraction was certain to make him forget the page existed.

Decision made, she gripped his coat's collar, yanked his head down, and kissed the all-too-real Robert's all-too-tempting mouth.

His cane clattered to the floor. His groan hummed against her lips. Powerful arms cinched around her like greedy ropes. Soon, her backside slid up. Up onto the desk, which scraped across the wood floor as Robert's urgency moved him into her.

God, even when she was furious with him, he tasted divine. A bit salty, a bit like coffee, and a lot like a man she wanted to devour. He felt enormous and powerful surrounding her. Yet she had hold of him. Her hands cradled his jaw. Her lips caressed his. Her tongue slid and hid until he invaded where she wanted him most.

Her desire frightened her. But it was the same heady sensation as standing upon a cliff above the ocean—all that force pounding through one's body, all that majestic beauty beckoning with power. She felt it. And he felt it.

She'd felt it yesterday when she'd trimmed his hair. It moved between them like a tide.

Now, his hands were roamers. Squeezing and tugging.

His tongue was an explorer. Pulsing and playing.

His thighs were seekers. Delving and spreading.

One of those thighs wedged high between hers. Pressed hard. Shocked a moan from her throat. The pleasure was ferociously eager as though it had waited years for an invitation. It spiraled out in sparkling waves from where he pressed and slid.

Nothing was solid. Except him. Robert. She tore at his collar. Distantly, she heard threads tear. But it didn't matter. Nothing else existed except his mouth and hers. His thighs and hers. His desire and hers.

Something squeezed her left bosom a breath before indescribably rich sensations burst from its center. She wanted to see. She wanted to keep kissing him, but equally, she wanted to see what he was doing.

Tugging and clawing at his shoulders, she pushed back to glance down.

His hand. Big, strong, warm.

Her breast. Bare, swollen, ripe.

"Damn and blast," he panted, his chest heaving. "Bloody siren."

His eyes were blue flames. They were riveted upon her breast, which he stroked and teased. His thumb danced over the hard, red tip with obsessive repetition. Each pass wound her tighter.

"You drive me mad," he growled. His cheeks were flushed, his eyes mirror-bright, his wondrous lips swollen. "Need a taste."

He kissed her shoulder first, having apparently bared it along with her bosom. Sliding damp lips to her throat, he then tickled his way down across the slope of her breast. There, bold as can be, his thumb moved aside in favor of his mouth. And his mouth claimed her nipple with breathtaking force.

Her entire body seized. Keened. Lost what was left of her sanity in an explosion so sudden and ferocious, she had to bury her mouth against his neckcloth to stifle her screams. The pleasure pulsed in wave after wave. And, like the ocean, it rocked her to and fro until she tumbled and lost her hold on the ground.

But he held her, his arms strong as ropes, his thighs hard as stone. His mouth explored her throat and eased her bodice from her other shoulder, which gave him access to her other breast.

Her body loved everything. His hands. His lips. His breath and the coolness of her nipple after he'd suckled it. A part of her was satisfied with what they'd already done, and like a kitten in a warm pool of sunlight, she wanted to stretch out and laze.

But he was not finished.

No, he seemed to have something to prove to her. As soon as both her breasts were exposed, he set to work like a man possessed. His mouth claimed one nipple. His thumb reclaimed the other.

Her head fell back on her neck as the pleasure started up again, slower this time, but with more urgent purpose.

His teeth scraped and nibbled. His hand traveled to her knee. Yanked at her skirts. Slid to her inner thigh, where she was soaked and soft. Firm fingers found a spot that only her own fingers had ever explored. The intimate touch gave her a start, but within seconds, she was writhing for him to deepen the contact.

His mouth was at her ear, now, his other hand testing her nipple's tenderness with a gentle, rolling pinch. "Say you're mine, love." His growl rippled against her ear as his finger circled and slid between her folds. "Say you'll be my wife."

Her heart pounded. She couldn't catch her breath. What was he doing to her? "Robert?"

"Say yes, and I'll make you come again." He didn't sound like himself. He sounded growly and hoarse. Rough.

It made her want him more.

"Oh, God. Robert." His name was one long moan. She hooked an ankle behind his good leg. "I need you."

"Damned right, you do."

His finger slid through her opening and snugged deep into her sheath. The fit was tight and foreign, but the relief of having something fill the aching emptiness was almost as good as the pleasure she'd experienced earlier. Almost.

"Feel that, Bumblebee?"

She grunted and dug her fingers into his shoulders.

"You can have more. Just say yes."

"I want you so much," she panted.

"Say it." His finger surged deeper. His other fingers plucked and pressed her nipple until it felt afire. "Or shall I leave you like this? Starving for a meal you'll never have."

"No, please."

"Marry me, Annabelle. Be my wife."

The tension was no longer an ocean. It was pure fire. Her skin prickled. Her nipple burned. Her sheath clenched and wept around his finger. Her hips rolled in an attempt to force even greater pressure from his hand.

She couldn't remember how this had begun. She scarcely

recalled the word he wanted her to repeat. Or why it seemed so important to him.

Everything was too bright. Even the air felt like velvet, weighty and soft.

She groaned.

"Give me your promise. Say yes."

"Good heavens."

"Say, 'Robert, I will marry you.'"

"Oh, God. Your hands feel soooo good."

"Go on, Bumblebee. Repeat the words."

"I can't ... I can't ..."

The hand between her thighs jerked as he buried his face in her neck and gave a long, deep growl. "Yes. You will."

His finger slid impossibly deep even as his thumb pulsed against her most pleasurable spot and his other hand squeezed her nipple with a firmness he hadn't used before. He drew the nipple out, lengthened it before engulfing it in the heat of his mouth. With brutal determination, Robert worked the pleasure points of her body until she was mindless.

Begging.

Chanting his name.

Exploding in shameless, luminous ecstasy.

She was buoyant as sunlight. Floating like a cloud across soaring peaks.

When she finally descended to the ground, Robert was there. If she hadn't been so befuddled by her own climax, she might have been prepared for what she saw.

He loomed above her, his face shadowed, his eyes gone black. His gaze was riveted to her bare breasts.

Faintly embarrassed now that her lust had eased, she started to tug the lilac silk and the cups of her stays back into place.

He stopped her. Met her eyes. "Let me look at what's mine."

Both her heart and her eyelids fluttered. He sounded beastly, as if he'd do violence to anyone who stood between them.

"Robert," she began softly.

"I can wait to take you," he rasped. "But let me look."

She nodded.

He looked. Every inch his gaze touched felt tingly and ripe. "You will marry me," he murmured before finally stroking the swells of her breasts with his knuckles and putting her bodice to rights. "You must."

"Only a blackguard makes such demands of a woman when she is ..." Her eyes traced the beloved lines of his face, the jaw and brows, the lips and freshly trimmed hair, so dark and thick. "Do not use my weakness against me," she whispered.

"I will do whatever it takes to keep you ... safe."

Was it her imagination, or had he hesitated before the last word? Dash it all, it didn't matter. A husband should respect his wife, not pity her. Did she want a lifetime of this? Did she want a man who looked on her as a charming pet best suited to confined spaces and dull cutlery?

Did she want Robert?

Oh, heavens. Yes, she wanted him. But no, she didn't want his pity.

"I've survived well enough these last seven years." She managed the lie with aplomb, though her voice was thin. "I suspect I'll do the same once you've remembered I'm not worth the trouble."

He stroked her cheek with his knuckles the same way he'd caressed her bosom moments earlier. "There's the problem, Bumblebee," he said. "To me, you were always worth the trouble."

Chapter Ten

*"Most expected I would object to Mr. Aimes's portrayal of me
as a dragon, but I fail to see the insult. On the contrary,
I suspect the hand that drew me as a fearsome,
fire-breathing creature knows me rather well."*

—THE DOWAGER MARCHIONESS OF WALLINGHAM in a letter to the
Marquis of Mortlock on the topics of amusing sketches, societal
hypocrisies, and unusual talents.

Dearest Robert,
*I made Major Colby laugh today. Fancy that. We met in the village,
and I showed him one of my sketches. He laughed.*

I think I may be getting good at this.

Ever yours,
Annabelle

—Letter to Robert Conrad dated November 5, 1812

TWO DAYS LATER, WHEN ANNABELLE ENTERED THE PARK FOR a ride with Jane, she was still fuming. Robert had followed her yesterday and the day before that, tracking her across Mayfair like a hound chasing a fox. He'd left her no opportunity to return to Mr. Green's offices unobserved, so she'd sent her last few sketches through a messenger.

"I do wish you hadn't used me as an excuse to delay marrying Robert," Jane grumbled, shivering atop a white mare. She wore a fine riding habit of warm blue wool—similar to Annabelle's, though Annabelle's was brown—but the weather this spring had been abnormally cold. May felt like March, dark and damp. Heavy gray light glinted off of Jane's spectacles. "Cutting the season short seems a splendid idea."

Annabelle hadn't yet told Jane or Papa about breaking the engagement. She wasn't certain why—probably her daft heart hoping Robert would make a grand gesture, such as sweeping into a ballroom, dropping to one knee, and declaring his eternal love and veneration.

Silly daydream. Dropping to one knee would be awkward for a man with a cane.

Annabelle sighed and answered her sister. "You must make an effort, Jane."

"I have."

"No. Dancing is an effort. Smiling is an effort. Speaking with someone of the male persuasion is an effort—"

"I spoke with Ned and Papa only this morning."

"Whereas *reading* behind Lady Colchester's topiary whilst eligible prospects search for dance partners constitutes the opposite of effort."

"I beg to differ." Jane sniffed. "It requires ingenuity to locate the perfect reading spot. Potted palms and topiaries are not as plentiful as I would like."

"You cannot marry a potted palm."

"Even a dashing one? Lady Colchester's are rather handsome."

"Jane."

Her sister's lips tightened. "I know, Annabelle. Perhaps you think me daft as well as plain—"

"I think you neither, ninny."

"—but I understand my duty well enough." Her voice grew quiet. "If it were merely a question of effort, the task would have been done last season."

Sadness and anger squeezed Annabelle's heart. She glanced to her sister—her charming, amusing, intelligent sister—and wished with all her might that Jane could be cured of her shyness. Then, others might see what she saw: a young woman of uncommon worth and wit. Objectively, Jane might be considered plain, yes. Her spectacles made her eyes appear bigger than they were, distorting her face's proportionality. Her nose, like Annabelle's, was round rather than refined. Her skin was pale, given to flushing red at the slightest provocation. Her brown hair refused to curl. And she was a bit plump.

Yet, Annabelle had never seen her sister as plain. She'd seen her as what she was—beautiful. If only the rest of the world were not so blind. If only gentlemen preferred charm above comeliness.

If only wanting and having were the same.

"In any event," Jane continued, nudging her spectacles with a gloved finger. "You have more urgent matters to consider than my wallflower status. Have you heard from your dreadful publisher?"

Annabelle shook her head and directed her mount closer to Jane's. "Not for over a week."

If she didn't know better, she would assume Mr. Green was avoiding her. But he had published her revised sketch of Lady Victoria and Atherbourne. Since then, she'd sent him several new caricatures with different subjects, but hadn't received so much as a note in response. Of course, she'd had no opportunity to venture to Catherine Street, either.

Because she had a hound upon her heels every time she left Berne House.

Jane glanced behind them and raised a brow at Annabelle. "Is it customary for one's intended husband to follow one about with such ... vigilance?"

Annabelle simply glared ahead. She would ignore him. She would.

"What, precisely, is his purpose?"

"I have no earthly idea."

"Does he think you will cry off?"

"Let us change the subject."

Jane frowned at her. "It is curious, Annabelle."

Not as curious as Jane supposed.

"I never knew Robert to show such intensity," Jane continued. "More a steady sort, I thought, like a great block of stone. And just that expressive." She chuckled wryly then resumed her musing tone. "Though, I do recall him being quite protective toward you." She nibbled her lip. "That time you followed him whilst he and John were hunting. When you wandered between his shot and the ducks. My, he was incensed, wasn't he?"

"Jane."

"Or, the time you rode Papa's stallion to catch Robert before he departed for Eton. He was furious then, too. So were John and Papa, to be fair. You might have broken your neck. That horse had a devilish temper. He threw Papa every other ride."

"Let us speak of something else."

"Come to think of it, Robert has always been rather intense where you are concerned." Jane eyed her with speculation. "Interesting."

As usual, Jane's insightful nature drew her too close to the bone. Annabelle would have to give her answers, or she would simply continue digging. And, as much as she loved her sister, she would not have her drilling for water where there was only blood and pain to be found.

"I ruined his life, Jane." She kept her eyes upon the path before them. A sharp wind came to bite her skin.

"But, you were a child then. Genie's age. It was an accident. Surely he's forgiven you. Else, why make you his wife?"

She glanced at her sister, who seemed genuinely perplexed. She had no further answers to offer, so she held her silence.

After a while, Jane said gently, "You never speak of that day."

Because she could not bear to touch it. To remember.

"John said you and Robert quarreled."

Annabelle closed her eyes. Stopped her horse. Swallowed against the sick. "I loved him more than I should," she whispered. "He loved me less than I wanted." She should have used the present tense. *He loves me less than I want.* Wasn't that the heart of the matter? When she opened her eyes, light rippled gray and white as tears came.

Jane drew her mare close enough to reach out and grasp Annabelle's hand. She said nothing, merely held her hand and let her regain her composure. If Annabelle hadn't already adored her sister, that single kindness would have earned her devotion.

Looking past Jane to the trees rustling along the path through the park, Annabelle worked to pull away from the memories. The bridge. The sigh of water and leaves. The stark realization of how much of her heart she'd given away and how much he'd pitied her for it.

"You were so young," Jane murmured. "He was what? Eighteen? Five years is a trifling difference now, but back then ..." She shook her head. "He saw you as a girl, which is as it should be. That does not mean he didn't love you."

Annabelle looked down at their clasped hands, let the cold wind whip away her tears, and forced her lips into a smile. "It is all in the past, now," she lied. "His strength has improved." An understatement. One need only glance at his shoulders to realize that. Or be held in his arms. A pleasurable shiver stole across her flesh at the memory. "If anything, his heretofore undiscovered talents for land management have been honed to a remarkable degree." She released Jane's hand and nudged her mount forward. "He cannot stop working long enough to trim his hair. Heaven knows what other tasks he's neglected. Something must be done."

Before Jane could reply, a deep, masculine voice came from behind them. It rippled with irritation. "What is everyone's preoccupation with my hair?"

Annabelle stiffened.

Jane stopped and turned her mare to face him. "Mr. Conrad. My, that is a sizable horse you have, there."

"He is a recent acquisition."

Knowing that Robert had never been the loquacious sort and Jane's shyness would slow her conversation to a halt within moments, Annabelle took pity on them both and turned her mount to join them.

Heavens, he was handsome with his hair properly trimmed. Brooding blue eyes glinted like steel in the gray light. A hard jaw flexed as he touched the brim of his hat. "Lady Annabelle."

"Mr. Conrad." His gaze held her captive for a long, lingering silence. Suddenly, the bite of cold wind became heat. Melting, liquid heat. Searching for a distraction, she examined his horse.

She blinked. Was it her imagination, or was the horse's face lopsided? And the eyes. The eyes were at half-mast, as though the gigantic hunter wished for nothing more than a field of daisies to munch at its leisure. "Your horse appears a bit ... drowsy."

"He prefers a slower pace. I've come to appreciate such circumspection."

Ignoring the veiled reference to her own nature, she blinked again, tilting her head. Had the horse just winked at her? "It is the blaze, I think."

"What of it?"

"Makes him appear a bit off balance."

Robert stiffened, his shoulders rolling, his brow glowering. "He is a sound mount."

"Oh, I quite agree. Stout as a great oak. And equally fast, I'd wager."

"Speed is overrated. Stamina is what matters."

"Perhaps you should inform all the horse-mad gents who bestow their mounts with such names as Highflyer and Phantom."

"Those are racehorses. A hunter must last longer than mere minutes. He must traverse rough terrain over hours. He must be strong. Determined. Patient and fearless." He patted his horse's neck. "Names are a frivolity for a hunter."

She narrowed her eyes upon Robert then his lopsided, sleepy mount. "What is his name?"

Robert's glower deepened into mulish lines. "Why do you wish to know?"

"Because you clearly wish to keep it from me."

"Rubbish."

"That's his name? Rubbish?"

"Stop being cheeky."

"Tell me."

Ruddy color painted his cheeks. She'd bet every pair of silk slippers she owned that it wasn't due to the cold.

"Robert. What is your horse's name?"

He muttered something beneath his breath.

"Pardon?"

"Dewdrop," he barked, his eyes flashing. "It is the name he came with. I plan on changing it."

She tried to keep herself from laughing, and she almost succeeded. But Jane let a giggle escape, and that was that.

"Oh!" she gasped, covering her unruly mouth with one hand and clutching her belly with the other. "Y-you mustn't. Too ... p-perfect."

Jane was snorting now, knuckling beneath her spectacles as she fought the same mirth that had taken hold of Annabelle.

Robert, by contrast, was far from amused. "His prior owner's daughter named him as a foal. He can hardly be blamed for that."

Annabelle pressed her lips together and nodded her understanding, though another giggle did manage to escape. She avoided looking at the big, sleepy, lopsided Dewdrop for fear it would set her off again. But Robert's expression also tickled her. He was offended on behalf of his horse's dignity, a very *Robert* reaction. He'd never liked for innocent creatures to be harmed, even when they were oblivious.

Dewdrop was certainly that. The gelding gave a slow blink, a snuffling sigh, and shifted as though settling in for a long wait.

Annabelle controlled her laughter long enough to grin at the man astride Dewdrop's back. "He is splendid, Robert. Positively splendid."

He glared as though she were being sarcastic.

"No, really!" She guided her own mount alongside Dewdrop so she could run a hand along his stout, brown neck. Lazily, the animal turned his head to sniff her skirts. "You are unique, aren't you, boy?" she murmured. "Too many mounts haven't the patience to stand still."

The horse gave her another slow blink then, oddly, appeared to nod.

Once again, she laughed, this time with delight. "Did you see that, Robert? He agrees with me." When she raised her eyes, however, laughter quickly faded.

Good heavens, he looked like he might snatch her up and carry her away. Brooding blue fairly singed her. Suddenly, the air was thin and her wool habit both too hot and too tight.

Jane cleared her throat. "I do believe the Aldridge sisters are headed our way."

Annabelle tore her gaze from Robert's to view the curricle approaching from the east end of the park.

"Shall we attempt a swift exit?" Jane asked hopefully.

She shot her sister a chiding glance.

"Drat," Jane muttered.

By the time the curricle rolled to a stop, Annabelle had positioned herself to greet Lucinda and Margaret Aldridge with a smile. The twins wore matching blue spencers, though Lucinda's gown was lavender muslin and Margaret's was primrose silk. Lucinda, who always wore large pearl earbobs, waved excitedly while her sister clutched her lap blanket and shivered.

"Lady Annabelle! Just who I had hoped to meet!"

Annabelle moved her mount to the side of the carriage where Lucinda waved a newspaper to and fro.

"Have you seen this morning's edition? Scandalous! Simply scandalous."

Margaret nodded her agreement. "*Outrageous,* I daresay."

Not to be outdone, Lucinda bobbed up and down like a duck on choppy water. "Oooh. Yes, outrageous. That is precisely the word, dearest Margaret."

Annabelle sighed. "Good heavens, Lucinda. Do calm yourself before you topple your curricle." Calmly, she took the newspaper from her friend's hand.

Behind her, she heard Jane introducing Robert, followed by more excitable chatter from the twins. Voices faded from notice, however, when she examined that morning's edition of

Green's Daily Informer. On the front page was the usual gossip, the usual drivel about beautifying cures for spots, notices of furnishings for auction, and offers to hire cooks with "knowledge of genteel households." But inside the folded pages, tucked in its usual location, was a print signed by Edward Yarrow Aimes.

Hardly noteworthy, except for one small thing. Well, two small things, really. First, the caricature was inferior work. Cruel rather than witty, mocking rather than wry, a lie rather than truth. It featured Victoria Lacey as a poisonous flower conspiring with Atherbourne's sinister highwayman to lure a handsome hound—obviously Stickley—first to the altar then to his death. The caption held no subtlety, simply a dialogue between Lady Victoria and Atherbourne describing their conspiracy to "make you a duchess ere we sup together at His Grace's table." The implication was as foul as it was absurd. Lady Victoria had never met Atherbourne prior to the Gattingford ball, let alone conspired with him to first marry then murder Stickley.

This was libelous. This was, to use Margaret's word, *outrageous.*

And this was *not* Annabelle's work.

Her throat tightened into a choke. Wind rushed in her ears.

How could this be? She examined the drawing. The curves were all wrong. The noses were flattened, the eyes lifeless. Hands were difficult to draw, particularly when styled as leaves or animals' limbs. She'd worked forever to master them.

These hands were amateurish. Disproportionate. Awkwardly angled.

The least Green might have done was to hire somebody competent. As it was, he was using her name—well, her fake name—to legitimize hackneyed rubbish.

Worse, *slanderous* hackneyed rubbish.

Oh, God. She was going to be sick.

ELISA BRADEN

"Annabelle." His voice drew her, as it always had. He'd pulled up beside her upon Dewdrop, broad and solid, steady and strong. Blue eyes were shadowed by a concerned frown. "What is it? What's wrong?"

She longed to tell him, which was pure idiocy. He would never understand. Worse, it would confirm his assertions about her recklessness. He'd think her mad for posing as a male caricaturist. Perhaps she was. But Edward Yarrow Aimes was *her* creation. And someone had stolen him. Made his work—*her* work—into a lie.

Robert sidled closer, clasped her upper arm and bent his head to hold her gaze. "Tell me," he murmured.

She couldn't. She wanted to. But even Jane thought her work was ill-advised. How could she expect this man, of all men, to accept the risks she'd taken? To understand the betrayal she felt?

Still, she nearly confessed. Right there in the middle of Hyde Park, she wanted him to gather her close, wanted to rest her head on his ridiculously broad shoulder and feel his strong arms surround her again.

"Do you suppose Blackmore has seen it, dearest Annabelle?" It was Lucinda's voice, high and grating.

Annabelle blinked and drew away from Robert to return the wretched paper to her friend. Gathering her composure enough to offer a placid smile, she replied, "Doubtful. I suspect his grace prefers *The Times.*"

"I thought yesterday's edition was scathing, but *this.*" Lucinda clicked her tongue and shook her head.

"Outrageous," Margaret repeated.

Annabelle frowned at Lucinda. "Yesterday's?" She hadn't seen it, too preoccupied with Robert's pursuit of her and Jane all the way to a bookshop on Piccadilly. "What was in yesterday's edition?"

"Oh, you remember the bad bit of business with Sir Harold Standish and that charlatan, Mr. Bickerstaff, don't you? Well,

Mr. Aimes implied ..." Lucinda fluttered her lashes in Robert's direction. "Of course, I wouldn't wish to spread untoward rumors."

Annabelle rolled her eyes. "Just tell me, Lucinda."

Margaret took Annabelle's demand as permission to pick up where her sister had left off. "He implied that Sir Harold knew Mr. Bickerstaff planned to flee to the Continent with the funds he'd swindled from his investment scheme."

Lucinda nodded emphatically, her earbobs bobbing. "Indeed, Mr. Aimes's drawing suggested Sir Harold was Bickerstaff's partner."

Her stomach churned and fired hot. A *second* fraudulent caricature? How long had Green been planning to replace her with this talentless imposter? The wretch could not even invent new themes, playing the same tired note twice. One would think all members of the ton were plotting dastardly deeds in asinine conversations. Had the wretch any familiarity with the beau monde, he would quickly realize most of them were too sotted, slothful, or stupid to engage in convoluted schemes.

No, it was the Mr. Greens of the world—the ones driven by greed and unhampered by conscience—who deserved exposure.

The bitter cold of the day caused the Aldridge twins to shiver and depart. It caused Jane to insist on returning to Berne House. It even caused Dewdrop to snort and shake his head.

But Annabelle did not feel it. She felt rage. And the only remedy was to confront its source. She glanced to her side, where Robert continued sending her brooding glances from beneath heavy brows.

Yes, she would deal with Mr. Green. But first, she must stop the most determined man she'd ever known from following her like a shadow.

Chapter Eleven

"Watch the sunrise? My dear Mortlock, do not let impending mortality render you an imbecile. Two good things occur before breakfast: Servants clean, and I slumber. All else is rubbish."

—THE DOWAGER MARCHIONESS OF WALLINGHAM in a letter to the Marquis of Mortlock admonishing said gentleman for suggesting a change in routine.

Dearest Robert,
My newspaper habit has grown such that Papa insists I must choose between subscriptions and slippers. Naturally, I chose slippers. However, my interest in matters political has persuaded me to try

sketching new subjects. Judging from the outrage toward gentlemen producing similar work, I have begun contemplating names under which I would publish, should such an opportunity arise.

I would like the name to be something true about me. Something unchanging. The only thing that matches this description is my love for you.

Must think on this further. Artists use initials, don't they?

Ever yours,
Annabelle

—Letter to Robert Conrad dated January 30, 1813

ANNABELLE'S MOOD WAS BLACK AS CHARRED BEEFSTEAK. This was the third morning she'd awakened at an atrociously early hour. The third morning she'd attempted to evade Robert Conrad.

But it was the first morning she'd made it this far.

A wagon full of caged hens clucked and rattled past as she neared a noisy tavern. Lurching to a halt, she waited, heart pounding, as a slovenly drunkard stumbled through the tavern door onto the walk in front of her. The red-nosed wretch squinted a bleary grin and meandered toward the adjacent alley. He smelled of ale and sweat.

She glanced up and down the Strand. Fifty feet ahead was D'Oyley's Warehouse. Around the corner and fifty feet farther was Green's office. Most shops weren't open at this ungodly hour, but Green would be onsite to oversee production of the

Informer's latest edition.

She'd written him thrice so far demanding an explanation. No reply. Not even a curt, "Leave off, Miss Aimes." Infuriating.

The morning was misty, but for once, it wasn't raining. The Strand's usual traffic hadn't thickened yet. Instead, the street was quiet, save for occasional donkey carts and wagons laden with wares for Covent Garden, along with the odd coal cart ambling by on morning rounds. Rather than throngs of pedestrians eyeing shop windows, the few souls braving the dawn went about their business with brisk purpose.

That's right, she thought. Pay no attention to the lone woman making her way toward D'Oyley's Warehouse. Just doing a bit of shopping—three hours before the place opens. One never knows when one might need a dozen dessert napkins.

Twenty feet. Ten. Almost there.

She reached the nearest corner of the brick warehouse by the time she saw him—a wide, squat fellow in a dark coat and tall hat. He'd rounded the corner from Catherine Street, her destination, and now stood half-turned away from her. He pulled a watch from an inside pocket and flicked it open. Had she not recognized him, she might have breezed past without a care.

But she knew him. This was Thomas Bentley, Matilda Bentley's father. With coats that always appeared oversized and graying whiskers extending from his temples to his jaw, the paunchy man was unmistakable.

She halted. Scarcely breathed.

He was frowning at his watch, now. Glancing left.

Oh, heavens. His head was turning in her direction.

She spun on her heel until her back faced him and walked west. Slowly. Steadily.

Breathe, Annabelle. Just breathe and walk. No reason to take notice, Mr. Bentley. No reason whatever.

Bloody hell, this was the opposite of where she should be

heading. But she couldn't let anybody recognize her near the *Informer's* office. She'd have to find somewhere to idle away the time until Mr. Bentley left. But where?

Ahead, she spotted the tavern she'd passed earlier and wrinkled her nose. The sign above the door displayed a rough likeness of either a dog or a fish. It was weathered and hanging crooked, so she couldn't read the name. Perhaps she should keep walking.

She took three steps before noticing an enormous horse emerging from a side street. The horse had a lopsided blaze and a broad-shouldered rider.

"Drat," she muttered beneath her breath. She glanced behind her. Mr. Bentley was still milling outside the warehouse. "Drat, drat, drat."

The tavern would have to do.

Quickly, before either man turned in her direction, she rushed to the old, scarred door marked either with a dog or a fish. Or was it a snail?

Inside, the place was shockingly small—smaller than the drawing room at Berne House. It stank like burnt wood soaked in bad ale. Crowded around a long, central table were three men, all intoxicated if the listing and backslapping was any measure. They appeared to be brothers, as they were similarly large and flat-nosed.

"If you're lookin' for your man, he ain't here."

The voice came from a man behind the bar. He was small— no taller than she. And he wore spectacles. She didn't know what she'd expected from the proprietor of a tavern, but he wasn't it. He looked like one of Jane's booksellers.

She cleared her throat and skirted past a smaller table near the window. "Have you any tea?"

The little man stared at her and wiped the rim of a wooden cup.

"Or coffee. Coffee would suffice."

A mild brow puckered. "There's a coffee house across the street, miss."

"I should like to stay here for a short while."

He glanced over her shoulder. A mild brow cleared. He adjusted his spectacles and raised his chin with a little smile. "If he allows it, I shall be surprised. But if he does, we've decent ale you might fancy."

She blinked. "He?"

The little tavern keeper moved away to clean more cups.

Behind her, she felt a damp breeze. Then, she heard the door close and a cane thudding on the plank floor.

Briefly, she closed her eyes.

"How many times have I told you not to run from me, Bumblebee?"

He was so close the words shivered from her ear down her neck and into her breasts. Good heavens, she really must stop letting him affect her this way.

"If you would cease following, my errands might seem less like running." She spun to face him. His skin was damp. His shoulders, too. She wanted to kiss him. What a mad, desperate idiot she was. "Why *are* you following me, Mr. Conrad?"

"You need watching." He muttered it in that deep voice that made unmentionable parts of her body tingle.

"Don't be ridiculous. Long before you arrived in London, I was taking hacks—to the market, the theatre, the shops—without mishap. Well, mostly. Drivers are dreadfully rude, aren't they? Yet they demand higher fees than ever for more arduous rides."

"Trouble follows you like a shadow, Annabelle. You'll soon be my wife. If trouble dogs your heels, so shall I."

"For the last time, our engagement is canceled. Finished. At an end."

"Why are you here?" He tapped his cane on the floor.

She looked around at the dingy interior, the smoke-stained

hearth, the low, beamed ceiling discolored somewhere between gray and brown, the three sotted brothers singing a pleasant tune about a lady with unusually large bosoms. "I've heard they have fine ale. I wanted to try it."

A glint of humor entered brooding blue eyes. "Is that so?"

Her chin went up. "Indeed."

"At six in the morning."

"I am an early riser."

This time, he outright chuckled and shook his head. "Ah, Bumblebee. If there's one thing you're not, it's an early riser. Have you forgotten the swans?"

Bloody hell. She rolled her eyes and sighed. "That was a long time ago."

"You begged me to meet you in Mr. Eggleston's northeast pasture, where the swans gathered of a morning."

"I remember."

"You intended to sketch them, as nothing else would properly represent the long-necked Mrs. Hopkins. How long did I wait in a muddy pasture with only the rising sun to keep me company?"

"I was there by nine," she grumbled.

"That's right. Three hours. I sat and waited, long after the swans were gone." He moved closer and lowered his head. "Do you know why?"

She shrugged, though his nearness was making her breathless and tingly. "A fascination with long necks and surly dispositions?"

"I couldn't leave you."

All air fled her body. The last bit of it carried his name. "Robert."

"I wanted to be where we'd promised to meet in the unlikely event you awakened before six. And I wanted to be there when I knew you would arrive—too late for the swans, but not for one last ramble before I returned to Eton." His grin was wide and real. It made his eyes crinkle and brought out the faintest dimples in his cheeks.

It lit her heart on fire. "Robert," she repeated, incapable of more.

"That's how I know you would not rise earlier than the sun for anything but a dire cause." He crowded closer. "So, what is it, Annabelle? The truth, now."

Behind him, a chair clattered to the floor. One of the large, sotted brothers reeled back while another shoved to his feet. The third remained slumped in his chair, eyeing both siblings with confusion.

There appeared to be some disagreement about which of the two had a larger cock. She wondered why the argument produced such offense. Surely, the matter could be put to rest with a simple comparison.

"Bloody hell," Robert muttered, positioning himself between the belligerent brothers and Annabelle. "We need to leave." He reached back to offer his hand.

She didn't take it. "I think I'll stay."

The glower he shot over his shoulder nearly shriveled her bravado. But she couldn't leave yet. Mr. Bentley might still be outside.

"Annabelle," he growled. "This is about to turn violent. I'll not have you in the middle of it."

"I fail to see the point of violence or even of arguing. If these gentlemen wish to determine who owns the bigger cock, I should think objective measurements a more proper solution."

Several sets of wide, disbelieving eyes turned in her direction. Had she spoken too loudly? And what had she said that was so outrageous? It was basic reasoning.

With a thunderous-yet-apprehensive expression, Robert's eyes darted to the men then back to her. He rubbed his forehead between thumb and fingers then sighed. "Now you've done it, Bumblebee."

"Don't be silly. All I've done is suggest a solution." She met the incredulous stare of the brothers. "If you wish to know for certain, you must first establish a mutually agreed standard," she advised them. "Shall it be length? Oh, but where to start and where to finish? Perhaps girth is better. But, again, at what point should one measure to ensure an accurate comparison? Circumference varies widely by location upon the anatomy. I know—weight! A scale shouldn't be hard to find. Covent Garden is nearby. Yes, surely weight is—"

"Enough," Robert snapped, grasping her arm in one hand and his cane in the other. "Apologies, gentlemen. We'll be leaving now."

"No, no," slurred the third brother as he lurched to his feet. "She 'as a fair point."

"'Oo's she, now?" asked the second brother.

"T'ain't right. This here's men's business," groused the first brother.

"Indeed," she replied. "You shan't find women arguing over the size of their cocks, that much is certain."

"Bloody hell, Annabelle."

Although Robert's groan was rather amusing, she ignored it. "And if we did, we'd have the good sense to measure first. Resorting to violence over a matter that can be so easily settled is the height of foolishness—"

Robert yanked her into his side and covered her mouth with his palm before she could utter another word. "We're leaving. Good day, gentlemen." He dragged her through the door and several feet down the walk before she managed to yank free. She suspected she only succeeded because he allowed it.

"What do you think you are—"

"What the devil are you thinking—"

"I said I didn't wish to leave."

He pointed toward the dog-fish-snail tavern. "You have no business entering a place like that, let alone engaging in vulgar conversations with three drunken men."

She frowned. "Vulgar? Sensible, you mean. I prevented them from coming to blows over a meaningless disparity."

Jaw flexing, he glared at her with puzzling incredulity.

"Robert, this cannot be your first time discussing the proper measurement of livestock. You've managed Rivermore's farms for the last seven years, and before that, you caught fish with your bare hands. You're far from ignorant about such things."

At her mention of livestock, Robert's scowl cleared. By the time she'd finished, he was smiling. A relief, to be sure. She much preferred a smiling Robert.

He wiped a hand over his mouth. "You thought we were discussing livestock. As in, the male counterpart to chickens."

"What else?"

Sighing, he started to chuckle. Which became laughter. Which soon had him bracing himself against his cane and shaking his head.

She took advantage of his distraction to glance toward D'Oyley's Warehouse. Thank heaven Mr. Bentley was gone. The tension she'd been carrying all morning began to ease.

She turned back to Robert and raised a brow. "I am glad you find me so amusing." She sniffed and smoothed her skirts. She'd worn leaf-green wool in deference to the early morning chill. "Now, I have errands to attend, and they do not involve you."

"Annabelle."

"I suggest you retrieve Dewdrop and return to—"

"I know your secret."

Her earlier tension returned in a flood. With a fluttery blink, she tilted her chin. "Don't be silly. I am not the sort to keep—"

He leaned into her, leaving scant inches between their mouths. "I know about the drawings. About Edward Yarrow Aimes." His voice was soft and low. At this early hour, no one was around to hear, but she felt the impact of his words and the intensity in his eyes as a blow to her midsection.

"You—you know?"

A faint smile curled his lips. "You sent me dozens of sketches through the years. Did you suppose I wouldn't recognize your pen at work?"

For a moment, all thought fled but one: He knew. Blast. Of course he knew. It must be why he'd been following her everywhere, why he'd known where she'd gone. Why he'd entered the snail-fish-dog tavern to retrieve her.

"It has not been my pen these past few—"

"I know that, too."

"Well, if you know so much, then why haven't you said anything?"

"I waited for you to trust me. I'm still waiting."

Trust? What rot. Lying to a girl because he thought her too pathetic to see reason was a better foundation for lifelong loathing than trust. Add to that his following her because he thought she was too helpless to survive a routine meeting off the Strand and hiding his knowledge about Edward Yarrow Aimes, and she wanted to laugh. Instead, she blew out an exasperated breath and straightened her spine. "Regardless, I need to speak with my publisher, so I shall bid you good day."

"Even for you, that is an exceptionally bad idea."

Her eyes flared wide. Good God, did the man *want* to incite her temper? "Even for me?"

Seemingly realizing his error, his head snapped back. He rubbed at his nape. Glanced at her bodice then her chin. "I—that wasn't what I meant."

"What did you mean, Robert?"

"I am not good with words."

"I'll save you the trouble, then. Go home. Leave me to bumble about and fall into unseen pits where I'll surely languish helplessly for want of male guidance and good sense." She waved her fingers at him in a queenly fashion. "I hereby absolve you of responsibility, Robert Conrad." Spinning on her heel, she started toward Catherine Street. Once again, she'd taken no more than five steps when another obstacle appeared.

This time, it was the biggest of the three flat-nosed brothers. He stumbled through the door of the fish-dog-snail tavern just as she passed. She tried to leap out of the way, but he plowed into her with bruising force. Her bonnet flew despite its pins. Her ear, which had collided with the man's thick arm, rang. Her forearm screamed pain where a hand seized hold of her.

"What's this? Ah, the sweet li'l morsel. Want to measure who's bigger now?"

A cloud of musty ale and sour sweat filled Annabelle's nose. She tried to pull away, but he had hold of her. And he was listing badly.

"I've got a cock ye'll not soon—*oof!*"

Abruptly, the sotted oaf loosed his hold when he needed both hands to clutch the spot below his sizable belly where a cane had struck with lightning force.

"Touch her again, and my target will be your throat. This blow was pain. The next is death."

Annabelle rubbed her ringing ear and marveled at the man she'd known her entire life yet apparently had never seen before. At least, not like this.

He was calm. Utterly calm. Though his attack had been swift and brutal, he stood with deeply rooted assurance, as though similar tasks must be attended every day. *Answer correspondence. Collect rents. Attack a drunkard's nether regions with a cane. Threaten him with death. Review the accounts.*

She shook her head. What a confounding, remarkable man.

When his gaze shifted to her, the only change was a familiar furrow of concern. "Are you all right, Bumblebee?"

She nodded. "Fine. He knocked me off balance, that's all."

Robert looked to where she cradled her arm. Then, his eyes narrowed with vicious intent upon the poor wretch huddled in the shadow of the unnamable tavern, emitting wheezing gasps and occasional whimpers.

She reached for Robert's wrist. "Don't," she said softly. She didn't have to say more.

He nodded and turned his hand to interlace his fingers with hers. "I cannot let anyone or anything hurt you." Blue eyes met hers. "There is no absolving me of that. It is as much a part of me as my bones."

Her hand tingled where he held it. Her chest ached. Her throat burned. God, how she loved him. Wanted him. How it hurt that he cared enough to watch over her yet could not love her as she wished.

With an effort, she looked away. Bent to retrieve her bonnet. Glanced down the length of the Strand. "I need to speak with him, Robert." She didn't have to mention Green's name. Robert understood.

His hand tightened. "I cannot let you."

"It is not your place to prevent it."

A long silence. He tugged her away from the tavern toward the alley where, evidently, he'd left Dewdrop tied. "Have you told your father you've attempted to break the engagement?"

She closed her eyes. Damn and blast. "No."

He took the bonnet from her fingers and placed it on her head. His fingers tickled her skin as he retied the silk ribbon. Brooding blue had gone dark and resolute. "Then nothing's changed."

She sighed. "Robert—"

"You will stay away from Green. And you will marry me."

"Saying it does not make it so."

The quirk of his lips was more ominous than amused. "But this does." He lowered his head until her bonnet's brim and his hat formed a shadowed canopy. "I will tell your father everything, Bumblebee. All about Edward Yarrow Aimes. The caricatures. How you kissed me in the Bentleys' closet. Seduced me in your family's parlor."

Her cheeks prickled. "Seduced? I most certainly did not."

The quirk grew into a grin. "Oh, I assure you, love, you most certainly did. Even now, I'm more intoxicated than those tavern vermin."

"You're blackmailing me again."

"Yes."

"Don't you find that scurrilous?"

"Yes."

"Don't you care?"

His eyes blazed into hers. "No."

She bit down on another protest. Blast. He had her cornered. If he told her father, Papa would insist they marry anyway. The only option was to play along, bide her time, and look for opportunities to contact Green. Keeping the betrothal intact ... well, she suspected that would likewise be a waiting game. Right now, Robert was driven by his desire to protect her and his grandfather's demand that he marry. But sooner or later, those two forces would ease, and he would come to the same conclusion he'd reached seven years ago—that keeping Annabelle Huxley in his life was asking for trouble.

Chapter Twelve

"Time wears away all disguises. The essential question is not what will be revealed but when."

—THE DOWAGER MARCHIONESS OF WALLINGHAM in a letter to the Marquis of Mortlock explaining the importance of timing in any deception.

Dearest Robert,
Mama has hired yet another dance tutor in anticipation of my debut. For an event which is at least a year away, she has beggared Papa and exhausted me. All this preparation for husband hunting makes my stomach hurt.

How can I contemplate marrying anyone but you?

Ever yours,
Annabelle

—Letter to Robert Conrad dated March 22, 1813

DURING THE SIX WEEKS SINCE ANNABELLE'S FAKE IDENTITY had been stolen, fifteen more inept-yet-cruel caricatures had been published. She'd sent eight more scathing letters to Mr. Green.

And Robert had not kissed her again. Not once. Not even her wrist or her cheek.

She glared at him now across Lady Darnham's drawing room. He glared in return. Perhaps he was vexed that she'd spoken to Martin Standish earlier—her most casual greeting to the unremarkable captain seemed to set him off. Or, perhaps he was simply displeased to be standing next to Lady Wallingham. The dowager did go on in the most high-handed fashion.

Annabelle sipped Lady Darnham's surprisingly palatable lemonade and fumed at Robert's behavior. They were engaged to be married, for pity's sake. He'd spoken to her father weeks ago. The settlements had been finalized. He'd dined with her family no fewer than eleven times.

In other words, the betrothal might as well be inked in the parish register. That's how difficult it would be to undo. So, why in heaven's name, hadn't he kissed her? Had his prior kisses been mere ploys to compromise her judgment? If so, they had worked splendidly.

For all that he watched her like a wolf watched its next meal, they were never alone together. When they weren't dining with her family or riding with Maureen and Jane or conversing with

Lady Wallingham, they were drinking more-or-less palatable lemonade at yet another ton gathering.

She sighed into her cup and took another drink. At least she'd found him a competent tailor. His new coat—black wool lovingly fitted to those broad, broad shoulders—made her want to cross the room and kiss him in full view of everyone from Lady Wallingham to Matilda Bentley. Particularly the latter.

Frowning, she rolled her shoulders against the surge of possessive lust. Of late, every dream plaguing her sleep involved some variation of Robert being naked and demanding to touch her. Every waking fantasy, meanwhile, involved her making shocking demands of him—namely that he disrobe and touch her with those large, competent hands. Or those delicious lips. Either would work, really.

Good heavens, his thighs were thick. Like dashed tree trunks. She sighed again as she examined them inside black breeches.

Perhaps she should agree to a July wedding, after all.

Perhaps she should have brought her fan.

Lady Darnham, whose wrinkles curved upward in a permanent smile, appeared in front of her, breaking her concentration. Despite the interruption, Annabelle greeted the delightful old woman warmly and complimented her lemonade.

"I add a bit of orange and a dash of honey," Lady Darnham whispered. "Don't tell Lady Wallingham. She is forever after my secret."

Beside Annabelle, Jane protested, "Oh, but you never mentioned the honey." Jane had long ago forgotten her shyness around Lady Darnham, who frequently kept company with the wallflowers at society functions.

Lady Darnham giggled and gave Jane a conspiratorial wink. "Better to throw the dragon off the scent." She returned her attention to Annabelle. "What is this I hear about you and the Conrad boy?"

Annabelle raised a wry brow. "Apparently, we are to be married. A shocking turn of events."

"Only to those who haven't known you both since you were infants," the lady said. "That boy never could keep his eyes off you."

"Little has changed in that regard," Jane interjected.

Annabelle blinked, a bit perplexed by their observations. Robert watched her now, yes, for reasons she found infuriating. But when they were children, *she'd* always done the chasing. He'd tolerated her, taken care of her when necessary, but to imply he'd felt the same obsessive devotion as she ... well, that was simply wrong.

If he'd loved her as she loved him, he could not have banished her from his life.

She met his eyes over Lady Darnham's shoulder. Brooding blue had riveted upon her. Over the past several weeks, she'd chafed beneath its weight—she could not very well confront Mr. Green while Robert watched her every move.

Yet now, she wondered if she'd been unfair. Perhaps he was doing as he'd done before the accident—standing sentry between her and danger.

If trouble dogs your heels, so shall I.

While Jane and Lady Darnham discussed the dreadful weather, Annabelle looked upon Robert with new eyes. He'd followed her everywhere—to her Bond Street modiste, to Jane's favorite Piccadilly bookshop, to the Covent Garden Theatre and Lady Wallingham's Park Lane parlor. None of those places were Robert's sort of entertainments. London itself could disappear into the Thames, for all it mattered to him. Yet, like a soldier performing his duty, he'd kept his vigil.

What if he really did want this marriage? What if he wanted *her*?

The mere thought filled her with heat. It flushed her skin, fired her belly, and quickened her breath. It incubated a seed of hope inside her heart, where she'd long ago ripped away every trace of that poisonous weed.

She mustn't let it prosper. She must remember what she knew—that he'd found her love pitiful. That he'd been hurt and broken because of her. That he'd demanded never to see her face again.

That he hadn't kissed her in weeks.

"... Matilda Bentley?"

Annabelle turned a questioning glance toward Jane.

Her sister arched a brow and cast a wry grin between her and Robert before repeating, "I asked why it seems ages since you've spoken to Matilda Bentley."

Rather than lie, Annabelle shrugged. "The Bentleys arrived late. I've not yet had the chance to speak with her." It was true, so far as it went. Mr. Bentley had entered Lady Darnham's drawing room an hour after the fete had begun. In contrast to his usual demeanor, he'd looked red and agitated. Mrs. Bentley and Matilda had been calmer, though stiff and unsmiling.

"So, it's nothing to do with her seeking Mr. Conrad's notice at every opportunity," Jane said.

Annabelle noted the willowy blonde stood a few feet away from him—much too close for her liking. "Perhaps she enjoys making a cake of herself. Who am I to stop her?"

Lady Darnham clicked her tongue. "Poor Mr. Bentley. I had no idea he'd suffered such losses. The family must be reeling."

It was another Edward Yarrow Aimes fiction, published only yesterday. The caricature had suggested Mr. Bentley was on the brink of bankruptcy, an outrageous falsehood. According to Annabelle's sources—Matilda among them—his finances were quite robust, despite losing a fair bit in the investment scheme that had ruined several prominent men the previous winter.

The man responsible, Zachariah Bickerstaff, had persuaded dozens of gentlemen to invest in a series of depleted coal mines on the promise of a "marvelous machine" capable of locating vast new veins where easier bounty had run dry. It had all been a lie, of course, sold by actors Bickerstaff had hired to portray seasoned colliers and a pair of "inventors." Suspicions had fallen on Bickerstaff after one of his actors was spotted on stage at the York Theatre Royal. Bickerstaff had fled to the Continent shortly thereafter, leaving his investors with emptier pockets and shares in a handful of worthless mines.

He'd also left them humiliated, a fact the person posing as Edward Yarrow Aimes seemed to relish. So far, nine of the talentless wretch's prints had been in some way related to the Bickerstaff swindle.

She wanted to know why. She wanted to give Mr. Green the scathing set-down he deserved. She wanted to demand he cease publishing a talentless wretch's work under *her* nom de plume.

But to do any of that, she must speak with the publisher in person. Thus, she needed to escape Robert Conrad's relentless surveillance.

Easier said than done.

She met his eyes again. Shivered at the intensity of his regard. And took a deep breath as she reviewed her plan for the evening.

Step one: distract.

Step two: plead a headache.

Step three: leave Robert Conrad behind and do what must be done.

"CAPTAIN STANDISH!" LIKE THE CAW OF A CROW, LADY Wallingham's voice echoed across the expanse of Lady Darnham's drawing room. "I scarcely recognized you without your uniform, young man!"

Robert winced and ground his teeth as Martin Standish—garbed in black rather than scarlet, for once—headed reluctantly in their direction.

"Explains why he appears so much smaller," the dowager muttered. "His shoulders aren't half the width of his epaulets."

The old woman had spent the past hour opining about the ubiquity of rosewood settees in Mayfair drawing rooms. "Perhaps if they bothered to glance at their ormolu clocks, they might notice when a fashion's time has passed," she'd groused before sipping her lemonade and complaining that Lady Darnham guarded the beverage's formulation "with the fervor of a nun guarding her virtue."

He hadn't bothered to reply, instead focusing on Annabelle. She was even lovelier than usual this evening, glowing and flushed in the candlelight, her rose silk gown clinging to her hips and bosom.

Despite his inattention, Lady Wallingham had nattered on, her trumpeting voice and superior manner wearing on his nerves until he'd contemplated tossing Annabelle over his good shoulder and abducting her to Nottinghamshire.

It was a sad state of affairs when not even Martin Standish could make a conversation more tedious.

Standish approached them with a cautious air. "Good evening, my lady." His narrow nose curled into a sneer as he eyed Robert. "Conrad."

The dowager offered minor pleasantries before launching into tart castigation. "If you are avoiding Miss Bentley because of those scurrilous rumors, Captain Standish, might I remind you your own father's reputation was similarly besmirched."

Standish wilted beneath the woman's sharp green gaze. His father, Sir Harold Standish, had, indeed, been publicly humiliated. Unlike Bentley, however, he hadn't the funds to sue Green for libel.

Green had made numerous errors over the past month. His first had been engaging Annabelle in a dangerous ruse. That alone had earned Robert's wrath. But before Robert had a chance to confront the man, the caricatures had changed in ways Robert noticed immediately. Green obviously had hired someone else to produce the sketches. Then, he'd begun publishing dubious accusations about powerful men. The new caricatures were largely rubbish, so the risk Green was running could only result in short-term gains before he was sued into oblivion. Annabelle was lucky to have been cut out of such an enterprise before it collapsed.

Robert knew she was distressed about Green's actions. He also knew that, if he relaxed his guard for even a moment, she would rush to confront the publisher, and damn the consequences. He could not allow that to happen.

He would have married her a month ago, would have absconded to Nottinghamshire or the nearest church or even to Gretna Green if he'd thought her father would consent. But Lord Berne adored his daughter, and she'd convinced him they must remain in London for the remainder of the season.

So, rather than fight both her and her family, he'd watched her and waited. The distance he'd kept between them had been agonizing but necessary.

He couldn't possibly touch her and not take her.

Gradually, his desire for her had grown from confusing longing into lustful madness. His dreams were nightly riptides of eroticism. He'd never do half the things his mind conjured. Not with his Bumblebee. She deserved better.

Yet, looking at her now, the chocolate swirls of her hair brushing lightly along her nape, the round swell of her hips begging for his hands to grip and squeeze, he was tempted to try everything. To push her the way she liked to push him.

Tearing his gaze from her, he drank his lemonade and gritted his teeth.

God, the hunger was killing him. The season could not end soon enough.

Lady Wallingham's plumes brushed his shoulder as she continued her set-down of Martin Standish. "Your father's baronetcy may grant you a title one day, Captain Standish, but if you wish to possess more than your uniform for clothing and more than gruel for sustenance, you will have to marry a well-dowered girl." She nodded toward Mr. Bentley, who bristled in a corner of the room, tossing back a swig of brandy. "Matilda Bentley is your best hope, and you have just given her father the cut direct. Perhaps you've misplaced your good sense along with your epaulets."

His cowardly gaze slid away. "I assure you, madam, I bear no ill feeling toward Mr. Bentley or his daughter." His shoulders twitched and his chin tilted to a pompous angle. "My uniform is being laundered."

"Hmmph." She arched white brows. "A uniform is not required for honorable conduct, young man."

Was it Robert's imagination, or had the other man's skin gone whiter? Perhaps it was the change of coat. Standish's cravat bobbed as he swallowed. He turned to address Robert. "How is your mount, Conrad?" A petty smile curled thin lips. "On his last legs, I trust. Like his master."

"On the contrary. The hunter I purchased from Tannenbrook proved well worth the price."

After a spark of surprise, Standish's sneer returned with a bitter twist. "Tannenbrook sold, did he? Well, I reckon he did me the favor. Only a man of your ... limitations would need a horse so slow one could mistake him for a trestle."

Robert resisted the urge to shut the other man's mouth with his fist. Standish was goading him, probably to distract Lady Wallingham from offering further critique.

The dragon was not so easily distracted. "Now that Mr. Conrad and Lady Annabelle Huxley are betrothed, I daresay the field is wide open for less impressive gentlemen to partake of the season's remainders." She blinked calmly at Standish. "A prime opportunity for one such as yourself, Captain."

Never one to fight when he could slither away instead, Standish took his leave, tight-lipped and stiff as he bowed to Lady Wallingham and ignored Robert.

"Why does he spew such venom toward you, dear boy?" she asked as Standish exited the drawing room. "Apart from venom being the natural weapon of snakes, I mean."

Robert shook his head. "It has been this way since Eton. Whatever I had, he wanted. Whatever he could not steal for himself, he sought to poison. He even attempted to turn John Huxley against me once." Robert gave her a small smile. "That went poorly for him." Huxley had pummeled Standish in front of forty other boys. Standish's aggressions had quieted afterward—until recently.

"Ah, yes. Sir Harold owns a hunting lodge near Rivermore Abbey, if I recall."

"I suppose."

"Two adjacent properties, one large and impressive while the other ... well, let us say the contrast is unflattering. Much like the two of you."

Robert frowned into Lady Wallingham's sharp, green gaze. "You think he is jealous of me." He tapped his cane against his right boot. "Of this."

"I think it is fortuitous you took my advice and secured Lady Annabelle's hand." She tapped his arm with her fan. "Wouldn't you agree?" Lady Wallingham enjoyed nothing better than being told she was right—repeatedly.

"Yes, my lady. Fortuitous."

The mention of Annabelle sent his gaze automatically searching for her again. It seemed he could not stop himself. But she wasn't where she'd been. Jane and Lady Darnham were there, sipping their lemonade and chatting. But no Annabelle.

"Ah, Meredith!" Lady Wallingham's fan tapped his arm again as Lady Berne and Lord Berne approached. "Mr. Conrad was just telling me how *beneficial* my advice has been."

Lady Berne grinned and rose up on her toes to kiss his cheek. "If your advice led him to join our family at long last, then I must agree."

"As must I," concurred Lord Berne, shaking his hand and patting his shoulder. "We've been trying to persuade Annabelle to marry you before we leave London, son. I'm afraid she insists the wedding be held at Rivermore Abbey."

"But that does not mean she cannot be persuaded," assured Lady Berne, her eyes twinkling. "If anyone can convince her, it is you."

Lord Berne invited him for dinner the following evening while Lady Berne went on and on about how thrilled John would be when he learned of the match. Meanwhile, Robert listened with half an ear while he searched the room for his intended bride.

She was nowhere to be found.

"... do hope John makes as auspicious a match as—"

He interrupted his future mother-in-law as his gut grew cold. "I beg your pardon, my lady—"

"Meredith," she corrected pertly. "Or, better yet, Mama. You have long been a son to me. It is past time you called me by my proper title."

His heart squeezed as he gazed into the merry eyes of the woman who had, indeed, lavished him with motherly kindness from the moment John had dragged him home for Christmas pudding. He smiled and bent to kiss her cheek, as she had earlier kissed his. "Mama."

Her eyes glossed with tears. "Oh, that sounds splendid, Robert."

"And I am Papa from now on, son," added Berne, clapping his shoulder.

Robert grinned and nodded to them both. "Mama and Papa." He met Berne's lively hazel gaze, his grin fading. "Now, I hope you'll forgive me, but where the devil is Annabelle?"

Lady Berne—or, rather, Mama—blinked and sniffed and glanced up at her husband. "Oh! Well, she said she had a headache." Together, Mama and Papa looked at him. "Poor dear. A footman summoned a hack to take her home. I am certain she'll feel better after a lie-down."

He was not. Darkness and urgency were a gathering storm inside him. Without another word, he stalked out of the drawing room, down the stairs, and outside to the center of the quiet Mayfair street as swiftly as his blasted leg would allow.

"Bloody hell, Annabelle," he growled through gritted teeth as he searched the dark, empty street. No hack. No Bumblebee.

But he knew where she was going—straight into trouble. Which meant he knew where he was going—to stop his future wife from risking her neck yet again.

Chapter Thirteen

"Daring is no great feat. Countless fools have dared and lost. The test is not whether you can plunge headlong into dark waters, but whether you have exhausted superior strategies before risking both your head and your dignity."

—THE DOWAGER MARCHIONESS OF WALLINGHAM in a letter to the Marquis of Mortlock reflecting upon the valorous legacy of said gentleman's bloodline.

Dearest Robert,
Do you remember the great thunderstorm that felled the ancient oak near the churchyard? That night, we were caught out after dark. I feared we might never find our way. Yet, you held my hand and made me believe you could see everything, do anything.

That is how this feels. Except that you are gone. And I am lost.

Ever yours,
Annabelle

—Letter to Robert Conrad dated July 30, 1813

RAIN BEGAN SOAKING UP WHATEVER MEAGER LIGHT COULD be had before Annabelle's hack left Mayfair. Now, as she stepped down onto the north side of the Strand, she felt the damp seeping into her skin.

"If you wait here until I return," she told the driver, nodding to the stretch of walk in front of D'Oyley's Warehouse, "I shall give you an extra shilling."

"Aye, miss." The driver fingered his dripping hat's brim in a salute she didn't entirely trust.

She tugged her woolen cloak's hood tighter around her ears and started toward the inky maw of Catherine Street. Occasional lamps lit the Strand, and a short distance away were several theatres filled with people—Drury Lane among them. But at this hour of the night, on a side street flanked by multi-storied buildings, she felt like she was entering catacombs.

Darkness thickened. Rain pattered onto cobbles. Shivers invaded until her belly went cold. *Only a little further,* she told herself. Green's offices were in a narrow brick building near the uppermost end of the street. *Where it is darkest, naturally.*

She gasped as her foot slid on something she would prefer not to identify. Blast. Her best pair of slippers would have to be burned. Perhaps she should have waited for daylight. Perhaps she should forgo confronting Green altogether. She paused. Glanced back toward the corner where she'd told the hack driver to wait. He was there, or at least the coach's backside was.

Sighing with relief, she fisted her skirts and resumed her foray into the catacombs of a dark London street. Good heavens, she could barely see a thing.

After a few minutes, her eyes adjusted well enough that she spotted Green's printing shop window. From inside, the faintest light glowed, though it was difficult to see through the glass panes, plastered as they were with prints of her work and that of the imposter. Reminded of her purpose, she stalked toward the door. First, she knocked. Green, who lived in apartments on the third floor, often worked late into the night, which was how she'd known he would be there. But surely the door would be locked.

No answer. She frowned, knocking again. A strange tickling sensation chilled her nape. She glanced nervously up and down Catherine Street, wondering if someone was lurking inside all that thick darkness—a pickpocket or footpad, perhaps. Once again, she adjusted her hood. Knocked again.

A faint scrape reached her ears. Queasiness struck. She spun around, placing her back against the door. Heart pounding, she scanned the street and shadows. God, she was going to be sick. What a foolish thing to have come here alone.

What else was I to do? she wondered. Bring Robert? He would pack me onto Dewdrop's back and haul me straight to Nottinghamshire before letting me near Mr. Green again. Still, she might have bribed Ned into accompanying her. But she hadn't had time. Robert tracked her every movement, and Lady Darnham's fete had offered the only opportunity she'd had in weeks to slip away unnoticed.

Swallowing away her rising fright, she peered into the dark. Was someone there? She did not know, but she thought she heard ... breathing. Without thinking, her hand found the doorknob. Twisted. The door swung inward, sending her reeling off-balance. Panic made her reactions jerky but quick. She stumbled inside, slamming the door against whatever—or whomever—waited out there in the dark. Then, she leaned against the wood for a moment to catch her breath.

The interior was a familiar warren of printer's paraphernalia. Immediately in front of her was a small counter where customers could purchase Edward Yarrow Aimes's prints or arrange a custom printing job. Behind the counter loomed two large, black-iron presses, multitudinous shelves, and several large, oak cabinets with tiny, labeled drawers and slots. During the day, this place would be hectic with typesetters and pressmen cranking page after page through Mr. Green's fancy, modern presses. Now, it was quiet and deeply shadowed, lit only by a lamp in one of the two rear offices.

Green's office. He must be here.

Casting off her earlier fright—really, she felt a bit silly about her reaction to a little darkness and rain—she lowered her hood and slowly made her way past the counter and between the presses.

"Mr. Green? It is Miss Aimes." The corner of her mouth curled up as her outrage resurged. "But, then, you know that isn't my real name, don't you?" She skirted around a large cabinet full of slim drawers. "Perhaps we should dispense with lies of all sorts. Though honesty may be asking too much from one such as yourself."

She expected him to come stalking out with his usual brisk energy. He did not.

"Mr. Green?" She frowned. "Are you here?"

Only silence answered. As she drew closer, she saw his arm splayed next to the lamp, white sleeve rolled up to his elbow. He must have fallen asleep at his desk. Or was feigning sleep to avoid her.

"Mr. Green," she called, raising her voice to be heard. "There is no use pretending. I have come all this way to speak with you about your disgraceful actions, and I shall not leave until ..."

Along with an oddly foul, metallic odor, several colors struck her senses all at once, halting her breath and heart and feet.

White—the white of his hair and his shirt and the paper near his left wrist.

Black—the black of the inkwell that had toppled onto its side, splashing the lamp's glass and soaking his stacked pages.

Red—the red of blood. From his head. In his hair, which was white. On his skin, which was gray. A drop had trickled into his eyebrow. Beneath that, his eye was open.

Not closed. Open.

Light dimmed. Wavered like water.

Her mouth moved, forming the letter M over and over. She couldn't breathe, yet breathed too fast. Couldn't gather enough air to scream, which was all she longed to do.

Mr. Green was dead. His head had been damaged. The black was not black. Not ink, but blood. Pooled and spattered. Too much to be anything natural.

Dear God. Light dimmed further. Sound whooshed. Her head swiveled back and forth. Slowly, as in a dream, she backed away from the white-haired man slumped across his desk.

Dead. Still. Gone.

If her heart had not been pounding so loudly, perhaps she would have heard the door behind her open. Perhaps she would have heard the staggered footfalls or sensed someone much bigger and stronger approaching.

As it was, the first scream from her throat came when she backed into a wall of muscle and wool, and a steel arm wrapped around her waist.

"Annabelle!" It was a growl, low and deep, beside her ear.

He smelled of rain and wind. He held her so tightly, she could scarcely move. Yet, she managed to whimper his name. "R-Robert?"

"What's happened, Bumblebee?"

That was all it took—that word. Everything it meant. The concern in his voice. She turned in his arms and buried her face in his shoulder.

And shook.

She didn't realize how hard she was trembling or how loudly she was gasping until he cupped her cheek and forced her gaze up to his. He looked ferocious, like a warrior preparing to battle an army. Yet, his touch was gentle. Swiping her cheek with his thumb, he brushed her lips and rested his forehead against hers.

"Tell me," he murmured. "Now."

"Dead," she rasped. "M-Mr. Green is ... dead." A sob took her by surprise. She seized her throat muscles around it and clutched Robert tighter. He was a rope between her and the abyss. "Oh, God. Someone killed him."

One moment, a warrior flash shone in his eyes, and the next, she found herself lifted. Pivoted. Carried several feet away and deposited with her back to a tall oak cabinet.

"Stay," he growled. "Do not move from this spot, Bumblebee. Do you hear me?"

She blinked several times. Her head was spinning. Fogging like a London street near dawn. But she nodded.

He was gone for what seemed a very long while, but it must have only been minutes. Every time she blinked, she saw red and white and black.

A warm, dry hand cupped her cheek. "I'm taking you home." He did not ask if she wished to be virtually carried. He simply tucked her against his side and lifted so that her slippers barely touched the floor. Then, moving much faster than a man with a cane should be able to move, he swept her out onto Catherine Street.

In the dark, she saw a lopsided blaze, heard Dewdrop's welcoming snuffle. Her throat tightened as tears burned. No. She mustn't let it out. If Robert could be calm after seeing a man who'd been murdered, she must be, too.

He set her on the ground, turning her and lifting her onto Dewdrop's back like a doll.

"Heavens, you are strong," she murmured without thinking. "Stronger than I remember."

Pausing for a long series of heartbeats, he rested his hand on her knee, held her tightly, and lowered his head. He wore no hat, as though he'd left Lady Darnham's too quickly to bother.

She reached out to run a hand through his hair. It was damp, already growing too long. Tenderly, she brushed her knuckles along his temple, traced his ear with a fingertip.

His nostrils flared and his grip tightened on her leg. Then, he raised his eyes to hers.

She couldn't see the blue, only a faint gleam of light from the Strand. But she felt something of his ferocity. It made him seem bigger. Dangerous.

Struggling to think clearly, she shook her head. "I—I asked the driver to wait—"

"The hack is gone." He slid his cane into the saddle's loop, gathered the reins, and used his left leg to mount behind her. Suddenly, she was surrounded by sixteen stone of furious male. He nudged Dewdrop forward.

She cleared her throat. "You're going the wrong way."

"No. I'm not."

He took a series of turns leading them deeper into darkness. She'd lost her sense of direction the moment he'd turned off Catherine Street into what looked like glorified alleyways. Dewdrop's gait was slow but remarkably smooth, rocking them as gently as a nurse rocked a babe. Shivering, she rested against Robert and closed her eyes. She felt a tug on the neck of her cape before her hood came up.

She'd forgotten it was raining.

Her hand searched for his. Found it flattened along her belly. Squeezed. "Robert," she whispered.

His jaw stroked her cheek like a cat marking its mate. "You've taken intolerable risks. This can never happen again, Bumblebee." His words were tender. His tone was not.

"I—I needed to speak with him—"

"Coming here alone at night was pure recklessness." His fury rumbled from his chest, vibrating through her back and cheek. "I was patient too long."

Only part of her chill was from the rain.

Once again, his jaw nuzzled her. And once again, his touch felt oddly possessive. "I shan't make that mistake twice."

She wondered why his statement sounded so much like a threat. Robert was rather bearish, growling and grousing and glowering a great deal. But he was a gentleman, honorable through and through. When she'd been small, he'd often treated her like fine china, careful not to squeeze her hand too hard or speak harshly and damage her feelings.

A shiver coiled up her spine. Had tonight's dreadful circumstances pushed him past his restraint? Had she provoked him one time too many?

"Robert?"

He did not answer, simply rubbed his jaw along her cheek and turned Dewdrop down a new street.

At this point, she was utterly lost. "Shouldn't we alert a watchman? Or a constable?"

"No."

"But, he ..." She swallowed against rising nausea. "He was murdered."

"And he will be found in the morning by his employees."

"Surely it would be better if—"

"It would be *better* for you not to be seen near the place where a man was murdered," he snapped. "It would be better if nobody associated your name with his. Or with Edward Yarrow Aimes."

Her head spun. "You think he was killed because of the caricatures?"

"I don't know."

In the distance, she glimpsed lamplight. Though the fine mist softened it into a hazy glow, she thought it might be Covent Garden. "But you suspect it is true," she whispered, her fingers sliding between his.

He was silent for a moment. "If it is, then Green would not be the killer's only target."

"All the more reason to alert some authority. Bow Street isn't far. Perhaps—"

"And how would you like to explain your discovery? You went to his offices late at night to confront him. Bow Street runners are far from daft, Annabelle."

"They will think I killed him, won't they?" she whispered.

"Yes. But their suspicions are not the greatest danger. If the real killer knows you were Edward Yarrow Aimes, he will come after you. Bad enough that you took a hack. The driver will need to be silenced."

"Robert," she said when she'd recovered from the shock of his implication. "You must never harm anyone in my name. Promise me."

"What the devil? I intend to pay him, not kill him."

Cold dread drained away, leaving her slumped against him in relief. "Thank heaven."

"Bloody hell, Annabelle."

"Well, what am I to think? I scarcely recognize you in this state."

"What state?"

"I don't know! Intimidating."

"This is who I am. You'd best accustom yourself to it."

"I'd rather not."

Silence settled behind her, thick with the very intimidation she'd referenced. He seemed immense to her. Stronger. Far too implacable. She preferred the old Robert, the one she could tease. The one who hesitated to bruise her feelings. The one whose reluctant smiles and rare laughter turned her heart inside out.

He guided Dewdrop along a series of darker, smaller streets, skirting the central square of Covent Garden. After an eternity, he spoke again, but not to comfort her. No, indeed, his words were a warning.

"Here is what will happen. I shall take you home, where you will lie to everyone about where you've been—your maid, your sisters, your mama and papa. In the morning, you will inform your parents we have decided to wed sooner than expected, and we must return to Nottinghamshire straight away." She began to protest, but his hand squeezed her belly. "They will understand, and Jane won't mind. You have one week, Annabelle. That is how long I require to ensure the danger to you is minimized." His jaw stroked her cheek again, and his hand slid lower. "We shall marry as soon we reach Rivermore." His lips caressed her ear, their tenderness at odds with the hardness of his words. "I've waited long enough, Annabelle. I will wait no longer."

Breathless and warm, she grasped his wrist and shook her head. "At least a fortnight remains before the season is—"

"Go on, then. Defy me." His fingertips curled into her lower belly, pressing and possessing. He sounded eager for her to push him. Eager to retaliate. "Discover how intimidating I truly am. I know how you love to test my limits."

"It's not that." She drew a shuddering breath. "After the damage Edward Yarrow Aimes caused, I've been trying to set things right. For Atherbourne and Victoria. For Blackmore. Lady Wallingham is helping them. So is my family. I must stay in town longer. It is only right."

"No." A dry chuckle. "As usual, you wish to have everything your way. But that is not how this will go." His hand had stopped its southward explorations, but his fingers continued to press and stroke in the most stunningly pleasurable way.

"You are behaving like a tyrant." Her accusation might have carried greater heft if it had not been followed by a tiny, helpless moan.

His teeth nibbled her earlobe, sending further waves of heat ricocheting between his mouth and her breasts and down to where his hand claimed its territorial dominance.

"Now you have it, Bumblebee," he murmured. "Now you understand."

Chapter Fourteen

*"I've little liking for publishers who print slanderous gossip.
The enjoyment of slander is ruined when its purveyor has no
standard of accuracy."*

—THE DOWAGER MARCHIONESS OF WALLINGHAM in a letter to the
Marquis of Mortlock regarding the appropriate use and distribution
of gossip.

Dearest Robert,
I have it. My name shall be Edward Yarrow Aimes.

It is perfect, don't you agree?

Ever yours,
Annabelle

—Letter to Robert Conrad dated September 4, 1813

DAYS LATER, ROBERT LEFT WHITE'S THINKING THIS WAS HOW it must feel to lose a war. He'd battled with everything he had, and ... nothing. A broad shadow merged with his as he waited for his horse.

"Conrad. You seem a mite perturbed," observed Tannenbrook. "Do you hate the clubs as much as I?"

Robert shook his head before shaking the earl's hand. As usual, Tannenbrook's expression revealed very little. "I have a ... mission to complete." He gritted his teeth and looked for the boy who was supposed to fetch Dewdrop a quarter-hour ago. "There have been obstacles."

"Obstacles, aye. I've some experience with those. Deuced inconvenient."

Robert shot him a frown. "You've no idea what I'm talking about."

Tannenbrook clapped his shoulder. "No, indeed. I've been accused of making poor conversation. I'm attempting to commiserate."

"Accused by whom?"

"Lady Wallingham."

Robert grunted.

So did Tannenbrook. It appeared they were in agreement about Lady Wallingham in general.

He glanced up at the giant. Tannenbrook was a good man, solid and reliable. He had a sound mind inside that enormous skull, had even helped Robert with valuable advice on improving an estate with limited resources. Perhaps he could offer a suggestion. "Tannenbrook."

"Aye?"

"Suppose you wished to discover a killer."

Green eyes went from idly squinting at the street to widening upon Robert. "A murdering sort?"

Robert nodded, thinking through what he knew, wondering how much to say without revealing anything that might implicate Annabelle—or himself. "Suppose this was vital, a matter of life and death."

"Where murdering sorts are involved, death tends to follow."

"The man he killed was despised by many people. Yet I've eliminated all the most likely attackers." He shook his head again, marveling at the sheer number of dead ends.

In the five days since Green's murder, Robert had scoured the man's past with methodical determination. First, he'd questioned Green's employees. Then, he'd tracked down his business partners—strictly financial shareholders quite pleased with their profits. Finally, he'd discovered Green's ongoing patronage of a Covent Garden lightskirt. She'd been most informative, particularly after he'd paid her twice her usual fee to tell him what she knew.

Orphaned at fourteen, Horace Green had worked first for a Manchester cotton mill then for a series of printers. He'd come to London seeking his fortune after a long stint writing for a radical newspaper that went out of business.

Three years ago, *Green's Daily Informer* had started as little more than listings for auctions and theatre productions and advertisements for household servants. Within a year, Green had hired two writers to pen salacious reports about the comings and goings of the city's aristocrats. Both writers turned out to be women. Both had written under assumed names—male names.

The following year, Edward Yarrow Aimes's first caricature had sold fifty copies in one week. Not even the newspaper itself sold at such a pace, let alone so profitably. Green could charge two shillings each for hand-colored prints, one shilling for the uncolored version. Within weeks, he'd pressed Annabelle to produce more frequently. Then, he'd used her sketches to sell his rubbish newspapers.

And he'd paid her five percent. Five. Measly. Percent.

Robert had been furious when she'd told him. In fact, the more he'd learned about Horace Green the more he'd struggled against deepening hatred. Green had deliberately targeted women—some talented, some less so—and paid them virtually nothing for their labor. They'd agreed, of course, keeping his secrets and rarely complaining, all for the promise of seeing their work published.

"So, you've taken it upon yourself to find this man's killer," Tannenbrook said now. "Why not let the constables handle it?"

"It is personal to me. It must be done right."

"You've a fondness for the victim?"

"God, no. The opposite."

Tannenbrook rubbed his jaw. "Have you considered hirin' a Bow Street man? Might offer some expertise you lack."

"I'd prefer Bow Street wasn't involved."

"Right." He shot Robert an assessing glance.

"So far, I've employed methods that served me well when investigating thefts and the like at Rivermore Abbey."

"Sensible."

Robert nodded. "I've queried everyone who knew the victim personally. In my experience, the culprit is most often one with ready access. Somebody close."

"Aye. When a theft occurs, I've found that to be true. But killin' takes a particular set of circumstances. A grudge. Something to be gained. Was the victim wealthy?"

"Not enough to warrant murder. And for those with a

financial interest, keeping him alive far better served their purposes."

"Could it have been a woman? Jealous wife or lover?"

Robert shook his head. "No wife. His lover was a lightskirt only too eager to tell me everything she knew." He gripped his cane and decided sharing more detail was worth the risk. Tannenbrook could be trusted. "But this man was widely hated by some powerful men. One of them is a duke."

Green eyes sharpened. "Blackmore?"

Alarm ran up Robert's spine. "How did you—"

"A guess. Aren't many dukes more powerful. Or any, truth be known. He employs a Bow Street man, name of Drayton, for sundry tasks. I shouldn't pursue that line of inquiry if you wish to keep things discreet. Blackmore's not to be trifled with." Tannenbrook rolled enormous shoulders and rubbed his jaw again. "Last man he killed was a friend of mine. I've every reason to want Blackmore hanged for murder. But the only way he'd kill anyone is in a duel. Fancies himself too honorable to do otherwise."

"Could he have hired it done? The Bow Street man, perhaps."

"Doubtful." Tannenbrook squinted at him. "This victim. It's that publisher, isn't it?"

"Bloody hell." Perhaps he should have kept the details vaguer.

"Be easy." A giant hand clapped his shoulder again. "I'll hardly be flappin' my jaws about it. Besides, the blackguard deserved what he got. Atherbourne's wife is gentle as a lamb. What Green did to her was detestable."

Robert frowned. "Is it possible—"

"No. If Atherbourne were going to kill anybody, it would be Blackmore. He hasn't. That's a measure of his reluctance to see death again."

Indeed, that had been Robert's thought. Most men who'd

seen war had enough of killing before they ever left the battlefield. Atherbourne had struck him as that kind of man—damaged, darkened, but fighting to surface, not return to the blackest depths.

He sighed and murmured, "If not Blackmore or Atherbourne, then who?"

"You were right to say Green had enemies." Tannenbrook gestured toward the gentlemen's club behind them. "It's all they've talked about for days. Worse gossips than the old women who run the haberdashery in my village. Bluidy gaggle of hens, they are."

Every now and then, an oddly Scottish inflection entered Tannenbrook's speech, usually when he was disgusted or vexed. Robert had his suspicions about the giant's origins, but he respected him too much to bring it up. Apart from which, he didn't fancy receiving a set-down in the form of a boulder-sized fist.

"If you're bent on finding his killer yourself," Tannenbrook continued. "Which I cannot recommend, mind. But if you are, I'd start by making a list—all the men who wanted him dead, less the ones who were known to be elsewhere when the murder happened."

Robert nodded, though frustration plagued him. "Already done. Even with Atherbourne and Blackmore eliminated, there are simply too many."

"Have a time limit, do you?"

"An urgent one. I leave for Nottinghamshire in two days."

Tannenbrook grunted. "Aye. That's a steep one."

"Steep. *This* is your sage advice?"

Crossing massive arms across a massive chest, Tannenbrook glowered down at him. "No. My advice is to leave it be. Man got what he deserved."

Robert couldn't argue with that, yet neither could he abandon his hunt. The killer might, even now, have Annabelle's name. He might come after her. Hurt her. The very thought made his skin burn with urgency.

"It's clear you intend to keep on as you were before, whatever my advice may be. Bluidy granite is more pliable." The giant's square jaw hardened as his eyes narrowed. "This is about a woman."

He slanted a glance at the giant. "That's a leap."

"Not much of one. If a man isn't watchful, he'll find himself tangled up in a woman's skirts so fast, there'll be no time to question how he arrived at such a pass. Before long, he's doin' mad things for daft reasons. Or daft things for lustful reasons." He held up a hand. "Not to worry. I'll say nothing. Merely wish you good hunting." A brief smile quirked the man's lips. "And good luck."

Behind them, a group of gentlemen exited White's. They were followed by Lord Atherbourne, who came to greet Robert and Tannenbrook. The black-haired viscount looked well, his color strong, his dark eyes glittering with good humor. Evidently, marriage agreed with him.

"Gentlemen. My, you do make quite a pair. Matching frowns the new fashion, are they?"

Tannenbrook grunted.

Robert was about to reply when a loud laugh nearby caught his attention. The group of five gentlemen stood several yards away. The laugher was Thomas Bentley. Beside him stood Martin Standish.

Atherbourne followed his gaze. "Ah, I see Standish has abandoned his penchant for outlandish misrepresentation."

Robert slanted him a questioning glance.

"The coat," Atherbourne clarified. "He's no longer wearing it."

Indeed, Standish was once again without his scarlet uniform. Robert wondered if someone had shamed him into dispensing with it. "Did you know him? During the war, I mean."

Atherbourne paused, his eyes flashing with something other than good humor. "We were in different regiments. But I knew of him. Many of us did."

Robert frowned his confusion. "I was given to understand he did not serve with distinction."

Chuckling darkly, Atherbourne replied, "Hardly. Unless it is a distinction to be caught hiding in a cottage while better men are dying in battle."

"He always was a coward," Robert muttered.

"Worse than a coward," Atherbourne corrected.

That brought Robert's head around. "Worse?"

The viscount's expression was a mix of contempt, disgust, and anger. "It was all rumor. Nothing confirmed. Are you certain you wish to know?"

Robert turned fully to face the man, meeting his hard gaze directly. "I must know. That scapegrace had eyes for the woman I ..." He bit down on the rest of it, avoiding Tannenbrook's knowing gaze before demanding, "Tell me."

A sardonic brow lifted. "Very well. Never say I didn't warn you."

HOURS LATER, AFTER THE FLUSTERED GROOM DELIVERED Robert's horse with profuse apologies for Dewdrop's "uncanny slow pace," and after Robert had digested Atherbourne's revelations about Martin Standish's black soul, he was still no closer to finding Green's killer.

He sat down on the wooden chair in the small bedchamber of his rented house. Then, he set about the task of forcing his bad leg into a boot. His old boots had been softer, easier on his stiff muscles. Likewise, his old coats had some give to them, allowing for the flexing of his bad shoulder when the damp weather caused it to ache.

But Annabelle liked his new boots with their gleaming polish. She liked his new coats, her voice taking on a husky tone whenever she described how well they complimented his shoulders.

His shoulders fascinated her, for some reason. She called them "ridiculous" but then sighed the prettiest sigh.

God, he wanted to see her again. He'd kept his distance for the past few days, determined to discover the killer's identity and remove every possible threat to the woman he ... well, his wife.

Or, rather, future wife.

Blast. Tannenbrook was right. His head was a muddle.

He did not even know who Green had hired to imitate Annabelle's work. He'd wager it was a woman, but details were difficult to gather. He'd visited Catherine Street after leaving White's, hoping to speak with some of the printer's employees. The place had been empty, locked tight. He'd spotted a hound-faced man in a greatcoat scribbling in a notebook while questioning one of the prostitutes who plied her wares nearby.

Hovering as close as he dared, Robert had pretended to peruse linens and lace in the windows of D'Oyley's Warehouse while he'd listened to their conversation. The hound-faced man had told the prostitute his name—Drayton. Hadn't Tannenbrook said Blackmore employed a runner named Drayton? If Bow Street had taken an interest, any direct inquiries Robert made likely would turn suspicions upon him.

Which was why he was now dressing in new boots and a new coat, preparing to ride from Knightsbridge to Mayfair. A short while later, he stood in front of a grand house on Park Lane, trying to decide if desperation always led to insanity or if it was only his lot.

"Mr. Conrad. Good evening, sir. Is her ladyship expecting you?"

He handed the starchy butler his hat and entered the house with the distinct feeling he should be somewhere else.

Anywhere else.

"No," he answered. "Is she at home?"

"Robert Conrad! It is about time you came to your senses, young man." Lady Wallingham's trumpeting voice echoed into the entrance hall from the staircase. "I expected you days ago." She was gowned in violet velvet and a silver silk turban with lavender plumes. As usual, her chin tilted to a haughty angle. "Perhaps I overestimated your intelligence."

"I need—"

"My help. Yes, yes." She waved her hand dismissively. "Come, let us have tea while you explain why you are not yet testing the structural integrity of Rivermore's beds with your new bride." She sniffed and looked him up and down. "One hopes it is a temporary affliction."

He sighed and followed her up the stairs and into her yellow parlor. Like a monarch in her throne room, she seated herself on a rose velvet chair and waved him toward a striped settee. Dutifully, he sat, though he wished with every bone and fiber there was another way.

He'd racked his brain. There wasn't.

"I must ask a favor, my lady."

"Then ask it. And do stop frowning, boy. Reminds me of your grandfather. At your age, he'd already fathered a son. You cannot afford to frighten the girl away before you've managed to yoke her with your ring."

"Lady Annabelle is the reason I'm here. Her safety is at risk."

A white brow arched. "I am confident you can control your baser impulses, Mr. Conrad. If all else fails, picture Sir Barnabus Malby. Such a vision will cool the most extreme ardor."

Damn, she was blunt. "The risk is not from me," he clarified. Well, not entirely. Before she could make their conversation more uncomfortable, he explained about Green's death, about his hunt for the killer, and about the need to winnow down his list of suspects.

"That vile publisher deserved to die," she said. "Surely you have better uses for your time. Weddings. Beddings. Begettings. Why not leave solving murder to the feckless constables and magistrates?"

"Because they are feckless."

"Precisely. As I said, the man deserved to die."

He gritted his teeth. "Nevertheless, I must identify his attacker."

She sniffed. "If this is about Annabelle and her little sketches, I doubt you have cause to worry. It is unlikely anyone else suspects her connection to Aimes."

Freezing into focus, he stared at the old woman he had obviously underestimated. "You know?"

"Of course I know," she snapped. "Meredith Huxley is my dearest friend. I take a keen interest in her children, and they have benefitted *greatly* from my influence. Did you think I would miss something so crucial as one of them masquerading as a man to publish her amusing scribbles?"

It took him some time to regain the ability to speak. "You knew. And yet, you did nothing to stop her."

Emerald eyes sparked and narrowed. "What do you suppose *you* are doing here?"

He frowned his confusion.

"I advised you to make yourself into a shield. And so you have." At his continued silence, she elaborated, "A lady who remains sheltered inside the bounds of convention has little need for one, wouldn't you say? No, when a notion takes her, Annabelle has all the circumspection of a hare flushed by hounds. She requires strong hands. Yours were being wasted on counting livestock. Besides, your grandfather and I agree you need a wife, dear boy. *Desperately.* I can put it no more plainly than that."

Suspicions and recollections swam inside his mind, coalescing around every interaction he'd had with this formidable, manipulative woman.

His grandfather had coerced him into an aristocratic wife hunt using his failing health as extortion. Lady Wallingham had volunteered to be Robert's guide, insisting that he attend Lady Gattingford's ball. Then, time after time, she'd neatly positioned him to conclude what she and his grandfather had predetermined—that he must marry Annabelle.

Good God. Everything had been about maneuvering him into the role of protective husband. His grandfather's demand. Lady Wallingham's instructions regarding the season. Even the world's slowest barouche ride. Now everything that hadn't made sense suddenly did.

A footman entered the parlor to deliver a tea tray. Lady Wallingham calmly poured herself a cup then set about sipping as though nothing were amiss.

"Tea?" she inquired.

"You might have bloody well asked me," he gritted.

"I believe I just did."

"Not about the tea. About Annabelle."

She placed her cup on the table beside her chair and rested her hands on the arms of her chair in a queenly pose. "The last time she put herself in jeopardy, what was your response?"

"That was ... different."

"You cut her off. Abandoned her." Glittering emerald went cold. "I shan't tolerate a similar outcome in this instance. Or ever again, Mr. Conrad. I trust I am clear."

"I did not *abandon* her, for God's sake. Bloody hell! I was keeping her *safe!*" He didn't realize he'd been shouting—indeed, roaring—until he heard his words echo off yellow walls. Shoving off the settee, he grasped his cane and made for the door. "Coming here was a mistake."

"Is Thomas Bentley on your list, by chance?"

The question stopped him a yard from the door. "Yes."

She raised a brow and resumed sipping. "His is the one name I would *not* eliminate too hastily, were I you."

Despite his fury, despite everything she'd done, he nodded his thanks before leaving the dragon to her tea.

"THIS SEEMS AN EXTRAORDINARILY BAD IDEA," JANE HISSED IN Annabelle's ear. "The worst. And I was there when Genie made that atrocious reticule with the tassels and—"

"Shh." Annabelle stood on her toes and craned her neck to view the woman selling flowers at one end of Covent Garden's crowded piazza. "I only want to speak with her."

The woman wore a mushroom-colored gown that had once been white. Tied over her shoulders was an equally dingy shawl. Her hair was light beneath her cap, her features more interesting than pretty. Annabelle thought it must be her dark brows and crooked nose—they reminded her of Dewdrop.

Still, the woman who had stolen and soiled the name of Edward Yarrow Aimes was attractive, in her way. Trim figure. Well-shaped hands.

"Let's go home, Annabelle." Jane fidgeted with her brown pelisse and glanced up at weighty clouds. "Before it begins pouring again."

"I only need a moment," she murmured, gathering her skirts a bit higher as she sidestepped a pile of donkey leavings. Passing shed-roofed stalls filled with dispirited asparagus, dulled radishes, and diminutive cabbages, Annabelle turned her shoulders sideways to avoid jostling a maid carrying a basket of cauliflower on her hip. "You may return to the coach if it distresses you so much."

Behind her, Jane snorted but stayed on her heels.

The flower seller counted coins a gentleman had given her for a bundle of blue flowers. She glowered and said something he didn't like. He dug out another coin and took the bouquet. She gave a deep, mocking curtsy as though on stage.

As Annabelle drew closer, she heard the woman's voice—scratchy and hoarse—calling out to passersby, "Sweet hyacinths, penny a bunch!"

"I shall take two," Annabelle said.

The woman looked her over before bending to retrieve the flowers from the large basket at her feet. "Fine bit o' springtime, they are, miss. And much needed after the soggy one we've had."

Making a show of digging in her reticule, Annabelle inched closer and murmured softly, "Now, I might be convinced to purchase the whole lot, if you were amenable to a short conversation."

The woman's brows flew up then crashed down just as swiftly. "I ain't a doxy. All I sell is flowers."

Jane, who had taken the bouquets from the woman's hand, turned to Annabelle and blinked. "I don't understand."

Annabelle, too, felt bewildered. Did "conversation" mean something different in Covent Garden? Apparently so. She cleared her throat and clarified, "I only wish to engage in intercourse with you. Briefly."

As though she'd made a lewd proposition, the woman's dubious expression deepened.

Annabelle tried again. "I wish to speak with you. Ask some questions. Nothing vulgar, I assure you."

"You ain't a bawd?"

She'd heard the word rarely, but she thought it meant procuress.

Jane choked. Evidently, her sister understood the meaning, too. Good heavens, their vocabulary was taking on new dimensions today.

"No," Annabelle replied. She gathered coins in her palm and let them clink together. "A few minutes. That's all I ask."

The woman chewed her lip, eyed Annabelle from bonnet to boots before casting Jane a dismissive glance. Then she shrugged and held out her cupped hand.

Annabelle gave her half the amount. "The rest comes after we've concluded our conver—our talk."

Nodding, the woman gestured toward a table and chairs a few feet away. The leavings of someone's meal—bread and fried eel—had not yet been cleared away. Once the three of them were seated, Annabelle wasted no time.

"I know who you are," she stated calmly.

"Do ye, now?" One dark brow arched above cynical eyes. "Seen me onstage, I reckon. Some said my Cordelia made them weep. Been years since I trod the boards, though. What ye wish to know?"

Annabelle blinked as though surprised. "Oh, but you've taken on a role more recently, have you not? A certain caricaturist, if I am not mistaken."

The woman's eyes shifted to Jane and back to Annabelle. She swallowed and looked around the teeming piazza. Then, she plunked the coins Annabelle had given her onto the table beside half-eaten fried eel. "Ye can have 'em back. We're done," she said coldly, moving to shove out of her chair.

Annabelle grasped her wrist, tightening her grip when the woman tried to yank free. "We are not nearly done." Her voice was low with fury. Though she'd dreaded coming here, dreaded this confrontation, righteousness put steel in her veins. "I said I know who you are, not merely who you pretend to be." She pulled the woman close. "Mrs. Bickerstaff."

The woman's backside hit the chair with a thud. Shrewd eyes rounded. A grimy hand came up to swipe a suddenly pale forehead. "Who—who're ye talkin' about? I've no acquaintance with—"

"Come now, Mrs. Bickerstaff. Let's not pretend."

The woman's expression hardened. "Stop callin' me that."

"Shall I call you Edward Yarrow Aimes, then?"

"Bugger all. Keep your voice down." Her eyes darted to the nearest stalls with porters and barrow boys coming and going. "What do ye want?"

"I want to know how you came to work for Mr. Green. I want to know if you killed him."

"Killed him?" She huffed in disbelief. "Man was payin' me two percent for the etchings. Think I'd rather be here sellin' flowers for a penny a bunch instead?" She shoved the plate of eel away with a disgusted swipe. "Bloody nobs. You haven't a clue what it means to be desperate. To fight the hunger in your belly and know you'll lose in the end."

Her patience wearing thin, Annabelle drummed her fingertips on the table and snapped, "How did you meet Green? Did he approach you?"

The woman crossed her arms and sank back into an insolent pose. "Why should I tell you?"

Jane chose that moment to intervene. "Because if you do not," she said quietly, "one of the greatest gossips in London will tell everyone your secret. Everyone you've maligned. Everyone your husband swindled. They will all learn precisely who you are."

Annabelle looked at her sister—her plain, beautiful, shy sister—and felt pride swell until she might as well be glimmering with stardust. Jane was brave and loyal. She was bold when it mattered most. And she was the reason Annabelle was here today, confronting the thief who'd stolen Edward Yarrow Aimes from his rightful owner.

Two days ago, they'd been playing charades in the parlor with the rest of their sisters. While Maureen tried to coax Genie and Kate into guessing General Cornwallis rather than Cornwall, Annabelle had stewed over Robert's absence.

"He's visited once," she'd whispered to Jane. "After everything that's happened. Once. Lady Wallingham's turbans are more attentive."

"Mmm. Those plumes do have that air about them, always bobbing about as if to say, 'I do concur, my lady.'" Jane chuckled then cast her a glance. "Didn't you say he is worried you might be at risk? Perhaps he is occupied with finding the attacker. Your safety does seem Robert's most ardent concern."

She waved away Jane's assumption. "Nonsense. If Green's killer intended me harm, I should think the deed would have been done by now. No, the matter that requires investigation is finding whoever has been perpetuating lies and slander in my name."

"Your fake name."

"I need to know, Jane."

Resettling her spectacles, Jane sighed before giving Annabelle's arm a soothing pat. "I know."

"I put everything I had into those caricatures. Do you realize how many nights I went without sleep?"

"Yes."

"Countless, that's how many. So much thinking and planning—the selection of each creature to properly represent my characters took me days. Days! Not to mention all the new sources I had to cultivate. Good heavens, I danced with Sir Barnabus Malby. Thrice!"

Jane wrinkled her nose. "His mother?"

"She gushes information when sotted. A gigantic, fizzy bottle of secrets, uncorked and unfiltered."

Turning thoughtful, Jane's brow furrowed. "Perhaps we've looked at this the wrong way round."

"How so?"

"I've read a great many novels."

"I hadn't noticed."

"There is always something of the storyteller in the story.

You said you put everything you had into your work. But I would phrase it differently—you put everything you *are* into those drawings, Annabelle. Your funny way of seeing the world. Your insight into the character of people around you. Even your delight in their foibles."

"People amuse me. We are all so ... full of little quirks."

"If you were not the original Edward Yarrow Aimes, what might you surmise about him? Think only of his work."

Annabelle mulled the question while watching Genie attempt to roll on the floor without mussing her gown. Maureen struggled to interpret her wild gesticulations as having gathered no moss.

"Assuming his veracity, I would have guessed he had access to those he lampooned," Annabelle murmured. "But not just access. Servants have that. He *sees* them. Understands their positions and their troubles and their ... their lives, I suppose. Therefore, he must be among their ranks. Gentry at the very least."

"Now, what would you conclude about the imposter?"

"A talentless wretch."

"Annabelle."

She watched Kate bow deeply before an invisible audience then stroke her chin as though she had a beard. Kate chose the same subject every time they played charades. Genie liked to torment her by pretending she'd never heard of William Shakespeare, but Maureen always stepped in to put everyone out of their misery. The routine had become as predictable as a quadrille's forms.

"Repetition," Annabelle whispered. "The imposter returns over and over to the same subject—Bickerstaff."

"Bicker who?"

"The swindler who fled to the Continent. It happened last year, remember? And yet the talentless wretch keeps circling old ground. Circling and circling."

Her suspicions had begun in that moment. And once she'd had a starting point, she'd discovered the rest by using tactics a grand deliverer of gossip mastered over the course of time.

Paying Mr. Green's most resentful employees for information had led her to conclude the imposter must be a woman—the publisher had preferred those he exploited to be female, as they were less likely to create a fuss.

Next, she'd raised the subject of Bickerstaff's swindle ever-so-casually within earshot of Mr. Bentley, being sure to include erroneous details. Mr. Bentley had interrupted to issue corrections, which had led her to identify Bickerstaff's swindling partners.

Of course, upon confronting them, she'd pretended to know more than she did, so they would tell her more than they should. The actors had been very helpful, indeed. Mrs. Bickerstaff, a former actress, had brought them all into the scheme.

Bitter people made excellent sources.

Their divulgences had led her here, to Covent Garden, where Bickerstaff's wife had been reduced to selling hyacinths by the bunch.

"You've been hiding a long time, Mrs. Bickerstaff," Annabelle said now. "One wonders why you did not simply flee with your husband."

The woman glared her resentment. "He took all the blunt we had. Fled London while I slept." Her mouth curled contemptuously. "Left me with nothin'. Couldn't return to the stage. Everybody there hated me. Those who'd purchased shares—"

"You mean those you swindled," Jane interjected.

"Aye, well. They were after me, too. Thought I'd know where Zachariah went with their money. I don't."

"How did you come to work for Green?" Annabelle asked.

"I wanted those who were after me to be fearful for a change. I'd seen Green's paper about. Went to his office to suggest he write about the men who'd lost fortunes in the mining venture."

"And on that basis, he offered to hire you?"

"Nah. I kept after him. Offered details, suggested ways to make the story more interesting, like a good play. I used to sketch scenes from the plays I was in. You know, the stage, where all the actors would stand. I sketched a few scenes for Green to show him how entertaining it could be. Couple months ago, he bit. Said I could tell any story I wanted, so long as I took over sketchin' the prints he'd been selling."

"What did he tell you about the original artist?" Annabelle asked carefully.

The woman snorted. "Closemouthed about it. I gathered he'd been the one to do the drawin' before me. He wrote the captions, you know. Said my writing was muck but my drawin' was passable. That was the word he used. 'Passable.'" She shrugged. "No matter. He paid me for doin' what I would have done for nothin'."

Annabelle looked at Jane. Her sister's eyes shone with sympathy. Annabelle's outrage, her loathing of the imposter, had carried her this far. But hearing that Green had taken advantage of a desperate woman—albeit a swindling one—to reduce the portion he had to pay "Edward Yarrow Aimes" from five to two percent made all the steel inside her soften. She sighed and examined Mrs. Bickerstaff's worn, stained shawl and grimy, well-shaped hands.

Then, she took five pounds' worth of coins out of her reticule and placed them beside the others on the table. "Do you know who killed Mr. Green?" she asked.

The woman looked at the money, glanced around nervously, then shook her head. "Would that I did. I've a fear Mr. Green might've given him my name before he died."

Annabelle's eyes met those of the imposter and saw her own fear there. It was disorienting to feel empathy for such a creature. But she did. "Leave London," she told her, nodding to the coins. "It is all I can give you—all I *will* give you. It won't be enough to take you to the Continent. But it should be enough for a mail coach. Start over somewhere else. Somewhere ... far."

Mrs. Bickerstaff blinked several times before a bewildered frown creased her brow. "Who in blazes are you?"

Annabelle pushed back her chair and stood. Jane followed suit, crowding closer and linking their arms.

"It doesn't matter who I am," Annabelle replied. "Only that I know who you are. And while I abhor the things you've done, I've no wish to see you end as Mr. Green did."

The woman stood and gathered her coins. Then, as they started away from her, she called them back. "Don't forget your flowers, miss."

Annabelle turned.

Mrs. Bickerstaff held out two bouquets, one for each of them. With a flourish, she placed them in their hands then bowed her head and offered the elegant curtsy of a dancer. "A fair bit o' springtime brings ease to the darkest days."

Chapter Fifteen

"If Annabelle Huxley is a bee, then Matilda Bentley is a moth.
Some creatures seek out ever more abundant gardens, create
intricate homes in geometric order, build cooperative societies,
and make life sweeter for their presence. Others perish because
they repeatedly knock into the lantern."

—THE DOWAGER MARCHIONESS OF WALLINGHAM in a letter to the
Marquis of Mortlock on the benefits of cleverness in a potential wife.

Dearest Robert,
In this sketch, I have given you a new shield. A knight might use a
cane in place of a sword, but he would have to be quite skilled, I think.
Something tells me you are just such an exception.

Ever yours,
Annabelle

—Letter to Robert Conrad dated January 28, 1814

CLEARLY, THOMAS BENTLEY HAD THE WRONG IDEA ABOUT Robert's visit. The whiskered man had mentioned his Northfield connection several times, once while complimenting Mortlock Manor and twice more while touting Matilda's "excellent teeth." All this before Robert had managed to remove his hat.

Robert accepted the chair and declined the brandy Bentley offered. "Mr. Bentley, I—"

"She requires a jot of patience now and then, I grant." Bentley released a jocular laugh and sank into the opposite seat. The ornate rosewood chair creaked in protest. "But name me a female who doesn't, eh, Conrad?"

"I've a few questions for you, sir."

"Of course, of course." Bentley drained his glass of brandy. "First things first. Is it true Rivermore Abbey has produced thrice the profit since you took over its management?"

Robert frowned at the abrupt change of topic. "No."

The eager glint in Bentley's eye dimmed as he glanced at Robert's bad leg. "Ah. I was misinformed, then."

Why it mattered, Robert didn't know. "Rivermore is much more profitable than that."

Bentley's eyes bulged. "More?" Once again, he glanced at Robert's leg.

"Much more. Now, I do beg your pardon, sir, but I must—"

"Well, this is splendid."

"—speak to you about—"

"Her dowry is generous, mind. I'm no miser, and she is my only daughter."

Robert paused. A mistake, as it turned out.

"Nevertheless, she'll need reminding of budgetary matters from time to time. Favors amethysts, you know. Gold and amethysts." Bentley chuckled fondly. "Daresay she takes after her mother in that regard." He shifted his bulk, and the chair groaned. "I'll tell you a secret. Every other month or so, I select one piece from her current collection and simply have it wrapped up like new. She's never the wiser, and it keeps matters well in hand. You'll find these sorts of stratagems useful, Conrad. You're a skilled manager, so I've confidence in your capabilities. More than thrice?" He shook his head. "Damn me, I should have you working for my company."

"Mr. Bentley, I really must—"

"What would you say to an apprenticeship, my boy? Chances are excellent you'll inherit one day. My son hasn't the head for anything more complex than bowling."

Robert sighed. "I am already betrothed, sir."

"What's that you say?"

"I am not here about your daughter. Lady Annabelle Huxley and I intend to marry. Quite soon, actually."

Bentley squinted at him. "Are you certain? Forgive me, Conrad, but Matilda reported Lady Annabelle has been filling her ears with rather unfavorable depictions of your character. Last I heard, she implied you suffer a digestive complaint which sends you to the privy at all hours of the night."

Bloody hell. This explained at least half of his bizarre exchanges with Matilda Bentley over the past month. "Nevertheless, we are to wed shortly. The reason for my visit is—"

"Damn me, what a disappointment, Conrad. Now I'm forced to reconsider that arrogant milksop, Standish."

"Standish?" Robert stiffened, his stomach going cold. "You

shouldn't, sir."

"He's shown interest, and she tolerates his company. He'll inherit a baronetcy—"

"He does not treat women well."

Bentley's chin went up. Shrewd eyes assessed Robert. "How do you know this?"

The things Atherbourne had told him burned his throat. Accusing a man—even Standish—of such depravity without proof would garner only charges of slander. Still, he could not in good conscience let Bentley consider matching Matilda with a villain. "If you regard me as a gentleman of good judgment, I must beg your trust in this matter," Robert said carefully. "Reject Standish's suit. You'll have no regrets, I promise."

Bentley laced his fingers across his belly. "Matilda will enjoy another season, I suppose." His gaze sharpened upon Robert. "*He* was not who I wanted for her, in any case."

Robert inclined his head, accepting the compliment.

"Now, then. If you did not intend to negotiate a marriage to my daughter, what did prompt your visit?"

"A recent death, sir."

"Oh?"

"A publisher, name of Green. He was killed in his office several nights ago."

Bentley's expression shuttered. He strummed his fingers upon his belly.

"Green's list of enemies is long," Robert continued. "It includes an acquaintance of mine. Lord Atherbourne." Yesterday, after leaving Lady Wallingham's house, Robert had realized he'd need a story to tell Bentley that kept Annabelle safely out of the picture. He also needed Bentley to believe they were on the same side. "Green viciously maligned Atherbourne and, more importantly, Atherbourne's new wife. His lordship is keen to know who might have attacked Green, as he has no wish to be accused of the deed, himself."

"Hmm. And what makes you think I can help?"

Robert leaned forward and held Bentley's gaze with bold directness. "Many good men have been harmed by that blackguard's pen. Whoever put an end to him has done us all a service."

Bentley frowned. "He targeted you, too?"

It was the first sign of an opening. Treading cautiously, Robert nodded. Not entirely a lie. By hurting Annabelle, Green might as well have targeted Robert.

"Bastard," Bentley spat, shoving to his feet so fast the chair rocked on its legs. "That piece of filth was a liar and a thief." He stomped to the sideboard and refilled his glass with a generous portion of brandy. After several swallows, Bentley continued ranting. "He stole my good name. Did likewise to Atherbourne. Others. I'd planned to sue. Would have won, too. Bastard." He drained his glass then refilled it again. Then, pointing at Robert, he nodded. "You understand, don't you? Aye. You do. I can see it. I always knew you were a good sort, Conrad. Good man."

Bloody hell, he needed details, and all Bentley gave were generalities. But he had to remain careful, keep the older man talking without compromising his own position. "I do," he confirmed. "I do understand. Did you speak to him? Green."

Bentley threw back another swallow and nodded. "Several times. I threatened suit. He laughed. Said his backers wouldn't care; they'd start a new publication under a new name. He'd done it before, he said. Bastard."

"A man like that is fortunate to have lasted as long as he did," Robert prompted.

"Right you are. Right you are." Bentley finished what had to be his third or fourth brandy then slammed the glass down on the sideboard. "Never meant to kill him, though."

Tightness coiled in Robert's chest. With great effort, he remained still. "How did it happen?"

"Bastard pushed too far. I only went there that night to give

him one last chance. Print a retraction. Tell the bloody truth."
Bentley shook his head. "He wouldn't. All but spat in my face.
So I ..." He paled. Wiped his mouth then his graying hair. "I
struck him. He fell to the ground. I thought he was unhurt. He
even shouted at me as I was leaving. But he must have cracked
his head on the floor or something. Next day, I read that he'd ...
he'd been found dead."

Trying to recall Green's injuries, Robert frowned. "Where
did you strike him?"

Bentley pointed to his own cheek. "Here, I think. In any case,
reports suggest his head was injured. Must have been from the
fall."

It was possible, Robert supposed. Still, a head wound as
severe as Green's would have rendered the man instantly
unconscious. Shouting would have been out of the question.
Perhaps the wound had not been as severe as he remembered.
Or perhaps Bentley's recollection was confused. The only
alternative was that two men independently attacked the
publisher the same night—extremely unlikely.

"Sounds accidental to me," Robert commented. "Did he
reveal anything about his backers—or perhaps those who
worked for him?"

"You mean Aimes." The shrewdness was back. "Don't bother
with that line of inquiry, Conrad. Green *was* Aimes, near as I
can determine. And good riddance."

Slowly, relief unraveled the knot in his chest. Annabelle was
safe. That was all that mattered.

"Do you intend to report this to Bow Street?" Bentley asked.

Robert examined the older man, whose color had returned,
though he steadied himself against the sideboard. "No. You
might wish to speak to them, however. A runner named
Drayton works for the Duke of Blackmore. He should prove
sympathetic. I'd wager he'll conclude the matter should be
regarded as an accident for legal purposes."

Bentley stared at him for a long moment then lowered his head. "Good man, Conrad," he murmured. "Good man."

A short while later, Robert donned his hat while glancing up and down the length of Brook Street. One of Bentley's servants had been tasked with retrieving Dewdrop, which invariably took longer than it should. For once, Robert was in no hurry.

Annabelle was safe. Green was dead, and his attacker had been discovered. Edward Yarrow Aimes was no more. And soon, Robert would make Annabelle his wife.

He blinked up at a tiny sliver of blue amongst shifting clouds. Perhaps, after battling everything that stood in their way, he and his Bumblebee were about to triumph at long last. Perhaps it was time to hope.

Faintly, he heard the lazy clop-clop-clop of Dewdrop emerging through the gate from Bentley's mews. The groom looked apologetic. "Begging your pardon for the delay, Mr. Conrad."

Robert felt himself smiling. Fancy that. He was smiling. "No need. Dewdrop prefers a steady pace over a swift one."

He closed half the distance to where the groom held his mount before he heard the clamor behind him. A loud pop. A man shouting a curse. Horses screamed. Wheels ground against cobbles in a rolling drum.

Without thinking, Robert spun on his bad leg. Fierce agony gripped his muscles.

"Whoa, boy. Whoa!" It was the groom, now behind him.

But Robert only saw the coach. It raced toward him. Twenty feet. Fifteen. The driver looked panicked, teeth gritted and reins gripped. Ten feet. Five.

Five thousand pounds of uncontrolled horseflesh. Another two thousand of muscular black coach. They were going to hit him. Now.

Planting his feet and using his cane, Robert tried to stagger out of their path, but his leg was weak. Useless. A heartbeat before the collision, everything disappeared—sound, memory, the street and the strip of blue sky—everything except the one thing he could not bear to leave.

Annabelle. His heart. God, how he loved her.

The strike lifted him into the air. Deflated his lungs. Sent him plowing into the black iron bars of the mews gate. He hit the ground with unforgiving force.

Couldn't breathe. For a moment, then another, he couldn't bloody breathe.

Christ, he remembered this feeling. Closed his eyes and forced himself to relax. He'd done this before. Slow. Easy. There. His first breath wheezed. The bruising pain in his back and shoulder and hip were likewise familiar. He'd fallen farther and suffered worse.

Something warm, moist, and sizable swiped from his chin to his forehead. The swipe repeated. Then came a snuffle. A nudge.

He opened his eyes to a giant nostril surrounded by white. A wide, pink tongue licked his forehead. His hand came up to rub Dewdrop's nose.

"... terribly sorry, sir. He just ... bolted! Knocked you out of the path right as you were about to be flattened. Never saw the like."

"It's all right," Robert managed, patting the horse's cheek. "You did well, Dewdrop. Well, indeed."

"The coach appeared frightfully sudden, sir. And at such speed!"

Robert raised a brow at the young groom, who stood with his hands on his knees. "Did you see where it went?"

"Toward the park, I reckon."

Robert looked for his cane and found it several yards away. "Fetch that for me, won't you?" He gripped the gate's iron bars and used his left leg to lever himself to his feet.

"Here you are, sir. Your hat, too."

"My thanks." Robert donned his hat and tucked his cane into its loop on Dewdrop's saddle. After checking to ensure the horse wasn't injured, he stroked his neck in one final gesture of gratitude and mounted up.

"Sir, should I ... that is, it did appear the coach was aimed at—"

Robert glared at the boy calmly. "Nonsense. An accident, that's all. No harm done."

But minutes later, as he made a second pass along Park Lane, scouring the area and finding no sign of a runaway travel coach, he had to concede what was becoming increasingly apparent.

That sliver of blue sky had been a taunt.

There were no accidents. Only threats hanging heavy and dark along the edges. Waiting for him to make a mistake.

No, someone wanted him to let the matter of Green's murder die, and they were willing to kill again to ensure he complied. It wasn't Bentley.

So, who?

Once again, he felt the battle slipping away from him. He had one last maneuver. A retreat, some might say. But it would safeguard the one thing that mattered. Yes, his mission was clear: Claim his woman. His heart. His wife. And protect her from whatever came next.

"YOU'VE A VISITOR WAITING IN THE DRAWING ROOM, MY LADY," said Estelle as soon as Annabelle and Jane arrived at Berne House. The lady's maid took their bonnets and gloves, along with their flowers, and nodded toward the stairs. "Lady Berne ordered tea."

"Who is it?" Annabelle asked.

Before Estelle could answer, Genie flew from the corridor toward the front entrance. Her arms wheeled as her feet slid. "It's not yours, Kate! He never said it was yours!"

"Where is it, Genie?" Kate yelled, charging after her sister with red-faced rage. "Where did you hide it?"

Genie skidded around Annabelle and ducked behind her back.

"Eugenia, I make a dreadful disguise," Annabelle pointed out. "Apart from which, Kate has already seen you. Now, what have you done?"

"Only what's right." A slim arm shot out to point toward the heaving ball of fury that was once their youngest sister. "It doesn't belong to her, and she needs to learn—"

"Give it back!" Kate screamed.

"Girls! That is quite enough!" Mama's warning tone brought everything to a halt. She took the last few stairs and bustled into the entrance hall. "What have I told you about such carrying on? You know your father prefers a peaceful, quiet house."

Annabelle quirked a smile at Jane and murmured, "How would he know? He's never had one."

Jane snorted. "A man must have aspirations, I suppose."

Mama gathered her two youngest viragos and explained why she must now cancel the Bond Street excursion she had planned for them, because "I cannot possibly take two such ill-tempered, ill-behaved young ladies into respectable shops, can I?" Then, having chastened them both, Mama sent them to their bedchambers.

She sighed before turning to Annabelle and Jane. "Perhaps I should hire a governess."

Annabelle frowned. "You swore you'd never hire another after the last one ... well, you know."

"Yes." Mama looked weary, her smile strained. "But John is rarely home these days."

Their last governess had been young, pretty, and wildly

ambitious. She'd worked for the family only a year before she'd crawled naked into John's bed and attempted to elevate her rank by way of begetting a child.

John had always been a deep sleeper, near impossible to awaken without a great deal of shouting or jostling or both. After being alerted to the governess's scheme by Estelle, Papa had entered John's chamber to warn him. Annabelle had later—years later, following a campaign of wheedling and bribery—persuaded Estelle to reveal what they'd found. Reportedly, John had still been asleep, and the governess had attempted to mount him in the way one sat astride a saddle.

Annabelle had tried to puzzle out the mechanics of it, but she always grew a bit nauseated—he was her brother, after all—so she'd never quite made it past the naked, scheming governess part before her skin started crawling.

Thereafter, Mama had determined governesses were unnecessary, as she and Papa could educate their daughters themselves. Still, managing five girls with willful, independent spirits must be trying.

Annabelle looked at her mother now, shoulders curled forward, lines beside her mouth deeper than usual. And a strange thought occurred to her—this might be Annabelle's future.

She'd agreed to marry Robert.

Which meant she would be a wife.

And, should they be blessed with children, a mother.

Why reality should take this long to sink in, she did not know. She'd thought he'd come to his senses, she supposed. But he hadn't. And now, all she could think about was babies and orange blossoms.

Well, kissing, too. Kissing Robert was sublime.

Yet, being a wife and mother also meant *managing* things—keeping a proper household, planning meals for hard-to-please visitors like Lady Wallingham, deciding whether to hire a governess for your termagant daughters, and weighing your love of cats against your husband's sneezing.

Or dismissing an upstart, scheming harlot who'd tried to trap your son.

Annabelle thought about what that must have been like. She imagined her own son. Robert's son. With Robert's eyes and his rare smile. If anyone tried to harm her son, she'd not have the restraint Mama and Papa had shown. Dismissal would be the least of the schemer's worries.

Behind them, Estelle asked, "Begging your pardon, my lady, but should I send Ned to the drawing room with fresh tea and biscuits?"

Mama's eyes went round. "Dear me, I nearly forgot. Annabelle, you should go up at once. He is most exercised. Well, so far as one can tell from the glower."

"Robert?" The word sounded hoarse. She cleared her throat. "Robert is here?"

"He was adamant about waiting. It has been hours, dearest."

She swallowed her apprehension, ran her hands over her skirts and hair, then started up the stairs. The moment she entered the drawing room, she simply stopped and let her earlier realization take root.

This man—the one standing at the window with the broad, broad shoulders and solid bearing—would be her husband. The thought made her head swim.

Would they be happy? *Could* they be? Once, she would have shouted *yes* in a resounding drumbeat to match her foolish heart. Now, she wondered whether happiness was even possible. The very best of marriages suffered ravages from time to time. Wives lost their tempers; husbands lost their patience; mothers were forced to watch their children fall ill; fathers were forced to carry their daughters after they'd broken a toe.

Without the kind of love that bound Mama and Papa together, how much battering could a marriage take before it broke apart?

She did not know.

How much worse might matters be if a husband wanted his wife but would suffer a daily reminder of how she'd harmed him?

She did not know.

How fragile might their family be if she loved her husband but had little hope he would ever feel the same?

She did not know.

She'd promised to marry him because she loved him madly. Possessively. Hopelessly. Her reasons were selfish but understandable. His reasons, by contrast, were incomprehensible. Did he want her? Or was she a habit he'd fallen into? How long before resentments made their union unbearable?

Perhaps this had been a mistake.

A cold flush soaked into her skin.

Dear God. What if this marriage was the biggest mistake either of them ever made?

Long minutes passed before she could breathe properly. She eyed his shoulders and the way he grasped his cane. His fingers gripped it over and over when he was agitated. Her foolish heart squeezed and ached.

"Robert," she called softly.

He turned. Oh, heavens. *Exercised* was not the word she would have chosen. Explosive, perhaps. Enraged, certainly. Blue eyes blazed fire beneath heavy brows.

"Where the devil have you been?" he barked. Rather than waiting for an answer, he charged toward her like a storm.

Her heart kicked in her chest. Her belly swooped and clenched. "R-Robert." As he came for her, she automatically stepped backward, raising a hand only to have it meet his chest.

Everything happened at once. He grasped her nape. Used his cane to shove the door closed. Backed her into it. Then brought her mouth to his with passionate purpose.

Her moan hummed against his lips. Her tongue tingled as it met his, sleek and sliding.

Her hands grasped. Clutched.

Her hips yearned. Thrust.

Heat detonated as he cupped her jaw and went deeper.

How had she lived without his taste? His touch? His hands? For six. Bloody. Weeks.

He withdrew his tongue, gripping her face firmly between his warm, dry palms.

"No, no, no," she panted, reaching for him. "Come back. Kiss. Please."

"Where ..."

"Here."

"Where were you?" he grated as though anguished. Blue seared into her as he lowered his forehead to rest against hers. "I waited hours. Have you any idea what I imagined ...?"

She kissed him. Just stood on her toes and claimed those irresistible lips. And he kissed her back, sliding and caressing. She loved how they fit together. Their hands had always fit the same way, like puzzle pieces.

Now, his hands gripped her waist. Ground her body against his, flattening her breasts and aching nipples in the most relieving way. She heard the clatter of his cane upon the floor. Felt the panels of the door at her back. Savored his flavor—tea and dusk.

"Where were you?" he growled. "Tell me." His lips claimed her throat, trailing suckling kisses down and down and down. She'd dispensed with her pelisse earlier, so all she wore was her walking gown, which was light, sheer muslin over apricot silk petticoats. The neckline was a scoop, which gave him perfect access to the upper third of her bosom. Her head fell back at the sheer pleasure of feeling his mouth there, against her softness.

"Tell me," he panted, his breath hot.

She threaded her fingers through thick, dark hair. Groaned

her need and writhed against his thighs.

Once again, his hand gripped her nape, and suddenly, blue eyes were blazing into hers again. He looked wild. Rakish and hungry. He seemed on the edge of madness. "Where were you?"

Her head felt thick like she was underwater struggling to surface. She clutched his shoulders, dug her fingertips into him. He was the only solid thing that existed. In that moment, for the first time, she heard his question. Slowly, her fingers traveled to his lips. "Robert," she sighed. "You—you were worried?"

He shook her using only the hand at her nape. "Answer me."

"Covent Garden. I wanted—"

"What did I tell you about going near the Strand?"

His hands were so big, one at the small of her back, the other on her neck. They didn't hurt, but for the first time since he'd swung her to the middle of a river rather than watch her fall onto rocks, she realized the enormity of his strength.

"I didn't go alone." Her voice was too thin. She mustered some force by tightening her abdomen. "Jane went with me."

"Why were you there?"

"It doesn't matter."

"You will tell me everything, or so help me—"

"I discovered who the imposter was," she blurted. "She sells flowers most mornings."

"At Covent Garden. Do you realize how near that is to where Green was—"

"No," she snapped, tugging at his wrists. "Apparently, I am daft as a carriage wheel."

"Who is she?"

"Why do you care? You've never approved of my work. And you'll never understand the importance of learning who stole Edward Yarrow Aimes from me."

Despite her tugging, he kept his hands where they were, warming her neck and lower back. "Tell me what you discovered."

After a moment's hesitation, she explained how she'd found Mrs. Bickerstaff. Then, she described their encounter and her reasons for giving the actress funds to leave London. "She is not a good woman, and I despise what she did. But the one who truly betrayed me was Mr. Green. I'll not have further violence done to anybody because of Edward Yarrow Aimes."

He sighed. "It was a woman, after all. A desperate one. I knew it must be," he murmured.

She frowned. "How?"

"Because I have spent the last six days scouring London for answers about Green's death. Did you think I was sipping brandy with the chaps at Boodle's? I am trying to keep you safe. God, woman, don't you understand yet? You are in danger. That is bloody unacceptable."

Her hands stilled, now lightly clasping his wrists rather than clutching. "I needed to know," she whispered.

"Now you do," he said grimly. "And the risks you're eager to take have grown past my tolerance. We are leaving."

She blinked. "What?"

"I've instructed Estelle to pack you a trunk sufficient for the journey to Nottinghamshire. She and your family will bring the rest of your belongings when they return to Clumberwood at the end of the month."

"Robert. Don't be foolish. We cannot travel alone together. We are not yet married."

The hand at her nape tightened. He lowered his head until his lips hovered a breath above hers. "You are mine. You have been from the moment you agreed to become my wife. No clergyman's approval will make that truer. And no protests about propriety will make it any less so."

Her heart both melted and rebelled, a strange, contradictory sensation. "I was yours long before that," she said achingly.

His head jerked back. It appeared she'd surprised him.

"You wanted nothing to do with me. Yet now, I am meant

to toss aside every sensible notion and follow your commands, simply because you've—what, precisely? Changed your mind?"

Jaw tightening, expression hardening, he replied softly, "You wish to know my reasons, do you?"

The cold sensation in her stomach told her she wouldn't like his answers. She nodded anyway.

"I shouldn't want you. I shouldn't dream of having you beneath me. Or all the things I will do once you're there. This … need. It disturbs me. Yet, I cannot rid myself of it." His chin tilted until the angle reminded her of a conqueror's portrait. A small smile curved the right side of his mouth. "In your sketches, I was always a knight, is that not so?"

"Yes."

"Wrong," he whispered, that smile growing while blue glowed with purpose. "You never understood, Bumblebee. Never saw the truth."

She swallowed. "Th-the truth of what?"

"Of me. I am not some noble knight but a warrior. Knights joust for show. I fight. Savagely, when I must. I claim territory and hold it with every weapon at my disposal, noble or not."

"You believe I robbed you of the chance to be an officer. Is that what you're saying?"

"No." The hand at the small of her back suddenly forced her hips into his, pressing a thick, hard ridge against her belly. "No, love. I'm saying my claim has been made. You are mine. And I will fight to protect you, fight to keep you, fight as brutally as I must. Even when you defy me." His gaze dropped to her mouth. "Especially then."

She gasped as the hard ridge against her swelled. Heat seared her cheeks. "Robert." His name was both a plea and a protest. He could not mean half of what he was saying. Robert had always been honorable. Tough, yes. Strong, certainly. A bit of a bear, particularly when he'd gone without eating. But his decency had never been in question. He was not brutal or ruthless, as he'd described. He was not possessive or territorial.

She was possessive. *She* was territorial. So, she knew the signs—jealousy of the women he'd considered for marriage, a desire to monopolize his attentions, constant cravings for his voice and hands and brooding gaze.

No, his nature was noble. Even the lies he'd told her had been for her protection. All this talk of ruthless warrior impulses must be aimed at intimidating her into obedience. Yes, that was it.

"You do not frighten me, Robert Conrad," she said with mustered bravado.

She expected his smile to fade. Instead, it grew. So did the infernal glow in his eyes.

For that matter, so did the hard, male ridge that seemed to want its freedom.

Oh, dear. Perhaps she'd miscalculated.

"I should frighten you." He kissed her long and deep. Suddenly, *possessive* and *territorial* seemed the only words capable of describing him. He devoured her, invaded and claimed. He took her mouth with ownership.

When he was done, she was boneless. Weightless. There was nothing left of her but heat and want. Certainly nothing left of her will to resist him when he muttered hoarsely, "Be ready to leave in an hour. The coach will be waiting outside."

Chapter Sixteen

"I would sooner eat mud for supper than travel in it."

—THE DOWAGER MARCHIONESS OF WALLINGHAM in a letter to the Marquis of Mortlock expressing her conviction that foul weather and carriage wheels are fundamentally incompatible.

Dearest Robert,
Do you ever wish the rain would either cease or carry you away in a flood? It seems the in-between is most trying.

Ever yours,
Annabelle

—Letter to Robert Conrad dated March 2, 1814

IN FAIR WEATHER, THE JOURNEY FROM LONDON TO Nottingham took two eight-hour days. However, while reliving the biblical Great Flood as they currently were, Robert thought they'd be fortunate to arrive at Rivermore within a fortnight— provided they arrived at all.

He muttered a curse as one of the carriage horses staggered through shin-deep mud, causing the travel coach to lurch to the right.

"If only someone had recommended waiting another week to travel," came a tart voice from the opposite seat. "But who would be so prescient as that? Hmm. I suppose we'll never know."

Glaring at the woman who vexed him like no other, Robert pounded on the ceiling of the coach and shouted at the driver to stop.

"Oh, must we?" Even her pout dripped sarcasm. "I find being thrust from one side of the coach to the other so ... what's the word? Invigorating."

She had her arms extended outward, bracing dainty hands wide on the wall and seat. She wore a blue pelisse and matching bonnet. Her gloves were white, her lips tight and pursed in displeasure.

Why was she so beautiful to him?

Even now, with her fury manifesting in sarcasm and wrathful glares, she made him hard. It was a bloody illness, this mad desire to take her body with his. Part of being a territorial sort, he supposed. And male. Yes, everything male in him wanted to claim everything female in her.

God, she was soft. Tasted like honeysuckle. Sweet and wild and—

"A shame Lady Wallingham couldn't accompany us," she grumbled. "One of her diatribes about England's roads would be cathartic right now—and all too accurate."

"She lent us her coach," he pointed out, reaching for his cane as the coach came to a sliding stop. "Asking her to chaperone us might have been too far."

"Well, so long as we're not making *unreasonable* demands of anyone."

He sighed and threw open the door.

"Where are you going?"

"To untie Dewdrop and Methuselah."

"Why?"

He climbed down, wincing as his boots sank deep into slick mud. Rain drenched his hair and shoulders within seconds. "Stay here."

Closing the door upon her reply, he first spoke to the coachman, a pleasant fellow he'd hired from a livery stable in London. He gave instructions for the remainder of the journey, to which the sodden driver nodded agreeably before climbing down to help him ready Methuselah and Dewdrop for riding. God, what a relief it was to have someone respond to his commands with cooperation rather than vitriol.

He and Annabelle had spent two days in that coach together. The first day had been bad enough. She'd demanded to know his findings about Green's murder. He hadn't wished to frighten her, so he'd kept his brush with death to himself, though he'd relayed his conversation with Thomas Bentley.

"Nonsense and rubbish," she'd replied. "Mr. Bentley would never kill anyone."

"Not intentionally, but if they argued and things got out of hand—"

"He was at Lady Darnham's fete the night the murder occurred."

"He arrived late, remember? Besides, he's already admitted

striking the man."

"I still don't believe it. Are there others you suspect?"

"Some."

She'd waited, strumming her fingers on the seat. "Robert, I have been most patient with you."

He'd sighed. "Patient is not the word I would use."

That had infuriated her, which had led to six hours of cold silence. They'd stayed in separate rooms at a coaching inn last night. This morning, she'd been in better spirits. Then, the rain had begun, and matters had slid downhill at an alarming clip.

Now, he and the coachman led the two geldings around to the middle of the road, where the mud wasn't so deep. Robert went to open the coach door and found a fuming Bumblebee inside.

"Come," he said gently. "If we ride straight through, we shall be at Rivermore before nightfall."

Brown eyes flared wide. "Ride? It is a deluge out there, Robert."

"In a carriage, it will take us another two days to reach Nottingham. The wheels will keep getting mired." He shrugged casually. "But, if you prefer to stay dry—"

"Oh, God." She rubbed her forehead with her fingers and thumb. "I cannot bear another hour, let alone two days."

He nearly grinned, but in the interest of keeping her anger within manageable proportions, he forced himself to frown instead. "Come along." He extended a dripping hand. "It is only a few hours' ride."

Grudgingly, she placed her hand in his and descended onto the coach's step. There, she halted, grimacing as she saw how deep the mud was. She shook her hem and pulled her skirts up high enough that he could see her lightweight half-boots. She sighed. Already her bonnet's brim was dripping. "Well, I suppose a bit of mud won't hurt. Apart from my pelisse. And petticoats. And the boots, of course."

He eyed the distance to the horses, then the mud, then his cane. "Wait," he muttered before presenting her with his back. "Climb on."

"Robert, I didn't mean—"

"Climb on." He glanced at her over his shoulder. "You remember how, don't you?"

"This is silly."

"Never stopped you before."

She clicked her tongue and swatted his shoulder, which made him grin. Then, her arms wrapped around his neck. Her breasts flattened against his back. When he turned his head to the side, her lips were right there.

He used the repositioning of her hands as an excuse to caress her. "Lock them like this," he murmured.

"Yes. All right."

"Hold on to me."

"I shall."

He started forward, using one hand to grip his cane and the other to secure her thigh against his hip. He thought he heard her gasp, but he was focused on maintaining his balance in the slippery mud. He managed to carry her without incident the ten paces to where Methuselah waited.

"Y-you put a side saddle on him?"

Gently, using only his good leg, he lowered them both until her feet touched the ground. "I assumed you'd need one. Or, do you prefer to ride astride?"

She either missed his dry tone or was somehow distracted, because she didn't answer for the longest time.

He spun and found her eyeing his shoulders. "Annabelle."

"Hmm?"

"I'm going to help you mount, now."

"Yes." Her gaze moved to his lips. "Mount."

"Bloody hell, you're getting soaked."

She sighed. Then, her tongue darted out over rain-wetted

lips. "Robert?"

"Yes?"

"I want you."

For a moment, all he heard was rain and his own thundering heart. Then, right there in the midst of a biblical deluge, arousal flooded him until his legs shook.

"Did you hear me?"

He ran a wet hand over his face, hoping to cool himself down. "You have the damnedest timing, Bumblebee."

A little smile curled her lips then disappeared. "Why have you not kissed me since we left London?"

"Because."

"Tell me why."

Because if he kissed her, he would not stop until he was buried deep inside her. And he wanted to reach Rivermore first. She deserved a bed and a fire, a ring and vows. Not to be taken against a door or on a desk or in a closet or a blasted coach. He was not a barbarian.

Well, he was. But she didn't need to know precisely how barbaric she made him.

He swiped his face again, shifted his weight to accommodate his aching cock. "We should go."

Her brow crumpled. She dropped her gaze then nodded.

Before he could change his mind, he lifted her onto Methuselah's back and ensured she was settled before climbing onto Dewdrop. With a nod of thanks to the coachman, he led the way, keeping to the center of the road. Both horses were heavy-boned and strong, but he'd thought Methuselah's stamina would hold out with Annabelle's lighter weight.

Within an hour, however, he heard her call his name from too far behind. When he glanced back, she was nudging the horse with her heel, bending forward and patting his neck. "What is wrong with your horse?" she asked. "He appears to be ... napping."

Robert glanced skyward. At least the rain had eased to a drizzle. "He *is* napping."

"I—I cannot seem to move him. Or wake him." She laughed. "Oh, my." Another burst of laughter. "This is the most ..." More laughter. Her eyes filled with tears. Overflowed. "The most extr—extraordinary ... Oh, heavens." She covered her face with both hands. Her shoulders shook and shook.

At first, he thought she was laughing the way one did when fatigued—a bit uncontrollably. Then, he heard a sob, and something vicious clawed at his gut. Within seconds, he'd spun Dewdrop and raced to her side. His only thought was to hold her. Now.

Now, now, now.

He must stop whatever was causing her distress. He took Methuselah's reins from her hand and wound an arm around her waist to lift her onto Dewdrop. Into his arms, where she belonged.

"God, you're drenched," he muttered. She was. Her woolen gown was sodden, her bonnet dripping and discolored.

She kept her face buried in her hands. They muffled the sounds of occasional shuddering breaths and tiny, heartrending gasps.

He enfolded her as tightly as he dared, his arms around her elbows and waist. He kissed whatever he could reach—mostly her jaw and forehead. "Bumblebee," he whispered. "What's wrong?"

"I am an idiot," she choked.

"No."

She shook her head then let it drop onto his shoulder. "I am." Her voice was a thread, her sniff damp and clogged. Her hands slid away from her face, and she gently clasped his wrist where he held her. Her round nose was red. So were her sweet brown eyes, glimmering and sad. "I am," she repeated. Then, she kissed the inside of his wrist. Gazing into the distance, she wiped her cheek and said, "It has been too much, that's all. Mr. Green and Mrs. Bickerstaff and, well, everything. I am fine, now."

A lie. She was not fine. She seemed ... hollow.

But he needed to get them home. He needed to get her warm and dry. He needed to marry her so he could kiss her properly. Then, he'd discover the truth about what had caused his Bumblebee to go listless and sad. He wouldn't stop until he knew. Until he'd done everything in his power to make her glow with happiness.

Behind them, he heard the clatter of Lady Wallingham's coach. Blast. With Methuselah's nap, they hadn't saved much time. He waited only long enough to transfer the old horse into the coachman's care before urging Dewdrop forward.

The gelding might not be the fastest mount, but he was steadfast and strong. With any luck, they'd be home in a couple of hours.

Home.

He tightened his arms around his wife ... or rather, his soon-to-be wife. How easily he kept forgetting. The words circled his mind like a bird's repeating song. *Home. Soon. Wife.* He nuzzled his Bumblebee's cheek and whispered that she should sleep awhile. "I shall wake you when we arrive, love."

She lifted his wrist to her lips again and nodded.

But, while her kiss was sweet and her body pliant against his, her sadness pulled at him like a rogue current. So he held her tighter. Pushed Dewdrop harder. In his head, a bird's song repeated—*home, soon, wife.*

He was bringing Annabelle home. And very soon, she would be his wife in truth. He need only be patient a little longer.

AWAKENING IN ROBERT'S ARMS MIGHT HAVE BEEN HEAVEN IF she weren't such a sodden, miserable mess. Soaked wool was heavy and heat-sapping. Her bonnet was an utter ruin, the satin ribbons lifeless yet choking. Her petticoats plastered her legs. Even her stays made her breasts itch.

The miseries of wet clothing aside, her backside was numb, along with one of her legs. Sitting sideways on a man's saddle might look like a grand lark, but it was far from comfortable over a two-hour stretch. And her neck had developed a crick that made itself known when she jerked awake and tried to lift her head from Robert's shoulder.

"Bloody hell," she muttered, rubbing the sore muscles.

"Easy. We're almost there." Robert's voice was rusty, his teeth gritted against an obvious chill.

Heavens, if she was stiff and sore, she couldn't imagine how he felt. His bad leg must hurt like the devil after such a long ride. She glanced down at his knee and thigh. Her hand moved to stroke it automatically.

He hissed in a breath between his teeth.

The sound made her heart lurch. "Did I hurt you?"

"No, love." He grimaced, his jaw flexing as he kept his gaze on the road. "I just ... we are almost there."

She smiled. "You said that already."

"Perhaps you could repeat it back to me."

Her smile grew. "We are almost there, Robert."

"God. Say it again."

She chuckled. Despite her misery and his. Despite the echoes of her earlier despair. Despite everything, he made her laugh. "We are almost there," she whispered, stroking his arm.

Brooding blue dropped to her lips then came up and started glowing. "That close, are we?"

"So close."

"It's a damned good thing, Bumblebee. I don't know how much longer I can wait."

She wasn't entirely sure what they were talking about, but she suspected Robert referred to something other than riding fatigue. "Dewdrop will surely be relieved to have a proper stable to sleep in."

His answer was a grunt.

Just then, they passed through a patch of trees, rounded a bend upon a small rise, and Rivermore Abbey came into view. It was the first glimpse she'd had of the place in seven years. The structure itself appeared largely unchanged—same sprawling sandstone square with a courtyard in the center and the odd brick wing here and there. Same ancient priory edifice with its octagonal towers and pointed arch straddling the drive. Same brick outbuildings and stables a short distance away.

But the land was different. The rail fences were new and in excellent repair. The trees to the west had grown into thick woodlands. The pastures to the east were filled with plump sheep and dairy cattle. Vast fields of wheat and barley appeared to have benefitted from improved drainage, particularly given the dreadfully wet spring.

Rivermore Abbey was thriving as never before.

She peeked at Robert's face, noting how he gazed upon the estate with something like possessiveness. A twinge of envy struck her. Yet, it was drowned out by her pride in this man. She'd heard he'd done well as the estate's manager, of course. Her sources had always been excellent.

But seeing Rivermore's prosperity for herself, knowing how much harder every task must have been for a man injured as he'd been, overwhelmed her.

"It's splendid, Robert," she murmured.

He shot her a questioning glance, his mouth quirking. "It's the same as ever. A great pile."

"No. You've made it better."

He didn't answer, didn't smile. But she sensed her words had pleased him.

They made their way past the great, pointed arch and into the stable yard. An old, grizzled Mr. Colby limped forth, his wooden leg looking more weathered than she'd last seen it.

"What's this?" the old man said to Dewdrop. "A new resident, have we?" As she recalled, Colby preferred speaking to horses rather than humans.

Robert performed brief introductions then waved over a pair of young grooms to assist Annabelle down. She groaned in both relief and discomfort as soon as sensation rushed back into the numb spots in her lower half. Robert dismounted on his own, but all she heard from him was a grunt.

Heavens, he must be so accustomed to pain. She winced against the guilt.

A large, strong hand clasped her elbow. "Come. It is not yet six. Grandfather may still be awake. He will wish to see you."

He led her inside through the main doors. The interior of Rivermore Abbey was a blend of square-patterned wood paneling and thirteenth-century stonework. Every room echoed. She'd always thought more carpets and draperies would soften the old house's lines. Not that it needed much adornment—the place was both vast and magnificent.

After introductions to the housekeeper, Mrs. Cleary, and the head footman, Benjamin, Robert ordered tea and baths before escorting Annabelle to the Marquis of Mortlock's sitting room.

"Blast you, Ben. I was about to have a nap," came a grizzled old voice from inside. "Now it will take me another hour to find a comfortable position."

Robert opened the door. "You've gone soft, old man." He guided Annabelle into the oak-paneled chamber, where a frail, much-older Mortlock sat in a winged chair before a low fire. "I recall stories of a captain who could sleep whilst cannons fired overhead."

Stooped shoulders straightened. Mortlock tossed away his lap blanket and shoved slowly to his feet. His arms shook. His lips were white, his eyes a milkier shade of Robert's vivid blue. Those eyes glossed and blinked. "S-son? My boy, I hadn't expected ..."

Robert moved swiftly to his grandfather and, with heartbreaking gentleness, helped Mortlock back into his chair. Their hands lingered and held before releasing. By the time the exchange was done, Annabelle wasn't certain who was shaking more.

Robert dragged two wooden chairs closer then gestured to her to take the one nearest the fire. "Grandfather, this is Lady Annabelle Huxley. You remember her, don't you? The Earl of Berne's daughter."

Milky blue raked her up and down. "Aye, indeed. You've grown, girl. Last I saw, you'd fit in a teacup." He frowned. "You're drenched, though." His frown deepened into a glower, and it refocused on Robert. "What the devil are you thinking, boy?" He gathered up his blanket and held it out to her. "Taking a lady out in a squall like this."

"We are to be married, Grandfather. That is what I came to tell you."

She accepted the blanket with a grateful smile. "Lord Mortlock, it is a pleasure to see you again. We've had a long journey from London, but Rivermore Abbey is a splendid sight after our travels."

He snorted, sounding oddly like Lady Wallingham. "An infested madhouse would seem a haven after my grandson dragged you through hell's own rainstorm." Again, he turned a wrathful gaze on Robert. "What the devil were you thinking?"

Robert rubbed the back of his neck. "You've asked that already."

"And?"

"The coach kept getting mired. It would have taken us an extra day—"

"You said you're to be married. Not that you are."

Robert's hand moved from his neck to raking through his damp hair. Ruddy color flashed on his cheeks. "Yes."

"I assume you left the young lady's chaperone out in the corridor."

"No."

"What's Lord Berne think of this, eh? That *this* is how you would treat his daughter."

Robert held his grandfather's gaze in what seemed a long battle, then answered, "I may have left him with the impression Lady Wallingham intended to accompany us."

The old man released another snort. "She'd sooner eat mud for supper than travel in it. Good God, boy. You're further gone than I thought." He shook his head and shot Annabelle a gently chiding glance. "He's left you no choice, has he? Set his course and gave no quarter. Still, there's nothing for it. You'll have to marry the brute."

"We'll marry tomorrow morning," Robert answered for her. "In the chapel."

Mortlock kept his gaze glued to hers. "Is that what you want, girl?"

She swallowed. Earlier, when she'd told Robert she wanted him, she'd hoped for ... she didn't know what. A sign, she supposed. That he felt as much as she did for him. That he was not simply marrying her to fill a role that needed filling, or protecting her out of long habit. She wanted him more than she wanted to breathe. Loved him until nothing else existed. Just Robert.

But sitting there on a dozing horse in the middle of a muddy road, she'd realized he couldn't possibly want her or love her in equal measure. Oh, he cared for her as one cares for an amusing, accident-prone neighbor girl who insists on making a pest of herself. He'd always been gallant. He'd always ridden to her rescue.

And that was what this marriage truly was. A convenience for him and safety for her. He'd been alarmed by the death of Mr. Green, by the risk that she might be attacked in a similar fashion. So, he'd brought her here. To Rivermore Abbey. His home.

Admittedly, his insistence that they travel without a chaperone was puzzling. She'd chalked it up to his urgency to leave London immediately. Still, they could have taken Maureen or Estelle or even Eugenia and Kate. And, at the very least, he could have taken her to Clumberwood, instead. She had clothing there. Extra slippers and stays. Kindly servants who would have served her delicious broth to warm her bones.

She frowned at him now. His grandfather had a point. She should have had a chaperone. She should have been taken to her home, not his. Perhaps Robert considered her unworthy of such courtesies. Perhaps he held her in even lower regard than she'd imagined.

Was marriage to Robert what she wanted? She sighed, the chill in her flesh warring with the blooming ache in her middle. Her eyes dropped to her hands where they wrung the edge of Mortlock's blanket. "I consented to marry Robert weeks ago, my lord. The wedding seems almost an afterthought." She chuckled, the sound echoing strangely in the large room. "I've long admired the chapel. So lovely, the way the light shines through the glass."

A long silence was broken only by the low crackle of the fire. "And you shall be a lovely bride," Mortlock said finally.

She tried to smile, but she couldn't raise her eyes.

"Best get you warmed up straight away, my dear. We don't want you catching your death before the nuptials." He rang a small bell on the side table. "I shall ask Mrs. Cleary to take you to the southwest chamber. Splendid view of the garden."

Robert gathered his cane to stand. "I shall take her—"

"No," Mortlock said with a commander's stern bark. "You'll

keep your backside planted in that chair, boy. We have a great deal to discuss."

Annabelle blinked at them both, wondering at the thick tension, the seeming battle of wills being waged between two such similar men. But, then, Mrs. Cleary arrived, and the promise of a hot bath and a hotter pot of tea beckoned. There'd be time enough later to unravel the mysteries of masculine behavior. For now, being warm and dry would be a welcome improvement.

Chapter Seventeen

"For a man who knows what he's about, ruthless is simply another word for effective."

—The Dowager Marchioness of Wallingham in a letter to the Marquis of Mortlock regarding the proper arrangement of events to achieve preferable outcomes.

Dearest Robert,
Last night, I dreamt of you again. You wore only breeches—not even a shirt—but you carried a sword. When I awakened, I was too restless to lie still. I wanted so very much to fall back to sleep. Part of me longed to know what your kiss would feel like. And by "part," I mean "all."

Ever yours,
Annabelle

—Letter to Robert Conrad dated May 14, 1814

"BOXED HER IN TIGHT, HAVEN'T YOU?"

Robert's skin prickled beneath his grandfather's condemnation. "It's not as though I don't intend to—"

"Damned ruthless, boy."

"—marry her."

"I said you should find a wife. Not lay siege to her like a French armory."

"Not a siege. An assurance. She is mine."

Grandfather ran a hand over his face and released a hoarse bark of laughter. "Bloody hell. Worse than I thought."

"She kept delaying. First, it was finishing the season for her sister's sake. Then it was because I vexed her. Then—"

"Has it occurred to you that she might have needed reassurance? A bit of gentle handling?"

Robert frowned. "I asked her to marry me. She agreed."

"Asked or coerced?"

"Either way, the matter was settled months ago. Delays are simply her way of needling me."

"Hmmph. What did Lady Wallingham have to say about all this?"

"She lent me her travel coach."

Grandfather snorted then chuckled. "Typical Dorothea. Forever rearranging things to her liking." He narrowed his eyes upon Robert. "The girl should have her family at her wedding."

Instantly, everything inside Robert rebelled. "No. That would delay it again. Another week, at least. Perhaps a fortnight."

"Is there a reason you cannot wait such a short time?"

"Yes."

The old man's expression took on a resigned cast. "So, she is with child." He sighed. "I suspected as much."

Robert glowered. "She is not with child."

"Then why the urgency?"

Robert didn't want to answer. Even he had trouble understanding it, sometimes. As similar as he and his grandfather were, Nathaniel Conrad's marriage to Helena Northfield had been more duty than attachment. They'd lived separately for long stretches before her death, Helena residing at Mortlock Manor with their son while Nathaniel remained at Rivermore. Clearly, Grandfather had never known the kind of consuming need Robert felt for Annabelle.

He explained in the only way he could. "She belongs to me. I've waited too long already."

"Fine way to treat someone you aim to make your wife."

Again, his neck prickled. "I told you, she's not with child."

"There's more to caring for a lady than controlling your lust, boy."

"I've kept her safe. Protected her—"

"She's an earl's daughter, not some dockside wench you can set up as your mistress."

His skin heated. His chest burned. "You don't understand."

"Think you're the first man whose blood lit on fire for a woman?"

He heard his own voice deepen to a growl. "You cannot know what this is like."

"Can't I?" A corner of the old man's lips curved. "I'll have seen eighty-one years on this earth before summer's end. You'd be astonished by what I know."

"I lost her once. I'll not do it again."

"Aye. And I had the misfortune to watch my grandson wither into a husk without the girl who made him laugh. Why do you suppose I sent you to London?"

"Lady Wallingham told me. Admirable scheming for a pair of old—"

"Don't go insulting your elders, boy. Dorothea said you'd resist more direct approaches, and she was right." Grandfather's chin came up to a stubborn angle. "You ought to be grateful we intervened, else your Annabelle might have wed another man."

Suddenly, Robert couldn't sit still. He shoved to his feet, fisting his cane and moving to where Grandfather's desk sat beside a window. His gut churned. His skin fired hot. He wanted to crack something in half at the mere notion of his Bumblebee with another man's ring upon her finger. Another man with the right to kiss her, touch her pearlescent skin, and breathe her honeysuckle scent.

"You think I don't understand." Grandfather's voice was graveled. Weary. "You think I've never felt it because I didn't for your grandmother."

Stiffening, Robert leaned into his cane and pivoted. He peered at the old man he'd known his entire life, wondering how much he *didn't* know. A great deal, evidently. "Who was she?"

"No matter. By the time she made her debut, I was already seven years married with a son. She was ..." An odd light entered milky blue—affection, admiration. And yes, a flicker of hunger. "Extraordinary. The kind of woman weak men fear and strong men desire. Brilliant. Dauntless. A dragon amidst sheep."

"Dragon," Robert murmured, startled by the description. Could it be? The ages were right. No. Surely not.

"Had she returned my regard, I would have sought a divorce. Would have done anything, honor be damned. Anything to claim her as my own." Grandfather appeared to have fallen into a reverie, staring at the fire with an unblinking gaze. "But she did not feel as I did. At least, not about me."

Bloody hell. Grandfather and *Lady Wallingham?* Robert returned to the wooden chair Annabelle had vacated and collapsed with a thud. He didn't know whether to be amused or horrified.

"Suffice to say," Grandfather continued, "I understand enough to assure you of your good fortune. Lady Annabelle hasn't set her cap for another man. If Dorothea's reports are to be believed, she didn't much bother to resist your cloddish efforts. She's agreed to wed you and, presumably, bear your offspring. Waiting another week won't kill you, my boy, however dire the prospect may seem."

If Grandfather believed that, then he understood nothing. Annabelle Huxley had belonged to him since they were children. Granted, things were different now. Once he'd seen her as a woman, his feelings had become tinged with lust. But they'd always been bound together by a force beyond this world. Good or bad, right or wrong, that hadn't changed. But the bond could be damaged. He'd done it before, thinking he was protecting her.

No, he could not wait another week. He could not allow her to slip through his fingers. He needed her fully bound to him before God and man and every bloody creature that might seek to come between them.

He needed more than her promise. He needed to solidify his claim.

And nothing on earth—not dragons, soldiers, or biblical floods—would stop him now.

ANNABELLE HAD GROANED MULTIPLE TIMES SINCE ENTERING the southwest chamber. The first had come when she'd finally been liberated from her damp stays. The second had been when she'd sunk into a tub of steaming, rose-scented water.

The third came presently when a pile of piping-hot crumpets dripping with melted butter and honey were delivered upon a silver tray. Beside the crumpets sat a plate of bacon, roasted pheasant, buttery herbed potatoes, and yet another pot of tea, this one made of china with delicate pink roses.

"Oh, good heavens, Mrs. Cleary," she moaned as her stomach rumbled its approval. "I think I adore you."

The cheerful housekeeper gave her a rosy-cheeked grin. "'Tis truly our pleasure to see to your comfort, my lady."

Annabelle couldn't help herself. She plucked up one of the soft griddle cakes and took a bite. Dear. Sweet. Heaven. Another groan. She closed her eyes and savored the funny little nooks and crannies, the buttery-sweet burst of warmed honey on her tongue. She took her time swallowing, but as soon as she did, she wanted answers. "How did you know?" she asked, collapsing into the chair beside the small, marble-topped table. "Crumpets are my favorite. Butter and honey. Always with butter and honey." She waved to the tray and laughed. "And bacon! Sweet and salt—perfection. How did you guess?"

The housekeeper chuckled. "No need for guessing, my lady. Mr. Conrad sent one of the lads to the kitchens as soon as you reached Rivermore. He was most specific."

Robert had done this? She took another bite and shook her head. How had he remembered? It had been so many years since she'd even mentioned crumpets, let alone precisely how much she loved them with butter and honey and a side of bacon. Even the teapot with the little roses was perfect.

Her chewing slowed. She swallowed hard. Sweet crumpet

stuck in her throat, so she took a sip of tea. Steeped just the way she liked it, of course. Not too strong, no hint of bitterness.

Perfect.

Breaths quickened. Heart pounded.

She shivered and leaned forward to set the half-eaten crumpet on the plate.

He'd noticed much more than she'd realized. Remembered details she'd nearly forgotten, herself. The way she liked her potatoes, for instance. Her favorite color—pink. That was the color of the rosebuds in the little china vase. Pink.

She glanced down at the gown she'd assumed had belonged to a maid or even to Mrs. Cleary. As simple as a chemise, it had long sleeves and a high waist. It caressed her bosom lovingly, even without her stays. The skirt swept without ornamentation to her toes. The gown was beautifully made. And it was ... pink. Soft, pink silk. A housekeeper wouldn't own such a fine garment.

"Mrs. Cleary?"

The housekeeper and three maids were busy cleaning up after her bath. "Yes, my lady?"

"Where—where did this gown come from?"

"From London, I presume. Mr. Conrad brought it with him." Mrs. Cleary murmured something to the maids and sent them on their way before turning to Annabelle with a puzzled smile. "I thought it must be yours. It fits so—"

"Perfectly." The word was soft on Annabelle's lips.

"Well, yes."

A short while later, after the footmen had hauled the tub away and Mrs. Cleary had encouraged her to ring if she needed anything else, Annabelle sat alone in the southwest chamber of Rivermore Abbey, full of crumpets, bacon, and turmoil. Slowly, she walked around the marble-topped table with its tray of perfection. She wandered to the bed with its bounteous feather mattress, satin-woven ticking, and layers of fine linens. The coverlet was rose damask. The bed curtains were a darker shade of the same silk with pink-striped, white cotton facings.

She ran fingertips over the fine, whorled leaves in the damask. Then she wandered to the spot near two diamond-paned windows, where she'd looked out upon the damp gardens earlier. Here, a pretty, marble-topped dressing table sat with its oval mirror and eight small drawers.

"Perfect," she whispered.

Why *perfect* should result in such panic, she could not say. But that was how she felt. Her skin was hot, and not from the bath. Her heart kicked faster and faster. Her chest was tight, too constricting to draw a full breath.

She looked at herself in the oval mirror. Mrs. Cleary had helped her plait her hair over one shoulder. Her cheeks were flushed, her lips oddly plump. She licked them and tasted honey and butter, smoke and salt. She noted her breasts beneath the pink silk. Her nipples were swollen and jutting. As if the silk itself excited them.

As if perfection were more arousing than a kiss.

Beyond the windows, she heard masculine voices. One was deep and made her eyes drift closed on a sigh. The other she barely heard. Drifting to the glass, she looked down and saw Robert speaking with Mr. Colby and a young, light-haired man, likely a groom, given his plain clothing. The sun was setting behind turbulent clouds, casting the gardens in shades of purple and gray.

Carefully, she unlatched the window and pushed it open.

"... oats once per day. Any more, and he'll make a pig of himself. Colby, has the northernmost stall been repaired?"

"Aye, sir. Last month."

"Good. We'll need it when the travel coach arrives tomorrow afternoon." Robert, whose hair was damp from a recent bath, turned to the young groom. "Take the cart to Clumberwood Manor at first light. The items should be ready for transport when you arrive. I want everything here by seven, understand? No later. The wedding is at nine."

"Yes, Mr. Conrad. Shall I send Billy to retrieve the vicar, as well?"

"No. The vicar's been informed. Colby, Lady Annabelle will require a mount of her own soon. A mare, I think. Gentle but with good speed. And not too old. Methuselah gave her some trouble on the ride here. I don't want my wife stuck in the middle of a road whilst her mount amuses himself with a doze and a spot of mischief."

Colby grunted. "The old ones do enjoy their wily tricks from time to time."

Robert's lips quirked. "Indeed." He sent the men on their way, but he lingered on the gravel path near a stone bench. His free hand first rubbed his neck, then braced on the back of the bench. He seemed tense. Restless.

From her vantage point, she could only see his profile. Thick, damp hair. Wide, wide shoulders. Tapered waist. He wore a shirt and waistcoat with his buff breeches and boots. Her fingertips traced the faint swirls in the glass while she absorbed heat generated by the sight, the sound, the very idea of Robert.

For, he *was* an idea. One she'd had forever. Her knight. Her love. The boy who never failed her.

God, her heart was pounding. Because he wasn't an idea any longer. He was a man. One with tired eyes and rolled-up sleeves. One who needed sleep and frequent hair trimmings. One with thick thighs and a leg that always pained him after a ride. One who gave orders and expected them to be followed.

He'd survived everything she'd done to him. The endless chasing. The relentless letters. The accident.

Her eyes squeezed closed. How could he remember something as tiny and forgettable as crumpets with butter and honey? How could he not hate her too much to give her a gown of perfect pink silk?

"Annabelle." The word was thick, gritted from below. But it opened her eyes.

There he stood. Her man, riveted upon her. Brooding blue was shaded violet by the waning light, but he looked ... ravenous.

And for the first time in her life, she was afraid of him, of what he might do to her heart. Why in blazes had she agreed to *marry* him? She'd have no protection, no one to rescue her from her foolishness. No barrier left, not even the gloss of girlish adoration.

He was real. A man. He could be hurt again. He could hurt *her* again.

Oh, dear God. What had she done?

She slammed the window closed and stumbled backward. Her heart raced so hard, she thought it might break loose of its moorings. Clutching handfuls of pink silk, she backed up until her backside collided with the bed.

The panic grew worse moment by moment as she contemplated how very much Robert was a real man and not an idea. The moment felt familiar.

Similar to another moment of panic seven years earlier in a tangle of thorns and leaves on the banks of the River Tisenby. When she'd realized that he could die.

These things should not be revelations, and in one sense, they were obvious. Of course he was real. Of course he could die.

But her heart—the one that had recognized him as hers from the first—only understood the connection, golden and pure and unbreakable. Not harsh realities of pain and risk and foolish words spoken in haste. The man in the garden was not a god, nor even a knight.

He could fall, crack his bones, acquire some dread illness. He could turn bitter or cruel. He could stop laughing at her jests, stop inviting her to do silly things like ride upon his back so she didn't muddy her hems. He could stop caring that her favorite color was pink.

He could deal her a deathblow. All he had to do was fail to love her.

A commanding knock made her jump and squeak. Breathing through the panic, she shook her head at her own foolishness. He was in the garden, for pity's sake. A man with a cane could not race up stairs that quickly. This was probably Mrs. Cleary, who'd probably forgotten some small thing, and Annabelle was probably an absolute ninny who should probably open the door.

She smoothed the silk over her hips and called, "Coming."

But by the time she'd spoken, the door was already opening.

And Robert Conrad—the real, fallible, ridiculously-broad-shouldered man—was charging into her bedchamber. Locking the door. Coming toward her with a look that made her tingle like a hot bath after a cold ride.

Moments before he tossed his cane aside and his lips captured hers, he growled words she scarcely understood. They resounded like battle drums.

"No more waiting."

Chapter Eighteen

"As a virtue, patience leaves much to be desired. It is useful when waiting for fruit to ripen. Otherwise, it serves as an excuse for inaction when more decisive measures are needed. Boldness wins the day. Patience only makes it duller."

—THE DOWAGER MARCHIONESS OF WALLINGHAM in a letter to the Marquis of Mortlock on the merits of skillful timing while meddling in the affairs of one's offspring.

Dearest Robert,
Well, I delayed as long as possible, but now Mama has declared I shall make my debut this season. Papa has agreed. Jane was elated, thinking she might wait until next year for her debut. Alas, Mama and Papa insist we must share seasons, as the budget requires it.

Now, I am tasked with finding a husband who is not you. I think it would be easier to fly.

Ever yours,
Annabelle

—Letter to Robert Conrad dated February 11, 1815

"WAIT." SHE PANTED THE WORD WHILE LYING ON A FEATHER mattress beneath a hard, heavy, heated Robert Conrad. Upon entering the bedchamber like a charging bull, he'd kissed the breath out of her, tossed his cane across the floor, then tipped her onto her back before she'd so much as spoken his name. Now, squished beneath his body, she cupped his jaw in both hands. "Wait, wait, wait."

His lips trailed to the pulse in her throat. "Bloody hell, Annabelle," he rasped. "Haven't I waited long enough?"

"The wedding is tomorrow."

"I want you now."

She squeaked when his big, warm hand slid to her breast. She felt naked with only pink silk between them. Her nipple had no such qualms, peaking and zinging as his palm squeezed and his thumb stroked.

"God, you're soft, love."

"Robert."

He nibbled her neck, stroked her breast. Nibble, stroke. Nibble, squeeze. Nibble, press.

"Robert!"

Grunting, he propped himself above her. "What?" Almost-black hair fell across a furrowed forehead. Brooding blue was a thunderstorm.

"What is happening?"

He blinked. Frowned deeper. "What do you think is happening?"

"You are lying on top of me."

"Right."

"And kissing me."

He looked at his hand, still covering her breast. "Among other things."

She wriggled to free herself.

He groaned. The thick, hard, lengthy ridge pressing rather insistently against her thighs grew thicker, harder, and lengthier. "Stop moving."

"We need to discuss this."

"Devil take it, Annabelle. Stop. Moving."

She went still. "Did I hurt you?"

His breaths were slow. Deep. Deliberate. "In a manner of speaking." His eyes finally opened. They were a cauldron, the blue nearly swallowed by black. "It hurts to look at you. Hurts to touch your skin. You smell like summer. Did I ever tell you that?"

The way he was looking at her slowed time to a trickle. Heat swelled to a blaze. She whispered his name.

"Earlier, you said you wanted me," he murmured.

"And you said I had poor timing."

"Because I need to be inside you. And I couldn't very well take you in the middle of a muddy road."

Another flare of heat flashed from her scalp to her breasts. She felt his words pulsing through her skin. "So you ... you wanted me, too."

For a moment, he appeared genuinely perplexed. Then frustrated. Then resolute. Without a word, he repositioned himself so he could grasp her thigh, pulling her leg up alongside his hip. He did the same with her other leg, ignoring her gasps and the way she dug her fingertips into his shoulders.

"Feel that?" He ground his hips into her, stroking hard so she could not possibly fail to *feel that*. It was as flagrant as a lone oak in a barren field.

Her cheeks went hot. So did everything else. She nodded, swallowing against a dry throat.

"That's been with me since the Gattingford ball."

"Is—is it ... painful?"

"Yes." He imbued the single word with towering intensity.

"And we must ... in order to ..."

"Yes."

"Oh."

They breathed together for a moment before he sighed. "Blast." His eyes flickered to her bosom. "Reassurance."

"Pardon?"

"Grandfather said perhaps you need reassurance."

A small smile curved her lips at his disgruntled expression. "He wasn't wrong."

"Bloody hell. I—bloody hell."

"You said that already."

"Give me a mission to complete. A job to do. I'll carry you for miles. Buy you a better saddle. Fetch you flowers to decorate the chapel." His head dropped until their foreheads touched. "But I've never been good with words, let alone reassurances. You know that. You know *me*."

She did know him. She examined his consternated brow, his tight, flushed features, his molten eyes. Cautiously, she swept her hands across his shoulders, measuring their width. Everything in the past few hours had happened so quickly, she'd felt the ground beneath her quaking into a different shape.

Her hands explored his muscles, so large and hard beneath the linen of his shirt. She wanted to see him naked. She wanted to brush his skin with her lips. Apparently, he wanted her, too.

She'd realized that weeks ago, of course. The signs had been clear—passionate kisses, hardness, urgency. But did he want her the way she wanted him? Or was this merely the normal needs of a normal male who had gone too long without female companionship?

She traced the strained cords of his thick, strong neck before trailing curious fingertips down to his collarbone. Then, without meaning to, she spoke aloud thoughts that should have stayed buried where they belonged—inside her head.

"This was broken, too."

A wave caught her unawares. Surged upward as she traced warm, tough skin over bones that had been shattered. Because of her.

Oh, God. Suddenly, she was dangling in midair. Below her were jagged rocks and rushing water. Above her were leaves and sky, a frantic boy trying to save her, a narrow bridge with moss-covered stones. Next, she was staring down at her heart lying fractured and still and bleeding.

Like a demon loosed from hell, nightmarish memories surged out of darkness to strangle her. Everything hurt. Her chest. Her eyes. Her skin. Every part of her remembered, and every part felt torn open.

She heard a gasp. Keening. Felt trickles from her eyes flowing down her temples. Nothing seemed real. She couldn't stop the words.

"How I want to kill that day," she mourned through gritted teeth. "Tear it from existence like a horrifying page from a sketchbook. I want to burn it to ashes. How I wish I could." Her throat closed, tight and burning. She shook and shook. Lost in a memory she rarely allowed to surface, she raised up to kiss the spot at the base of his throat, where his bone had cracked. Though it had been years since the injury, she took the greatest care, giving his skin a trembling brush.

His hand scooped beneath her neck. Suddenly, he reversed

their positions so she straddled his lap. Then, he sat up on the bed, powerful arms banding her tightly against him. "It was not your fault, Bumblebee."

She squeezed her eyes shut and wrapped her arms around his neck. Buried her face against linen and whiskery skin. Words formed a lump in her chest. He was wrong. It was all her fault. If she hadn't followed him and John that day, he would not have been forced to save her. He would not have fallen and nearly died.

"Listen to me." The rumble of his growl resonated throughout her body. "None of it was your fault, do you hear? It was just a mad accident."

Kissing his skin over and over, she stifled a rising sob. "No," she moaned, her fingers digging into his nape. She could not get close enough. She held him tighter than she should, clung and squeezed to keep him with her. Keep him safe. "No."

He rocked her to and fro. Stroked her hair and held her tight. "I never blamed you, love. I know it seemed like I did. I am sorry for that. So sorry. I—I thought I was doing right. Nothing has ever hurt so badly."

She heard his words, but they made no sense. The memories had come to drown her. "No." The sound was low and raw. Mournful. Pain wanted out. "Noooo."

"God, love. Please believe me. Please forgive me." He continued rocking her. Back and forth. Back and forth. He kept stroking her hair, now somehow loosened from its plait. Stroke and breathe. Stroke and breathe.

"Robert." His name quavered, but she managed to squeeze it out through a swollen throat. "I cannot lose you again."

"You won't."

"You mustn't ever send me away."

"Never."

"Even when I do foolish things. Even when I vex you so much you want to toss me in the Tisenby, sketchbook and all."

He grunted. "I expect you to vex me. It is what Bumblebees do."

She squeezed his neck tighter. Turned her lips to whisper in his ear, "You mustn't ever fall or die, my dearest love. I shall have no choice but to follow you."

"Do not say that."

"It is true."

"Annabelle ..."

"I cannot lose you," she repeated. "I won't survive it again."

For a long while, he simply rocked them together until his heat and heartbeat and strength seeped into her, surrounded her like a fortress. Every breath filled her with the fresh-air scent of his skin. She held him and swayed. Back and forth. Back and forth. Back and forth.

Slowly, when the dark waters of memory receded and her cheek rested upon his shoulder, she smiled. "This is all the reassurance I require," she murmured. "Your arms around me. Your ... nearness."

His arms tightened. He turned his head and brushed her lips with his. "I'll give you anything. Everything you desire. You need only ask."

Her smile grew. She returned his kiss. Deepened it with a playful flicker of her tongue. "I thought you said you couldn't dance."

He frowned. "I can't."

She propelled their swaying to illustrate her point. "Then, why does this feel so much like dancing, Mr. Conrad?"

Blue eyes flared into a deep burn. Then, he gave her a slow, wicked grin she had never—*ever*—seen on Robert Conrad's face.

It made her melt into him like butter over a crumpet.

"This isn't dancing," he rumbled, licking those delicious lips. Big, possessive hands stroked up and down her spine, ending in a position at the top of her hips. There, he gripped firmly and ground her softest center against his hard staff. "As I said, love, if dancing is what you desire"—he began tugging at her skirt, pulling the silk up past her knees until warm, dry hands gripped her bare thighs—"you need only ask."

BY ALL RIGHTS, ROBERT'S ERECTION SHOULD HAVE FADED BY now. Earlier, his lustful fervor had been thwarted, though not ended, by Annabelle's strange remoteness. Annabelle was a passionate woman. She'd confused him with her lack of response. Then, she'd seemed to get sucked into a whirlpool of painful memories.

That had bloody well torn his heart out.

He could not allow his Bumblebee to hurt that way. The wrenching cries. The anguished regret. Never again. He'd sacrifice his three remaining limbs to prevent it.

The only thing he could think to do in the moment, however, had been to hold her fast, keeping as much contact between their bodies as possible. The closeness had soothed him, too. As she'd calmed, so had he. As her distress drained away, he'd simply absorbed everything about her. Summery scent. Lush curves covered in pink silk. Pearlescent skin. Gentle breaths and dainty fingers playing with his hair. In time, his cock had reacted as it always did whenever she was near. Or when he thought about her. Or when he woke from a dream about her. Or when he caught a scent similar to hers.

Bloody hell, perhaps this was madness.

And perhaps he didn't care.

Now, she pulled back to cup his jaw between her hands. A small, pink tongue darted out to wet her lips. "I've dreamt about dancing with you," she whispered, her cheeks blooming the sweetest shade of rose.

"Have you?" He found himself grinning wider.

She nodded.

"Are you certain you don't wish to wait until tomorrow?"

She shook her head.

Thank God. Of course, the question was largely rhetorical. With her straddling him as she was, all it would take was releasing his fall, and he'd be poised to slide inside her.

But that was deceptive. Because his wife—blast, his *intended* wife—was innocent and required special consideration.

Soft lips explored his neck. Slender arms gripped and clung. Bountiful breasts pressed and rubbed. "I long to see you naked," his siren whispered in his ear.

"Bloody hell, Annabelle."

Her laugh was husky. Wicked. "It's true."

He threaded a hand through the soft waves of her hair. Wrapping a length of the brown silk around his wrist, he cupped her nape and replied, "I must be mindful of your innocence, love. How am I to do that when you behave like a temptress?"

She pulled back. Gave him a fierce frown. "Am I not to enjoy this dance as well?"

"Yes. You are."

"Then, I should like to see you naked, Robert Conrad. Presently."

He sighed. "We don't want this dance to reach its crescendo too soon."

"Why not?"

"Trust me."

"No," she said with exaggerated patience. "Explain."

"It will hurt. When I take your virginity. The better you're prepared, the more pleasurable it will be. That takes time."

Her lips pursed. Her eyes narrowed. "I want to see you naked."

He dug his fingers into her hips while groaning his arousal.

"Every time you say the word 'naked,' I get harder."

Slowly, his siren grinned. Sweet brown eyes went both soft and mischievous. Soft, pink lips hovered within a breath of his. In fact, he felt damp breaths fall against his chin as she whispered, "Naked." A low, sensuous chuckle. "Naked, naked, naked."

Abruptly, he lay back on the bed and rolled over until she was tucked beneath him.

She first squeaked her surprise then started laughing. "Oh, heavens. Dancing, indeed." She laughed again, the sound like a balm in his ears.

He needed her laughter. Her grief earlier had wrecked him. Now, he propped on his elbows and stroked her cheeks with the backs of his fingers. "First, I will remove your gown."

She bit her lip and nodded, obviously not listening. Her hands were measuring his shoulders again.

"Then, I will make sure you're ready for me."

"Mmm-hmm."

"When that's done, I shall remove my—"

"Take your shirt off, Robert." She was tugging at the linen, pulling the hem from inside his breeches. "I want to see."

"Bloody hell, woman."

Again, she laughed, her eyes dancing.

He looked closer. She was aroused. He hadn't even touched her yet.

Blinking, he examined as much as he could see—mostly her eyes, which had darkened to black as the centers expanded. Her lids were half-lowered, her focus shifting in a circular route between his lips, neck, and shoulders. Rolling to one side, he eyed her breasts. Hard, needy nipples pouted inside pink silk.

He swallowed. "God."

"The way you look at me," she murmured. Her breaths quickened. Her hands tugged harder at his shirt. "It makes me burn."

Speech abandoned him. He pulled back enough to grasp the hem of her skirt and toss the silk northward. When her lower half was exposed, he stopped to gaze upon her.

White thighs, soft and curved. A thatch of brown hair. And hips—oh, God, her hips were heavenly. Diabolical. Designed to torment mere mortals like him. He groaned. Circled her waist with one arm. Slid her higher on the bed so that he could grip the backs of her knees and spread her wide.

She squeaked and clutched his hair.

He could scarcely breathe for her beauty. Pink folds glistened with arousal. Dark and lush and swollen with need, they welcomed his sliding fingers as he traced perfect lines. Danced alongside her most demanding center. Then, he let her pleasured moans lead him through his explorations. A sweet, honeyed glide. A slow, silken slide.

He bent and gave her his tongue, glorying in her shocked gasps, her trembling arch. She chanted his name. First, her voice was a query. Then it was a revelation, filled with wonder.

Sweet, womanly honeysuckle. Summer rain and pure intoxication. That was his Annabelle. He tasted her in long strokes. Slid a finger deep inside her channel, reveling in the virginal tightness, the demanding clenches of silken flesh.

By God, this would be his new obsession. Hips were merely the frame. This was his prize.

"... cannot ... bear much more. Oh, dear heaven, Robert." She arched upward.

He gripped her thigh and held her against his stroking, flickering tongue. He felt her pulses coiling higher. Saw her belly rippling. Heard her cries and wanted more.

More. God, more and more and more. Would it ever be enough? No. He'd always want more of her.

Her pleasure broke over him as she reached her climax, seizing around his finger, sobbing his name. Fingers gripped his hair as she writhed against the mattress. He kept at her.

Everything else disappeared—the room, the bed, the waning light. There was only his Annabelle. Pink and white. Wet and soft. An enchanting siren he could not resist.

He suckled the sweetest part of her, the swollen nub that fairly pulsed with her recent climax. Faintly, he heard her cries, felt her tugging his hair and clawing his shoulders. He knew she must be sensitized after coming so hard. But he couldn't stop. He wanted more.

He slid another finger inside, stretching her sheath as he drew upon her swollen nub. Hard shudders wracked her small frame. Slowly, he became aware of the desperation in her voice.

And the pain in his cock. Bloody hell. One stroke and he'd be done.

Soothing her thighs with gentle kneading, he gave her one last lap of his tongue then withdrew his fingers.

"Robert," she groaned, trembling badly.

"I'm going to remove your gown now, love." He scarcely sounded human. Nothing remained of his voice but an animalistic growl. Nevertheless, he stripped her of her gown by simply pulling the thing off over her head.

Then, another obsession began. Her breasts. Full and round and pearl-white. Tipped with berry-bright nipples that stood up and demanded his complete attention. How very Annabelle. He smiled and traced them with wet fingertips.

"Please," she sobbed. "Please."

He couldn't help himself. He cupped her. Kneaded her flesh until her breasts were even fuller, flushed pink with arousal and begging for his mouth. He gave her that, too, tasting the essence of his woman there.

How long precisely he'd been suckling her when his patience broke, he could not say. He knew she was arched and gasping. He knew she'd come again. He knew she'd torn the hem of his shirt trying to get the thing off him.

He stripped it in half a second. Another tick and he'd ripped his fall loose enough to grip his cock. Then, he splayed her wide, rolled fully between her thighs, and positioned himself to enter paradise.

That was when she cupped his jaw, and he felt some indefinable force compelling his gaze to meet hers. The force was golden. Pure. Inexorable.

Tears had streaked from her eyes at some point in the past few minutes. Ecstasy, he hoped. She was smiling up at him, but that was not what made his entire being light up like a sunrise filled with swans. No, it was the moment between them. A fusion of his soul with hers.

This was no mere coupling, no simple claim. It was a reknitting of something precious that had been torn asunder. They belonged to the same whole. She'd been born to bring him joy. He'd been born to keep her safe and happy.

He wanted to tell her, but as usual, he had no words for it. Instead, all he could do was kiss her. He worshipped her mouth, stroked her soft cheeks with his thumbs, paid homage to the woman who'd always been meant for him. Finally, he leaned his forehead against hers and whispered, "Now, Bumblebee. It must be now."

She nodded, wrapped her arms around his neck, raised her hips, and squeezed him with her thighs.

With that, he slid inside her tight, silken sheath in a swift stroke. Gritting his teeth as he felt a brief resistance and heard her small gasp, he held still while she adjusted. As soon as he felt her relax, he went deep, driven by lust too long denied. She bit her lip and clutched at him, but she was slick and wet, welcoming his thrusts even as he drove harder than he should. Deeper and stronger. Over and over. Pounding at a mad pace.

Before long, a miracle happened. That golden thread between them began to glow. And she began to tighten. To squeeze. To ripple. And then to shout. Her little fist landed on his shoulder then pounded onto the bed. Her hips frantically sought his, as though she needed more.

More of him. More of them. More of the luminous bond that seemed to be stoking them both.

Three strokes before he detonated, her back arched high and his siren sang a song formed of his name and pleas to God for mercy. She came around him, gripped him so hard, he instantly followed her, filled her sweet body with an explosion as fierce as his love for her. Inchoate sounds burst from his chest as he held her. Kissed her. Thrust deep inside her rippling sheath and felt the wonder of that golden thread, now a golden cord, pulsing with power.

Luminous waves of it washed over him in the aftermath. He lay with his head upon her splendid breasts, reveling in the simple knowledge that she was his. His hands could not stop roaming across her skin. He stroked her hips and her waist, her arms and thighs. She did likewise, her fingers trailing to every part of him she could reach.

When she spoke, her voice was frayed. "For a man with a cane, Mr. Conrad, I daresay you are a masterful dancer."

Perhaps his laughter was louder than it should be. But he could not help it. No one had ever made him laugh like this. No one made him happier than his Bumblebee. And she was finally his again. Finally back where she belonged.

Chapter Nineteen

"In the end, vows are promises. Promises may be kept or cast into the refuse pile. Marriage initiates at the altar, to be sure, but the choice to sustain it is made every day of one's married life. And, for some of us, every day thereafter."

—THE DOWAGER MARCHIONESS OF WALLINGHAM in a letter to the Marquis of Mortlock answering his kind admiration of her character and regrets for opportunities left unexplored.

Dearest Robert,
John says I must cease writing these letters, as they can do no good.
How can I stop when they are my only connection to you?

And how pitiful must I be to keep on with them, knowing you will never read a word?

Ever yours,
Annabelle

—Letter to Robert Conrad dated May 25, 1815

LEAVING ANNABELLE'S BED JUST BEFORE DAWN WAS DOWNRIGHT painful, and not merely because he'd overworked his bad leg the previous day. He didn't want to stop touching her. With her wrapped in his arms, he'd slept better than he'd done in years— or ever.

Throughout the night, she'd explored his body, marveling at this muscle or that trail of hair. She'd wept again after seeing his leg, and he'd held her and murmured assurances that he was grateful to have it, that the accident had been a fluke, and it was not her fault.

She'd gone silent after that, kissing his scars and plastering atop him like a protective blanket.

Their night together had healed a part of him that had been raw and starving. Now, he must marry her.

After dressing in his torn shirt, breeches, and waistcoat, he sat on the bed to don his boots. Behind him, he heard rustling bedclothes and a sweet little sigh. The sounds made him smile.

"Is it morning already?" his sleepy siren inquired.

"It's early yet."

"Must you go?"

"I must. It's better if no one finds me here."

A pause. "I become your wife today."

He finished pulling on his second boot and turned to look at her. She was beautiful. Lips swollen, cheeks blushing, hair a tangled mass. Beautiful. He leaned down to steal a kiss. "You became my wife last night. Today is a formality."

"Hmm. An important one, though."

"Yes."

She nibbled her lower lip. "Do you suppose—"

A knock sounded at the door. Robert frowned, wondering who in blazes would be visiting Annabelle's chamber before dawn—apart from him, of course.

"Sir? Mr. Conrad?" It was Benjamin's voice, hushed but insistent. What the devil?

Robert immediately searched for his cane, snatched it up, and winced as he limped to the door. "What?" he snapped upon cracking it open.

Benjamin looked red about the cheeks. "I beg your pardon, sir. You have a visitor. An *urgent* visitor."

"Who?"

"Lord Huxley."

His frown deepened. "You mean Lord Berne?"

"No, sir. His son, Lord Huxley."

Robert could only stare at his head footman in silence.

"Er—Lady Annabelle's brother," Benjamin clarified. "Viscount Huxley."

"I bloody well know who Huxley is. What I cannot understand is why he is in England when he is supposedly traipsing about the Continent."

"I am given to understand he arrived at his family's home some days ago and was alerted to your presence here by the note delivered to Clumberwood Manor last evening."

Robert rubbed his forehead and nodded. "Where have you stashed him?"

"The library, sir."

"Serve tea. Strong tea. I shall be down shortly."

As soon as he closed the door, Annabelle demanded to know what was happening. He debated whether to explain this new wrinkle, but he wished to deal with John first, to get a sense of whether he must fight yet another battle before being allowed to marry Annabelle. Given the earliness of John's visit, he suspected so.

He kissed her and told her to go back to sleep for an hour or two. "Some of your gowns should be delivered shortly after dawn, love. Until then, you should rest."

Her frown spoke of stubbornness. Suspicion. "Robert," she said in a warning tone. "You are hiding something."

"Yes. But I shan't worry you until there is something to worry about."

"But—"

He laid a final kiss upon her lips before slipping out the door.

Upon entering the library, he braced himself for what was clearly ahead. From the back, John Huxley appeared much the same—though his shoulders had widened and his hair was sun-streaked. But he still stood with the same hand propped on his hip, the same insouciant posture.

Except that today, tension tightened the other man's neck and filled the room with an air of foreboding.

"Hux," he greeted his friend. "This is ... unexpected."

Huxley turned. Hazel eyes burned with nothing short of wrath.

Bracing for imminent attack, Robert shoved the door closed behind him and advanced into the room. "We are to be married this morning."

"No, damn you." Hux stalked toward him, looking older, harder, and more bronzed than the last time Robert had seen him. "You'll do no such thing. You will deliver my sister to me, and I will take her home."

It was rare to see John Huxley this enraged. Ordinarily, he was a charmer, impossibly difficult to rile, even when sotted.

But this was about Annabelle. He was protective of all his sisters, but especially her. Especially after the accident.

"Your father and I already negotiated the settlements. Annabelle has consented. We've been betrothed for months—"

"I don't bloody care."

"Your family approves, Hux."

"Of *this?*" Huxley bristled as he gestured in the direction of the front drive. "Absconding with an innocent girl so she'll have no choice but you?"

Robert ran a hand through his hair. "You've been away a long time. Things ... changed between me and Annabelle."

"I'm certain they did. She's a woman now. Bit of lust added to the mix, no doubt." With long strides, Huxley approached, his every step snapping with ire. "I'll not allow it, Con. I'll not stand by and watch her be damaged again."

Preparing for battle, Robert automatically adjusted his stance so his good leg took the bulk of his weight. They hadn't had a physical confrontation in years, but he knew Hux's capabilities well enough to imagine neither of them would come out unscathed. "And I will not let her go," he said. "Not ever."

"That's a bloody big change from seven years ago."

"A lot has happened. When I sent her away—"

"You mean when you allowed a thirteen-year-old girl to carry a burden she had *no business carrying!*" Hux bellowed the final few words.

Robert felt them like blows. "I regret what I did. I believed it was necessary."

"Necessary." Disbelief colored Huxley's features. "You blamed her for your fall. You cut all ties with her. Had I been less of a pigheaded bastard, you'd have done the same to me."

"It appeared that way, yes."

Hux stared at him in silent incredulity.

"I never blamed her. Nor you. Persuading her to leave me behind was the only way to protect her."

Robert could see Hux was frustrated. The other man raked stiffened fingers through his hair, pacing back and forth with his hands stacked atop his head. He looked ready to throttle someone. Probably Robert.

Hux halted with his back turned. His hands came down to prop on his hips. Then he returned to where Robert stood, hazel eyes flashing with a grim light. "So, you lied. To her, to me, to our family."

"Yes."

"Do you have any idea how badly you wounded her?"

Robert gritted his teeth. Last night, when she'd wept in his arms, he'd been given a glimpse. Even that had torn him apart. "Yes."

"Wrong," Hux barked. "You know nothing because *you* didn't have to stand by and watch her break apart. How bloody convenient."

Robert waited for Hux to pace out his fury, waited for signs that his old friend had regained hold of his temper. Then, he attempted to explain his reasoning. "Remember the time she climbed the tree?"

Huxley, half-turned in the middle of the library carpet, cast him a dark glance. "The one by the old mill."

"Yes. She went chasing us after we'd warned her to stop."

A few seconds passed before Hux's expression eased. "Must have told her twenty times we'd take her fishing the next day if only she'd stay where she belonged. How long did she wait before following us?"

"A quarter hour, perhaps."

She'd watched them from the nursery window at Clumberwood. Then, like the determined little Bumblebee she was, she'd donned a pair of boots too large for her tiny feet and trailed after them.

Robert hated the rest of that memory. He'd hated her fear. Her pain.

"What is your point?" Huxley demanded.

"She nearly died. It was not the first time. It was not even rare."

The tree was near the river, its roots snaking down into the bank. Hux had shouted at her, calling her Anna-smell and trying to goad her into running home. Ever determined, ever undaunted, she'd continued climbing, sweet brown eyes turned upward toward Robert. Then, she'd slipped. Her brother had reached her first, scrambling down from his perch halfway up the giant beech. He'd risked his own neck to slide down the bank and retrieve his tiny sister from tangled roots before she was carried into the mill's giant wheel by the river's current.

"I was furious with you that day," Robert continued. "Do you remember why?"

"Because of the way I spoke to her."

"I hated to see her hurt. But you knew she *needed* to be afraid, Hux. She should have been, by God, but I was always ..." Robert ran a frustrated hand through his hair. Annabelle would admonish him for letting it grow too long again. "Protecting her. Far too much. I never let her feel a fraction of her own foolishness."

"Yet, in the end, you were the cause of her greatest pain."

For a moment, his head swam. It felt light and detached from his neck. "Not without a damned good reason."

"Which was?"

"Sparing her a life tending an invalid." For that, he'd wounded her. He'd wounded himself in the process, of course, but that didn't matter. He'd assumed she would change once he was no longer in her life.

She hadn't. Same Bumblebee. Same indomitable will.

"You saw me after the fall," Robert continued. "Mad, starving badgers are better company. More useful, too."

Hux drew close. They were nearly of a height, so his gaze met Robert's directly. "Do you love her?"

Robert felt his temper prickling his scalp. "Of course I love her."

"Do you? Because I recall you stopping me every time I tried to mention her in the last seven years. Perhaps you had your reasons. I'll grant you, I thought it defensible at the time. But not now. Not if you never blamed her for the accident."

"She was a young girl. It would have been senseless to blame her."

"Yet you let her believe you did. You let me believe it."

"Because she would never have stopped." Robert's fist clenched and twisted upon his cane. "Damn and blast, Hux, I thought you, of all people, might understand. She would have ruined herself trying to help me. I was a prisoner of my bedchamber for a year. She was thirteen. What do you suppose would have happened if I hadn't forced her away?"

Huxley's jaw flexed. "She would have plastered herself to your bedside."

"Yes." Robert glared at his friend. "A girl that age would not have realized how her mere presence in a young man's bedchamber would compromise her prospects in a few short years. And Annabelle? She would not have cared a whit. She would have dashed her reputation—indeed, her very life—to pieces on the rocks of *my* misfortune. You think saving her from the odd scraped knee or broken toe was worth wounding her feelings, yes?"

Huxley nodded.

"What was preserving her entire future worth?"

"That explains why you did it in the first place. Not why you refused to hear so much as her name spoken in your presence for seven years."

That he couldn't explain. Not without sounding mad. "It took everything I had to survive. I could not afford the distraction."

"Damn and blast, man. Do you understand nothing?" Huxley

shook his head. "No. No, I don't think you do. She turned herself into a gossip for you. Do you realize that?" He didn't bother to wait for a response before answering his own question. "Of course not! Because you never wondered what she got up to after you tossed her out on her backside. You never thought to ask whether Annabelle Huxley would simply give up and forget about you the way you did her."

Robert felt his chest tightening, his breathing grow faster and shorter. "No. That's not what—"

"She sought every piece of information she could glean about you. From me, from the vicar's wife, from old Mr. Parnell. Anybody who would share the slightest morsel, she'd turn them into one of her 'sources.' She did this for years, Con. *Years.*"

"She gossips because she enjoys—"

"It is a habit. Being cut from your life became intolerable, so she settled for scraps from the table."

Dark, cold fingers lengthened and seized his insides. They curled and dug with an icy grip. "What are you saying?"

For a moment, grief flashed across his old friend's brow. "I'm saying she loves you more than you love her. Always has."

Everything inside him rose up with a fierce battle cry. No. By God, *no*, that was not true. "She cannot love me more than I love her." He said it quietly, though he wanted to roar. "It's not bloody possible."

"No? She's spent her life cultivating her obsession. While you were here, tending your grandfather's estate and ignoring her existence, she was still following you. She never stopped."

His muscles froze. He felt both hot and cold at once. Like he'd been poisoned.

"My father may have consented to your betrothal, but I'd wager it is only because she hid all this from him and from my mother. Perhaps Jane knows, but the others?" Huxley shook his head. "I knew. Because I saw what you'd done to her. I'll not sit there in a chapel pew while she marries a man who loved her so little he was willing to crush her heart beneath his boot—"

Suddenly, his oldest friend's loosely tied cravat was wrapped inside Robert's fist. Their noses were inches apart. "Try to take her from me. Try it. See what happens."

"Stop." The reedy, feminine voice came from behind him. It sounded choked.

He released Huxley and turned. His heart fell into an abyss.

Paper-white cheeks were streaked with tears. She'd wadded pink silk into clenched fists. Her hair was haphazardly knotted atop her head. Her toes were bare beneath her hem.

"Bumblebee," he murmured.

"Don't call me that. Please." She didn't seem angry. Only sad.

"God, none of it is true, love."

She held up a hand then cupped it over her eyes. Her chest shuddered for several seconds before she lowered her hand to her mouth. "John," she mumbled behind her fingers. Her eyes glossed with fresh tears.

Huxley sidestepped Robert and rushed to her, wrapping his arms around his sister as she hugged his neck. The siblings held one another for a moment before Hux drew back. She sniffed and patted his shoulders with affection.

"Why did you not say you were coming home?" She smiled through her tears. "Mama will be over the moon." She patted his cheek. "So long as you haven't married a Spaniard."

For the first time since Robert had entered the library, Hux grinned. "They are a handsome people. Alas, no bride. Only me."

Her smile trembled. "You are more than enough." She embraced him again before asking, "Now, would you be a darling brother and give Robert and me a moment alone?"

"Annabelle, he is—"

"Please."

After a long hesitation and a longer glare at Robert, Huxley nodded and kissed her cheek before leaving the library.

In the silence that followed, dread filled Robert's veins until he wanted to howl.

Annabelle stood there in her pink gown, lips downturned as though she teetered on the edge of weeping. She stared down at her hands, which could not seem to decide where they wished to settle.

"What he said," Robert began when he could breathe. "You must know it was wrong."

"No. Unpleasant. But not wrong."

"I love you. I have always loved you."

She raised her eyes to his. Her quiet anguish knocked him flat. "But not as much as I love you. Never that much."

"You don't know ... you cannot comprehend—"

"I've always known." The tremulous smile returned as tears spilled over. "I've taken whatever you gave as the gift that it was." She pressed a hand flat over her heart. "But here? I've always known we stood on uneven ground."

"Annabelle."

"I want you more. I love you more." She chuckled. "To an unwholesome degree, some might say. Like a daft sickness. Be grateful you haven't been infected, too. I chased you so blindly it drove you off a bridge. Heaven knows what might have happened if you felt as I do in equal measure. We'd probably both be dead."

Anger flooded in on a boiling tide. Seethed and churned. Opened a door he'd kept locked. The vicious instinct to seize and claim surged forth unbound. It propelled him closer. "A few months in my bed, and you'll realize how very wrong you are. Until then, mark me well, Bumblebee. If you think to escape this marriage, think again." He moved within an inch of her and lowered his head. "The moment you agreed to be mine, it was far too late for both of us."

EMPTY AND ACHING, ANNABELLE GAZED UP AT A MAN WHO utterly confused her. She'd known him forever, seen him stubborn and disagreeable, laughing and content, brooding and vexed. Yet this particular expression—possessive rage, focused and primitive—was as foreign as watching him don Roman robes and dance around a bonfire. It simply did not happen. Yet, here he was. Not a valiant knight content to win her favor, but a warlord set to sack her village and claim her as his battle prize.

When she'd followed him here to the library, she'd been curious. Then, she'd heard her brother's voice through the door. Elated, she'd nearly opened it, but John's angry shouting had stopped her. And, as she'd listened to her brother speak the truth she'd always known, pain had pummeled her belly in a series of blows.

The previous night in Robert's arms had allowed her to fool herself again. Even now, she still felt him inside her. Smelled his fresh-air scent on her skin. Remembered the look in his eyes when he'd taken her. Brooding blue had been a wild tempest, demanding nothing less than her total surrender.

She'd given it gladly. In exchange, he'd ravished her with pleasure, and for a few sweet hours, she'd forgotten.

Now, despite his protestations, the truth had been spoken aloud. There was no denying it. Even John understood. "Robert, this …" She gestured between them. "This has already hurt us both so badly. Perhaps it is time to consider—"

His arm circled her waist, drew her tight against him. "No. You will hold to your promise." His lips breathed against hers. "Or I will tell everyone where I spent last night. John, your family. I will announce it to the bloody congregation."

Stricken, she pushed against his chest to gain some distance, but he refused her the barest inch. "I cannot believe you would stoop so low—"

"Believe it," he growled. "Think we traveled here alone together by chance?"

"You—you were concerned about my safety ... in a rush to leave London ..."

"I was in a rush to claim you."

Her skin began to heat. Her thighs began to soften. The places he'd touched last night tingled and swelled. The longer he stared at her, the worse her reaction became. "Why?" she wondered aloud. "We would have married in a month or so anyway."

He tilted his head, the posture deeply thrilling—or, rather, *intimidating*. Yes, intimidating was a better word. Not thrilling. Or enflaming. Or so compelling she wanted to lie down on the library floor and lift her pink silk gown for him.

"Because of this," he answered softly. "Your reaction. What's between us frightens you. For months, I've been worried you would withdraw. Obviously a sensible concern."

She jerked back. "Absurd. I've dreamt of marrying you since I was a girl."

"You wanted to marry your knight, love. Not me."

"No. I—I love you. I have forever."

A small smile curled his lips. Combined with his commanding air and possessive, flickering glance over her bosom and lips, he did, indeed, appear more warlord than knight. "Does that include this moment, Bumblebee? Now that you see what I am."

Silence fell as she considered his question. Did she even recognize this hard, ruthless man? The Robert she knew would not threaten to reveal what they'd done last night. He would not insist they dash off alone together like youths eloping to Gretna Green. And he would not be standing here now, looking at her this way.

The desperation was stark and raw. For the first time, she saw a mirror of her own feelings.

"What are you, then?" she whispered, more to herself than to him.

"*Uncivilized,* Grandfather calls it. The past few years haven't improved matters, I grant, but this is who I have always been."

Swallowing against a dry throat, she lifted a hand from where it rested on his chest and gently stroked that hard, familiar jaw. He hadn't shaved yet this morning. Dark whiskers chafed her fingertips. "We've hurt each other," she murmured.

He didn't answer, merely breathed against her wrist and held her waist between his hands.

"I don't know ..." She couldn't finish the whispered thought. Her head spun with warring love and longing and bewilderment. The world had just reordered itself, and she needed to catch her breath.

Her indecision seemed to ignite something dark inside him. His hands tightened. Gripped her waist like a rope. His voice dropped to a growl. "By God, Annabelle, you will marry me—"

She slid two fingers over his lips. "Shh. Be easy, my love."

His hands loosened, sliding down to cup her hips. He propped his forehead against hers.

She continued stroking his cheek, as it seemed to calm him. "John will not countenance a wedding today. He will want to take me back to Clumberwood."

He grunted, closed his eyes, and nuzzled his cheek into her hand.

Watching him, she smiled. A tiny glow of hope flickered to life. When he clasped her hand and kissed her inner wrist, that glow surrounded her heart. Perhaps he did not love her as much as she loved him. But that did not mean he didn't love her enough.

Blue eyes opened. They stole her soul in a single, time-stopping moment. Love unfurled its wings inside the cage of her ribs, awakened by everything she saw in him—desperate longing, deep need, strength, tenderness.

She held his jaw with her hands. Stroked his lips with her thumbs. Stood on her toes to kiss him. "All I ask is a bit more time."

Scowling, he shook his head. "No."

"Listen to me."

"I need you, Annabelle."

"And I you."

"I cannot wait any longer."

"Yes, you can."

He enfolded her in powerful arms and buried his face in her neck. "No."

She held him. Breathed him. Stroked his hair, already grown too long. Together, they swayed slowly to one side then the other.

"We're dancing again," she teased into his ear.

Releasing several deep breaths, he kissed her neck, her temple, her lips. "How long?" he demanded.

"Let's delay the wedding until my family arrives. That will give us a chance to ..." She grinned up at him with a deliberate twinkle. "... further our acquaintance."

He groaned.

"Meanwhile, John will come round to the idea of his best friend and his sister as man and wife."

"Think he will reconcile himself to it, do you?"

She raised a brow. "I am most persuasive when I wish to be. Besides, John is headstrong, but he hasn't the nature for sustained fury. When he realizes you are the only husband I will accept, he'll recover his good humor."

Robert's expression remained sober. "Do you believe I love you?" The question was hoarse.

She didn't know what he felt because, as it turned out, she'd never known *him* quite as well as she'd assumed.

Yet, she could not forget the crumpets, the honey and butter, the pink silk gown. She could not forget the way he'd held her, with such remorse and patience, or the way he'd touched her as though her pleasure was the only thing that would satisfy him.

Looking at the man now—unshaven face, overlong hair, desperate longing, and perennial frown—she believed he did love her in his way. Which allowed her to answer truthfully, "Well, I should hope so. Only a madman would go to such lengths to trap a woman he does not love into marriage."

Slowly—as slowly as the sun rising—a smile curved his lips, first tender then sensual. "Perhaps I want you for your fortune."

"Sadly, my fortune consists of a modest dowry and a vast collection of slippers. Papa has five daughters to launch, and I am merely the first. Budgets are confining."

Brooding blue eyes lightened further. "Perhaps I have lecherous intentions."

"Mmm, that sounds splendid."

His grin broadened. He chuckled, eyes dancing. "Or perhaps I intend to exploit your talent for caricature to profit myself whilst humiliating my enemies."

"A poor investment on your part. In Mr. Green's employ, I spent more on sketchbooks and slippers than I earned."

His frown returned. "Truly?"

"A bit of an exaggeration, but not by much."

"Bloody infuriating."

His low grumble made her heart light up. "You believe I am worth more, Robert Conrad?"

This time, his eyes glowed with intensity that made her wish the wedding were, indeed, this morning instead of a week or two away. "You are worth everything," he said. "Everything."

Chapter Twenty

"A common mistake, I daresay. A man in high dudgeon and a raving lunatic do bear a striking resemblance. However, the distinction is meaningless, for the remedy is the same—good brandy, sound sleep, and reassurances that nonsense is sanity."

—THE DOWAGER MARCHIONESS OF WALLINGHAM in a letter to the Marquis of Mortlock regarding the value of wifely comfort in the prevention of madness.

Dearest Robert,
Attended the theatre with Jane and Maureen three nights ago.

Today, the pond was frozen. We went skating.

Outside my window, snow has started.

I miss you.

Ever yours,
Annabelle

—Letter to Robert Conrad dated December 24, 1815

THE MOMENT ANNABELLE SAW THE TWIN OAKS FLANKING THE drive to Clumberwood Manor, another dratted lump formed in her throat. Clumberwood was no palatial stone sprawl as some country houses were. In fact, one might be forgiven for thinking it an overgrown cottage, with its three black-and-white, timber-framed stories; five steep gables; countless diamond-paned windows with old, rippled glass; and an ivy-covered brick wing that was at least a hundred years newer than the rest.

The house nestled on a gentle knoll above a too-small fish pond containing no fish whatsoever but, rather, an overabundance of frogs. Surrounding the pond were two clusters of birch trees. Maureen had thrown a rare tantrum to save them from Papa's ax. Down a long, gradual slope sat the coach house, a crooked, pint-sized version of the manor house with whimsical framing that Annabelle fancied as bright, orderly stars. Nearby was a brick stable, which Papa had reconstructed when Annabelle was seven so she could have a pony. Ivy covered that, too.

Heavens, how she'd missed this place.

"You're not going to weep, are you?"

Deliberately, she let her lower lip quiver and pressed the

back of her wrist to her forehead. "Oh, John," she mocked. "Have you any smelling salts? I feel a swoon coming on."

Her brother snorted, rolled his eyes, and urged the horses pulling the curricle a bit faster. "Mama will be the one swooning once she realizes the scandals you've been courting, little sister."

She ignored his aggravating observation in favor of reminiscing. "Do you remember when we would sledge down the hill to the coach house?"

John chuckled. "You loved it so much, you wanted me to pull you about even when we hadn't a flake of snow."

"That was Genie."

"No, that was you. The Christmas before you broke your toe."

A memory tugged. "Oh. Perhaps you are right."

"Sisters," he grumbled. "Nothing but trouble." His tone was teasing, his manner charming as always. John could charm the moon from the sky, she'd often thought. But then she glanced at his hands. One held the reins. The other fisted upon his knee.

Her heart squeezed. Not knowing what to say to ease his mind, she patted his arm. "I'm glad you are home, John."

He cast her a glance, hazel eyes both twinkling and turbulent. "As am I."

Less than an hour later, Annabelle stood in her bedchamber trying to decide which of her second-best gowns she should wear while attempting to coax her overprotective brother to see reason. She was torn between a blue muslin frock with uneven tucks along the sleeves, and a pretty green cambric gown with a faintly stained hem.

Fanny, one of the few chambermaids left behind at Clumberwood during the season, flitted around the lilac-draped room opening windows and gathering up garments. "Begging your pardon, my lady. What would you have me do with this?"

Annabelle turned. Fanny held the pink silk gown.

Slowly smiling until her cheeks warmed with memories, her

breath caught as a new vision replaced the old—there would be the light through the chapel windows, of course. Ivy and orange blossoms. A bit of lace for her hair. And now, this. Pink silk. Perfection.

"A proper cleaning should do. But have a care. This shall be my wedding gown."

After washing, dressing in the green gown, pinning her hair into a semblance of order, and having a spot of tea, Annabelle went in search of her brother. She found him in an unlikely place—the herb garden outside the kitchen. John was in his shirtsleeves, bent over a bed of rosemary. He held a sprig to his nose.

"Good heavens, John. Gardening? What have the Athenians and Spaniards done to you?"

He shot her a wickedly charming grin over his shoulder. "That is hardly a subject for your ears."

"Hmm. These ears might surprise you. I shall be a wife soon, you know."

His grin died. His jaw flexed. He stood and planted his hands on his hips. "Not Robert's wife. Not after what he's done."

She sighed and picked her way past fragrant thyme and lavender that should have already bloomed. "Yes. Robert's wife."

"I forbid it."

Moving to stand beside him, she looped her arm through his and squeezed. "Whether you do or not, the wedding will happen."

He looked away, his lips tight. "Have you forgotten so easily, Annabelle? Because I have not."

She swallowed a lump and rested her head on his upper arm. "No. I remember everything. Including how many times you defended me to him. You nearly lost your friendship over it."

A damp breeze came up and ruffled John's hair. It was lighter than when he'd left, now the color of Maureen's—brown streaked with gold. He gazed out toward the woodlands on the eastern horizon, hazel eyes both angry and sad. "Should have done," he murmured. "Should have thrashed the stubborn cur."

"It would not have solved anything. He thought he was doing right." She ignored the ache in her chest. "Who knows? Perhaps he was."

"There were other ways—"

"Were there? I've never been particularly biddable."

He fell silent as the breeze picked up and carried the scent of rosemary to her nose. He tossed the sprig back into the garden bed.

"In any event," she continued, "he realized his error weeks ago and has since gone to great lengths to convey his regret."

John looked at her askance. "Regret. Is that what this is about? He thinks to make amends by *trapping* you in leg shackles—"

"No. Nothing like that." Unbidden, a smile came to her lips. If there was one thing she knew, it was that Robert was not marrying her as compensation. He did want her. He did love her. Their connection was deep and complicated by many factors—mistakes, unruly impulses, regrets, and wounds that had been disguised rather than healed. Beyond that, she only knew one thing: She loved him. The whole man, both knight and warlord, gentleman and conqueror. She loved the friend he'd been to her as a child. She loved the man he'd become before the accident—the one who revered his grandfather and caught fish with his hands. More than anything, she loved the man he'd become since then. Harder, quieter. Stronger. She even loved the ruthless parts.

"God, Annabelle. Don't go weepy on me."

She blinked. Sniffed. Felt her cheek and found it wet. She hadn't realized tears had spilled. "Not to worry. This is happiness, John. Truly."

"Odd sort of happiness. Can't you laugh instead?" Her brother rolled his shoulders.

"Apologies."

"He made you cry before. He cut you in half."

Yes, he had. And knowing how easily he could do it again was a vulnerability she must live with, for she could not live without him. She simply could not. "I wasn't blameless, you know."

"You were a girl. You had trouble controlling your impulses. What he did was akin to hanging a child for eating too many peach tarts."

Wondering if she was making the right decision, she argued with herself for long seconds before saying quietly, "Look at me, John."

When he did, he was frowning.

"I am no longer a girl, am I?"

"Precisely my point. You're now a lady deserving of every care. A man should show you respect if he favors keeping his teeth in his head."

She bit down against her instinct to guard her secret, to keep her brother's good opinion of her intact. But she could not. John had been with her the day Robert had banished her. John alone had held the shattered pieces together.

John deserved to understand.

"I have something to confess." And with that, she explained about Edward Yarrow Aimes, about Mr. Green and the imposter, about Robert's efforts to protect her, once again, from the consequences of her decisions. When she finished her tale, her brother was pale beneath the bronze of his skin. He paced away from her and came back looking grim and tightly coiled.

"You took a grave risk, Annabelle," he rasped.

"Yes."

"Why?"

"Because I needed it. I needed to ... fill the emptiness with something I had created. Something clever and true." She glanced down at her hands, clasped over a white sash and green cambric. "Robert discovered what I was doing. He did everything in his power to protect me, just as he's always done. You may fault him for his tactics, John." She lifted her eyes to meet his. "But never doubt that he cares for me."

He didn't believe her. She could see it from the twist of his mouth, the narrowing of his eyes. "Very well, if you're so certain of him, let's go for a visit."

She frowned. "To Rivermore?"

"Tomorrow morning. You can wander about the chapel and plan the wedding decorations, if you like."

"What will you be doing?"

"Chatting with your paragon of protectiveness."

"Oh, for ..." She sighed. Rubbed her suddenly aching temples. "At least wait a few days for tempers to cool. Otherwise, this will end very badly."

John grinned. "For him, perhaps."

"I really think it best to remain here until—"

"Shall I go without you, then?"

She rolled her eyes. "As if I would stay behind even if you did."

"DEVIL TAKE IT," ROBERT GROWLED TO NO ONE IN PARTICULAR. His hammer had struck the fine nail with such force it bent in half and dented the oak board he'd just spent an hour smoothing with a rasp. He muttered a curse before pulling the nail and replacing it with another. This time, he controlled his temper enough to lightly tap it into place.

No small effort. After four days without Annabelle, he wanted to break things, not build them.

He glanced up when the door to Colby's workshop opened. A surprise sauntered inside. "Huxley," he muttered before turning back to his project. "What brings you here?"

Slow steps carried him deeper into the workshop's gloom.

"Brought you something." A small, flat, leather-covered box appeared on the workbench beside Robert's elbow.

"What is it?"

"Everything you missed."

Robert frowned at his old friend. Huxley looked weary, his usual polish missing. "I don't understand."

A small smile lifted one corner of Hux's mouth. "No. You never did." Huxley patted the box. "Perhaps now you will."

Robert set aside his hammer and folded his arms, turning to lean against the workbench. "I will marry Annabelle. She's already agreed the wedding will occur as soon as your family arrives."

"She told me."

"We will be brothers, Hux."

"We always were."

Clenching his teeth, Robert dropped his gaze to the leather box. "What's in it?"

"Letters."

His gut went cold. "I've already realized the pain I caused her."

Weary hazel eyes caught his. "Just read them. Call it a reassurance. I need to know you understand. I need to know I will never have cause to piece her back together again."

For a moment, Robert considered keeping quiet. He'd never been good with words, and articulating his feelings for Annabelle—particularly to her brother—was impossible on the best day. But John Huxley was also his best friend, the one who'd drawn him into the Huxley family in the first place. So, for his sake, Robert tried.

He leaned across the workbench and retrieved his cane. "Walk with me."

Hux nodded and followed him outside. The workshop was a small building connected along one side to the stables. Robert led the way past the yard then out beyond the gardens to a field several hundred yards away. As they topped a small rise, Robert halted and turned back toward Rivermore Abbey.

"Look there," Robert said. "What do you see?"

Hux shot him a questioning glance. "Is this a jest? As I've said for years, a pint of ale tells better jokes than you do, Con."

"Just tell me what you see."

Bracing his hands on his hips, Huxley scanned the vista before them. "A great pile."

"And?"

"Fences. Fields. Gardens. Woodlands."

"All in good condition, yes?"

"Exceptional. You've worked miracles with the place. If this is about your finances, I've little doubt you'll keep Annabelle quite comfortably—"

Robert shook his head. "Now you're the one who doesn't understand."

Hux's face hardened. "Then, explain."

"I wanted to die," he said. "The surgeon wanted to take my leg. But I wanted to die."

"Anybody would. You'd broken bones. You were in a lot of pain."

"No. Bodily pain was nothing. I'd lost the only thing that mattered, Hux. The only thing that made this life worth enduring."

Frowning, Hux's eyes sharpened upon him. "Annabelle?"

Robert nodded. "It wasn't ... like it is now, of course. But you'd have found it strange if you knew how much I loved her. She was my joy."

"Very well. You loved her." Hux glanced toward the abbey. "What has that to do with—"

"Grandfather knew. He knew what I'd given up. He knew why I was languishing."

"Con, I—"

"So, he gave me a job. I put everything I had into it. Every bit of care I would have given her."

For a long while, Huxley stared at him. Hazel eyes assessed and probed. Finally, he asked, "Why did you never let me mention her name?"

Robert swallowed before answering. "Hearing about her was torment. A reminder of what I'd lost."

Huxley lifted his hat and ran a hand through his hair. "You should have told me."

"Our connection was impossible to explain. Stronger than friendship. Too innocent to be infatuation. At least, until recently."

Hux held up a hand. "Let us not delve any further, hmm? I just finished breakfast."

Briefly, Robert smiled. "I need her, Hux." He took a deep breath and shifted his gaze to the woodlands beyond Rivermore. "Rest assured, I would sooner carve out my own heart than break hers."

"Well, you're right about one thing," Huxley replied. "I don't understand this mad connection the two of you share. But neither do I doubt it. Annabelle has spent the past four days filling my ears with similar sentiments. The nausea has yet to abate."

Robert chuckled and settled a hand on Hux's shoulder. "One day, you'll find a woman who makes madness a pleasure. When that day comes, I shall take great satisfaction in mocking your prior ignorance."

His friend released a disgusted grunt. "Good God, I pray you're wrong. I'm a wanderer, Con. All this deathless devotion twaddle sounds appalling."

As Robert started back toward the workshop, he reminded his friend, "You'll need an heir sooner or later."

"Later will do nicely."

They were halfway across the field when an insect buzzed loudly next to Robert's ear.

Ten yards ahead, mud flew upward.

Then, he heard the echoing crack.

"Down, Con! Get down!"

Easier said than done. Heart racing and blood boiling, he put all his weight on his left leg and dropped into a crouch. Forcing his right leg to bend, he turned in place. Huxley crouched a few feet away, scanning the woods behind them.

Robert cursed.

"Did you fail to pay your gamekeeper, perchance?" Huxley gritted.

"Colby is Rivermore's gamekeeper. And no."

"We've about twenty seconds before the devil finishes reloading. Assuming he doesn't have a second rifle." Hux clapped Robert's shoulder. "Ready?"

Robert nodded. "You go left. I'll go right."

"You always take the right."

"Favors my good leg."

"Bloody hell. Ten seconds." Hux picked up a fist-sized rock from the dirt and hurled it twenty feet away. Moments later, a thudding ping struck near the rock's landing spot. The shot resounded like thunder. The flash had come from just inside the tree line, behind a sizable boulder. "Now!"

Hux sprang to his feet and sprinted. Robert was slower, but his blood thrummed with power, driving him into a swift, staggered lope.

Had to reach the shooter.

Had to stop him.

Had to protect everything that was his.

The pain of pushing his leg too hard uphill was a distant flicker. All his senses sharpened upon the boulder behind which a craven killer hid. His boots dug into mud, ground into grass. His cane propelled him harder.

Huxley reached the trees first, but Robert wasn't far behind. Using the cover of trunks and underbrush, they closed in from right and left upon the shooter's position, searching for signs of a killer fleeing—or circling back upon them. As Robert neared the boulder, he braced his back against another tree and peered around, finding nothing but brambles and hawthorn. From behind a thick beech, Hux gave a shrill whistle. It was a signal. The shooter was gone. They were both panting when Robert rounded the boulder.

Hux crouched nearby, retrieving a scrap of cloth from the ground. "Patches."

Robert nodded. The remnants of firing what must be a Baker rifle, given the weapon's accuracy at two hundred yards, had flown several feet from the shooter's position. Deep footprints in the mud gouged the ground where the shooter had stood. He'd clearly used the boulder as a prop.

"We can safely rule out an accident, I think." Hux's tone was wry.

Robert gazed out from the shooter's vantage, noting how clear and wide was the view of where he and Hux had been. "My thoughts, as well."

"What do you want to do?"

Turning away from the open field to meet his friend's gaze, Robert's wrath boiled up and out, hardening inside his gut. Senses sharpened by his brush with death coalesced upon a single purpose. "I want to find him."

Satisfaction curled a corner of Hux's mouth. "Oh, yes."

"I want to kill him."

"Indeed."

"We'll need men."

Hux glanced around the wood. "An army of them if we're to search Rivermore's lands properly. Perhaps I should ride back to Clumberwood. We've a handful of footmen who might be useful—"

"Leave them there. But send word. They must guard Annabelle."

Hazel eyes met his. And there, shining gold and grim,

Robert saw something that stopped his heart cold.

"No," he whispered.

"She is here, Con."

"No."

"She came with me."

He went cold. Every piece and part. For the first time, fear iced his body until his teeth nearly chattered with it. "God Almighty. Where?"

"The chapel."

It wasn't fear that drove him to a dead sprint. Fear had flown like dross from a fired rifle. No, this was certainty.

He must get to her first. Nothing else mattered. Any other outcome was unthinkable.

He must get to her first. He forced his bad leg to move, endured distant agonies as bone and muscle warred against his will. Whatever it took—pain was nothing, she was everything.

He must get to her first. The field was gone, now, a span of several hundred yards passed in a haze of cold horror and hot urgency. The gardens were coming. The chapel was on the opposite end of the abbey, but it seemed miles away.

He must get to her first. All he knew. All that mattered.

Annabelle. His wife. His heart.

He must get to her first.

An hour earlier

AS ANNABELLE STOOD INSIDE THE OLD OAK DOORS OF THE ancient chapel, she breathed the scents of stone and wood and beeswax candles. For a moment, she closed her eyes and listened to the reverent hush.

This time of day, the chapel was empty. Slowly, she meandered up the center aisle, letting her fingers brush lightly along the backs of the pews. It was a small place, only seven rows on each side of the nave. But everything about it felt sacred—the timeworn stone beneath her feet, the ornate pulpit and lectern, the tapestry on the east wall. Most of all, the light. Even on a cloudy day, brilliant rainbow light shone through six stained-glass windows, casting walnut and beeswax and stone in magical hues from red to blue and back again.

Annabelle paused as she reached the front pew and gazed up at the altar. Here, she would marry Robert. Here, she would become a wife. His wife.

What once sparked uncertainty now filled her the same way light filled this chamber. Helplessly, she smiled. She could not wait to be his. The past four days had been both wondrous and agonizing. She'd missed him terribly. Ached for him. But as she'd attempted to persuade her brother to abandon his concerns over Robert's feelings for her, crucial realizations had solidified inside her own mind.

How unfair she'd been to Robert, thinking he did not love her as much as she loved him. Ridiculous, she'd realized. Robert might not show his love in precisely the same way, but he was a different person. He'd lost his mother before the age of six. He'd been raised by the gruff Lord Mortlock, not by affectionate parents. He was a man with a man's pride and protective instincts. And he was five years older. As Jane had observed, that age disparity had been far more significant before she'd grown to womanhood.

That he loved her as much as he did was a miracle.

She gazed up at the nearest window. It depicted a pastoral scene with a haloed shepherd carrying a lamb. Green, blue, and yellow glass transformed the light that landed on her blue muslin skirt. The next window was richer. Darker. It depicted one of the apostles, who had bronze and red in his robes.

Both windows were beautiful, but they were different.

She smiled, imagining her wedding. How real it all felt, now. She could almost smell the orange blossoms.

A cooling breeze rustled the curls at her nape just as she heard the chapel doors squeak open. She turned, and her smile grew. "My lord. How well you look today."

Mortlock did, indeed, appear better. He was not in good health, but his pallor was less, and sharpness had returned to his eyes. She'd wager Robert's presence had a great deal to do with the improvement.

She stood and moved to his side.

"Now, now, my dear," he grumbled. "No need to fuss over an old man."

"Nonsense." She braced his elbow and helped him to the front pew. Together, they sat, and she patted his arm. "It is splendid to have your company."

"Have you any word from your family?"

She nodded. "They'll arrive Friday next. I should like the wedding to be the following morning, if you are amenable."

An old hand patted hers. Blue eyes smiled. "You've more patience than my grandson. If he had his way, you'd be married this very hour."

"I've long thought of Robert as the patient one."

He huffed out a dry chuckle. "Ordinarily, yes. I once saw the boy stand in the middle of a brook for hours merely for the chance to catch a larger fish. Did you know he catches them with his hands?"

"Yes. He and my brother used to make a contest of it."

"Takes patience, to be sure. And that he has in abundance. But when it comes to you, the boy might as well be on fire, so acute is his urgency."

Speaking of fire, Annabelle's cheeks began to burn. "Are not all young men a bit ... eager in that regard?"

Mortlock shook his head. "No, no. Long before he saw you

as a woman, he had trouble with distances. 'Twas always so."

"Distances?"

Blue eyes focused on her. "Aye. Any distance from his Bumblebee was too far." He grunted. "Time, too. The longer it went on, the worse it was."

Perhaps Mortlock's age had addled his memory. As Annabelle recalled, Robert had often been glad to see her, but no happier than he'd been to see John or Mama and Papa. His grandfather made it sound as though he'd sought her company specifically—as though he'd needed her as much as she'd needed him. Which could not have been true unless he'd gone to great lengths to disguise it. No, Mortlock must be misremembering.

"I can see what you're thinking, my dear. But you're wrong." He tapped his temple. "Happens this is the one part of me that's still functional."

Puzzling at the contrast between her memories and Mortlock's, she considered the possibility that he was right. Robert had always been the stoic sort, even as a boy. One rarely knew what was going on behind those beautiful blue eyes—apart from brooding, of course.

She gave Mortlock a considering glance. "Let's suppose you are right."

"Hmmph. No supposing about it."

"That would mean after the accident, when he sent me away, he was ..." Her stomach dropped into her feet. Her hands went cold, and her chest went tight. "No."

"Yes."

She shook her head. "He—he would never have—"

"Not deliberately. But neither did he wish to fight."

She squeezed his arm. "But you made him fight. Please tell me you insisted."

"Aye. Gave him a role here at Rivermore. He took to it rather well."

"Yes. Yes, he did." The tightness in her chest began to ease.

She breathed through it, reminding herself Robert was strong and resilient. That both of them had endured. "I am mad for him, you know."

Mortlock released a graveled chuckle and slanted her a grin. "That much is plain, my dear."

"It's a bit ... frightening, sometimes. To know one's happiness is so very reliant upon another person. The thought of losing him again ..."

Silence fell between them. As trees rustled outside, rainbow light rippled and danced. Finally, Mortlock said, "Wind is a powerful force."

She blinked, wondering if perhaps it was time for his lordship's nap.

"It can madden the sea, turn water into an enemy. It can pull the strongest trees out by their roots. Ungoverned, wind may destroy what it touches." Mortlock gazed up at the tapestry while light danced across his features in shades of blue and green and yellow. "But if you build a proper ship with proper sails, that same wind will take you across oceans."

"I'm afraid I don't quite—"

He nodded toward the altar. "This is where you'll start building. The vessel is neither you nor Robert. It is a third thing. The most important thing." Old eyes met hers. "Construct your ship properly, and you'll not fear the wind but welcome it."

She blew out a breath and examined the altar, solid and plain. The tapestry, which depicted Conrad ancestors kneeling at the foot of the cross. Finally, the windows, one gentle and pastoral, the other vivid and strong. "You're saying our marriage must be built to carry both of us."

"Not just you. Your children, too." Mortlock shook his head. "No room for sacrificial claptrap when you're in the middle of the ocean, my dear. Every hand is needed. If decisions must be made, the ship is the thing."

Gently, he patted her hand. They sat for a time while she

mulled his words over in her mind. Her connection with Robert was powerful, and yes, it had the potential to do great harm. Her mistake had been failing to control her impulses. His had been sacrificing everything for her sake, including the connection itself. Both of them had let the winds whip them about willy-nilly, and heartbreak had been the result.

But they were both older now, and they could make different choices. Better ones. They could love one another just as passionately, yet this time, they would travel in the same vessel and chart their course together.

She and Robert *would* build a ship, she decided. A great, stout ship. One strong enough to carry a family, a legacy. Strong enough to survive whatever tumult came their way. She could imagine no better partner for such an endeavor than a man who'd decided to fight, even when he'd lost hope.

"So tell me, my dear," Mortlock said. "Any chance of Lady Wallingham attending your nuptials?"

She raised a brow at the old man's odd tone. "I expect so. Would that please you?"

His gleaming grin was his answer.

Just then, the chapel doors flew open, and Benjamin entered with two other footmen bracing a figure between them. The poor wretch's face was swollen and bruised, but though her head hung forward, she appeared conscious. Her skirts were sagging rags, her bodice torn scraps hastily knotted together. The only thing left of the filthy creature's modesty was a shawl.

A discolored, knitted shawl.

With a horrified chill, Annabelle recognized that shawl. She recognized light hair and dark brows. Her nape prickled. Her skin writhed.

The woman raised her chin.

Oh, dear God. "M-Mrs. Bickerstaff?"

Swollen eyes appeared shocked. Dazed.

Annabelle   rushed   forward   while   Benjamin   began

stammering explanations to Mortlock. Villagers had found the woman stumbling about in the woods south of Rivermore's lands. She'd begged for help, claiming a man had abducted her.

The villagers hadn't known what to do, so they'd brought her to Rivermore.

Slowly, Annabelle reached for the woman's hands. The nails were torn as though she'd fought with everything she had—and lost. "Mrs. Bickerstaff," Annabelle murmured softly. "Please tell me what happened to you."

The woman flinched away. Then blinked. Recognition flickered. She tried to speak, but her voice was a ragged whisper. "H-he found me."

"Who? Who found you?"

Mrs. Bickerstaff began swaying, her swollen eyes fluttering.

Annabelle looked to the footmen. "Help her sit."

As soon as Mrs. Bickerstaff was seated on the last pew, Annabelle heard Lord Mortlock ordering Benjamin to fetch Major Colby and organize a search. Annabelle sat next to the other woman and carefully caught her eye. "What can you tell me, Mrs. Bickerstaff? Do you know his name?"

The woman's poor, battered features contorted and a tear streaked through the grime on her cheek. "No. He were the one that killed Mr. Green. That much I know, for he bragged of it whilst he ..."

Her hands wrung at her skirts, the heels of her palms digging into her thighs repeatedly. Her shoulders shook beneath the shawl.

Annabelle leaned as close as she dared, for the poor woman flinched whenever anyone tried to touch her. "You are safe, now. Lord Mortlock is arranging to have the area searched. The black-hearted demon who did this will be found, and he will be punished." She did not doubt it. Robert would hear about this, and he would see justice done. Meanwhile, all Annabelle could do was offer small reassurances, small comforts. She dug her handkerchief from inside her sleeve and held it out on her palm.

"I am so very sorry this happened to you, Mrs. Bickerstaff."

The woman hesitated for long minutes. But, finally, she took the scrap of linen, inclining her head in thanks.

"Can you remember where you were when he abducted you?"

"Outside my rooms. I was set to leave London. The mail coach, as you advised. He bashed my head, I think. Next thing I know, I'm waking on the floor of a post-chaise. He kept me tied and gagged for two days."

"Where did he take you?"

"A cottage. In a wood. It were dark there. Smelled of rats."

Annabelle nodded, noting the woman hadn't yet used the handkerchief. Slowly, she moved her fingers closer, hovering so as not to cause alarm. "May I?"

Mrs. Bickerstaff glanced down at the handkerchief then at Annabelle's hands, and finally, Annabelle's face. "I—I wouldn't wish to soil it, miss."

Annabelle's heart cracked. Good heavens, she wanted to scream her fury at what that violent, miserable, black-hearted demon had done. But she could not. She could only take the scrap of cloth and dab lightly at Mrs. Bickerstaff's cheeks, the corners of her swollen lips, and a scratch along her forehead. "Do you remember anything else about him? What he looked like, or what others called him?"

The woman took a long time to answer, and when she did, her ravaged voice shook. "Not tall, nor short. H-hair were neither light nor dark. Had I seen him in Covent Garden, I'd have taken no notice." She swallowed hard as Annabelle gently wiped dirt and old blood from her chin. "As to what he were called, he only let me call him by one name."

Annabelle froze, lowered her hand, and held Mrs. Bickerstaff's red, swollen gaze. "What was that?"

"Captain," she replied. "He insisted I call him Captain."

Chapter Twenty-One

"Although many ladies admire a gentleman in uniform, this effect is markedly reversed when said gentleman is outsized by his epaulets. One cannot help wondering what else may prove underwhelming when measured against expectations."

—THE DOWAGER MARCHIONESS OF WALLINGHAM in a letter to the Marquis of Mortlock regarding the benefits of valor and the detriments of diminutive character.

Dearest Robert,
The second season promises to be a repetition of the first. For Jane's sake, I am making the best of things. My work for Mr. Green is diverting, and I've found some amusement in Society's entertainments.

Occasionally, I encounter gentlemen—kind or witty or handsome—
whom I find unobjectionable. Yet, invariably, I end a dance or
conversation hoping to turn round and discover you have appeared.
My suspicions have proved true, dearest Robert. For me, there is only
you.

Ever yours,
Annabelle

—Letter to Robert Conrad dated April 17, 1816

ANNABELLE'S HEART GALLOPED PAINFULLY IN HER CHEST.
Dear heaven, she hoped she was wrong.

Robert would kill him. He already hated the man with an
unreasoning fervor. And, if Green's murderer—the man who'd
savaged Mrs. Bickerstaff—was, indeed, Martin Standish, he
would certainly deserve death. But she wanted no taint upon
Robert for putting him down.

Unfortunately, she suspected she was not wrong. Too many
pieces fit too neatly. Standish's father owned a hunting lodge
south of Rivermore lands. The place was a dilapidated cottage
quite useless for hunting since Sir Harold had sold the
surrounding land to purchase Martin's commission.

Beggared by the Bickerstaff swindle, Sir Harold Standish's role
within polite society had gone from fool to outcast after Edward
Yarrow Aimes had suggested he'd been one of Bickerstaff's
partners. Martin hadn't taken kindly to his family's humiliation.

But, could he have murdered Mr. Green for it? She'd
dismissed the possibility early on because she'd spoken to him
at Lady Darnham's the night of the murder. He'd seemed exactly

the same—bland with a hint of pompous. He'd done his usual boasting about unlikely exploits, mentioned a play he intended to see, and stared at her blankly when she'd quipped about a well-known actor's beard falling off during King Lear's lamentations about his age. Apart from Standish's attire, he'd been the same man who'd danced attendance on Matilda Bentley at all the other ton functions he'd wheedled his way into. How could he have committed murder then blithely changed his coat and attended Lady Darnham's fete, no more bothered than if he'd spilled his tea?

She examined Mrs. Bickerstaff's hunched, shaking shoulders and bruised, bloodied face. There was her answer, she supposed. A man who could do this to a woman had no conscience.

"Mrs. Bickerstaff," she said gently. "Did the man say why he abducted you? Did he know about your work for Mr. Green?"

The woman nodded.

Annabelle dreaded the answer to her next question, but she had to know. "Did you—did you tell him about me?"

"Never," she rasped, a spark of defiance flashing. "Night he murdered Green, he returned to the *Informer's* office to gather what he could about Aimes. Saw a woman enter, but it were dark, so he didn't spy her face. I told him it were me."

For a moment, Annabelle couldn't speak. How much more had Mrs. Bickerstaff suffered while protecting Annabelle, whose name she didn't even know? "How did he find you?"

Shaking her head, the woman's gaze dulled and dropped. "Same as you, I expect. Said an actor told him where I lived."

"We must go," barked Mortlock's graveled voice from beside her. "Now, ladies. If you please."

Reminded that Lord Mortlock had also been Lieutenant Colonel Lord Mortlock, Annabelle nodded and helped Mrs. Bickerstaff to her feet. "We shall take you inside Rivermore Abbey, Mrs. Bickerstaff. We'll ensure you have something to eat and a place to wash up a bit."

The woman nodded, and together, the three of them made their way through the chapel doors. The breeze had picked up. It blew cool and damp across Annabelle's skin, giving her a shiver. Mortlock urged them out of the churchyard and toward the gardens that led to the abbey. He scanned their surroundings as they hobbled along a brick wall to where an iron gate stood open.

"The east entrance is closest," he said, his breathing labored. "Once inside, take her to Mrs. Cleary. I'll gather footmen and ..."

Annabelle had already passed through the open gate into the walled garden by the time she noticed Mortlock lagging. She glanced back. He'd braced a hand on the gate, his head craned forward as he peered out.

"My lord?" she called. "Are you well?"

When he didn't answer, she murmured to Mrs. Bickerstaff to continue on and wait for her at the opposite gate. Then, she rushed to Mortlock's side, bracing his elbow. His skin was ghostly, but his eyes were sharp, squinting toward the eastern fields.

"What is it?" she asked.

"Heard something," he muttered. "A shot."

Another chill rippled through her. "Are you certain?"

He glanced down at her. Yes, he was certain. These were the eyes of a warrior who'd seen battle, a commander of men. Their glittering hardness was familiar—she'd seen it in Robert frequently of late.

"We should go," she said, tugging his sleeve. "We'll be safe inside the abbey."

He nodded. They soon crossed the walled vegetable garden and, pausing to join Mrs. Bickerstaff, they passed through the gate into the abbey's orchard. Old apple, pear, and plum trees rooted in symmetrical rows across a vast field. Beyond the orchard was a wide lawn, then another small garden near the east entrance. As slowly as both Mrs. Bickerstaff and Lord Mortlock moved, the distance might as well miles.

Annabelle tightened her abdomen and tried not to think. But, though her feet kept moving forward, her mind had riveted upon one thought.

A shot. There had been a shot. Oh, God. Where was Robert? Was he safe? Had he heard it, too? Was he wounded? Bleeding?

She shook her head to cast off the ugly visions. No, she mustn't assume he was in danger, or she would lose her mind. She must reach safety, for that was what Robert would want her to do.

As they approached the last row of plum trees, Mrs. Bickerstaff stumbled to a halt. She was gasping. Lord Mortlock had gone gray.

"Just a bit farther," Annabelle assured them. "Can you make it?"

Lord Mortlock grunted and Mrs. Bickerstaff nodded, though she swayed as she nudged away from the trunk of a gnarled apple tree. Annabelle grasped the woman's elbow and urged her forward.

Just then, a violent burst of leaves and bark showered from overhead as a booming crack sounded behind them. Mrs. Bickerstaff screamed. Annabelle ducked and shoved her behind a nearby trunk.

Mortlock closed in upon Annabelle and herded her behind a second tree. "Stay low, girl. Run when I tell you to run."

"Bad advice, Colonel," shouted a voice from ten yards away. "I've a pistol. She'll only die sooner."

Annabelle closed her eyes briefly as she recognized Martin Standish's nasal, bland tone. Slow footfalls through grass and leaves reached her ears, which still rang from the shot. He was drawing closer.

She glanced up at Mortlock, who nodded reassurance and leaned carefully to one side so he could view Standish's approach.

"You're a bloody disgrace," the old man barked. "Little wonder you no longer wear the uniform."

"Coat was a mite stained. Had to burn it. Printer's ink. Printer's blood. Neither washes clean from wool, as it turns out."

Dear God, he was close. Within twenty feet, by the sound of it. Annabelle heard Mrs. Bickerstaff whimpering.

"What do you think will come of this?" Mortlock challenged. "You'll be hanged, Standish."

"No. I'll have what I deserve."

"Right. As I said, hanged."

"Teaching the whore her error was satisfying, but not so satisfying as this will be, I think. Robert Conrad deserves everything he's about to suffer."

"What's Robert ever done, apart from being your superior in every way?"

Footsteps paused. Metal scraped metal. "He refused to let the Green matter die, for one. And he cost me Matilda Bentley, for another. A single recommendation to her father, and I was rejected out of hand. Have you any idea the size of her dowry, Colonel? Lady Annabelle does." A snick and a click. He was reloading his gun. "Tell us, my lady. Tell us precisely how much your beloved Robert cost me."

She forced air into her lungs, though her insides felt weighted. Compressed. "Matilda would not have chosen you regardless of Robert's advice," Annabelle pointed out. "She'd already set her cap for another—"

"Ten thousand. He cost me ten thousand and a wife with Northfield connections." Another click sounded as a hammer was cocked. "These are no small matters, are they, Lady Annabelle? I'd thought to make you my wife, but it soon became clear you'd have no one else but him. So I'll take you from his grasp another way. Then, he shall die. That is what I deserve. A proper victory."

Mortlock's eyes were frighteningly grim when they found hers. He grasped her hand in his, warm and dry. "Run when I tell you. Don't stop." He squeezed, and it felt like he was squeezing her heart. "Don't stop, little Bumblebee. You and my boy have a ship to build."

She was shaking her head when he released her. Clutching the tree's gnarled trunk to rise when he shifted. Rounded. Rushed toward the black-hearted demon. Her mind screamed a denial.

But all she could do was watch as an old warrior charged into the fight. Mortlock grasped Standish's rifle, forcing the barrel up. The shot boomed. Mrs. Bickerstaff screamed.

Run. He'd told her to run, and she must, or this would be for nothing. With a sickened heart, Annabelle crossed to the battered woman, yanked her to her feet, and shoved her toward the abbey. Then, Annabelle ran. Past trees and onto lawn. Heart pounding, lungs heaving. Propelled by a single purpose: She must save herself, for she was half of a greater whole. Robert needed her just as she needed him.

The thought drove her harder. She shoved and yanked at Mrs. Bickerstaff until they were halfway across the lawn.

A second shot rang out. She glanced over her shoulder, and what she saw pierced her soul with grief. A wail tore from her throat, but she didn't stop.

Run. He'd told her to run. So, she would. She would save herself. Robert needed her.

She kept on, didn't slow, although she heard Standish's pounding steps and shouted threats closing in.

Just inside the high hedge bordering the east garden, she saw a flash of white, a powerful arm reaching through the shrubbery. She would have screamed in fright.

Except she knew this arm. She knew the hand that took hold of hers, warm and dry. They belonged to the man who had rescued her from the abyss over and over.

"Robert!" she sobbed, letting him pull her through a gap in the hedge and into his arms. Both of them were gasping. His heart thundered even faster than hers beneath her ear. "Oh, God. My love."

"Annabelle," he groaned, clutching her desperately tight.

She struggled to pull back, frantic to tell him what had happened. "It—it is Standish, Robert. He murdered Mr. Green. He—"

"No time," he said, shifting her toward the east entrance. "I need you to go inside. Please, love. I need you safe."

One look into his eyes, and she knew his intent. He was going to kill Standish. And no doubt Standish would try to kill him. She grasped his waistcoat and growled an order of her own: "You'll live for me, not die. Do you understand, Robert Conrad? I'll do as you ask, so long as you promise to stay alive. I need you safe, too."

He lifted her by the waist and turned, depositing her behind him. "Understood, my lady. You have my solemn promise. Now, do as you're bloody well told."

She retrieved the confused Mrs. Bickerstaff and did as she was told. As she ushered the other woman through the east door, she turned back to see her husband—blast, her *almost*-husband—waiting for his enemy to arrive. The broad, broad shoulders. The dark, overlong hair. The stance of a warrior, a commander. The cane that was more a weapon than a necessity.

Suddenly the fear twisting her inside out transformed. Shifted. Rooted and grew into an odd certainty. She had no need to fear for Robert, she realized. He was born for this—to protect all that belonged to him.

No, the one who should be frightened was Martin Standish.

She closed the east door and leaned against it with the faintest smile.

Martin Standish should be very frightened, indeed.

ROBERT'S FIRST STRIKE WAS THE BLACKGUARD'S KNEE. HE jabbed his cane through the thick hedge at such an angle that Standish collapsed instantly, howling like the weak, pathetic worm he was.

Striding through the gap in the hedge, Robert assessed the damage before delivering his second strike to the worm's upper thigh. Another howl.

It was not enough. Robert drew his cane back for a third strike.

"Con."

Robert glanced up to see Huxley striding toward him. Hux's face was flushed from his long sprint. Robert supposed his own face was similarly flushed, but who could tell? Everything was red, now. His heart pounded, his blood thrummed. His ears only heard war drums.

"Is she safe?"

Realizing Hux was asking about his sister, whom he also loved, Robert nodded. "She went inside."

Hux frowned. "Are you certain she'll stay there?"

Oddly, he was. "Yes. Now, would you care to help me deal with this worm?"

Huxley gave Standish a contemptuous glance. "Certainly. Would you prefer to kill him yourself, or shall we involve the magistrate?"

"Excellent question," Robert replied, ignoring the worm's mewling about his knee. "On one hand, killing him would be most gratifying."

"Indeed."

"On the other, worms such as this suffer more when subjected to humiliation. It is their greatest fear. Being exposed for the cowardly worms they are."

"A public trial should accomplish that." Hux tilted his head and came to stand beside Robert as though pondering the possibilities. "Yet, there is always the chance of a worm slithering away. Notoriously slimy creatures. Death is more certain."

"Sound point, though I tend to favor the suffering bit."

Hux crossed his arms and propped a hand beneath his chin. "A true dilemma, I daresay."

Perhaps Huxley was jesting. Robert was not.

His third strike hit the worm's opposite knee, eliciting another round of howling. The noise drowned out more distant shouts at first, but soon, Robert and Hux turned to see what was going on. Five footmen carried something long and alarmingly man-shaped across the lawn. Leading them was Colby.

Robert had heard about Major Colby's exploits in war. But he'd never seen the man in full battle mode. It was an intimidating sight.

He frowned as the major approached. "What happened?" he began, noting the grief on the footmen's faces and the ferocity on Colby's. "Who is ..." He saw the hair first, iron gray and thinned. His legs went hollow. Then he saw the hand, an older, craggier, time-spotted version of his own.

That hand was covered in blood.

"Christ, Con. No. Ah, bloody hell, no." Hux's cursing faded to a faint buzz. Everything else did, too. Green hedges disappeared. The ground was gone, the air and sky. Everything but the wool of his grandfather's coat. The skin of his head showing through iron-gray hair. The knuckles of the hand that had held a boy together after his mother's death.

Distantly, he felt Colby squeeze his shoulder as he passed. Sensed the old major withdrawing a weapon. Heard the cock of the hammer. Flinched at the shot.

But he never took his eyes from the man he admired above all others. The man he'd striven to be.

Something empty and devouring took hold of him. Not pain, precisely. Pain had more substance. No, this was colder. Numb. Vast. It spread like roots into crevices, forcing weakness into solid ground.

The footmen carried him past Robert. Old knuckles brushed his. It drove him to his knees. His cane rolled. Time passed. He thought Hux tried to speak to him, but he couldn't hear past the buzzing. Rain came. His shoulders were soaked. His hair dripped onto his neck.

He didn't know how long he'd been there when he felt her arms surround him. Felt her lips at his brow, his cheek, his ear and jaw.

"Come inside, my love," she murmured. "Come inside."

He reached for her. Drew her around and clung. Buried his face in her and made his first sound of grief. She held him tightly. Stroked his hair. Whispered her love for him.

And rocked him slowly back and forth, back and forth, back and forth.

Wind sighed. Her warm breath caressed his neck. She slid to her knees and remained there. Holding him together. Rocking them together.

While he fell apart.

Chapter Twenty-Two

"Of course I shall be attending their wedding. Does a composer miss the grand performance of his symphony? I think not."

—THE DOWAGER MARCHIONESS OF WALLINGHAM in a letter to the Marquis of Mortlock answering said gentleman's inquiry about anticipated visits to Nottinghamshire.

Dearest Robert,
When I saw you this evening at Lady Gattingford's ball, every single thing came to a halt—the music, the chatter. Even time itself, I fancy.

But not my heart. Indeed, the moment my eyes touched you was the first moment in seven years I felt my heart begin beating again.

Ever yours,
Annabelle

—Letter to Robert Conrad dated April 20, 1816

WHY SHE WAS NERVOUS, ANNABELLE COULDN'T SAY. SHE smoothed her hands over her hips, admiring the pink silk gown in her dressing mirror. "I still think I should wear the black shawl," she said to Jane.

"His lordship would not have wanted you to be in mourning on your wedding day."

Annabelle sighed as Genie fussed with the lace veil, removing the combs and better securing the flowing panel to drape from the top of Annabelle's head down to her waist. "This needs pearls," Genie declared before disappearing, presumably to locate pearls.

"Here, dearest," said Maureen, offering an exquisite silver lace shawl. "Will this do? It is close to gray, but not so close as to be mistaken for mourning. Yet, you will know."

Annabelle accepted the shawl with a grateful smile.

Jane came to stand beside her, bending to view her own bespectacled face beside Annabelle's. "You become a wife today," she said softly, grinning until her dimples appeared.

Annabelle hugged her sister's waist and kissed her cheek. "In many ways, I feel I already am."

It was true. Over the past fortnight, she'd stood by Robert's side through everything that had followed that dreadful day. First had come the magistrate's inquiry into the death of Lord Mortlock and the subsequent death of Martin Standish. After testimony from Mrs. Bickerstaff and Major Colby, the inquiry had lasted all of five hours. Robert had shared what Lord

Atherbourne had told him of Standish's history during the war—that the cowardly officer had escaped battle by claiming he had informants in a nearby village with information on the French forces. He'd hidden in a cottage, taken the woman inside hostage, and abused her in unspeakable ways—just as he'd done with Mrs. Bickerstaff.

While the magistrate had been sympathetic to Mrs. Bickerstaff's plight, he'd been most persuaded by Major Colby, who had explained in the bluntest terms that Captain Standish attacked a superior officer, an offense for which the penalty was death. Given the esteem with which Lieutenant Colonel Lord Mortlock was widely regarded, the magistrate had expressed only regret that he hadn't been the one to carry out the execution himself.

Next had come the funeral. Ordinarily, ladies of a certain station avoided attending funerals, but Annabelle could not bear for Robert to endure the ordeal alone. She'd clung to his side like brambles to silk, lending him every ounce of love and strength she possessed—which happened to be a great deal.

He'd soaked it in, embraced her in return. She'd also stood by his side as he'd dealt with his father and brother, who arrived the day of the funeral and departed early the next morning. She'd held his hand as he'd listened to his grandfather's solicitor explain why Rivermore Abbey and all its lands were now his.

She'd spent every day at Rivermore, arriving at dawn, ensuring Mrs. Cleary understood Robert needed both coffee and toast for breakfast, that his beefsteak must be properly seasoned, and that airing his bedchamber was essential. Throughout each day, she'd simply sit with him, sketching away while he tended his correspondence and other duties. Every now and then, he would glance up at her with a haunting expression; she'd wait for him to speak, but instead, his eyes would turn tender, and he'd resume writing. Sometimes they rode together. Sometimes they sat quietly in the garden, his arms cradling her close, his jaw stroking against hers.

Late into the evening when hours of silence had done their work, and he was ready to share his burdens with her, she'd listen to his memories of his grandfather, his fears about running the estate in Mortlock's absence, his regret that his grandfather would not see them wed. On that point, Annabelle had assured him Mortlock would most certainly be attending their wedding, for she could not imagine the great commander letting anything keep him away—including death.

Robert's smile—sad but sweet—had been her reward.

John had remained close, too, taking long rides with Robert, driving Annabelle back and forth between Rivermore and Clumberwood at all ungodly hours of the morning and night. When the rest of her family had arrived, along with Lady Wallingham, they had gathered around her, too, a bustling phalanx of warmth and kindness, support and humor and love. Mama and Papa had comforted both her and Robert, offering baskets full of food (Mama's contribution) and sensible advice (from Papa, of course). Lady Wallingham had peppered them with amusing observations about the slipshod rules of mourning dress and the need for improved suspension schemes in travel coaches. Annabelle's sisters had busied themselves planning the wedding, with Kate gathering flowers and ivy, Genie plotting Annabelle's coif and headdress, Maureen arranging the wedding breakfast, and Jane composing letters to sundry acquaintances, notifying them of the happy news.

Today, all Annabelle had to do was walk down the aisle and marry the man she loved.

So, why were her hands shaking?

Jane adjusted her spectacles and sniffed. "Your life is about to change, Annabelle Huxley. Do not seek to minimize it. You may feel like a wife already, but as of noon this very day, you'll become mistress of Rivermore Abbey, wife of Robert Conrad, and future mother to multitudinous children."

Annabelle raised a brow. "Multitudinous? Really, Jane."

"We are Huxleys. I believe the polite word for it is 'prolific.'"

She rolled her eyes at her sister. "Hmmph. Next, you'll be claiming my hips and bosom are harbingers of my fecundity."

Jane glanced down at her own generous curves with mock alarm. "Oh, dear. Does this mean what I think it means?"

Laughing helplessly, Annabelle's nervousness began to ease.

Soon, Genie returned with pearls. Maureen and Kate brought her a nosegay of white orange blossoms, pink roses, and ivy. Mama stopped by to weep and hug and wish her great happiness. Finally, Papa arrived to collect Annabelle.

At her father's beaming smile, Annabelle's eyes started welling. "Oh, Papa," she whispered.

He opened his arms and gathered her close. "He loves you, my sweet girl." He kissed her forehead. "Nearly as much as I do."

By the time she entered the chapel on her father's arm, by the time she spotted John and her sisters standing attendance, smelled the sweet scent of orange blossoms perfuming the pews, and walked through rainbow light to the man she loved as no other, Annabelle felt nothing like nervousness.

There was no room. For, there stood Robert—*her* Robert—tall and handsome. With ridiculously broad shoulders clothed in dashing black wool. With almost-black hair trimmed to the perfect length and heavy brows showing no sign of a frown. With blue eyes glowing summer-bright. For her. All for her.

She spoke her vows and wore his ring—the ring his mother had given him—and finally, at long last, she became his wife. He belonged to her and she to him. A surge of love filled her until she wondered if she'd lit up like a lantern.

Perhaps she had. Robert, too, was shining. Blue eyes blazed down at her with ferocious possession.

Good heavens, he made her heat and flutter.

As she took his arm and they walked toward the chapel doors together, light through the windows seemed to brighten—so much so that she blinked as they passed through a particularly dazzling golden beam. Briefly, approaching the last pew, she thought she saw a figure watching them. It must have been a trick of the light because the last two pews were empty. Perhaps the flash from the windows and the play of shadows had confused her vision. But she would have sworn, if only for a few seconds, she'd seen a pair of smiling blue eyes and a head of iron-gray hair.

She squeezed Robert's arm, glanced up and noticed he'd riveted upon the same spot. "Do you see him, too?" she whispered.

He turned back to her. Swallowed visibly. Nodded.

She gave him her best grin—the one with the twinkle. This time, there was nothing false about it. "I told you he would come."

He answered with a slow grin of his own. "So you did, love. So you did."

HOURS AFTER THE LAST BITE OF CAKE AND THE LAST TEARY hug from Mama, Annabelle sat sideways on Dewdrop's back, wrapped in her new husband's arms. "Why am I not allowed to know where we're going?" she grumbled. "It would have been more sensible to have brought my own mount."

A hard jaw stroked against hers. "Perhaps. But I prefer you this way."

"At your mercy, you mean."

He groaned, his lips nuzzling her neck. "God, Bumblebee. Yes. That is it precisely."

Chuckling, she stroked his knee with her fingertips. "Rivermore is back there. If you intend to ravish me, I daresay you're headed in the wrong direction."

"No. I'm not."

She sighed at his low, arousing voice. Ran her hands over his thick arms. Rested her head on his wide shoulder. "I want you, Robert."

"And I you. More than I can say."

They entered the wood east of the abbey. Above, leaves fluttered the same way her belly did every time he touched her. "I changed my gown for this, you know." She now wore a blue velvet riding habit with a fitted bodice and silk-lined skirt.

He spread his palm across her abdomen, pressing and heating. "I know."

"I'm running out of patience."

"Just a little further, love."

"How much further?"

"Almost there."

"Do you even know where we're going?"

"Yes."

She blew out a breath of frustration. "Honestly, what is the point of a wedding night if a wife cannot expect a bit of ravishment?"

"Hmm. I can safely promise you more than a bit."

Arching a brow, she wriggled her hips against him, enjoying his groan and tightening grip on her waist. "If the scale of your *livestock* is any measure, I fancy you can."

Robert's hand froze in place. His posture straightened. "You knew—"

She snorted. "Of course I knew, silly. Who goes on and on about settling a dispute by measuring a chicken's *girth*, for heaven's sake?"

"Bloody hell, Annabelle. Those men were completely sotted."

"And distracted by my argument." She sniffed. "An effective approach, I daresay."

"Where did you learn that word?"

"You mean cock?"

Another groan.

"Oh, we caricaturists are quite keen to learn such things. A play on words is a favorite technique of humorists, particularly when prurient in nature. Though, I must say, 'conversation' did come as a surprise. Mrs. Bickerstaff alerted me to that one."

His hand slid down until his fingers nestled between her thighs and his palm pressed into her lower belly. His jaw stroked her cheek. His lips found her ear. "I think you and I need to have a long ... *hard* ... conversation, wife."

Now, she was the one groaning. "That is what I've been trying to tell you, husband."

Yet, despite his delicious threats, he did not stop then and there, did not pull her down and ravish her in a pile of leaves until neither of them could speak.

Disappointing, indeed.

Minutes later, however, she recognized their destination, and all thoughts of ravishment fled. Instead, she sat forward, bracing her hands on Dewdrop's neck. "Turn round," she said coldly.

"No."

"Turn round, Robert. I don't wish to go any further."

"We need to face this, love. Together."

"I don't want to face it. I want to forget."

"I know." His big, strong hand slid up from her belly to the space between her throat and her heart. He drew her back into his body. "We belong to each other. You to me, and I to you. Nothing can come between us." He rested his chin on her shoulder. "Except this."

Her chest went tight beneath his hand. She grasped his wrist and squeezed. "I cannot bear to remember, Robert."

"Can you stand with me as I remember, then? Will you do that for me, Bumblebee?"

She closed her eyes, gathered strength from his hand, from their connection, burning bright gold and humming with power. Could she? Could she stand with him, be his strength as he was hers?

Slowly, she opened her eyes. Heard the rustle of heart-shaped leaves. Looked up and saw white clouds drifting across a blue sky. Looked down and saw the Tisenby. Looked across and saw moss-covered stone and the arch of Packhorse Bridge.

"I don't know," she whispered, her heart twisting painfully. She threaded her fingers through his. "But I shall try, my love."

Dewdrop didn't move an inch as Robert dismounted and helped Annabelle down. She gave the horse a grateful pat before walking slowly toward the south end of the bridge. Robert came to stand at her side, taking her hand in his, warm and dry.

Her stomach swooped. Her breathing halted. Her legs went weak.

"Ready?" he murmured.

She swallowed. Nodded.

Together, they stepped onto the bridge. In many ways, it looked the same as it had that day. Brambles grew thick along the banks. Moss grew heavy along the stones. Water curled and meandered among the rocks.

"I nearly lost you here."

She should have been the one to speak those words, but Robert said them instead. Her eyes flew to him.

He stared down at the water, his brow furrowed, his jaw flexing. "You were sliding through my hands. I wasn't strong enough to pull you up, small though you were." One corner of his mouth quirked. "All I could think to do was let you fall where you had a chance of surviving."

She moved into him, tucked his arm close. "You saved me, Robert. I am alive because of you."

His eyes met hers. "I also hurt you. I am sorry, Bumblebee."

Pressure in her chest wanted out. It gathered and pushed. Tightened her throat. Tears swam, making the light swirl. They spilled over. "It is I who am sorry," she whispered. "For the accident. For needing you so much that I could not grant you any amount of distance. For thinking my love for you was greater than yours for me." She shook her head. "How little I truly knew."

He propped his cane against his thigh and reached for her cheek, brushing away the tears. "You were just a girl. Neither of us knew what to do with this."

"If I could change that day, I would. A thousand times over, I would do it."

"Close your eyes," he said, tenderly stroking her cheek. "Go on, then. Close them."

She took a shuddering breath and complied.

Firm lips settled upon hers. Gentle. Sensual. "We are alive, Bumblebee." His breath washed across her mouth. "You and I. Both of us survived, and we are stronger for it."

"I love you, Robert."

"And I love you, Annabelle."

Cradling his hand against her cheek, she opened her eyes. Endless, brilliant blue glowed with possessive ferocity. "Please forgive me," she whispered.

"Whatever needed forgiving, I forgave long ago."

She nodded. Kissed him. And slowly, the pressure inside her chest eased. Around her, heart-shaped leaves fluttered, water sighed against stone, clouds drifted through patchy blue. But she and Robert were here, alive, together, and that shimmering golden thread had grown into a rope—one strong enough to hold them both above the abyss.

They left the bridge, hand in hand. He lifted her onto Dewdrop and climbed up behind her. Then, he guided the horse across the bridge, heading along the road toward Clumberwood lands. Before long, he veered left, leaving the road behind and wending deeper into thick woodlands. At a small clearing, he pulled Dewdrop to a halt. They were surrounded by lime and beech and rippling sunlight. The ground was cushioned with leaves, half the clearing guarded by enormous, mossy boulders. The spot felt magical.

He dismounted and lifted her down. "I have something to give you," he said, looking far too serious.

"Does it rhyme with lock?" she quipped.

It only took a heartbeat for his smile to start. "No."

"Hmm." She stretched up and kissed his lips. "Perhaps it rhymes with miss?"

His smile grew. "No. Although, I shan't rule out either possibility in the very near future." He retrieved a sizable package from Dewdrop's saddlebag. It was perhaps eighteen inches long and twelve wide, wrapped in a wool blanket. He handed it to her with odd uncertainty. "I made this for you."

The thing was weighty, obviously constructed of wood, for it had hard corners. It was a box of some sort.

Robert rubbed the back of his neck. "Colby helped. He has a talent for such things, whereas I have more eagerness than skill."

She removed the blanket, revealing smooth, rich oak. The box had an angled top, a small ledge at the base of the hinged panel, and decorative trim with heart-shaped leaves. "Oh, my," she breathed, stroking fingertips along the sturdy edges.

"It is a travel desk. See there, I've added a leather handle to each side. You can carry it with you. For sketching."

She beamed up at him. "I love it."

A worried brow cleared. "You do?"

Nodding, she stroked her palm over the surface. "It is perfect."

Silence fell, filled only by wind and sighing leaves. "Look inside."

With a curious glance at her husband, she set the desk on a waist-high boulder. Lifted the top. And saw letters. Some were old—yellowed and careworn. They bore a familiar, flowing script. But others were new. Those had neat, bold writing in fresh, dark ink.

"Wh—what is this?"

"Hux gave me some of your letters."

She sifted through the stack. The older ones were letters she'd written to phantom Robert during their separation. The newer ones were—

"These are my replies," he said. "A bit late, I'll grant."

Quickly, she scanned the first three in the stack. Filled with wonder at the love of this man, she closed the lid, tears streaming, heart pounding.

"You don't like them. Blast, I knew it. I've never been good with—"

Forgetting herself, their surroundings, and his bad leg, she rushed him. Leapt into his arms. Buried her face in his neck. He caught her but stumbled back awkwardly against another boulder. Fortunately, he was able to lower them both so they were kneeling in leaves and grass with his back braced against mossy stone.

Good heavens, he was strong.

She did not care if her gown was stained. She did not care that their bed was a forest floor and their roof the sky. Proprieties be damned. She was *busy*. Her task was kissing Robert. Stroking Robert. Loving Robert.

She kissed his mouth, tangled their tongues, yanked at his cravat, and grunted her impatience to see him naked.

Now. She wanted him naked *now*.

"So," he panted as she straddled his thighs and frantically tugged at the buttons of his fall. "I take it you liked them, after all."

She growled in frustration. "You." Kiss. "Are wearing." Kiss. "Too many." Stroke and kiss and nibble. "Dratted clothes, Robert Conrad."

His deep laugh was deceptive, for his body did not seem amused. No, indeed, the hard, lengthy ridge pulsing against her inner thigh spoke of urgency beyond imagining. His fingers dug into her waist and hips. "Slow down, Bumblebee. Else I won't be able to ..." He touched his forehead to hers. "I cannot be patient much longer."

She cupped his flushed cheeks in her hands. "I don't want patient. I want you." Kiss. "Inside me." Nibble. "Now."

Something dark and primitive exploded in his eyes. A deep growl sounded across their magical glade. It rumbled through her body, inflaming her arousal to a fever pitch. Suddenly, she was tumbling backward, her riding hat rolling away. Powerful, masculine hands shoved silk-lined blue velvet up and up, tore delicate petticoats from his path.

Until she was bared to him from hips to toes.

Her breasts swelled inside her stays, jealous of the attention he paid her lower half.

"Fast," he panted, dark hair falling over dark brows. The blue lit her up like tinder. "Need you fast this time, love. Apologies." His words were nearly unintelligible, as though he'd abandoned civilization for hunger and lust. Perhaps he had. His hand loosened the last few buttons of his fall and withdrew the thick, long stalk of his manhood. Flushed and weeping, it made her lick her lips with inexplicable desire.

"Yes. Need you, too," she rasped. "Please, Robert."

He fell over her, bracing himself with one arm while positioning his cock with the opposite hand. She felt the blunt tip at her opening, circling once before stretching her wide. Her eyes flared at the size of him. How had she forgotten? Granted she'd been so wet and swollen the last time he'd taken her, sensation had all merged together. Pain had been nothing compared to her need.

Now, although she was slick, his first thrust made her gasp.

"Tight," he groaned, the skin over his cheeks and jaw tense and flushed. "So bloody tight." He gripped her thigh in his hand and yanked her up and forward into his hips as he forged deeper.

The sudden, pressured stretch inside her body was both unnerving and unbearably arousing. She reached for his neck, but he clasped her wrists and secured them above her head.

"Need you this way," he panted, powerful arms trembling as

he braced himself above her, sank his cock further inside her. His eyes glowed with possessive fire. "Let me."

Though it was a new sensation to be held captive beneath him, she nodded, trusting him to bring her pleasure. And he did. Oh, how he did. Shockingly, given the rough force with which his body began pounding away at hers, pleasure bloomed where they were joined. It began as pressure. Then heated from friction. It gathered momentum. Curled and coiled. Burned hot as a bolt from thunderous clouds.

He touched her nowhere else—only her wrists and where they were joined. His thrusts grew increasingly brutal, deepening. Taking. It felt like a claim.

Yes, this was Robert's claiming. And oh, how *taken* she felt. How thoroughly, wondrously *filled* until she couldn't imagine her body without his. As the pleasure gathered, building higher and higher, she held his gaze. And smiled. Wider and wider. Panting his name. Loving the deep, hard, relentless power of her husband's claiming.

The peak, when it came, was a launch from a precipice, sudden and explosive. One moment, her sheath quaked with spiraling pleasure. The next, she seized upon his cock with enough force to drive them both into a frenzy. Whirling, indescribable ecstasy coursed through her as she closed her eyes and cried to the heavens.

Two more thrusts, and Robert followed her over the edge into deep, rumbling waves of rapture. His seed filled her, warm and wet. His hands held her, secure and safe. His eyes devoured her, possessive and possessed.

They were one.

Their connection hummed with power.

Golden. Inexorable. And, at long last, whole.

Epilogue

"*If you can manage to tear yourself away from endless procreating, my boy, I should enjoy having your company and that of your dear wife at Grimsgate Castle this summer. Feel free to bring the children, provided they number fewer than twenty by then.*"

—THE DOWAGER MARCHIONESS OF WALLINGHAM in a letter to Lord Robert Conrad, the future Marquis of Mortlock, inviting said gentleman to a house party of some importance.

Dearest Bumblebee,
The first time I saw you, though you were tiny as a teacup, I knew.

The second time I saw you, a siren in silver, laughing your womanly laugh, I was reminded.

You have always been my happiness. And that is why I shall always and forever be yours, Annabelle. Your husband. Your knight. Your love.

With all my heart,
Robert

—Letter to Annabelle Conrad dated August 3, 1816

July 30, 1826

SUNLIGHT BLAZED YELLOW ACROSS GREEN FIELDS AND BLUE sky. The open carriage rocked and creaked as they traveled from Rivermore Abbey to Clumberwood Manor. Birds sang. Children giggled. A cooling breeze carried away thick heat.

Annabelle sighed as the scent of freshly cut grass tickled her nose. She kissed her youngest babe's sweet head and peered out at fields of wheat ripening to gold.

"You are not my nurse, Beatrice," complained six-year-old Nathaniel. "Stop telling me what to do."

"Sit still, and I shouldn't have to," seven-year-old Beatrice replied with a sniff. "Boys wiggle about too much."

Annabelle shared a grin across the carriage with Joanna Bickerstaff, who cuddled Annabelle and Robert's second youngest daughter. Hyacinth might have her father's coloring, but she had Annabelle's penchant for mischief. Just two years old, and she'd already stolen every heart within reach.

"Perhaps if certain boys had finished their lessons as they ought, they'd be riding with their papa as your brother is,"

Annabelle chided gently, nodding toward the pair currently on Dewdrop's back, riding alongside the barouche.

Robert, looking broad and dark and dashing while holding their sleepy youngest boy in front of him, merely raised a brow. "Your mother makes a sound point, son." Brooding blue eyes met their perfect reflection in Nathaniel. "A ride on a day like this is a fine thing, indeed. A worthy reward for tending one's duties."

"Driving in a carriage with ladies is *boring,* Papa," Nathaniel replied, crossing his arms.

"Hmm. In time, you'll feel differently, I suspect."

Joanna leaned closer and whispered in Nathaniel's ear. The boy's eyes widened. He nodded fiercely. Then, wriggling his backside against the seat, he settled in and behaved like a gentleman.

"Remarkable," Annabelle murmured. "How?"

Joanna merely laughed, winked, and bounced Hyacinth on her knee. "I have my ways, my lady."

Following the horror of Martin Standish's attack, Joanna had struggled to reclaim her soul from the black-hearted demon's grasp. It had been a hard battle, and numerous scars remained. But she hadn't let her ordeal defeat her. No, indeed. Over the past ten years, Joanna had performed many roles at Rivermore Abbey—lady's maid, nursemaid, charades instructor. Above all, she was a friend.

Beatrice tugged at Annabelle's sleeve. "Will Uncle Hux be at Clumberwood this time, Mama?"

Annabelle smiled at her serious, commanding little girl, the only one of their five children to have inherited Annabelle's dark eyes. "I'm afraid not, my darling. He is still in Scotland."

"It must be splendid there," Beatrice said. "Uncle Hux does not ordinarily stay in a place so long."

Kissing Beatrice's Huxley-brown curls, Annabelle sighed at her precocious daughter's observation. Apart from "ordinarily" being Beatrice's favorite word, it appeared even seven-year-olds could detect the change in John's pattern. Annabelle's brother had wandered from one corner of the world to the other in search of something he could not seem to find. Perhaps Scotland would be different. She hoped so. John deserved the sort of happiness she and Robert had built together.

And happiness it was. They had suffered their share of storms, to be sure. One, in particular, had tested them in ways they could never have anticipated. But that was why ships were necessary. Big, strong ships secured with golden, shimmering ropes. Testing the ropes only strengthened them more.

"Mama, I should like to hold her."

Annabelle smiled at Beatrice then looked down at the sleeping babe cradled against her breast. "Very well." Carefully, she transferred her youngest daughter into her oldest daughter's arms. "Gently, now. Mind her head."

With her hands now free, Annabelle's fingers itched to draw. She leaned forward and retrieved her travel desk from beside her feet. Then, with a lingering glance at her family, she opened her sketchbook and set pencil to paper.

First came her children—Beatrice was a mothering brown hen, Nathaniel a restless bear cub. Little John was a sleepy hedgehog, Hyacinth a sprightly fairy, and baby Dorothea a tiny teacup. Finally, with sweet sadness, she drew her sixth child—or, more rightly, her first. He'd been born two months too early, had departed a lifetime too soon. They'd named him Michael, and in her drawings, he was always an angel.

Next came Joanna, a resilient willow, and Annabelle, a fluttering bee. Last, she drew her husband, a towering knight standing watch over them all.

She drew her family on a ship—a fine, stout ship with golden sails. The winds blew powerfully strong, and waves licked the ship's railing. But their vessel was carrying them to a shore where Rivermore's ancient arch straddled a welcoming drive, where golden wheat and ripe grass rippled and danced, and where tall beech trees surrounded magical glades.

"Where are we headed this time, Bumblebee?"

She glanced up. Robert was smiling, nodding toward her sketch. She'd drawn many over the years—so many, she'd begun making them into books for their children.

Looking at her husband, so strong and vital, she reached for him helplessly. He moved Dewdrop closer to the carriage and clasped her hand in his, warm and dry. Love blazed down at her. Blue. Adoring. Ferocious. Her heart answered by filling past its capacity, flooding her with a golden shimmer.

"Home, my love," she replied. "Wherever else we may wander, our ship will always carry us home."

Have you read the story that started it all?
Don't miss Lord Atherbourne and Lady
Victoria's scandalous tale in the first book of the
Rescued from Ruin series, **available now.**
Read on for a sneak peek!

The Madness of Viscount Atherbourne

ELISA BRADEN

Chapter Two

"Virtue is its own reward.
But then, the same could be said for sin."

—THE DOWAGER MARCHIONESS OF WALLINGHAM to the Countess
of Berne upon said lady's refusal of a fourth lump of sugar.

HE WAS MOCKING HER. SHE KNEW IT, AND YET COULD SAY
nothing because she was quite ridiculously hypnotized. That
faint grin had grown into a full-scale smile. *Parliament should
declare his smile patently illegal,* she thought. *It is lethal to all
womankind.*

"I—I saw you earlier, when you entered the ballroom," she
said finally, kicking herself for the inane utterance.

"Yes, I was a bit late arriving. Caused quite a stir, I understand. But then, the only thing the ton enjoys more than its rules is the fever created by those who break them."

His rich baritone alone was enough to weaken an aged spinster's knees. Add the subtle lift of one dark brow and the half smile gracing his sinful lips, and it was no wonder a visible shiver ran along the surface of her skin.

Without a word, he stepped closer and reached for her shoulders, chafing his gloved palms along the skin of her upper arms between the edges of her cap sleeves and the tops of her gloves. It was a shocking breach of etiquette to touch her without so much as an introduction, much less her permission.

She stood motionless for several long seconds, unable to speak. That must have been why she failed to step back and rebuke him immediately for his cheek. It could not be the fizzing excitement in her belly at having him so close, feeling the warmth of his hands on her skin, his thumbs stroking gently and causing little thrills to shoot from her arms to her spine and, most concerning, her breasts. No, surely not.

"You should have a wrap if you intend to spend much more time out here, my lady. To call this springtime would be generous, indeed."

She blinked up at him, feeling weak and slow—enthralled. Even standing this close, she could not make out the color of his eyes, only noting they were dark and glimmered in the moonlight. He was so tall, the top of her head would barely reach his collarbone.

With Lord Stickley, her forehead came even with his nose. At one time, she had thought him the ideal height, not requiring the craning of her neck to look up at him. As an added benefit, they moved quite nicely together on the dance floor, his strides more closely matching her shorter ones. However, now she was less certain about how perfectly suited she and her fiancé were on a physical level. Something about this man's height and larger, more muscular physique made her feel oddly safe.

Comparing Stickley to a stranger was not wise, she chided herself. She was engaged and now must make the best of things, rather than finding fault with her betrothed at every step. Yet, she could not help noticing he stood in this man's shadow in numerous ways.

The errant thought seemed to break the spell the stranger had cast over her. She abruptly pulled away, breathing embarrassingly fast, heart racing. "Sir, you overstep yourself. I don't even know your name."

"Call me Lucien."

She reeled back a step further, her hip bumping the balustrade. Stiffening her spine and raising her chin, she retorted, "Your familiarity is insulting. We have not been properly introduced. I could not possibly call you by your first name."

"You must call me something if we are to continue our conversation."

"Perhaps I should call you presumptuous. It seems fitting."

His slow, wicked smile seemed to speak a foreign language, one she did not understand but which caused a flush of heat to wash through her. "I have not begun to *presume*, my darling."

For a moment, she was flummoxed, her open jaw working in a fashion not unlike a fish lying onshore. She had never been spoken to in such a manner. As the daughter and then the sister of a duke, no one would dare exhibit such disrespect for her station and the simple courtesies due her. No one except this bounder, apparently.

At last, she found her voice, stumbling and ineffectual though it might be. "I—I am not your darling!"

"My goddess, then?"

"Furthermore, your suggestive tone implies a much more significant acquaintance—"

Lucien tilted his head and spoke as though she'd said nothing at all. "I have it. My angel."

"—than I would ever allow. I will have you know I am engaged to be married—"

"Although it still fails to do you justice. You are quite beautiful, you know."

"—and your behavior is entirely inappropriate ..." Her breath stuttered to a full stop as she absorbed what he had said. His tone had been so offhanded, it took a moment to sink in. "You ... you think I am beautiful?"

"Hmm. Yes, quite. Has no one ever told you?"

She shook her head and then immediately corrected herself. "Well, several of my suitors did say they found my hair attractive. And one gentleman said my eyes were like pools. Of what, I am uncertain. But I assume it was meant to be flattering."

His mouth quirked in amusement. "And your betrothed? What does he say?"

Is he standing closer than before? Victoria wondered absently. Yes, he was. His massive body nearly surrounded her now, only inches away. He gave off such heat, she no longer felt the bite of cold, damp air. Her voice grew breathless and high. "Lord Stickley? Oh, well, he is not much given to poetry or flattery."

"Has he not said that your skin glows with the purity of fresh cream?" He stroked one finger delicately along her cheek, his dark gaze holding hers rapt. "Or that your hair rivals the last glorious rays of the sun just before dusk?" His fingers sifted through the loose curls behind her ear. "Has he not even mentioned your lips, how they are as full and luscious as a ripe peach? Come, now. He must have done so at least a dozen times."

She made an inarticulate sound that was vaguely embarrassing, but she was utterly helpless to prevent it. If she could have managed to draw air into her lungs, she would have groaned. Oh, he was simply divine. Divine and devilish.

Lucien's lips hovered so near her own, she felt his breath

with each word. "Surely he has kissed you, my angel. Has he not?"

"Yes," she whispered, staring at his mouth.

His head tilted. "And did it feel like this?"

This was heaven. He fitted his mouth masterfully to hers, his lips warm and firm, gliding sensually without a moment of hesitation. It was not the soft, gentle kiss of a man concerned with offending her. Nor was it the dry, obligatory peck of her fiancé. As strong arms wrapped around her waist and pressed her breasts to his hard form, she marveled at his confidence. Then all thoughts of assessing the kiss flew away like a dandelion tuft on the wind as his hot, slick tongue slipped along the seam of her lips.

Lucien pulled away for the barest moment. "Open for me, angel," he whispered, tugging at her lower lip with his finger. When she obliged, he swooped back in, this time thrusting his tongue inside her mouth and stroking along her own. She felt seared and shaken, the boldness of it shocking, unfamiliar in its intimacy.

She moaned into his mouth and clutched at his lapels. He drew her tighter against his body, his hands gripping her hips and sliding along her bottom as a flooded river of heat coursed through her. Her breasts felt heavy where they pressed flat against his chest, she ached low in her belly, and the muscles in the intimate place between her thighs clenched as though in great need of ... something.

Distantly, she noticed a hard and rather large object pressed against her midsection. But a moment later, she was distracted by one of his hands moving up over her ribcage and cupping her right breast. The most pleasurable tingles—yes, *tingles*—erupted from the center as he skimmed lightly over her breast with his palm, then returned to stroke insistently with his thumb.

Truly, she was awash in tingles of every sort, in every place she could imagine and some she tried not to think much about.

She could feel herself panting, the sensations overwhelming whatever faint notion of propriety might have flitted through her head. Indeed, her mind was sluggish and spinning, every sense singing to the tune only he could play.

Abruptly, both his hand and mouth were removed from her person. But it was no reprieve.

"I must feel your skin. Now," he gritted. He took the tip of one of his gloves between his teeth and pulled his hand free, spitting the glove onto the ground and immediately running the backs of his fingers along her collarbone. Then, as she stood hanging helplessly in his embrace, not knowing what to expect, his hand turned so his fingertips traced their way along the upper slopes of her breasts. They caught on her low-cut bodice, slipped beneath the silken layers, and tugged slowly downward. Her right breast popped free, the nipple hard and flushed.

She glanced at his face, seeing the muscles tighten in his jaw and no hint of his earlier sardonic smile. Was he displeased? She couldn't decide why he suddenly looked so tense. Then his head dropped forward, his hand cupped her breast from beneath, and his mouth covered her nipple, suckling it like a babe.

What in heaven's name was he doing? This was ... this was sweet madness. She heard herself squawk, but could not bring herself to care with his fiery mouth drawing so pleasurably upon her nipple. He licked and stroked, even glided his teeth gently along the tip, causing her legs to weaken in an alarming way. She feared she might collapse, were it not for the iron-like arm wrapped tightly around her waist.

He shifted her so that his thigh wedged high between her own as he worked and laved at her nipple. At first, this seemed to soothe the infernal ache she felt deep inside. Then, like a fiendish devil, it caused an even deeper emptiness and tension. Occasionally, his thigh would brush against a hidden spot and a sharp burst of pleasure would erupt, causing her to cry out and grind herself against him. This repeated over and over, almost rhythmically, and each time, the coil inside her wound tighter.

His mouth pulled away for a moment while he tugged her other breast free and latched onto her left nipple, giving it the same treatment as the right.

She moaned and threw her head back, clutching desperately at his hair as the torturous ache between her legs rose to an unbearable height. His thigh pressed harder at that sensitive center. Without warning, the tension gave way in an explosive spiral. "Oh, my stars. Lucien!" she shouted as her body spasmed in a crescendo of echoing pleasure.

A shriek from the direction of the ballroom doors pulled her rather rudely from the heavens down to earth. "Good gracious, Lady Victoria! Have you lost your senses?"

Warm lethargy weakened her muscles, filled her head like a steam cloud. Vaguely, she knew something odd had occurred, but she was dazed, shivering in the aftermath. Lucien pulled away slightly, but still clutched her waist. Her bare breasts were suddenly cold, exposed in a way they had not been when he had covered them with his mouth and hands. Slowly blinking up at his face, she noticed he was breathing heavily, flushed and wearing a fierce frown. He shook his head like a dog casting off water after a swim.

Distantly, a thread of sanity anchored on the edge of her mind, and she realized what must have happened: They had been interrupted. She froze, seeing the same realization in Lucien's face. Simultaneously, they turned in the direction of the shrill exclamation.

And there stood Lady Gattingford, the venerable hostess of one of the finest balls of the season and a notorious gossip, staring back at her from the open door. The expression on the matron's face was astounded, appalled. Scandalized.

In that moment, as Lucien pivoted so his back blocked Lady Gattingford's view and calmly tugged Victoria's bodice up to restore her modesty, the full horror of what had just occurred—

what she had *allowed* to occur—hit her with paralyzing force. She had let a man unknown to her touch and pleasure her in ways she had not even considered permitting her fiancé. This had been witnessed by none other than her hostess, who would doubtless relish notifying every member of the ton in hopes of enshrining her ball as the event of the year. The scandal would spread with the swiftness of fire through dry grass. Within a week, everyone would know. Everyone. Including Lord Stickley, who would surely cry off the engagement. And her brother, of course.

Oh, dear God. The duke would be enraged. She had shamed the entire family. Harrison placed great importance on honor and reputation. Her other brother, Colin, would be far more understanding. But then, he was hardly a stranger to less-than-dignified behavior himself.

There was no mistaking it: Her life had changed inalterably this night. And not for the better.

"Lady Gattingford," Lucien said as he turned, his tone nonchalant, even mocking. "A fine night for a stroll on the terrace, wouldn't you say?"

The tall woman's eyes narrowed on him, her mouth a flat line. "Do not imagine I hold you blameless, my lord. You are nothing less than a bounder!"

While Victoria had defined him with the same term earlier, she found herself bristling at the insult toward Lucien. They had experienced a moment of uncontrollable passion together. She suspected he had felt as swept away as she had, blind to their surroundings, and tossed amid a raging storm. There was no need to paint him as a villain.

"My dear lady," she began, "I do comprehend your dismay at what you have seen. But, please understand we were both caught up in the moment. It was simply a lapse of judgment. If—if you could see your way clear to—"

"Lapse of judgment? While that may be one acceptable

description of your behavior, my lady, it in no way excuses the shameful wantonness I witnessed."

Other guests began taking notice of the intriguing and heated conversation happening on the terrace, and the two remaining sets of doors were opened. Soon, an alarming number of people—perhaps twenty—crowded around Lady Gattingford, including Lady Berne, her two daughters, the Aldridge twins, and Lord Stickley. *Oh, heaven help me,* she thought, cold dread clenching her insides. *Stickley does not deserve what is about to happen.*

Before she could say another word, Lady Gattingford regaled the crowd with a summary of her observations. Snippets of the matron's monologue repeated in Victoria's mind—*kissing, shocking, inappropriate.* As though trapped in a nightmare, Victoria froze, only able to watch and endure. The woman appeared to savor each word, her descriptions growing ever more detailed with each gasp from her audience. *Fondling, bosom, exposed.* A flush of pure shame heated beneath Victoria's skin, burning and pulsing in her face and chest. The humiliation was almost too much to bear.

Then, it got worse.

Lady Berne paled to a sickly white as her eyes darted between Victoria, Lucien, and back to Stickley. Flags of ruddy color signaled the marquess's anger and embarrassment as he glared at Victoria. When Lady Gattingford reached her triumphant crescendo, and the shocked mutterings of the crowd burst forth, he simply turned his back and walked away, charging through the doors and out of the ballroom, shouldering several gentlemen aside as he went. The din of the crowd's chatter prevented her from calling out to him, begging him to stop and listen so she could defend herself.

Not that she had a defense. She was, in fact, quite guilty.

Lady Berne, bless her, courageously approached Victoria, risking much by further associating herself with a ruined young woman. She took Victoria's icy fingers in her hands. "Are you well, Victoria?" she asked gently.

Victoria nodded, then looked down at the flagstones, no longer able to hold her friend's sympathetic gaze. She swallowed hard, bothered by the tightness in her throat. She refused to cry. She simply would not.

"He did not harm you, then? Force you?" The softly spoken words were stunning, as Victoria had not imagined anyone would reach such a conclusion.

"No. Why would you suggest ...?"

"Because, my dear, he more than any other may have reason to wish you and your family harm."

She shook her head. "That makes little sense."

"Do you not yet know who he is, child?"

Victoria stared into Lady Berne's kind, steady brown eyes and knew she would not like this. Not at all. "Who is he?" she whispered hoarsely.

The countess took a deep breath and squeezed Victoria's hands as though to brace her for a great shock. "He is the new Viscount Atherbourne. He inherited the title after your brother, the duke, killed his brother in a duel last season."

Victoria reeled, the sounds of the crowd dimming, her head spinning with the possible implications. She had known about the duel, but Harrison had not explained why it had happened, only informing her it was a matter of honor that had been resolved, and had ended in the death of Viscount Atherbourne. He had refused to discuss it further. The incident had generated a shockwave among the aristocracy, but because it had occurred toward the end of last season, just before most families departed London for the country, the scandal had fizzled before it really began. Few of her acquaintances had brought it up after that—a testament to her brother's considerable power—and she assumed the matter had been largely forgotten.

But here stood a man who had every reason to remember, every reason to seek retribution. Could he have planned this? Was his impassioned embrace—she swallowed hard on a wave of sickness—nothing more than a cruel charade designed to ruin her? No, surely not. He must have felt the same tidal force sweeping away all reason; she could not have been alone in that. She could not have been such a fool.

She immediately sought reassurance in Lucien's gaze, shifting to look up at where he stood a few feet away, listening to her conversation. "You ...?"

The mocking smile and triumphant glint in his eyes confirmed her worst suspicions. "Yes, my darling. I am Lucien Wyatt, Viscount Atherbourne." He swept a graceful bow, his discarded glove now back in its proper place as though nothing significant had occurred. "And I must tell you, making your acquaintance has been the greatest of pleasures."

WANT MORE OF THE STORY?
THE MADNESS OF VISCOUNT ATHERBOURNE IS AVAILABLE NOW! FIND IT AT WWW.ELISABRADEN.COM

More from Elisa Braden

*Be first to hear about new releases, price specials,
and more—sign up for Elisa's free email newsletter at
www.elisabraden.com so you don't miss a thing!*

Midnight in Scotland Series
*In the enchanting new Midnight in Scotland series,
the unlikeliest matches generate the greatest heat.
All it takes is a spark of Highland magic.*

THE MAKING OF A HIGHLANDER (BOOK ONE)
Handsome adventurer John Huxley is locked in a land dispute in the
Scottish Highlands with one way out: Win the Highland Games.
When the local hoyden Mad Annie Tulloch offers to train him in
exchange for "Lady Lessons," he agrees. But teaching the fiery, foul-
mouthed, breeches-wearing lass how to land a lord seems impossible—
especially when he starts dreaming of winning her for himself.

THE TAMING OF A HIGHLANDER (BOOK TWO)
Wrongfully imprisoned and tortured, Broderick MacPherson lives for
one purpose—punishing the man responsible. When a wayward lass
witnesses his revenge, he risks returning to the prison that nearly killed
him. Kate Huxley has no wish to testify against a man who's already
suffered too much. But the only remedy is to become his wife. And she
can't possibly marry such a surly, damaged man...can she?

Rescued from Ruin Series
Discover the scandalous predicaments, emotional redemptions,
and gripping love stories (with a dash of Lady Wallingham)
in the scorching series that started it all!

EVER YOURS, ANNABELLE (PREQUEL)
As a girl, Annabelle Huxley chased Robert Conrad with reckless abandon, and he always rescued her when she pushed too far—until the accident that cost him everything. Seven years later, Robert discovers the girl with the habit of chasing trouble is now a siren he can't resist. But when a scandalous secret threatens her life, how far will he go to rescue her one last time?

THE MADNESS OF VISCOUNT ATHERBOURNE (BOOK ONE)
Victoria Lacey's life is perfect—perfectly boring. Agree to marry a lord who has yet to inspire a single, solitary tingle? It's all in a day's work for the oh-so-proper sister of the Duke of Blackmore. Surely no one suspects her secret longing for head-spinning passion. Except a dark stranger, on a terrace, at a ball where she should not be kissing a man she has just met. Especially one bent on revenge.

THE TRUTH ABOUT CADS AND DUKES (BOOK TWO)
Painfully shy Jane Huxley is in a most precarious position, thanks to dissolute charmer Colin Lacey's deceitful wager. Now, his brother, the icy Duke of Blackmore, must make it right, even if it means marrying her himself. Will their union end in frostbite? Perhaps. But after lingering glances and devastating kisses, Jane begins to suspect the truth: Her duke may not be as cold as he appears.

Desperately Seeking a Scoundrel (Book Three)

Where Lord Colin Lacey goes, trouble follows. Tortured and hunted by a brutal criminal, he is rescued from death's door by the stubborn, fetching Sarah Battersby. In return, she asks one small favor: Pretend to be her fiancé. Temporarily, of course. With danger nipping his heels, he knows it is wrong to want her, wrong to agree to her terms. But when has Colin Lacey ever done the sensible thing?

The Devil Is a Marquess (Book Four)

A walking scandal surviving on wits, whisky, and wicked skills in the bedchamber, Benedict Chatham must marry a fortune or risk ruin. Tall, redheaded disaster Charlotte Lancaster possesses such a fortune. The price? One year of fidelity and sobriety. Forced to end his libertine ways, Chatham proves he is more than the scandalous charmer she married, but will it be enough to keep his unwanted wife?

When a Girl Loves an Earl (Book Five)

Miss Viola Darling always gets what she wants, and what she wants most is to marry Lord Tannenbrook. James knows how determined the tiny beauty can be—she mangled his cravat at a perfectly respectable dinner before he escaped. But he has no desire to marry, less desire to be pursued, and will certainly not kiss her kissable lips until they are both breathless, no matter how tempted he may be.

Twelve Nights as His Mistress (Novella – Book Six)

Charles Bainbridge, Lord Wallingham, spent two years wooing Julia Willoughby, yet she insists they are a dreadful match destined for misery. Now, rather than lose her, he makes a final offer: Spend twelve nights in his bed, and if she can deny they are perfect for each other, he will let her go. But not before tempting tidy, sensible Julia to trade predictability for the sweet chaos of true love.

CONFESSIONS OF A DANGEROUS LORD (BOOK SEVEN)

Known for flashy waistcoats and rapier wit, Henry Thorpe, the Earl of Dunston, is deadlier than he appears. For years, his sole focus has been hunting a ruthless killer through London's dark underworld. Then Maureen Huxley came along. To keep her safe, he must keep her at arm's length. But as she contemplates marrying another man, Henry's caught in the crossfire between his mission and his heart.

ANYTHING BUT A GENTLEMAN (BOOK EIGHT)

Augusta Widmore must force her sister's ne'er-do-well betrothed to the altar, or her sister will bear the consequences. She needs leverage only one man can provide—Sebastian Reaver. When she invades his office demanding a fortune in markers, he exacts a price a spinster will never pay—become the notorious club owner's mistress. And when she calls his bluff, a fiery battle for surrender begins.

A MARRIAGE MADE IN SCANDAL (BOOK NINE)

As the most feared lord in London, the Earl of Holstoke is having a devil of a time landing a wife. When a series of vicious murders brings suspicion to his door, only one woman is bold enough to defend him— Eugenia Huxley. Her offer to be his alibi risks scandal, and marriage is the remedy. But as a poisonous enemy coils closer, Holstoke finds his love for her might be the greatest danger of all.

A KISS FROM A ROGUE (BOOK TEN)

A cruel past left Hannah Gray with one simple longing—a normal life with a safe, normal husband. Finding one would be easy if she weren't distracted by wolf-in-rogue's-clothing Jonas Hawthorn. He's tried to forget the haughty Miss Gray. But once he tastes the heat and longing hidden beneath her icy mask, the only mystery this Bow Street man burns to solve is how a rogue might make Hannah his own.

About the Author

Reading romance novels came easily to Elisa Braden. Writing them? That took a little longer. After graduating with degrees in creative writing and history, Elisa spent entirely too many years in "real" jobs writing T-shirt copy ... and other people's resumes ... and articles about gift-ware displays. But that was before she woke up and started dreaming about the very *unreal* job of being a romance novelist. Better late than never.

Elisa lives in the gorgeous Pacific Northwest, where you're constitutionally required to like the colors green and gray. Good thing she does. Other items on the "like" list include cute dogs, strong coffee, and epic movies. Of course, her favorite thing of all is hearing from readers who love her characters as much as she does. If you're one of those, get in touch on Facebook and Twitter or visit **www.elisabraden.com**.

Made in United States
Troutdale, OR
05/11/2024

19768692R00224